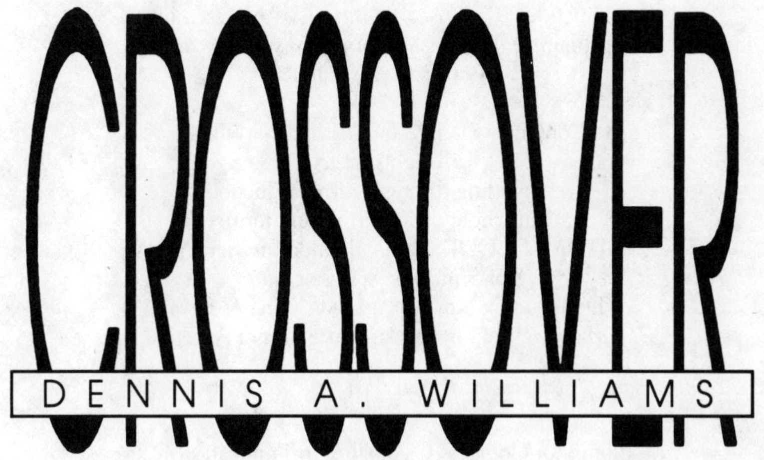

SUMMIT BOOKS
New York London Toronto Sydney Tokyo Singapore

SUMMIT BOOKS
Simon & Schuster Building
Rockefeller Center
1230 Avenue of the Americas
New York, New York 10020

Designed by Nina D'Amario/Levavi & Levavi
Manufactured in the United States of America

1 3 5 7 9 10 8 6 4 2

Library of Congress Cataloging in Publication Data

Williams, Dennis A.
Crossover / Dennis A. Williams.
p. cm.
I. Title.
PS3573.I448455C76 1992
813'.54—dc20 91-25501
CIP

ISBN 0-671-72640-4

For Cat,
and, at last, for Millicent

May 1954

Saturdays was the best day. All the other times she went to work and he had to go to old fat Miss Harris, or else they had to get ready for church and she came in and picked him up and he picked up Clyde and he got dressed and then she got dressed while he ate his oatmeal and watched the radio.

But on Saturdays he woke her up. First Clyde told him it was time to get up and they got out of bed and went into the living room and turned on the TV and said good morning to Uncle Sergeant Clarence on the top. Then he got the bowl of Cheerios out the fridgidator and the cup of milk and him and Clyde sat down to watch Captain Video. *After the Cheerios was gone and Captain Video was gone they went to wake her up. Sometimes Clyde whispered It's time to get up and sometimes he kissed her eyes open and sometimes they just yelled Boo.*

Then him and Clyde would jump in the bed and ask what they gonna do today and she would say how about we sleep. But Clyde wanted to go shopping so she said all right we'll go shopping. Can we go downtown? He liked to go downtown cause they rode on the bus and he had to pick the colors of things in the store cause he was good with colors and he gave the lady the plate and watched her put the paper in the can and send it away. She told him how they did it cause she used to be the lady who got the plate. And him and Clyde sat in the white chair and waited by theirself while she went to the bathroom and all the white ladies in church hats tugging on their clothes said how cute he was and what a big boy to sit and wait like that and they got a hot dog at Woolworth's if he didn't cry but he always let her finish it 'cause it took him too long to eat and they'd miss the bus. But if they didn't go downtown and just got food that was okay 'cause then they might get ice cream instead of a hot dog and Clyde didn't like waiting in the white chair that much anyway.

While she got up and started cleaning the house she turned on the record player and he said I know let's play "Kee-Mo Ky-Mo" and ran and got the purple record and she sang and danced and swept the floor.

Sometimes if they didn't go to the store she made a cake and he got his bowl and mixed his own dough and got real happy cause that meant that Uncle Hodge was comin and while her cake was in the oven in the kitchen and his cake was in the oven behind the couch he stood at the window and watched for Black Beauty. Uncle Hodge talked to Black Beauty like it was a girl and when he got out he took his hankerchif and licked it and rubbed a spot on the door or the top or the front and said Black Beauty gotta shine and put the hankerchif back in his pocket and came upstairs and said all right where's that boy at. He hid behind the couch till Uncle Hodge went by and jumped out and said Boo, wanna buy a cake and Uncle Hodge gave him some money and said My My My My My what a pretty cake and it taste good too maybe I'll have a piece for Black Beauty and he laughed and said it's a car, cars don't eat cake, silly!

Uncle Hodge sat and talked to her awhile and ate some of her cake and he sat on his lap and played with his tie, sliding the big gold H up and down the strings. Then he climbed down and pulled up Uncle Hodge pants to see what his socks were, sometimes they had stripes and triangles and sometimes they had a H and sometimes they had a girl in a swimming suit on them. When they got finished talking she looked at the letters he brought and Uncle Hodge came to play with the blocks or they would draw or play store and Uncle Hodge would give him pennies for his toys but just for pretend cause he always gave the toys back but he got to keep the pennies.

And then they went for a ride and sometimes they bought some stuff for Uncle Hodge house or they just went around and saw the houses get bigger and then farther apart and then sometimes they went so far there was cows and chickens instead of dogs and if nobody was mad or tired maybe they went to the Piggy. She liked the sandwiches and he helped Uncle Hodge with his ribs but really he just liked the big smiling pig in front. It made him laugh.

On Saturday night she went out. She put her hair up and walked around in her robe and put records on in the afternoon and he knew what that meant. Back to Miss Harris house. He got his toys and coloring book and started looking for Jack out the window. He was tall and had a little mustash and shoes the same color as his hat and she always smiled when he got there. He played with Jack while she finished getting dressed but he wasn't as much fun as Uncle Hodge and kept lookin up to see if she was ready. He didn't have to look. He could smell her comin. She grabbed him from behind and picked him up and he grabbed Clyde and the coloring book and waved good-bye to Jack and off they went downstairs.

Look like they was never gone very long. He could sort of hear her comin and smell the perfume and wine and smoke and he hugged Clyde and smiled in his sleep while she kissed him and carried him home.

It was Saturday when Daddy came. She was cranky all day and made him put on outside clothes even though they wasn't goin to the store and she fussed when she cleaned the house and didn't put on no music. She let him keep watchin TV and said she was glad he liked it cause that was all Daddy left him, she always forgot about Clyde. Then she dusted the picture of Uncle Sergeant Clarence in his hat and said Clarence told me not to marry that nigger. She hadn't said that in a while.

When he heard somebody comin up the steps he started to run to the door but she told him to sit down. She didn't yell but the way she said it hurt his feelins and made him want to cry but he was too excited. She opened the door and stood there while Daddy said hello and asked could he come in and was he there and he wanted to move so Daddy could see him but he was scared. She moved and Daddy smiled and said Hey kiddyo and walked right to him and picked him up. He smelled good and he wasn't yellow—he didn't think he was, so why did she keep callin him that? He smiled and said Hi Daddy behind his ear and saw her scrunch up her face and make that click sound with her mouth so he stopped for a minute then closed his eyes and smiled some more. What you bring me? He opened his eyes and saw her make another face. Daddy put him down and reached into his pocket and gave him a whole dollar.

Daddy told him how big he was and how he looked like a little man and a sharp cat—a sharp cat?—and then he said why didn't he take Clyde in the other room and play for a little while. He looked up at her cause he didn't wanna go and she looked like she didn't want him to either but she said Yeah go on, real quiet. He went in the bedroom and she closed the door. He put Clyde down by the door to see what was goin on through the crack at the bottom and started to play with a puzzle but Clyde wouldn't tell him what they was sayin so he came and sat there too. He was hungry but he was afraid to ask for somethin to eat. Then he got sleepy. Then he got scared 'cause they was yellin and he heard his name. They was talkin about what he could do when he got big but he didn't wanna get big and he didn't want no job, he didn't wanna do nothin but see Daddy and get somethin to eat. And he wanted them to stop yellin. They got quiet again and he asked her somethin and she said No, real loud, if you goin, go on and he said You tell him then and she said Uh-uh you tell him. That's when he grabbed Clyde and started to cry. They heard Daddy comin to the door and they jumped on the bed.

The door opened and they didn't look. He sat up on the bed. Tell me what? You heard some of that, huh? Tell me what? Where you goin? New York. For a while anyway. When you comin back? I don't know, gotta try some things. But you got some things to do too. What? Get ready. Get ready to be a man. That's a hard thing, kiddyo, hardest thing in the world for me and you. You gotta know what you want and know how to get it. The crackers'll try to stop you but you gotta try anyway. Ain't nothin else to do. I'm still tryin, that's why I gotta go.

He wanted to ask if he could go too but he didn't really want to. He didn't know what New York was. He didn't know why he was sposed to be 'fraid of crackers. And he didn't wanna leave Mommy. I love you Daddy. I love you too kiddyo. You bring me somethin when you come back? We'll see, man, we'll see. Come on, gimme some sugar.

Daddy carried him and Clyde into the other room and sat them down. You be good now. Both of you. She didn't say nothin. He went to the door. Bye, Daddy. Bye, son. The door closed. He heard Daddy's steps goin down the stairs. She got up. What's New York? Someplace else, that's all. Same world. She went to the kitchen and started makin crumble-in and makin a lot of noise. Same damn world. Her voice scared him and he took Clyde behind the sofa. They stayed there a long time. She left the kitchen and stomped into the bedroom and didn't say nothin.

Then she came out and went to the record player and he saw her put on the purple record. She looked over at the sofa and held out her arms. He ran out and jumped up and they danced and he smiled and held on to her neck real tight and felt the water on her face but she was smilin too and squeezed him till it almost hurt. When the record stopped she said let's get some ice cream.

August 1974

She didn't have to work **every** *Saturday, did she? No matter how good Friday night was, even if they hung out with the black mafia like she wanted, it usually turned out the same. She jumped out of bed just when he was about to roll over for her and wouldn't even wait to let him make them a quick breakfast before running over to the office to read the paper and talk about shit. Yeah, okay, so she was busy impeaching a president, or doing whatever a congressional intern did to help impeach a president. But what about him? What about them? This summer should have been a return to those glorious days of yesteryear, when they first got together ringing doorbells in Harlem, and a preview of real life, after law school. Instead it looked like they were going backward, or at least it* **felt** *that way, like back when it was just him and Al Green, tired of being alone.*

She should be out here with him checking out the folks—the we-the-people she was supposed to be doing for over on the Hill. Not just scoping real estate on Sundays, although that was something, kind of a promise of things to come. The idea of calculating investments in people's neighborhoods, though, and waiting for them to lose and go away, seemed a pretty cynical way to plan a future, even if it was the way of the world. It was like joining the other side, the people who tore down Jewtown for highrises and highways. What did she know about that? **Her** *house was still standing. On second thought, better not to have her along on the pilgrimage. She'd probably just talk down everybody—he'd heard* **that** *before—and worse, she'd be mostly right. Fuck it. He needed a haircut anyway, so he'd just go on and get him one.*

But damn, whose idea was it to put a capital here? The wet heat was worse than those muggy Saturdays back home in Onondaga when after a couple bike laps around the block, a few rounds of marbles or a game of catch, their skins would begin to melt so bad, even One More Time Tommy would start looking for reasons to collapse on the porch. The best excuse, always available on a summer Saturday, was to watch the flowered processions honk up the hill toward the rose garden in the park. Like official greeters of the block, they blew kisses at the brides and counted the cars. Twelve was the record, that was the daughter of J.T. Slater, the richest man in Jewtown, but they couldn't figure out who would want to marry the undertaker's daughter. Once, when it wasn't so hot, they jumped on their bikes and pumped up the hill to follow the parade. When they got to the edge of the rose garden the wedding party was already posing for the pictures that looked just like the ones in everybody's living room, or almost everybody's. The groom could have been Brook Benton or somebody with his powder-blue tuxedo and stagey pose. Tommy started calling him a dumb sucker, not quite loud enough for anyone to hear, and saying that the woman was ugly. But that was wrong. She was beautiful. The white lace and the flowers helped, but it was mostly the look on her face, and the thank-you-pretty-baby look on his. Besides, it **had** *to be love, standing out there in that humidity. Tommy didn't know shit anyway.*

Did people still do that? If so, where did they go? Not the White House rose garden, that was for sure. That was another country, and it got to be more of a rumor with every block. This was Hodge *country, Jewtown revisited. Women with rags on their heads and kids with ashy knees. Aimless men with picks sticking out of their heads like the bones in a cartoon African's, tipping at a forward angle on platform shoes. Elizabeth went off first time she saw those. Talking about sissies and sprained ankles. Hodge could dig it. Man got to have some style on his feet, even if it hurt. His own blue suede Adidas—go, cats, go—were a civilized compromise. No compromise out here, though. They acted like they had no idea the world was being reshaped a couple of miles away. Or maybe like they understood that the new shape wouldn't be too much different from the old as far as they were concerned. Every closed eye ain't asleep. Now when Martin was killed and all hell broke loose over on—where was it, 14th?—***that*** *was a change that meant something. They were all sure enough awake that night, just like they were on State Street. Same newscast, in fact. Roving bands of Negro youths burning and looting. Elizabeth didn't get it. They watched together and she called them all kinds of names. He didn't get it either. Not yet. They didn't know his time would come.*

But where was that place? Just past a liquor store and a check-cashing joint. There. The old-fashioned barber pole and hand-lettered sign. Duke's. When he found it on another safari last month he knew exactly what it was. Pete's. The place around the corner off Canal back home where Elizabeth wouldn't take him because it was too rough, so they rode the bus to Mister B's, where the deacons went and they had a lot of mirrors and booster seats for kids. Hodge didn't even mess with Pete's, either because Elizabeth bribed him not to set a bad example or maybe just because he owed people money in there. Looking out the window waiting for Black Beauty, he used to watch the men drift in and out. And he dreamed of the day he'd be big enough to swagger in, or better yet, step out, fix his brim just so, hitch his trousers and strut off down the street to another bright-sign man place.

That was the thing. This here was a man place. From the Players *calendar on the wall to the cigar butts in the ashtrays. Dark and dingy. Two chairs, one barber. Workingmen, used-to-be-workingmen and never-did-shit men. And him. It wasn't the kind she had in mind for him, which is why he never made it to Pete's. But he'd been to plenty of those, and recently, like the office shindig at the country club. In fact, she'd be surprised at the similarities, once you stripped away all the pretense. Both were about bullshit, basically. Fixing the world with your mouth. Anyway, she should be glad he was in a room with scissors. His third cut of the summer, counting the one before St. Thomas, was one more than in four years of college.*

The paper was raggedy—no wonder, it was yesterday's—but that was just a prop. He was there for the show. A neighborhood scandal. Maybe a fight the night before. Celebrity dirt from Jet. The Orioles, looking good as usual though a little light after Robbie. Or even the hearings; Duke seemed to stay on top of things. But today he took his text from the Atlanta shooting earlier in the week. Two cats had gunned down a federal judge, a black one at that. Killed a cop standing next to him. He'd heard about it but hardly noticed it at the time. Too much local shit going on. Duke and his men were all into it, though. Couldn't believe it, especially because one of the gunmen was black. A **brother** *hooks up with a* **white** *boy to shoot down a black* **judge**? *They ran through all kinds of theories. A mob hit, with the brother as a decoy (probably killed his ass too). The judge was crooked but ready to talk. A Klan thing (and maybe that was a white boy in blackface). You never know, but it was somethin goin on. Couldn't be what it look like.*

Waved into the chair and asked for his opinion, he reminded them that that bunch out in California kidnapped the rich girl, brothers in that group, too, had shot a black man first. School superintendent. More confusion. And he thought he was naive. Why couldn't they just accept that the bad guys could be black, too? Must be drugs, they insisted. Got 'em all turned around. Brainwashed by the commies.

Naw, I'll tell you what it is, said Duke. These young folk just mad, you know what I'm sayin. Don't know 'bout what. Used to be they just fuck with the white folks. Talkin 'bout Angela Davis, George Jackson, even somathese college kids usedtabe out here carryin on. Now they wanna mess with every goddamn body. Brother look like he done made somethin outta hisself, he the enemy too. No leadership, that's why. Got black judges, black congressmen, black lawyers, black everything, ain't got no black pride. Sense, neither. Ain't that right, young buck?

Couldn't argue with that; Duke had the razor. Besides, this wasn't no moot court. More of a tribal conference cum sermon. Half an hour of religion and a half inch off the top. He climbed out of the chair, just like a man, tipped too much and stepped outside. Still hot, even worse. No rush. A long, easy stroll back across the line. Maybe they'd do sundaes when she got home.

Just because you've become a young man now,
There's still some things that you don't understand now.

—Smokey Robinson

I'm taking care of business, woman, can't you see?
I've gotta make it for you, and I've gotta make it for me.

—The Isley Brothers

Ike stood at the window at the end of the corridor, more conscious than when he had perched at the edge of the baptismal pool that he was about to be born again. Elizabeth turned, spotted him and waved, a showy, carefree kind of wave, like the one she had used when she walked him to the corner on his way to kindergarten and was about to board the bus downtown. It was a gesture that had less to do with him than with her own pride in taking him that far and having the courage to let him go. Did he look so much the same to her now? Didn't she understand what was happening? Or was it because she knew that she deliberately conjured up that old image in a last-minute attempt to bind him?

She had tried about everything else. For the past month she had slowly been going soft on him, the frostiness from last spring melting like a popsicle that turns sticky and too sweet in the summer sun. She had dropped comments about how empty the apartment would seem, right in the middle of perfectly good conversations. She, who always complained about stores rushing the seasons, had begun considering Thanksgiving menus. And she had floated the names of people from school she had hardly mentioned and never invited all those years, suddenly anxious for him to continue friendships she knew barely existed. It had not been a subtle strategy, but at times it had nearly worked. Especially that Saturday they had gone shopping for school clothes (though he suspected he had far too many already) and stopped for lunch the way they used to and even picked up a box of Karmelkorn. He had almost let it take him back, until he remembered her disembodied voice cursing him the night he came home late and told her about Cheryl and she snapped off the light on her bedstand and he couldn't see her anymore. Keep waving, girl.

At least she still had Hodge, who whipped off a quick salute from the brim of his hat, pointed, grinned and kept stepping his don't-rush-me-baby-I'ma-get-there step. With his bolo tie, wide-shouldered jacket, forties-baggy pants and high-shine shoes, he probably looked to this crowd like an aging pimp. Of course, that didn't say much for his mother, who did swing it a little mincing over the gravel in her heels, but she certainly looked more dignified in her carefully chosen secretarial outfit than the others in their Long Island sportswear. Yeah, Hodge would help her play it off and pretend not to notice when it did get to her. He knew how to do. He'd had practice; they both had. It was the second time he had been there to rescue her. Good thing there weren't any more Isaac men, because the old boy was getting up there.

I think you really believe all that stuff . . .

Hell, yeah! And why not? It's true. They're the only ones who don't believe it, he thought as Black Beauty eased out of the dorm parking lot. They've got too many baby pictures, and they confused his with theirs. It was almost the seventies, and the eagle has landed. He turned and faced the empty corridor, the alien terrain. He had in fact been building momentum for years, had broken out of orbit at Southwest High. The clubs, cruising The Group, the elections, the awards, had all been in-flight training; now, at last, he had touched down on this new sphere.

Although no one was around, signs of life, presumably intelligent, were everywhere: a blue footlocker over here, a hand-lettered name sign on a door over there, a taped-up box probably holding records, books, maybe a favorite photo, some old *Playboys* or *Sports Illustrateds*, an alarm clock, a slide rule, a tennis racket. One door was ajar, revealing a typewriter in place beneath a Mets poster; the occupant was almost certainly nearby. Ike, in no hurry to make introductions, ducked into his own room across the hall and closed the door behind him.

Because the window was open, it seemed louder inside than it had in the hall. Amplified, Anglicized blues blasted through self-importantly from a close-by room on the other wing, carrying with it snatches of conversation from the sidewalk just below. Ike went to work immediately setting up the one-piece stereo with detachable speakers that had been his graduation present. It was a poor weapon, he knew, to battle the heavy components he'd seen others lugging in, and he was not used to playing his music loud—partly his own preference, partly Elizabeth's rules. *If I wanted the neighbors to know what we were doing, I'd invite them over, and you notice I haven't made any phone calls.* At least, there was a good chance that his roommate, whose rig was not much bigger, would be less obnoxious with his curious mix of Barbra Streisand and Crosby, Stills and Nash.

He had been informed that he would be sharing the room with Arthur Rosen, whose effects were already on display, and so he assumed that Arthur Rosen was also expecting him. That is, he was expecting Richard Isaac, but not *him.* They didn't send pictures. But his roommate did not appear in the time it took Ike to arrange the speakers on his bookshelf along with selected volumes from Baldwin to T.H. White. Although he liked the advantage of possession, he began to dread the moment Arthur Rosen walked in. The reaction, he knew, would not be one of outrage or shock or even discernible disappointment. But there would be a reaction, and he decided that he could wait to see it. He put out a stack of records on his desk with Aretha on top as a clue and went out to explore the campus.

The men's freshman dorms were a ghetto. His was one of a cluster of low brick buildings resembling the projects he had not lived in but passed every day as a child. These were hidden from the street behind a more impressive, and obviously older, array of Gothic buildings with odd angles, peaked roofs, lots of steps and small courtyards that recalled English private schools. The whole complex lay at the foot of a hill rising steeply to the main campus. Women's and upperclass men's dorms, Ike knew from the map he'd been sent, formed a separate community on the other side of campus.

Ike had seen the place once before, when he and Elizabeth rode down on a Saturday the previous autumn. He had wanted to check the school out because of the stories Hodge had told him about Bo Howard, a black All-American football player and Phi Beta Kappa student from the forties who had become the kind of credit to his race *Ebony* liked to feature behind the Dorothy Dandridge and Sidney Poitier covers. Howard was from nearby Auburn, and since there were few blacks playing white college ball at the time he had attracted a large local following. His success story, coupled with the academic reputation and impressive campus of the school, led Ike to make up his mind on the spot. He knew that day this would be the place, even though he hadn't told them yet he was coming. It never occurred to him that he might not be accepted.

Strolling across the quad, feeling very Ivy League in his glen plaids and Hush Puppies, Ike recognized a few buildings from his whirlwind tour. He remembered the administration building, a compact but intricate flag-bearing fortress where they had gone to seek information. That had given him a point of reference when the newspaper at home ran a photo of black students, fists raised in triumph, emerging from a two-day occupation of the president's office in April. They had looked old and, despite the concessions they'd won, unhappy. But there were only about thirty of them, and there were more than a hundred blacks on campus. The rest, no doubt, were real students. That was the argument he had made, anyway, to Elizabeth, who didn't seem to understand that it was too late for him to change his plans.

Not that he had been seriously tempted to do so, but the occupation had given him pause. It had come a year after the mess at Southwest, when Patterson and Walsh had gone at it the morning after King was killed. And that became a big deal, as if it had anything to do with anything, as if they hadn't hated each other since that brawl when they played football for competing junior high schools. Some black geniuses volunteered for detention by insisting on a separate after-school assembly while the whites discussed brotherhood in the auditorium. Ike, frustrated by the pointless talk of looting and vengeance, had surprised himself by walking out. *Guess you in the wrong room anyway, "Brother" I.Q.* The voices of his past had trailed him out of the building, and he spent the rest of high school trying to erase the sound. And then, just when it was nearly over, there they were choosing up sides again on the campus he was about to escape to. The prospect scared the hell out of him, but he couldn't say that to Elizabeth and Hodge, who were busy clucking about trifling Negroes raising hell instead of going to class.

He found the student union all by himself. For the most part there were only other freshmen on campus for orientation, and since he figured he knew his way around as well as anyone else he didn't bother asking for directions. The cafeteria had a cavernous dining room filled with long, heavy, wooden tables; the seals of all the Ivy League colleges adorned the walls. It was oddly dark, and the jukebox snarled its honky-tonk at a level that seemed excessive because the room was not yet filled with chattering lunchtime students. Ike got a burger that smelled as if the grease was left over from Bo Howard's days and sat down at a table by a window overlooking the freshman dorms. In an instant he knew—felt as much as saw—why this place was special, why people paid, dearly, to come, and kept paying and kept Homecoming and made up stupid songs. This was the college from the movies. The huge oak tree on the hill, the dorms—not his projects, the good ones—the lake and the farmland in the distance represented unruffled tradition. Old shit. Like a secluded, ancestral estate, but everyone who passed through owned a piece. You could take government courses anywhere; this was the kind of preserve that governments were about.

And down there, emerging from one of those baronial passageways, splitting the guardian flagpole (bad luck) and tilting up the hill marched a band of black students. Everyone else wandered alone or in pairs, having just shooed their parents away to make tentative contact with one another and eye the landscape like tourists. In comparison, this half dozen seemed a small army. They had obviously already made their connections—a secret caucus, a prearranged signal that no one had told him about? They were striking in their very blackness, which they wore easily and defiantly, like Roman cloaks. Though they moved at a relaxed pace, talking among themselves, the attitude was there with each stride, the dontfuckwitme, and it worked; others changed their walking angles twenty yards away to avoid them.

The effect was probably not deliberate. Ike remembered seeing the same looks on long walks home from track practice with Hez leading a chorus of "Say It Loud, I'm Black and I'm Proud." They'd strutted tired-legged through tipping neighborhoods, clapping, harmonizing, and Hez (at nineteen, a senior at last) would scream Black Power *Evry* Gotdamn Hour, then call to a passing white girl, *Hey* bitch, you know you want somathis sweet soul dick. Ike was happy to be in the band, happy that no one mocked his strained, airy, pseudo-bass, the only sound he could possibly contribute without losing pitch; happy that no one held his walk-out, his grades or his seditty mother against him; happy though he knew the impression he was making as part of this unruly black multipede ambling back to the quarters. But that was different. That was home. As the mean-stepping collegiate brothers who were *not* Hez or even Tommy surged to the top of the slope in their shades and army jackets, Ike dry-swallowed the last of his Bo burger and knew that he had his work cut out for him.

And so he headed back down to give Arthur Rosen his surprise. Enough solitaire. He had crossed over once before when he let Tommy talk him into joining the track team. He wasn't slick. Ike knew it was a challenge, a setup designed to confirm Tommy's physical mastery over the non–blood brother who was moving ahead academically. But Tommy had proved his heart by being glad, beneath the put-downs, when Ike made the team as a quarter-miler, proving he could hang with the brothers. Tommy had even helped him establish the public identity of "Ike" that he had invented for himself in high school to change his image from an anonymous egghead. (Between them, that had begun as boyhood payback. Years earlier, Ike—then Richard—had made the mistake of taking to school the family nickname of "Little Tommy." Tommy had responded—except around Elizabeth—with the label "Little Ike," taken from the name by which Big Tom and others had known Lonnie Isaac, his father.)

And in his second season, right about the time of the King assembly, he had connected with Cheryl, one of The Group he and his outcast buddy Janet used to run down at lunchtime though he desperately wanted their approval. But Jan, who was never wrong about anybody, had figured out that the tall, gawky transfer was okay—not really one of *them*—and had even served in her unsubtle way as matchmaker. That was probably an even bigger breakthrough, considering the corner-eye pressure from others at school, though it had seemed perfectly natural, almost inevitable, at the time. His balancing act had worked before; he could make it work again. He wondered, though, as he descended the slope, if after the spring disturbance the university had sent letters to the unlucky white kids warning them of their situation and lecturing them on their responsibility.

When he entered his corridor for the second time it was alive, and he found the door to his room open.

"Hi, I'm Richard Isaac," he said to the tanned figure with dark, curly hair he found standing inside.

"Art Rosen," the figure said, smiling uncertainly and extending his hand. "Did you just get in?"

"A while ago," Ike said as he shook the hand. "I was out looking around." They looked each other over quickly and Ike guessed that his roommate hadn't gotten any warning. But if he was upset it didn't show. He even seemed a little bit happy, which Ike hadn't counted on and which, it occurred to him, could be worse.

"Yeah, sorry I missed you, man. Our dorm counselor took us over to meet some girls from another dorm. I think he's got somethin goin with their counselor, so he used us as an excuse, you know? You didn't miss nothin. Alpo City."

Art flopped into the lone armchair, which he had positioned on his side of the room. Ike returned to unpacking.

"Tonight's supposabe somethin else, though," Art went on. "There's a mixer over at the student union. They're importin chicks from some girls' school. They say they're really good-lookin over there, you know, cause they don't have to be as smart as they do to get in here. Whaddaya think?"

"I don't know," Ike said with exaggerated weariness. "I thought I might just kinda feel out the dorm tonight, maybe wander around campus some more."

"Hey, the whole dorm's gonna be there, man. They're gonna

have a band and free beer. I'm only goin cause I figure once classes start I'll be bookin like a fiend, you know?"

"Yeah, me too. I'll think about it."

"That's cool. Hey, excuse me, Rich, I'm gonna go check out the neighbors."

He wasn't gone long. As Ike arranged his side of the room, Art drifted in and out, dropping pieces of his biography as well as an expanding tale of some ugly girl who kept sticking her big boobs in his arm at dinner—"like gettin goosed with one a them couch pillows but worse cause it had a face like a pothole." He was from Queens, which explained his accent and maybe his recklessness. He left the room door open, bopping in and out all evening, even after Ike thought he had signaled his desire for peace by stretching out with *Notes of a Native Son*. Still, Art was relentlessly friendly. He even brought other guys from the corridor into the room to introduce them. Ike chatted with them all a little but never put his book down.

"You're gonna get a headache, man," Art said at last, betraying a touch of a whine. "You sure you don't wanna boogie?"

Part of him, in fact, did want to make the effort, but he had put so much psychic energy into simply being there in that space with a stranger—he hadn't shared a room with anyone since the last time he'd slept over at Tommy's years ago—that he wanted nothing more than for all of them to clear out. Besides, he didn't trust Art Rosen's gregariousness. Maybe the dorm counselor had given him a pep talk. Maybe he thought having Ike around would do for him what colored girl backup singers did for white bands. No soul for sale tonight, Daddy Cool.

"I think I'll pass," he said. "I'm pretty wiped out."

"Okay, suit yourself. Say, what do you think I should wear?"

"I don't know," Ike said, mildly perturbed that Rosen had shifted focus so quickly. "Just throw on anything."

"No, man, that's no good. I gotta make sure the chicks know I'm from the city, you know."

"So are they."

"Hey, all the more reason I can't disappoint them."

Shortly, a slicked-up Art Rosen in his best party bells joined the troops converging on the hot imports. The mobilization left a peaceful vacuum in the cinderblock beehive, which Ike filled for a time with the downbeat notes of Baldwin's prose. Then, realizing he was wasting what might be a rare opportunity, he put on his favorite record, an Otis Redding album bequeathed to him by Jan, who had listened once and decided to stick to Motown and Simon and Garfunkel. He had remembered seeing the record in a bin at Louie's during lunch breaks from his summer job in the appliance stockroom of Hall's department store. He went in once a week to collect stuff he'd heard Elizabeth playing when he was a kid and to catch up on things he'd heard at Tommy's and to watch black kids play the latest James Brown single on the turntable and buy it as soon as they heard two notes that were different from the latest James Brown record they bought the week before, neither of which he'd ever heard on the radio. He hadn't been particularly interested, but because Jan was never wrong he had listened, and again in the far-side quiet of the dorm he marveled at how she knew the sweet-and-husky heartbreak was his. The horns more mournful than James's, the beat like a pulse creeping, then soaring. It was that beat, finally, along with the teasing insinuation of the guitar fills and the bold affirmation of the voice, that moved him out of the room.

Into the warm night, Ike drifted past the lights of the throbbing student union toward the brighter destination of the off-campus area known as the Village. Most students who didn't live in dorms or fraternity houses stayed in apartments there, above and next to the record stores, clothing stores, delis, diners and little incensed boutiques. It reminded him of Jewtown, a self-contained little hamlet with its own distinct population, in this case East Coast remnants of the Haight-Ashbury subculture, as opposed to the colored community displaced by the interstate.

As it turned out, the association was more literal than he expected; here, too, the image was darkened by spooks.

"Say, blood. Was*app*nin."

Three black students, who really looked like freshmen, snatched his attention from a display window of pipes and tie-dyed shirts.

"Loadin up for the par-tay, brother?"

"You mean the mixer at the union?" Ike said brightly, feeling suddenly wrong for not having planned to go.

"*Naah.*" The word was a sharp rebuke, but the face did not judge. "Down in the Valley. Number Three. Be jumpin off in about a half hour."

"Oh, yeah. Right."

"You weren't here this summer, were you?" said one of the others. "Name's Carl."

He lifted his hand and Ike watched the fingers closely; would they hang loose for a grab, close for a slap or form a fist for a pound?

"Ike. No, I just got in today." Uncertain at the last moment, he grabbed Carl's hand as it still descended, worked a quick thumb-wrap and pulled free. The other two kept their hands in their pockets. None of them had actually stopped moving; the whole exchange took place in a slow, circling shuffle, like prowling heavy-weights, so that Ike was left facing the way he had come.

"Come on down, man. Might as well get the year started right. In fact, why don't you come on with us. We're gonna fall by my room and do somathis wine."

Without actually considering the proposal, Ike took his next step in the direction they were going. The one after that came more easily, and soon he was falling into their rhythm.

"This here's Freddie, my roommate," Carl said, "and Zulu." Nods and grunts.

"So what was the deal this summer?" Ike asked.

"Nigger orientation," said Zulu, the biggest of the three, who moved his huge sneakers as if they weighed forty pounds each.

"They brought about thirty of us here for six weeks. Gettin ready for college, you know? Classes and workshops and shit."

"And parties," added Freddie.

"It wasn't bad," Carl continued. "But they had some white high-school kids stayin in the same dorm. Silly motherfuckers, man. First week they smelled one of the sisters' hot combs and complained that we were usin drugs."

"She ain't had no business straightenin that shit anyway," Freddie said.

"Yeah, but dig, they moved *us* out of the dorm. Said that was easier 'cause there were more of them. You know that ain't right."

"I know at least one a them was sorry to see us go, though, cause she was gettin her *own* orientation," Zulu said straightfaced.

They laughed and slapped, and Ike, back in stride with the pimping pace, knew that this was his chance. It had been a long time since Tommy had led him to hot-body functions at Douglass Center and in church folks' sweaty living rooms, with 45s stacked like pancakes and "Cookie" or "P.J." scribbled on each label. He'd stopped cold after Valerie of the shiny legs and sweaty dreams left him for dead. She had bopped around the red-lit room with him politely, then gone over to do amazing things with her brand-new body on the other side of the room. When he saw her grip one of the older boys' shoulders and let herself be slowly ground into a man's man's man's world he knew he was out of his league. Since then he had confined himself mostly to Jan's rec room with a dozen or so other misfits, cuddling with Cheryl on big pillows on the floor and denying the urges of his feet. Time for that shit to stop, and he knew he had to make his move before he slipped back into his old routine.

Carl's room, unlike his own motel setup, already seemed like somebody's home; everything had found a place to be that was more natural than where it belonged. Freddie shoved aside a stack of magazines and newspapers to make room for himself on one bed, Carl sifted through the albums spread on the other, and Zulu sat heavily beside a basketball on the desk to open the wine.

"Hey wait, man, let me get some cups," Carl said, fishing four from a desk drawer.

"That's right, Zulu, we don't know where your blue lips been," Freddie said.

"Your mama's pussy."

The wine came around, red and sweet but lighter than Hodge's holiday Mogen David, and the conversation ebbed and surged. They assessed O.J.'s pro prospects—Carl, from Buffalo, was missing the last exhibition game by being there—and Zulu held forth on the Panthers. It seemed a canned spiel, primarily for Ike's benefit, since everyone else had no doubt heard it to death. But the wine helped him challenge the wisdom of armed confrontation and risk Zulu's scorn. Shit, man, you think the po-lice care about you and me? Cause we in college or somethin? Just some more nigger heads to crack open, and I for one ain't turnin no cheek, dig. Talkin bout payback. Yeah, Ike answered, but where's the payback if you're dead or exiled in Cuba someplace? It's just not *practical*. We get in a position to run these cities, get control of the political machinery, the police will be working for *us*. As he spoke, a reefer floated by and Ike waved it off expecting a reaction but Freddie, still sipping, denounced drugs in the name of the Honorable Elijah Muhammad. Bean-pie, bow-tie motherfuckers ain't shit, Zulu scoffed, and asked Freddie how'd he like them ribs at the barbecue. I ain't no Muslim, he replied, but that don't mean they ain't right about some things. At least they ain't no revolutionary rapists like your boy Beaver Cleaver, and I'm tellin you, that dope's killin us, man. Not as fast as the honkies, said Zulu. Well, y'all done killed the wine, so what do you say? asked Carl, splashing Brut at the dresser. The music, which had been going in circles, had built to a climax and was now calling for Maceo. It was time to get down.

As they crossed the yard to Number Three, Ike noticed the lights in the union building up the hill and imagined the kind of weird, pagan, off-the-beat gyrations they were doing in there. Off the beat, off the pig, it was all the same to them. Anarchy. Ahead, other dark figures slipped into the low building that was an exact duplicate of his own—a meeting here tonight—and the vibrations spread out to meet them: Ike's right foot struck the ground on two and four.

The room was darker than the night. The electronic wails from the union did not penetrate the walls of the dorm lounge, which had been transformed into something Ike remembered almost painfully. The people were bigger, the knit shirts somewhat different. But the poses, the voices, even the faces were the same. *Caintgetnexta**you** girl, caintgetnexta**you** girl*. Ike felt like a sinner back in service. He even saw a guy looked just like ape-ass Wilbur Harrison, who had hated Ike ever since first grade, apparently because Ike could read and talk, which the teachers appreciated.

Be good or I won't let you suck my banana, he'd said, proud of himself, at the starting line in response to one of Wilbur's tired faggot taunts before beating him at last in the final city meet. So what if his teammates had had to pull Wilbur off him in the locker room later?

Ike drifted away from the others and eased along the wall like someone coming late to a movie and waiting for his eyes to adjust. But his eyes were the least of it. He was entranced by the ritual and watched for what seemed like a very long time. The floor space quickly shrank, but the room's boundaries expanded until they were nonexistent; there were people everywhere, and they were all moving.

Listen to the voices:

WEDON'T NEED NO MU-SIC
WEDON'T NEED NO MU-SIC
WEDON'T NEED NO MU-SIC
WEDON'T NEED NO MU-SIC

When rattlesnaking tambourines announced a tune he knew well, he reached out to a short sister who, he thought, looked like Sunday School. She grabbed Ike's hand and pulled him into the quicksand. Then she left him on his own. Had he not been high he might have wanted just to study her movements. But he was high, and he was tired of spectating, so he went after her. He didn't know what he was doing, but it didn't matter. He took his cue from the look on her face—the child was happy. She even paused to meet him halfway so that when the song ended and broke his heart they were getting off in unison.

"Thank you," she said smiling and not at all out of breath. "What's your name?"

"Ike."

"I'm Juanita. You weren't here this summer, were you?"

Ike laughed to himself and wondered if he should have a T-shirt made up: NO, I WAS NOT HERE THIS SUMMER. WHY WERE YOU?

"Nope," he said. "First time."

"Really? So how you like it?"

Ike gave an animated shrug. "Not too bad so far. This happen every night?"

"I don't know where you come from, honey, but this is college. Gotta hit them books, you know? But hey, Saturday night come, watch out."

"Okay. I guess that'll do," Ike said straightfaced.

"Listen, I'll see you later, all right? I have to take a break. I been workin hard, and it's *hot* in here. You know niggers can throw off some heat."

"Yeah, why do you suppose that is?"

"*Funk* genes, baby. What's the matter, ain't you never took biology?"

He watched her work her way through the crowd and the music began again, loud, and somebody screamed. People were getting serious about this. The sound of a whistle pierced the thump as the room whirled back into motion. Joyous voices climbed above the record to testify.

I said a HEY HEY . . . I feel all right *one time!*
huh!
Said HEY HEY . . . I feel all right! *two time!*
unh! unh!
HEY HEY . . . I feel all right! *three time!*
unh! unh! unh!
I said a-HEY HEY . . . I feel all right! *fo' time!*
TURN THIS MOTHERFUCKER OUT!
HEY HEY . . . I feel all right!
TURN THIS MOTHERFUCKER OUT! *YEAH!*
TURN THIS MOTHERFUCKER OUT!

The little old groovemaker with the whistle jumped up on a table. The people were summoning the spirits from behind the castle walls. Their funky temple jumped to warp factor 8 and soared, straight on till morning.

Hours later, long after the beer-soaked anarchists had been driven into hiding, Ike stumbled back to tranquility base humming. He spent about half an hour putting his key into the lock, cut a little step in the hallway, and spun into his room. With his bad self.

"If you're from upstate, you must know of Bo Howard," said Maier. "God, he was good. Never saw anyone that big move that fast, certainly not then. He made the end-around play an art form. One of our most honored students, too."

Ike smiled and wondered how fast Howard had moved clearing the tables at the fraternity where he worked. The end-around, he knew, never got him into the hotels when the team was on the road. Was this guy sugar-coating, or did he really not know what Ike could have figured out himself if *Jet* hadn't confirmed Hodge's rumors?

"He's in the administration now, as you probably know. Urban development, number two man. The only surprise is that I never knew he was a Republican, but of course that fits if you know him. Well." Maier looked down from the top of his neatly packed bookshelf and noticed Ike as if he'd just remembered why this kid was in his office. "What area of government do you think you might want to concentrate in?"

Wasn't it enough that he had a major planned? Nobody had said this would be a multipart exam. "I really don't know," Ike said. "I mean, I'm not sure what areas there are to concentrate in until I take a few courses. In the long run, though, I was thinking about law school and maybe politics." Halfway through the statement, Ike realized that the apologetic tone wasn't necessary; Maier didn't care.

"Of course, of course," Maier said, crinkling his eyes under the shaggy white brows in a way Ike supposed meant that he'd given the correct answer. "Most freshmen don't know exactly what they want to do. Most haven't any idea, just between you and me. You might not want to stay with government at all. Not too popular these days." He winked. "They all seem to want to get rid of it, not make it work."

"Well, I think I'll want to stick with it," Ike said, encouraged to the point of casual confidence. "I've given it some thought and it seems like the right thing."

"That's good, that's good. So." He leaned back in his squeaky swivel chair. "How did the first two weeks of classes go? Any problems so far?"

"Not at all. Nothing's really happened yet, but I'm adjusting pretty well."

"Fine, fine. You know, we in the faculty are par*tic*ularly concerned about the incoming black students this year. Whether or not they can get settled in light of the trouble we had in the spring. You know about that, of course."

"Yeah," Ike said, wondering if he was supposed to know any more than he had read in the paper.

"I was part of the faculty advisory committee that helped organize the Black Studies program. We had some last-minute snags about the degree of autonomy the program would have. That was the crux of the problem. The black students involved had some people they wanted to bring in and that's what they got. I assume they've put together a fairly competent staff over there."

"I really don't know. I don't have any courses there this semester."

"Well, that's probably good. You've got a lot of other things to get out of the way your first couple of years. I think they're doing a lot of political science over there, though, which may interest you."

"Yeah, I'd thought about that."

"In fact, this Bates is a political science man—he's the director over there, you know. I'm not too sure about his academic credentials, but the students were very adamant about getting him. He apparently was very much the activist out in California. That's what frightened some of my colleagues. They had hoped for a more traditional scholarly approach, and the students naturally were inclined toward a bit more, ah, relevance, as they say. I suppose that makes some sense. If you wanted any old fogey in there, I could teach the bloody classes, but that would miss the point, wouldn't it?" He laughed a quick, dry chuckle with his pale eyes leveled at Ike. "No, I think there's more to this fellow than meets the eye. You know anything about him?"

"No," Ike said, as it struck him: not only was he not going to get any advice from this man, but he was supposed to be providing *him* with information.

"Well, I'm sure you'll run into him. He talks about black students as if they were all his personal responsibility, so I suppose he would want to get to know as many as possible." Without warning, Maier sprang forward in his chair, rolled it a couple of feet closer to where Ike was sitting on the sofa—or was it a divan?—and poked him on the thigh with a wrinkled finger. Ike recoiled from the attack, and from the memory of the Vulture who used to snag in a Vulcan death grip eighth-graders carousing past his wood shop.

"That's what really *burns* me about this whole business," Maier said with threatening confidentiality. "The way students get sucked into the middle of it. Last year another of my counselees, a *brilliant* young black fellow named Eugene Mayford, got very involved in the planning of the program. I'm afraid he was mixed up with that takeover, too, although we're all supposed to pretend nobody knows who did what. I tell you, he used to come in here and discuss his ideas about politics—very well thought out, too, and of course very radical. We got into some interesting arguments. But I'm afraid he may be losing *perspective* on things." Maier rolled even closer, his voice hushed. "You know, some of these kids running around making trouble aren't going anyplace and they know it—

the white ones more than the blacks, frankly. But this Mayford can do things, I tell you, and he could seriously jeopardize his future with all this hoo-ha."

Ike had no idea what he was supposed to say, or if he was supposed to say anything, so he nodded understandingly, a little knit in his brow, and Maier backed off.

"Well," the professor said, bounding out of his chair. "I didn't mean to get you in here to listen to a whole lecture. I imagine you'll be getting enough of those, mine too. I think there were others waiting outside, weren't there?" Ike stood and moved the few steps to the door with Maier's hand on his back, steering. "Glad to have the chance to talk with you. If you have any problems or questions, just drop by. I'm always here, fossilizing." As Ike stepped outside the professor's office another student was already going in. "Well, you made it back, eh? What a surprise. Come in, come in. How was your summer?"

In the hall, Ike identified the scent he'd left behind: pipe tobacco, an especially rich and ancient blend that had matched perfectly the leather bindings on the books and the worn upholstery and the tweed and the hint of yellow in Maier's thick white hair. He'd been afraid they didn't have them like this anymore, the real thing, half Rex Harrison and half Rudy Vallee. Although he didn't quite know what to make of the exchange, or interrogation, he found it strangely satisfying. At least it had been a real human contact. The other instructors he'd encountered seemed dry and unimpressive or foolishly ingratiating. Those who fell into the first category, his calculus and chemistry professors, he'd wanted to show off for; he was, after all, a renaissance manchild, equally adept at numbers and his preferred humanities. But he had found himself, for the first time, uncertain, bearing down hard from his up-front seat in the large lecture halls and frustrated when some cocky bastard sitting even closer asked the questions he'd thought twice about. The younger instructors in his English and government seminars, on the other hand, seemed to expect certain things from him, some passion, some insight, some classic victim response, and he wasn't about to become a show-dog martyr for those trendy revisionists.

Which left him nowhere. In two weeks, he hadn't impressed anybody.

Especially students. On the second day of orientation, still high on his success at the party the night before, he'd felt more secure in spending time with Art Rosen. He had made his point, to himself, and could go on with his life. When he saw Carl and the others at dinner, he greeted them as everyone moved through the chow line. He thought he might ask about dropping by later, or even see if they wanted to come by his place sometime. But when they saw him walking to a table with Art they veered off pointedly in another direction. He knew immediately what game they were playing and knew there was no winning even if he had the heart to try. The next night he skipped dinner. Soon after, Art had assembled his own dining group from the dorm. Ike joined them mournfully on those nights he couldn't summon the energy to make excuses and eat alone. He would nod at the others if their paths crossed, but no words were spoken.

Passing through the dorm lobby, Ike glanced at his empty mailbox and muttered curses to Cheryl until he got to his door, which was open, meaning that Art was in. He found his roommate sitting with a bio book and Lenny from across the hall sitting on *his* bed reading out loud. "Get off my bed," Ike said almost before he was through the door.

"Hang on a minute," said Lenny. "I'm readin my daily mail from my girlfriend. Lookit, five different letters she wrote in one day and mailed together."

"Come on, Lenny, can't you read your mail in your own room? Nobody wants to hear that crap."

"Hey, Art, how come your roommate's such a spoilsport?" Lenny said, rising.

"How come you gotta be such a asshole?" Art said. "I just got finished tellin you I didn't wanna hear that shit either. Give it a rest, awready."

Ike smiled as he settled into his rightful place to read the campus paper. Apparently Lenny was beginning to get on Art's nerves, too—especially all the yammering about his sex life which nobody believed. Girlfriend talk bothered Ike anyway, even more than

Mets talk. He had promised to throw something at the next person to say the words "magic number." He had no idea, however, what he would do if anyone said something about the picture of Cheryl he had put up on his dresser.

"Okay, just for that, Rosen, I'm not gonna let you hear the hot fantasy part."

"She writes science fiction too?" Ike said from behind the paper.

"Yeah, sounds like a horror show to me," Art added. "Gowan, take a walk, Lenny."

"Awright, well screw you guys."

Lenny went out and left Ike and Art in the silence of their little homestead, which already had clearly defined lines. The telephone was on Ike's side of the room and was the only reason for violation of turf. On Ike's wall, above his head, was a huge black and white poster of Tommie Smith and John Carlos in their Olympic salute. Art had countered with Joe Namath and Raquel Welch, both in full color, which tended to steal the show. Ike had then hunted up a glaring color montage of Sly and the Family Stone, restoring the balance.

In spite of, or perhaps because of the fences, they had gotten along well. They had been to the movies together, and Ike had gone along to a party in the Village thrown by an upperclassman Art knew from home. Following the pattern established by dinner, Art did most of the socializing, and it was up to Ike to say if he wanted to join in. If he didn't, which was usually the case despite his lack of alternatives, there were no hard feelings. A pacer, Art left the room often but always closed the door so the hurly-burly of the halls didn't spill in. His gum chewing bugged the hell out of Ike, though; one day, forgetting himself, he'd nearly accused Art of sounding like a colored girl. But Art tried to be cool about that, too, so Ike never complained about his Ginger Baker drumming with highlighters on his math book.

"Hey, you read the editorial yet?" Art asked, breaking the silence.

"Uh-uh." The editorial, which Ike had just finished, was about the black students' sit-in and the controversy over the Black Studies program the previous spring. The paper applauded the administration's restraint in dealing with the protesters but chided it for forcing such action and thereby contributing to racial tension on campus.

"I heard a little about that back home, but it didn't seem like such a big deal, you know? Just like all the Vietnam stuff, like at Columbia and all that. I didn't know it was supposed to be so bad here."

"Neither did I. They might be exaggerating, though. I mean, they're probably not used to a lot of the other stuff in a place like this."

"Yeah, I guess like there's fights and things all the time in the city. There's the blacks and the Italians and the Jews and the Puerto Ricans, and every once in a while they all go at it, if somebody steps on somebody else's toes. But basically, you know, everybody gets along most of the time."

"Maybe the difference is it's all mixed together here. People don't have their own neighborhoods and schools or whatever."

"Yeah, you know, I hadn't thought about that. Like what's this, a Jewish room, a black room? Beats me. The whole dorm's mixed up. There's that crazy guy from Oklahoma or someplace upstairs and that Chinese kid on the next corridor." Art paused and looked puzzled. "I don't know, though. Shouldn't that make it better?"

Ike shrugged and went back to the paper.

"Guess I just don't get it," Art said. "You think there'll be any more trouble this year?"

"I don't think so," Ike said lightly. "Shouldn't be anything serious anyway." He hoped he sounded convincing, and he hoped that nothing he heard later would prove him wrong.

At exactly eight o'clock that night, Ike entered the Uhuru House, a small converted fraternity house on the south edge of campus, for the first time. He had found the notice in his mailbox the day before announcing an urgent meeting of all black students. It didn't surprise him that they had found him; the school seemed extremely conscious of keeping counts. He had already sort of decided that if something like this happened he would show up to see what was going on. Despite his experience in the dining hall, he knew he wanted to keep in touch and this kind of formal setting might be the best way. There wasn't much contact in class. That was worse than high school, in fact. It couldn't be tracking; they all got in, didn't they? Maybe somehow, with those lists they kept, they had found a way to disperse the hundred or so black freshmen throughout all the courses available so there weren't but a couple in each: busing by registration.

It didn't surprise him, either, that by being on time he was way early. The one social contact he'd made since orientation made him expect that. Hearing word of a Saturday night party, he had gamely showed up at the appointed time and watched stereo equipment be set up for about half an hour before he gave up. Luckily—lucky because he was able to ease his guilt—he caught Art out and Cheryl in and talked on the phone till one. So he had no hopes for timeliness when he walked into the deserted lobby, but had thought it better to leave before Art returned from his after-dinner pool game to ask where he was going.

The main room, off the lobby, looked like a large living room and had a map of Africa and cheap-looking paintings of blue-black people in profile, the men framed in fierce warrior headdresses, the women encircled by earrings, necklaces and elaborate headwraps. Two brothers were standing in the room talking, and one looked around at Ike's entrance.

"You here for the meeting?" Ike nod-mumbled yes. "Yeah, we'll get started in a few. There's some people downstairs. Why don't you try to start gettin them up here?"

Ike found some stairs and descended to a darkened lounge where a stereo was playing and about a dozen people were sitting around, a few playing cards and the rest talking. There were pictures of Malcolm and Huey Newton and Kathleen Cleaver lining the walls. "Uh, excuse me," Ike said. "I think the meeting's about to start upstairs."

There were vague sounds of acknowledgement but nobody moved. Ike faded into a chair in the corner. Several minutes later, the brother who had greeted Ike came bounding down the stairs. "Hey, come on, you all, let's make that move, all right? Man, you can play cards all night. People are comin in now, and we got to get the thing started."

Upstairs, a small crowd of people had formed and others kept dragging in. The upperclassmen, it seemed, could be divided into two groups: one sporting leather jackets or fatigues and berets, the other emulating the pictures on the wall with large jewelry, dashikis and braids. The freshmen, in their denim caps and sneakers, looked like guys from the Southwest track team, like people who threw rocks when Martin Luther King was shot and hadn't done their homework. Depending on their roles, they stood erect along the walls, sat thoughtfully in the folding chairs set up in rows, or slouched on the furniture and perched on radiators and windowsills. But where was she?

It was going on nine when a short, muscular, darkly handsome dude finally spoke to the gathering. He wore, Ike noticed, combat boots, jeans and a dashiki. "All right, this is the first meeting this year of the Black Liberation Front," he said, managing to get on top of the noise level and ease it down some. Ike was asking himself how he got to be a member of the Black Liberation Front. "I guess most of you know me, my name is Ken Hollyfield. For those of you who may be here for the first time, I want to welcome you to Uhuru House. I hope you'll feel free to make this like your second home, or your first home, really, while you're up here. It's here for all of us and it needs all of us to survive. Starting this year, Uhuru also houses our Black Studies program. Even if you weren't here last year, I'm sure you know about the hassles we went through to get it, and our primary concern this year is to make sure we keep it, right?"

The speaker, Hollyfield, went on to talk about sacrifices and building on a foundation and healing old wounds within the group. He claimed that although they had forced the university to give them the program, they still didn't want them there. As evidence, he mentioned a letter in the paper from a government professor whining about lowered standards and the coon calls some black students had received during the night.

"And just *today*," he said, his top lip curled in a sneer, "some of you may not have heard about this, but two sisters were over in the Village—where the *liberal* white folks hang out—and the cracker told them straight out they couldn't try on no clothes, *and then tried to accuse them of stealing when they left*. That's right.

Called 'em niggers, too, when they wouldn't let him search their stuff. Then *they* went to call the police and he backed off. See what I'm sayin? We been through this shit before, right? You know what I'm talkin about. It's still happenin. Every *year*, and this one ain't no different. Same shit, so get ready."

There. She appeared in the entrance from the lobby—the reason he'd gone to the party, and the reason he'd felt guilty afterward. Her hair was out farther than he remembered; the sweat must have pulled it back that night. She had on a dashiki, too, but it didn't look like a costume. She eased behind Hollyfield and filled a space that somebody made for her on the sofa. She didn't see Ike's reaching eyes.

"Brother Garfield Bates," Hollyfield continued, "the director of the program, is scheduled to be here to talk about it—kind of run it down for those of you who know very little about it and give a progress report for the brothers and sisters who were here last year working very hard to get the thing off the ground." He glanced at his watch. "Yeah, Gene?"

Someone leaned forward from his seat in the front, near Juanita. "Don't forget to mention the on-campus and off-campus tutoring programs," he said. "We need to get that going within a couple of weeks if it's going to do the job."

"Yeah, right," Hollyfield said. "We got a lot of tutoring needs, so anybody wants to help in any capacity, check with Brother Mayford there later on tonight." There was an unsettling in the lobby. Bodies shifted and a man of about forty entered the room in a collected rush. He had glasses and a lightly salted 'fro and wore an open-collared, short-sleeve shirt with lots of pockets that suggested an African communist. He stood noticeably straight. "Brother Bates is here now, so we'll let him talk about the program, then back to BLF business," Hollyfield said.

In the soothing, elegant voice of a well-educated preacher, Bates briefly traced his own odyssey from Nashville to Oakland, watching the revolutionary fervor of the civil rights revolt first spawn and then become overwhelmed by the antiwar movement. As brothers and sisters, of necessity, grew increasingly extreme in their agitation for justice, once-sympathetic whites grew increasingly distant, and finally hostile, to the point where every black man and woman had a choice: to be actively involved in the struggle, and therefore inevitably at risk, or, by withdrawing, to become an unwitting tool for the forces dedicated to their oppression. He had accepted this position, he said, because he believed it presented a unique historical opportunity. Here, employing the vast though perverted resources of the institution, the talented tenth of which Du Bois spoke could be educated, not to rise above but to serve the Afro-American nation. And, he said, in the process of defining that education, tailoring it to our own needs, we can begin to transform the power structure from within, in one of the citadels of Western thought that have long propagated the policies designed for our destruction.

The words, and their presentation, transfixed Ike, even though some of the uncompromising implications disturbed him. For better or worse, Bates was able to put this—what did Maier call it, hoo-ha?—in perspective and give it a more precise nobility than the outfits and pictures could hope to project. But once Bates began describing the program itself, somebody interrupted to question why two white students had showed up in one of his Black Studies classes. That struck a nerve. Bates, looking tolerant, tried to explain that at this point they were in no position to deny registration to anyone, that a few curiosity seekers were to be expected but that they probably would not opt to persevere throughout the term. It didn't help. Other voices jabbed in, referring to *their* program. They couldn't let the honkies just take over; that was the administration's way of killing the thing. They were spies, sent by the president, Ellsworth, and the government department. Bates reminded them that they were not about conducting midnight rituals. What they hoped to accomplish could only be done in the bright of day, with the full confidence that theirs was a valid, even transcendent, educational mission. Let them come, as long as no black student is denied; perhaps they will learn how corrupt and narrow-minded their own classes have been.

Applause and right-ons drowned the lingering notes of dissent as Bates concluded and prepared to leave. The sight of Hollyfield rising dropped Ike's spirits. Even if the mau-mauing did not continue, this would, at best, become another tired business meeting, like the ones he had conducted in high school. Except his meetings had always started on time. A few students trailed out in Bates's wake, suggesting that that, indeed, had been the main event. Ike checked his watch, reminded himself of the work he had waiting, and, with a last glance at Juanita, decided to do the same.

As soon as Uhuru House faded behind him he felt the thrill of freedom, like when he and Tommy had slipped out of church. And he realized, again, just how much he enjoyed walking across campus at night. Night itself was a revelation, a rediscovery he had earned by coming of age. He'd known it as a boy, looking out the rear window of Black Beauty at the tops of trees and chimneys and water towers, or the stars themselves when they went farther out, to the fair or the drive-in or Niagara Falls—*hitting the road, Jack*. And the sneaky night of summer vacations that kept Tommy from go-seeking him in the bushes or kept him from finding the baseball until it thudded on his chest. Then he went inside to read and watch television and separate himself from the bad boys who stayed out too late, past puberty, and he lost it. He found it again when he got his license: driving at night became a peaceful exercise in expansive isolation. Without exposing himself, he could study the city, noticing things that didn't interest him before and that had been hidden from him when Elizabeth feared they might interest him: the bopping in bunches, the drinking on corners. But walking at night, here, was like what walking in towns with village greens must have been like, a kind of real-world Disneyland where nice people were out strolling and there was no shattering glass and no sirens.

There he is!

Hold it, asshole!

Ike turned to the voices that exploded behind him. Two large white students pounded toward him, slowing slightly with the confidence that their prey was within reach. His legs stopped working. His breath had left him. His eyes, he feared, had gone Rochester, bugging whitely in the dark.

We gotcha now, boy.

"C'mon, lay off, willya?"

A third voice that was not his pulled Ike's head around. Another white student he had not noticed stood a few yards ahead of him, looking sheepish and annoyed. The first two moved past Ike as if he were a shadow. He felt a glancing shoulder and a rush of beery air.

"You can't leave now, kid. We got it all set up."

"Not tonight, okay? I got work to do."

"Bullshit, man, it's Thursday. Weekend's started."

"Come on back to the house. We need everybody to play."

Ike faded to the other side of the street, avoiding the human roadblock ahead of him and the shame of his own, brief terror. Forcing all thought from his mind, he carefully placed one foot in front of the other in a quickening sequence that he hoped would get him back to the dorm before the replays began. Behind him, one of the voices—were they that loud before?—caught his ear.

You see that colored kid? I think we scared the shit outta him, man.

Trying to keep a calm, leisurely pace as he moved toward the bus station downtown, Ike found it impossible not to absorb some of the Friday energy. People were out, playing touch football on what might be the last nice weekend of the year, and trekking to Village stores to stock up on beer and sangria. Even Art Rosen, finally, was on his way home. For days Ike had been urging him to take the weekend off, watch the playoffs with his buddies at home and catch the Monday game at Shea. Besides, Ike assured him, there was no use sticking around for Homecoming without a date, and it was no big deal for freshmen in any case. Art knew, of course, why Ike was so eager for him to go and teased him along, changing his mind repeatedly, fretting over the playoff tickets, pretending he had plans for Homecoming. At the last minute, there was some confusion about the ride, and Ike became so agitated Art had to calm him. *Look, it's okay, awright? I'm goin. You got the whole room for the whole weekend. Just remember, if I get lucky next Saturday, you're sleepin with Lenny.* Soon, but not soon enough, Art was gone, and Ike began trying to cover up the evidence of his roommate's existence, throwing Art's loose clothes into the closet and sticking all his books up on a shelf to make the other half of the room look, at least, neutral.

Ike paused for traffic at the top of the steep hill that separated the college from the small town it supported, and a car pulled up beside him. The driver, a black female, motioned to him, offering a lift. He didn't want one, but since he hadn't asked for the favor he didn't feel he should refuse. He opened the door and realized he had made a mistake. It was Juanita.

"Where you goin?" she asked with weekend feel-good charm.

"All the way through," he said. She didn't recognize him. She hadn't stopped for *him;* she had simply stopped for another black student. He felt even worse.

"Bus terminal?" she asked. Ike nodded. "You ain't got no luggage, so you must have somebody comin in, right?" She was smiling like a kid sister who knew all your business. "Hey, I know you. What's your name?"

"Ike."

"Yeah, that's right!" She turned down the loud eight-track. "I met you at that first party. I'm Juanita, remember?"

"Oh yeah," he said. "Hi."

"That was a month ago, brother. Where you been keepin yourself? I don't ever see you around. Way you were workin out that night, I expected to see you swingin from the chandeliers every weekend."

"I didn't know freshmen could have cars," Ike said.

"What? Oh, it's not mine. You know Gene?"

"Gene Mayford?"

"Yeah, it's his. He just lets me drive it once in a while," she said with a sly smile. "I need practice, just got my license. Don't be scared, though. I won't kill you or anything." But it was not her driving, scary though it was, that concerned him. "You takin any courses at Uhuru?"

"No, I've been pretty busy, you know, tryin to get all my requirements out of the way."

"Oh, you one of them niggers that does it right, huh?" She laughed. "That's probably a good idea. I been goin to so many parties and meetings, honey, I'm about a month behind already. After this weekend I'm gonna settle down, though. You goin to the thing at Dewitt tonight?"

"I don't know. I'll see what happens." He had ceased to be

amazed by the fact that everybody just automatically knew about these things except him. His grape was just *off* the vine, that's all there was to it.

"You oughtta try and make it if you can. Like, I figure we really oughtta get together when the whiteys have their shit, you know. Got to put out our own vibes to counteract theirs."

"Yeah, right."

They hit red lights going through town that were never there before, Ike was certain, and by the time they got to the bus station Juanita had dug into his hometown and his major and was closing in on his blood type.

"Thanks a lot," he said when he finally got out of the car. She wasn't in any rush and had taken him right to the door. Good thing buses never came early.

"Okay, Ike, take it easy. And you all have a good time." He watched the car disappear, then went inside.

The tiny station looked like a museum replica of an old rural railroad depot. Six pew-like benches sat back to back in pairs in the center of the hardwood floor; four others lined the walls that were decorated in elaborate, sandy tile beneath a stamped tin ceiling with a large, lazy fan. The ticket counter was made like an old-fashioned bank teller's window. Behind it, on another tiled wall, hung the arrival and departure board, the kind where the names of cities and the times slid into grooves and looked like a ransom note because the type faces were different. Perhaps, Ike thought, this sort of quaintness was typical in those places where white people, and not just poor ones, still rode the bus.

The place was filled with people waiting to get out on the six twenty-five to New York. That must have happened every Friday, but there was also a whole delegation of fraternity types waiting for their Homecoming dates: hometown stuff or girls' school imports. Ike took a seat and watched the turnover as the New York bus loaded up and the weekend goodies rolled in. A procession of trim and stylish girls with their overnight cases stepped out of ten-year-old *Life* magazine photos, met their escorts, their *Ivy men*, and promenaded out of the station beaming. Ike compared them to his five-week-old image of Cheryl walking from his car back to her house with that skating gait on Labor Day night. For a long time before that it had depressed him to drop her off at that corner, by a small playground, and slink back to his own side of reality combing the seat and his clothes for long hairs in the dark. But that night he had cut through the streets at sixty blasting his radio. It was over. They had made it. They would meet again in the next life. *We got the right foundation, and with love and de-termination . . .*

He looked up and saw her walking toward him. For an instant, a terrifying instant, she looked like the others. Taller, of course, but the same pale lipstick and mascara, the sweater, skirt and stockings—a yearbook picture—under an Easterish overcoat. Desperately, he focused more closely: in the heavy eyebrows, the almost cruel cheekbones, the spidery lines of gray in the deep auburn hair, he found her. In that searching moment he also saw himself in her eyes (lighter than they should be, they always surprised him) and knew the difference. The others wouldn't even look at him sitting there; she could see him.

"Hi," she said quickly, less a greeting than a statement of fact. Neil Armstrong should have been so profound: I'm here. *We're* here. He saw the skin stretch beneath the wide line of her mouth, promising a chin cleft that would not, in fact, appear even if she let herself smile all the way. What could Ike possibly have seen that would remind him of the others?

"How you doin?" He smiled easily but felt a twinge when he thought, for a second, that she wanted him to jump up and hug her, as he had never done.

"All right, I guess," she said, obviously resigned to playing by the old rules.

"You ready to go?"

"Yeah, unless you wanna sit here and watch people get off the bus all night."

"You look terrific."

"I feel stupid. This is like Barbies on parade."

"Well, the show's over. Come on." He got up, took her suitcase and led her out of the station. She took his free hand in hers, a small but significant change. He decided that a city bus would be quicker than a taxi, since the few lurking around had been snapped up, so they crossed the street to the bus stop. They had just gotten there when a blue Toyota flashed past them and screeched. Ike released Cheryl's hand, and Juanita backed up in front of them.

"Hey there, Brother Ike. Want a ride?" She grinned.

"No, that's okay, we're just—the bus'll be here any minute."

"Don't be silly," she said, flinging the passenger door open. "Get in." Ike crawled into the back seat with Cheryl's suitcase and Juanita passed him a bucket of Kentucky Fried Chicken. Cheryl got in front. "That was good timing. I just had to get some food to take to one of Gene's meetings. I'm Juanita," she added, looking at Cheryl.

"My name's Cheryl." She glanced back at Ike, who was sliding uncomfortably into a corner.

"How do you like it here, Cheryl?"

"I don't know. I've never been here before."

"Oh really? We don't see Ike around much, and I thought maybe he'd been spending time with you. I can see where he'd want to, you know. You're very attractive."

"Thank you," Cheryl said. She tossed her hair luxuriously, a completely foreign gesture, and smothered a smirk.

"Hey look, Juanita . . . You can let us out anytime."

"No trouble, brother. What are friends for? Which dorm are you in?"

"Six."

"Yeah, that sounds right. I didn't think there were any black people living there."

Through his anger, Ike thought he heard Cheryl giggle.

The car kicked up dirt and gravel when Juanita, at last, swerved sharply into the parking lot behind Ike's dorm. "Pleased to meet you, Cheryl," she said. "I guess you won't be at Dewitt tonight, Ike. I see you got other business to take care of. Knock yourself out, brother."

"Old flame?" Cheryl asked as the car spurted off.

"New pain. What are you smiling about?"

"I've never seen you squirm like that. It was funny."

Ike grunted, yanked up her suitcase and stalked into the dorm, pushing past a group of guys gathered in the corridor. Inside the room, he dropped the suitcase, leaned back against the door and exhaled.

"She really got to you, didn't she?"

"Oh no, I love harassment. I love it when people can't mind their own business."

"But they can't. I mean, they never do. So what?" She pinned him to the door. "If you're going to go out with a beautiful woman, you have to expect people to stare and be jealous. Now kiss me. It's all right, nobody's looking."

"You think you're pretty damn smart, don't you?"

"I missed you."

His fingers quickly reacquainted themselves with the back of her ribs, and after a breathbreaking clinch he gently extricated himself.

"So, whaddaya think of my place?"

She shrugged. "Looks a little like a jail cell. But a nice jail cell."

"Thanks." He flopped on the bed and pulled her down beside him. "So whaddayawanna do?"

"I was doing it."

"Well, I mean, don't you think we should *do* something?" he asked. "Look around, go someplace?"

"Not especially." She was stroking his good hair in back—his only inheritance, he had been told, besides the TV and his teddy bear. "It's enough just to be here with you, darling."

Ike made a noise, and realized as he made it that it was the same tooth-sucking, get-out-of-my-face-with-that-mess sound Elizabeth made when *he* was laying it on too thick.

"Uh-oh," she said. "You're not gonna sulk, are you?"

"No, I'm not. It's just so, you know, pre*dictable* to fall in here and roll around on the bed. We've got all night to do that."

"Excuse me?"

"You know what I mean. I kinda thought we should celebrate our independence."

"Okay. You're right," she said. "Get up."

"You got a plan?"

"Do I have a plan." She started swatting through his closet. "Take your clothes off. You're changing."

"Where are we going?"

"Come on, where's the good stuff? I know she made you bring a suit."

"What's the deal?"

"This'll do. Oh, I remember this jacket. Didn't you get some award in this? Very debonair."

"Cheryl . . . "

"We're going where they go."

"Who's they?"

"You know, the blazers and the debs. The bus people. I got all dressed to look like one, God knows why, so you can, too. I want to see them in their natural habitat."

"This is crazy, you know that," he said. "I don't know where those people hang out."

"So we'll follow the smell of flowers. I know they're out there someplace. Hundreds of them. Please?"

"All right, but turn your back. You may not be able to resist me when I take my pants off."

"Don't worry. That would be too predictable, don't you think?"

Outside, since Ike didn't have much to offer in the way of news, Cheryl talked about her roommate, who she thought was fabulous, and how they did everything together except tennis, because Judy was a good athlete but had pronounced her a hopeless klutz, and about how she couldn't decide among English, French and economics as a major because she loved all her classes. Ike listened dutifully, although he found the conversation troubling. It put distance between them. In just a few weeks, she had begun a new life. Why were these things so easy for her? It had taken her about two minutes to get in with The Group when she'd transferred from Michigan to Southwest, and then she glommed on to Jan—*his* friend. And now this wonderful Judy person.

"Oh, Richard, wait a minute," she said suddenly. They were crossing a bridge that spanned a deep gorge cleaving the campus. Not far away a waterfall, especially majestic by night when it sounded more Niagara than it looked, plunged into the depths below them. "This is *fantastic!* Why didn't you tell me?"

"I thought I did."

"Yeah, right. 'Scenic' was the word, I think. Nice try. Can we walk down there tomorrow?"

"Okay," he said, and put his arm around her. "It's a date."

The distance melted, and they were back. The summer had not been a waste. They'd both had Mondays off—she was working part-time at Sears, he had odd hours at the airport (where an aging skycap who used to hang with Hodge kept asking about white pussy at college). Every week he would drop Elizabeth off at IBM on the Parkway, then double back for Cheryl, who had taken the bus downtown, and they would drive out, away from the city in every direction to every park and natural attraction they could think of. He said he was getting her acquainted with the region, since she'd gone home to Michigan the summer before. But in fact, having huddled so desperately in the dark since they'd come together, they used those sunshine hours to create a fantasy courtship that went beyond the tacky confines of dates and proms, the routine options which, they said, they would have rejected even if they could have done those things.

Instead, they talked. Lying on a hillside or sitting by a lake, shielding the sun with each other's bodies, they shared the three-year-old hiding place, the six-year-old accident, the twelve-year-old birthday party. He told her about Hodge running the 100 in 10 flat in army boots during World War I and dating Lena Horne—she didn't believe any of it either—and about his Uncle Sergeant Clarence leading newly integrated troops in Korea, and about dancing with his mother to Nat King Cole and how that memory got him through those miserable thirteen-year-old hours at Douglass Center. And, when she asked, he told her it didn't bother him not knowing his father—except that his not being around was kind of a cheap cliché—because he didn't remember enough to miss him and everything had turned out all right anyway.

She talked of her father's struggle to overcome Italian stereotypes in Detroit, a struggle that won him her distantly Irish mother, who, she was sure, had not forgiven her for being born; his relatives thought starting a family would bring him back to earth. But her father had kept pushing by borrowing money from his brother, a jazz drummer—another obligation her mother regretted. A little night school, an MBA, a few promotions and finally the out-of-state transfer that took them away from the scent of garlic—a move that *she* had not forgiven her mother for engineering. She had gone as far as trying to rent a room at the Y so she wouldn't have to leave. Her father had talked her out of that with promises of frequent returns, which she often mentioned to Ike's dismay. But, as she was always quick to point out, meeting him had been worth it, especially since, even back home, she had already been programmed for a WASPy fate.

But that wasn't her. As she'd told him when they met, they weren't all alike. Even little things set her apart, like the way she'd started walking without lifting her feet when she was taller than all the boys in sixth grade. And her commitment to fashion became tenuous after she ironed her hair for a British look and some wise guys decided she resembled something out of *101 Dalmatians*. Why bother? That was why she'd let Jan, and then him, pull her away from that crowd her mother approved of at Southwest.

By summer they were alone together; graduation had removed the cover of classes, meetings and school-sanctioned activities. When Jan tried to get them to go to Woodstock they'd been all too eager to use their parents as an excuse; they went on their own picnic, got caught in the rain, too, and sang Phil Spector—he was the only human being who'd ever witnessed her biker-girl routine, and he'd been waiting years for somebody to hear him do both Righteous Brothers. Near the end they spent a day reliving his memories at the annual State Fair, where newfangled technology, mostly in the form of military exhibits, mingled with livestock shows as easily as the smells of cotton candy, sausage sandwiches and manure. They strolled the midway with their names stitched onto matching cheap cowboy hats and rode the two-tiered carousel over and over and over again. It reminded her of her favorite at an amusement park back home, where she always chose the black pony with the pink mane and severe nostrils and the strong neck curved down like a swan's. Next to the bumper cars, he became obsessed with popping a balloon with a water pistol to win her a stuffed animal; he didn't, so he spent the next week hunting down a teddy bear that looked something like the ones they'd both had and christened it Mr. McFat, in honor of Clyde.

He told her he loved her. He had thought about it, but said it before he'd planned to—said it instead of a kiss under a tree with a bluejay in it, in the state park with the bottomless lake where all the black people in the county used to go on the Fourth of July. She looked like she was thinking about it but didn't say I Love You too. To her credit, she never did; she didn't have to. The time ran out on them in Madison Park, after they'd seen *Romeo and Juliet* for the second time and were waiting in the Comet to see if "In the Still of the Nite" would beat out the Beatles for number one on the all-time Top 300 countdown. It didn't—it even finished behind "In-A-Gadda-Da-Vida," an outrage that distracted him for a while—but soon they were hardly listening.

"I knew you could do it," she said, as he led them into a bar, the Greek House, on the street bordering fraternity row. "It's okay, I won't tell anybody you knew about this place."

It was not impressive, a lot of old wood under dim lights, beer signs and fraternity emblems, a dart board and a simple bar swarming with people. Ike and Cheryl were both over- and underdressed. Although there were a few in the crowd who looked like a society ball, most were the sloppy prep variety, outfitted in uncreased corduroys, baggy sweaters and holey oxford button-down shirts.

They sat in a narrow, high-backed booth complete with carved limericks shellacked over by age-old beer. No waitress was forthcoming, so Ike elbowed up for a couple of drafts—since they didn't ask for ID, he didn't have to act on his briefly considered scheme of hollering discrimination—and returned to the booth as disappointed as relieved that no one thought their presence remarkable.

"There's something you don't see every day, Chauncy," Cheryl said, licking beer foam from her top lip.

"What's that, Edgar?" he responded, reflexively quoting the cartoon line.

"Over at the end of the bar." He followed her chin to a tall, balding, paunchy guy—a lineman gone to seed—holding court.

"Well, there's the real thing, all right," he said. "Homecoming hero. I bet he's not talking about plastics, either, or the stock market."

"The touchdown that beat Harvard in forty-nine, maybe?"

"Something like that, but *he* didn't score it."

"I wonder where Mrs. All-American is. Maybe he's hunting chippies."

"Nope. Over there."

"Bingo. Think she looks tight enough? God, she makes my mother look like a fun chick."

"Yeah, and we're not having a good time, are we? Look at her checking her watch."

"She probably remembers how she met him and doesn't want him to get *too* nostalgic."

"Watch it, here comes the blitz."

As the man hunched slightly and extended his elbows—the key block, no doubt—the woman moved in deftly, grabbed his arm, placed his drink on the bar and steered him toward the door. He recovered just enough to grab a few hands and wave before she rode him out into the street. The fans left behind, respectful enough in his presence, were laughing before he was back in his car.

"So much for heroes," Ike said, returning to his beer.

"You know, it seems awfully dead in here," Cheryl said after a while.

"You were expecting maybe outrageous debauchery?"

"Maybe it's too early."

"Yeah, like maybe at the stroke of midnight somebody will play 'Louie, Louie' and they'll all go crazy."

"Ooh, I have an idea. Wait here."

"Where'm I goin?"

When she returned, he thought he heard the bass intro to "My Girl."

"Shall we dance?" she asked.

"Where'd you find that?"

"Jukebox in the corner. There's always something. Come on."

He rose warily, shaking his head. It was just the kind of display he'd never put on for his friends. But these were not his friends, were they? She was. What the hell. He took hold of her long waist and began to shuffle his feet self-consciously. She seized his shoulders and pushed her pelvis into him, locking him in place, and worked an animated slow drag.

"You don't even like to dance," he protested mildly.

"No, you don't like to dance. You never asked me."

"They're watching, you know," he said. His lips were right on her ear; her head fit neatly onto his shoulder.

She flung her hair back—twice in one day—and stared at him. Her face was even with his. "Are they smiling?" she asked.

"No."

"Good."

"What do you suppose they're thinking?"

"They might think I was a hooker but you don't look like you have enough money, so I guess that makes me just a slut."

"That should make you very popular."

"I don't think so. It's obvious that I have high standards."

As Ruffin's vocal faded she took his head and kissed him hard. And they left arm in arm, her singing the violin bridge, him adding the chorus of hey-hey-heys.

They skipped and Smokeyed their way back to the room, where the curtains remained open to the electric moonlight, like the blue-tinted glow at Madison Park, and stripped each other, barely heeding the luxury of time and space and the prying eyes of Broadway Joe and Raquel and Sly and Smith and Carlos. Only after she had wrapped those forever legs around his hips, dug her bitten nails into his back and—he was sure—finally squeezed a dimple onto her chin, did it occur to him how far they had come.

Although it was December and the temperature was in the thirties, he was sweating as he watched the cheerleaders and the warm-up drills and the swarm of people spreading over the shiny orange bleachers. Cheryl and Jan had strolled in, studying the crowd, and started to climb up into the seats, then saw him. Janet waved and handed something to Cheryl, who headed back down toward him, her long legs looping easily over the bleacher rows like a horse taking a jump. He'd never seen her in jeans before.

"Looks like it's gonna be a good game," he said when she got there.

"Too bad. Come on."

"Don't you wanna wait for the introductions? Sing the national anthem? Maybe catch the first quarter?"

"Nope," she said and took his arm.

She walked briskly, and he kept the pace, mostly out of concern for being seen. Slipping out of the gym with a girl before the game even started looked like exactly what it was. Outside the door she broke into a run and he followed. It was beginning to snow a little and the sense of escape was getting good to him. The slamming car doors left only the sound of their foggy breathing. He turned over the engine, sat back for a moment and took a deep breath. She reached over and covered his hand, then slid over to kiss him on the cheek.

"Take me away," she said.

"Where?"

"Just get moving."

He had spent the previous Saturday afternoon checking out nearby parking spots. It was hard to tell in daylight, though, and Elizabeth had wanted him home by nightfall. This was his first nocturnal expedition. He pulled out of the lot, came to the first stop sign and wavered.

"Turn right," she said. He almost wished she weren't sitting so close; he didn't drive that well.

"You have a plan?" he asked, creeping around the corner. She dipped into the pocket of her suede jacket and pulled out something noisy. "What's that?"

"Keys."

"To *what*?" It came out more testy than he meant.

"Jan's house." He could tell by her tone that she was pretty proud of herself, but he couldn't look. It had become more difficult to stay on the road.

"What about her parents? She does *have* parents, doesn't she?"

"Gone for the weekend."

"Completely? Both of them? You sure?"

"Trust me."

He was impressed, and incredibly excited, and a little disappointed; he had smuggled an old comforter into the back seat. He wanted to ask how long they had planned this, but thought it better simply to grip the wheel and get there. On Janet's block, it occurred to him to turn off the headlights. It was a dumb idea. The snow was drifting right into the windshield, and he was temporarily blinded, and she asked what he was doing, and he almost missed the driveway and had absolutely no good excuse for being wrapped around Janet's tree.

"I thought I saw a light on in the living room."

"They always leave a light on."

"This is the right house, right?" Of course it was. She was already getting out of the car. She pulled out the keys and went straight to the side door, the one that led to the basement. He took a double handful of snow and threw it on the license plate. You never know.

"It's cold in here," he whispered.

"I'll find the thermostat. Why are we whispering?"

"Because somebody might *be* here, that's why."

"There's nobody here, Richard. Janet just left twenty minutes ago, and there's no car in the garage." She ran up the basement stairs and opened the door to the kitchen. "Hello? HELLO? See, nobody here but us chickens."

Seeing the room empty he was better able to recognize what it was—some man's finished basement that had been gradually taken over by his children. The bar was still there but the bar stuff had been moved. The tools and fishing gear looked lonely and outnumbered by the posters, books and records. He turned on the stereo, flicked on a low-watt lamp and switched off the overhead.

"Real furniture for a change," he said, stretching out on the sofa. It beat leaning up against file cabinets and painted cinderblock walls and blackboards for hasty clinches in after-school meeting rooms. "Good idea. Thank you."

She threw off her jacket, pulled off her boots, folded her legs under her and cuddled in tight. "My pleasure."

He kissed her all over her face. "You're pretty pretty, you know."

"No I'm not. My nose is too big and my ears are too big and

my chin is too weak. You're prettier than I am." She was stroking his hair. "And you've got the most beautiful hands in the world," she added, kissing one and pressing the other to her body.

"You've got good taste. And you taste good, too." He came off her neck long enough for both of them to peel off their sweaters, and he began to open her blouse. At least she had the good sense not to wear a turtleneck. He fingered her small breasts through her flimsy bra. She worked at his shirt buttons and got her hands under his shirt.

"You sure are skinny. I can feel your ribs, individually."

"Do you mind?"

"Mm-mm."

"You're not exactly fat."

"In some places."

"Where?"

"Look and see," she said, lying back.

He followed her, lifted her bra and licked her nipples.

"Oo, that tickles." He lifted his head, and she eased it back down. He nibbled down around her belly button and unfastened her jeans.

"Think I found one of the spots. We've got a little belly here."

"Who asked you?"

"You told me to look around."

"Yeah, but you're not supposed to say anything. Come back up here."

He stretched out over her but kept working his hand under her jeans and pantyhose. She had one arm around his neck, the other all the way up his back beneath his undershirt. And she lifted one leg up to the top of the sofa to give him more room.

"Didn't your mother ever tell you to look with your eyes and not with your hands?"

"Probably. I wasn't listening." His hand, in fact, was getting cramped, but he didn't want to stop until she made him.

"Richard?"

Thank God. "What?" he said, giving his hand a break.

She turned her head up and blew a hair away from her mouth. "That feels good." He smiled, although his hand was about to kill him. "You're sweating."

"You turned the heat up too high."

"No, you did."

He sat up and pulled her jeans off. He had never thought of her as particularly pale and was surprised by the contrast between her skin and the cinnamon pantyhose. He'd been feeling her legs for months under her skirt but never had so much room to roam before. He ran his hand all over them—feeling the glide of the nylon on his fingertips as much as the flesh he squeezed in his palms—and kissed the insides of her thighs.

"Oh, you found the other fat spot," she mumbled as she lay with her hands over head and her eyes closed.

He bit gently on her thigh. "It's delicious." Then he leaned up to kiss her some more, stopping at her nipples again on the way. He never did know which present to open and play with first. She rubbed her hand along his corduroy leg and pulled at his zipper. Her hand on him was like a cold breeze.

He caught the tops of her pantyhose, slid them under her butt and down past her knees, and reached for the box in his pocket. He wanted to watch her face but had to pay attention to what he was doing. He managed to pull out one foil packet—trying to do this as quickly and smoothly as possible—and found he couldn't tear it open. She reached out to help, he cut his eyes at her and she drew back with an embarrassed smile. By then it was hopeless; he was getting nowhere and handed it to her. She grabbed it, ripped a corner off with her teeth, extracted the rubber and handed it to him.

"Damn," he said, and they both started laughing while he tried to start it on the right side. "Excuse me?"

"I'm sorry." She covered her mouth to stifle the giggle and kept her eyes fixed on his crotch. Sometime that night he positioned himself above her, and she made him kiss her again while she helped direct him. It wasn't working. He began to melt. He got in just a little, and they both began to push, when he suddenly let go.

He didn't want to lift his head to face her. "Don't say anything," he muttered.

"Why would I say anything?" Her smile barely held back the laughter.

"I really hope you're having a good time here."

"I am. Really."

The phone rang. It might as well have been a grenade.

"Where are you going?" he asked as she twisted out from under.

"I have to get the phone. It's Jan." She walked to the wall phone trailing her pantyhose on one foot. She pulled her bra back down, straightened her blouse and answered laughing. "No, you're not interrupting anything," she said and couldn't help peeking back at him, his pants around his ankles and undershirt up in his armpits. "Okay. I got it." She hung up. "We won, 67-62. I thought we should know the score."

"Great. Southwest 67, Isaac nothing."

"Stop it. Come on, we better get dressed."

"That was quick," he said.

"I know," she answered. His eyes shot her dead. "Sorry."

"You look like hell. I look like hell."

"Heaven," she said. "Heaven must have sent you, precious."

"Don't try to be nice now. What do I do with this thing?"

"I don't know. Throw it away."

"Yeah, I bet you don't know." They got their clothes on more efficiently than they had gotten them off.

"Thank you," she said at the door.

"For what?"

"*Richard!* Look, you just hang on to the rest of those and we'll put 'em to good use. Okay?"

"Yeah, sure."

"Richard."

"Okay. Okay okay."

He didn't know he'd been asleep until her hand, tracing the lines of his face, tripped his eyes open.

"Thanks for the dance, handsome," she whispered.

"Anytime," he mumbled, shifting onto his back and noticing how little room there was on the twin bed.

"You feel properly celebrated?"

"Yeah," he said absently. There was something else, he thought, though it seemed silly to mention it. And then it hit him, and he climbed over her onto the floor.

"What is it?"

"I just remembered. I had a plan, too," he said and, suddenly wide awake, kneeled into his closet. He came out with a short stack of 45s, stolen from his mother, he explained.

In his excitement he didn't catch the look that flitted across her face as she gathered herself on the bed. It wouldn't have made any difference; he was into it. Bent naked over the stereo, he ran snatches of Nat, Brook and Dinah, Big Joe, Clyde, the Clovers. He sang half-remembered phrases and talked and sang some more and looked to see if she was digging it. It was his world now. He was planting his flag. *It doesn't matter,* he'd told her a year before, the day she'd been so pissed because her former friends were giving her grief over him, *you're not part of that anymore.* He settled on King Pleasure's "Moody's Mood," scatting his way back to her arms.

"Richard," she said, interrupting him.

"What?"

"You can't sing, but I love you."

As soon as she said it, he knew how much he'd wanted her to, needed to hear it despite his rationalizations. She kissed him before he could reply, reached for him and led him above and into her again as the mood recycled.

There I go there I go there I go there I go *theeere* I go.

10/17/69

CC Rider,

That's what I call a Homecoming.

I'm sorry it took so long, not just getting together but really *being* together after you got here. This is all so new, being away from home—you know about that already. I thought it would be no big deal, since I've been away in a lot of ways for so long. But people keep bringing that same stuff up here, like that girl in the car. Who needs that? You do everything you're supposed to to get someplace else, and then they want you to pretend you've never left. But it's even worse. They've got new rules. Nobody went around speaking to every other black person they saw back home. I finally got used to that, and somebody dropped an a-salaam-alaikum on me. What are you supposed to do with that?

With all that, I'm ashamed to say, I forgot what I knew. Being home is being with you. I guess I wanted it to be different somehow with us because of everything else going on. I forgot to remember that it was already different with us. How and Why don't matter. Those are questions for everybody else who doesn't get it, and who cares about them? You're the real thing (ain't nothing like it), and you're all I need to get by.

Love always,
Richard

Oct. 20, '69

Sweet Lovin' Baby,

What is all this talk about loving me, my sweet?
I am not afraid, not anymore.
Not like before.

CC

P.S. Say Hi to your uncle.

Funny how she knew she had an ally in the old man. She had only met him once. But Ike spoke of him often. Whenever they got finished trading mother stories and she turned to her father for sympathetic contrast, it was Hodge who filled the gap for Ike—never the sainted Sergeant Clarence, who was for all practical purposes Elizabeth's invention. He hadn't even told her, he thought, of how Hodge had salvaged graduation day, when the tension was tightest, just a month after he had stayed out late with her instead of going to the prom that Elizabeth had her heart set on.

Their undeclared truce for the occasion hadn't been working, even with the familiar rhythm of a lifetime of Sundays. He had gone to church to please her and had made sure to point out that Tommy hadn't done the same for Dessie; had stood up to be acknowledged as a graduate, although he had sworn for years that when the time came he wouldn't. Still, she barely spoke and when she did her tone recalled the one in which she always spoke of his father. Her attitude threatened to spoil his big day, big not because it was the culmination of achievements, as she thought, but because it was the starting line for his getaway. So he stared blankly at the sports page and listened to the sound of every car outside as he waited for Hodge. Just as he had done when he was a kid, but this time it wasn't so much that he wanted to see his uncle; he just wanted somebody else to take the weight.

Hodge, he knew, was the one to do it, although you couldn't tell by looking at him. The word jive came to mind. He was the reason—the excuse, really—that Elizabeth had come to town for secretarial school. A compromise: away from home, but under the supervision of an uncle she knew (better than her mother, who denied all evidence) was too much a gadabout to supervise anybody. She managed, without too much difficulty, to stay clear of his unwatchful eye until they went home together to Springfield for Christmas.

That was when she announced that she was going to have a baby—or at least could no longer hide the fact; Ike had received various versions in bits and pieces from his two sources over the years. Her mother, Hodge's little sister, became terribly upset and wanted Elizabeth to come home. Her brother, Clarence, a father himself by then and the stern protector Hodge was not, threatened to kill the cat. But Hodge was cool, and remained so even when Elizabeth, checking him with her eyes (Ike could clearly picture the look) explained that there had been no mistake, that she fully planned to marry when she finished her course and Lonnie got the job he was waiting for. They didn't buy it, apparently, until Hodge soothed his sister, told Clarence to worry about his own son, and confirmed her story, even adding a few embellishments about Lonnie's character and his own guarantee of their welfare.

It was the last time either of them saw her mother or brother alive. Her high blood pressure killed her suddenly within six months; the army kept moving him out of reach until some Korean took him away for good. But well before then, both Elizabeth and Hodge had made real their lies. During a dreary January snowfall three months before her nineteenth birthday, with Hodge as witness, she married Lonnie, a redcap who'd claimed her bags and her fancy when she got off the train the summer before. (By Hodge's account, delivered under heavy questioning much later, it was she who had resisted any suggestion of such a union until she had trapped herself in order to placate Clarence.) And on a bright July day, the kind she had wanted for a wedding, the pains came, and it was Hodge in Lonnie's absence who took her to the hospital.

He had been there ever since, and Ike had spent many hours awaiting his arrival. But this time the sound of the Lincoln eluded him, so the syncopated rap on the door made him jump.

"I'll get it," he called.

"They tell me it's some man here 'posed to graduate from high school today," the old man said. "You seen him 'round here anyplace?"

"You're lookin at him."

"Nah, I must have the wrong house."

"You better *get* in here. Hey, you didn't bring me no CC to celebrate?" Ike said as they hugged.

"Ain't that somethin," Hodge said, letting loose his Woody Woodpecker cackle. "You hear that, Baby?"

"Yeah, I'll C his C. How you doin, Hodge?"

"Not bad, baby. Everythin's chicken but the gravy. Lemme get in here and sit down. I don't like standin up next to this boy. Look like he done growed another inch on me."

"Well, you know bigger don't necessarily mean smarter. Make yourself comfortable. Dinner'll be ready in a few minutes."

It was a good meal—ham with macaroni and cheese and mustard greens for Hodge. Ike tried to convince himself that it was a peace offering but suspected she had really done it for herself—to keep up appearances and to mark *her* accomplishment.

"I sure am proud of you—both of you," Hodge said. "When Lizbeth got through school I was on the road and Clarence and his family was overseas, you know. But they'd've had to bury me sure nuff for me to miss this. I wish your mama and Clarence could be here too."

"I almost wish Lonnie was here," Elizabeth said acidly, "just so he could see how wrong he was about Negroes not bein able to get anywhere. Just cause he didn't have no ambition. Well, it hasn't been easy but thank the good Lord we got the brat this far. He better not go and mess up now."

"Now how he gon mess up, Baby? He got all them awards and

scholarships and everything, he gon be all right. Ain't that right, Richard?"

"See? He knows you got nothin to worry about."

"If he knew like I know he'd be worried. You goin over Tommy's later? Dessie says he's havin a little party."

Now she wants him to go to parties. She probably thought there'd be some nice colored girls there to save him. Truth was, it would be the same people she'd been keeping him away from for the past four years. The fact that they would be high-school graduates by tonight just made them seem classier. "Yeah, I thought I'd drop by. If it's all right with you."

"Nice to know you're still concerned about what's all right with me," she said, rising to clear the table.

"What time you got to be down to the War Memorial, son?" Hodge asked.

"About two hours."

"Go ahead and start gettin ready. I'll run you down and come back for your mother."

"Can I drive the Lincoln?"

"Boy, you ain't hardly that grown yet."

Shortly, Ike settled into the red plush interior of Black Beauty VI, all of them Ford products—*It was his idea, wasn't it?*—and once again felt the sensation of escape. The feeling had never been better than on their camping trip; he was eight, and it was to be his first night away from her. He could never remember, and Hodge never owned up, which of them had called it quits. Maybe both. One with his panama and leather shoes trying like a champ to pretend the mosquitoes weren't getting to him, the other with a book and three-year-old batteries in the flashlight and scared to death of the dark. Nice idea to make up for the Cub Scout trip he'd missed, but their last pork sandwich at the old Piggy drive-in, a happily agreed-upon compromise, was a better memory.

Now their voyage seemed almost more remote, not out of the city but into its haunted belly, what used to be the neighborhood before the interstate came through. It was Jewtown then, although it wasn't anymore, and who knew what it had been before that? Everybody probably just got tired of changing the name. It had seemed strangely prosperous, strange compared to what Ike now knew prosperity was. The only clue to the future was the low, blood-red projects that had been built shortly before he was born—and even they seemed more like bungalows than brewpots of urban blight. What he remembered was folks strolling the streets to go visiting on Sundays, hanging out in Madison Park on Saturdays and making dark, happy noises on the neon avenue that he heard sometimes on Saturday nights mingling with jazzy sounds from the radio in the back seat of a younger Black Beauty.

It was dusty and crumbly now, like old pictures of Southern poverty. The stores didn't have real signs and the homes left standing had no people or too many. Elizabeth frequently accused the "Bamas" of bringing the decay with them and running down the town, ignoring the mass dislocation of the highway and the fact that she herself had been in the city less than twenty years.

"So what's goin on with you and Lizbeth?"

"What do you mean?"

"I'm old, boy, I ain't dead. I seen people shoot friendlier looks at snakes."

"It's this girl I've been seeing."

"Well, I guess we're bout due for one of those. Your mama don't like her?"

"She's white."

"Oh, I see said the blind man. Guess that would get her goin a while."

"Why should it?"

"Man, you don't think she went through all that bother raisin you to let you go lay up with some white chick, do you?"

"I don't see why not."

"No, I reckon you don't. So what you gon do about it?"

"Keep seein her, I guess."

"You guess? That's the best you can do?"

"Well, yeah, I mean, I'm gonna see her."

"All right, that's what you gon do, go on and do it. I wouldn't worry too much about your mother."

"You gonna talk to her?"

"Shoot no, man. I don't want her mad at *me*. Look here, your mother's always gon be your mother, even if she don't talk to you for ten years—and she might not. I love her like my own daughter, but you know she can be mighty evil sometime. But she ain't the one you gotta worry about. It's all these other cats out here—these ofays, you know what I mean—that's gon give you hell."

"That's comforting."

"Look at it this way, buddy. You had a pretty easy time in school, but you didn't think it would all be that easy, did you?"

"Well, I was hoping."

Hodge pulled up in front of a restaurant that didn't look like much in a block that looked like less. "Man," he said, "you don't know how many times I had to run in here and have a real fast one while you was buyin funny books and candy down at the corner and gettin your hair cut over Mr. B's and whatnot. I'm just glad I'm finally able to take my time."

"You know I won't be eighteen till next month," Ike said, trying to focus his eyes in the dim, musty room.

"Old folks can't remember no dates, man. Say, Shurley," Hodge called to the silent man behind the bar, "give us a couple."

"Shurley?"

"Oh yeah, you don't know 'bout Shurley? He runs this place for the Greek now, but the cat usedta be somethin. Played ball with Snake Dumpson and them—you know, the housing commissioner—in school and over to the Douglass Center, back 'fore the war. Tore them white boys up, too. Ain't that right, Shurl?"

"You doin the talkin, Hodge."

"Word was they changed the district to split 'em up so they wouldn't all be on the same team in high school. Ran the line right down between Shurley's place and Ralph Joplin's. He's supposed to be some kinda writer now. See, you ain't the first nigger tryin to be somebody around here."

"Yeah, yeah, we've done that one before."

The man smiled, slid a couple of beers over and walked away.

"If they'd gone to white colleges like you they'd've been All-American for sure. Be up on the TV with O.J. Simpson and them. Course, wasn't none of 'em good as me when I was their age." Ike glanced down at the man still smiling and determinedly wiping glasses at the far end of the bar. "You heard of Red Grange? They called him the Gallopin Ghost. Well, they usedta call me the Skedaddlin Spook."

"*Hodge.*" Ike groaned.

"Lyin, I'm flyin," he declared. Shurley, unable to contain himself any longer, began flapping his wings.

The longer they sat there, the more Hodge seemed to belong. The sense of adventure, of this little coming-of-age ritual Hodge had probably planned for so long, began to chill. Drinking alone in a seedy bar on a Sunday afternoon. This, Ike supposed, was what his mother's uncle did after chicken and watching Jimmy Brown run over Sam Huff. Maybe on weekday afternoons, too, since he had stopped working regular, and possibly even before. He saw Hodge's face hang down toward his glass like a hound dog's and his runny eyes looking past the napkin—DRINK FAST WE NEED YOUR GLASS—and focusing through time. It was like looking closely at the sporty Johnnie Walker on the bottle over there and seeing an old man with toupee and lifts, trying real hard.

But then, into the second round—Hodge had moved on to CC and soda—he eased into a story about the time he and a buddy went fishing at the lake down by the college. As he spoke the old man went away. Johnnie was back, strutting his stuff. Ike peered into his glass, confused.

"Beautiful place," Hodge said, "and good fishin, too. So we was just gettin into it, you know, and heard this real loud *ba-doom!* Looked up and if it wasn't this old cracker with a shotgun, talkin 'bout get off his property. We said, man, you don't own the whole lake, and he just cocked and aimed, said, nigger I don't want no conversation, just move on. So we backed up and tried to nice-talk him, you know, said okay, man, but you don't wanna shoot a man 'bout no fish, now. *Ba-doom!* Like to took my foot off. We was back in the car 'fore he reloaded. This wasn't no trash, mind you. One of the professors with a house on the lake. Ornery old sonofagun."

"That *was* a long time ago."

"Yeah, but them folks don't change none too quick. Why you think them boys runnin all that Who Shot John down there now, struttin around with they fists all up in the air and takin over people offices?"

"I don't know, but they're not gettin much work done. I mean, that's the whole idea, right? Go down there and get thrown out of school, you don't change anything and you're back on the corner."

"Maybe so, son. They probly don't be shootin niggers no more, but everything must not be copasetic. I want you to get your work done, all right, but you just be ready to take care of yourself, too."

"Well, I don't think I'll have too much trouble—nothing I can't handle, anyway."

"How would you know?"

"What do you mean?"

"Man," Hodge said, leaning close to Ike's face, his own having regained its solidity, "you ain't never had to handle nothin. You know what I'm worried about? I know you'll do okay with the books, and I don't *spect* nobody's gon take a shotgun to you. But I tell you, son, I think you really believe all that stuff people say about you."

Just a few hours later, that caution seemed silly as he and Cheryl sat on top of the world. They had giggled through the ceremony, even though he knew that Elizabeth would pick him out and say something later, just as she'd always known if he was talking and chewing gum in church even when he was in the balcony and she was out of sight downstairs. She had gone home to submit herself to a small, terse celebration of parents and friends. He had gone by Tommy's and lingered, like somebody's unfriendly cousin from out of town, among people he used to know, finding no solace in the picture stuck in a mirror frame of Elizabeth, Dessie, a one-year-old Tommy and his eighteen-month-old self. They had met one last time at Jan's safe house, lying around the rec room talking scornfully about the class party that night at somebody's summer house. And then they had begun the journey forward by going back, riding through some of the same streets Hodge had covered that afternoon.

"Where are we going?" she asked.

"Madison Park."

"Didn't somebody get raped there last month?"

"Don't worry about it. Remember I told you one day I'd show you my old stomping grounds."

"Sure looks like somebody stomped it pretty good."

"Careful, now, you're talkin about my home. We used to live on that off-ramp back there, and I used to go to school in that drug treatment center."

"How educational."

"It wasn't that bad, really. It was a nice neighborhood."

"I guess you had to be there."

They cruised up Indian Head Hill to the park. If you spat on one of the engraved emblems embedded in the sidewalk and rubbed it with your foot, Hodge had told him, you'd get good luck. Past the rose garden where people posed for wedding pictures every summer Saturday afternoon stood the reservoir, a red brick pillbox on a hill overlooking the park, Jewtown and much of the city beyond. Hodge had brought him there one memorable afternoon—memorable, like the camping trip, because Hodge was a night person and usually left the outdoor stuff to Elizabeth's long-ago boyfriend, Jack—and told him the stories of Shine and the Signifying Monkey.

They parked the car and walked out onto the grassy slope. Ike looked down at the empty swimming pool and remembered the mass of skinny brown bodies thrashing up foam. But sitting with Cheryl, arms and legs entwined, he focused on a more recent, shared past, as they tried to pick out distant spots from the lights: the theater where they'd necked through *A Man and a Woman*; their high school, nestled in that corner way over there; the street leading up to Jan's house and hers on the opposite end of town.

"Okay, you win," she said. "This is not bad. I can see where it might be a little sad for you to leave all these memories."

"Are you kidding? I can't *wait* to get out of here. Especially since I'm taking you with me."

She turned and kissed him. "I do like the way you talk sometimes."

"My uncle's a talker. I come by it honest."

"I'd like to meet him sometime."

And so she did, but not soon. Just days before they returned to the reservoir for the last time, in the midst of their climactic outing at the State Fair, he took her to see him. Hodge always worked maintenance at the fair, usually at the Indian village—out of loyalty because of his Choctaw blood, he always said. It was one of the many odd jobs he picked up around town after retiring from GE, cleaning or attending something or other for a few weeks at a time. In his early teens, Ike had begun to avoid strange public restrooms out of fear that his uncle would hand him a paper towel. But it seemed okay, almost natural, to walk over with Cheryl and surprise the old man picking up soiled napkins and candy-apple sticks in his feathered headdress.

Hodge was surprised, though his reaction to Ike's tap on his shoulder was to turn, raise his pointed stick, eye their cowboy hats and say: "You better be cool, Kemo Sabe. You in Indian territory now."

"Peace, chief," Ike said. "Just stopped by to say hi. This is my friend Cheryl Costanza."

"Pleased to meet you, miss. My, they growin 'em big these days. Pick a lotta corn, this one."

"I've heard a lot about you, Mr. Hodges."

"Oh? Well, buffalo soldier speak with forked tongue, too, you know. Tell you what. Richard, go on over tell Joe at the stand there I said give you one a them beaded necklaces. This two-dollar hat ain't no souvenir for a fine squaw like this. Go on, I ain't gonna bite 'er."

When Ike returned, Hodge had his arm around Cheryl's shoulder, which was shaking in laughter. He had to stand a moment and wait for them to acknowledge his presence before he could tie on the necklace.

"There you go," Hodge said. "Princess Longleg. Now you children go on and let me work. 'Less you wanna pay me to do my special dance to keep that cloud from openin up. See, anybody can do a rain dance, but I got one to keep it *from* rainin."

"That's okay, we're on our way. I'll see you 'round the wigwam."

"Bye. Glad I got a chance to meet you," Cheryl said, adding as they walked away: "He's a riot. Is he really part Indian?"

"Who knows? You should see him at Oktoberfest. Uh, wait here a minute. I forgot there was something I had to tell him."

Ike jogged back to where Hodge had resumed his rounds. "What was that all about?" he asked.

"Scuse me? That's my private business, now ain't it?"

"Not when she's with me."

"Well, we'll see 'bout that, buddy. I asked her did she wanna come hang out with a real man and she said she'd think about it."

"Come on, Hodge. What you tell her?"

"You sure nuff got your mother's sense of humor. Look here, I told her same thing I told you. Said you ain't near as hot as you think you is, but she might wanna stick around. You got potential, boy."

"Goin to Boston now, baby."

"Keep talkin, Negro, you ain't there yet. I got somethin for you."

"You got squat, that's what you got."

"*Bap!* And I got your back, partner."

"All right! Beans and lobster!"

"Damn.. Who dealt that shit?"

Ike sat in his regular seat in the union cafeteria, the one he had taken by the window his first day on campus, listening to the card game over in the black section and watching the snow drop. It would have been no big deal to sit there. As with membership in the BLF, his face was his ticket. But the idea bothered him a little; it was just so obvious. And he did like the view from his original seat, so he kept to it. After only a few weeks in the semester, even the freshmen had become regulars, and he began to feel more like an outsider and then it *became* a big deal, a matter of pride or something.

Besides, he thought, they must be in here all the time. According to Rosen, they weren't much in evidence at football games or anywhere else large numbers of students gathered. Ike had seen a few of them at campus movies but not at guest lectures or political rallies. It was as if they were not really there, except, he supposed, for classes—just lurking and waiting. Someone approached his table.

"What's happnin, man. You're Richard Isaac, right?"

"Ike," he said, shaking hands.

"I'm Gene Mayford."

"Yeah, I know. How you doin?"

"Not too bad," Gene said, easing onto the seat. "You're on that student government committee, right? Minority affairs?"

Maier had told Ike about the committee and said they were looking for volunteers. They'd had two or three meetings discussing ways to promote interracial awareness and tolerance on campus. But as the semester progressed and there had been no outbreaks, the thing seemed to lose some steam; Ike had considered quitting, but nobody at the black tables had volunteered, and it was something.

"Yeah, right," he answered. "Haven't done much."

"But that's hip, though. I think more bloods should be in on that, cause the BLF's goin through some changes, man, you know, and we need some people on the inside like that."

"That's what I thought," Ike said. "But so far I'm up there all by myself."

"That's not right. But listen, anyway, what I want to talk to you about is, you've heard about the tutoring programs, haven't you?"

"Uh-huh. I was givin it some thought for a while, but I haven't had time to get into it."

"Yeah, I think you'd be good for that, man. It's a cooperative kind of thing. If somebody's good in one thing, they help out somebody who's not and vice versa. We need people bad, 'cause, you know, like with everything, a few people take it seriously and they end up carryin the load." He was watching Ike carefully.

"You really hustle for that, don't you?" Ike said with genuine admiration. He liked Gene. Part of it was the flattery—he appreciated what Ike was doing and thought he could make a contribution; part of it was that Maier had praised him. But even more,

Ike saw possibilities in Gene, hope that one could be righteous and rational at the same time.

"Hey, it's important," Gene said smiling. "Specially the way niggers be droppin out of here like flies."

"Maybe they should do more work," Ike said.

"Well, some of us need help, brother." Gene's smile eased up, a subtle rebuke that Ike felt sharply. "Listen, we're havin a meeting later on today to try and get the shit together for next semester —"

"Sounds good, but I won't be here," Ike said without shame, sensing that he had already blown a chance to make good. "I'm goin out of town."

"I see. You goin to catch Sly, huh?"

"Yeah, if I can get outta here."

"I hear you. Lotta people makin that move. With all this whitey winter weekend bullshit goin on the folks are just scramblin to get away. It's a bad time for the meeting, but like I said, I want to get things straightened out ahead of time so we won't be fuckin around next semester. We want to get the program goin downtown, too."

"Well, look, I'll keep it in mind, and maybe I'll have more time next semester."

"I think you should make time, bro," Gene said, still smiling and standing to go. "Like I said, we need you. But I'll be in touch. You take it light, Ike. Hope you can make it to the show."

"Hey, wait a minute. Can I ask you a question?"

"Shoot."

"How come there aren't more black people involved in things around campus? I don't mean the committee so much, but that's one example. It's like, I go to stuff and expect to see other folks there and nobody shows up."

"Oh, I see," Gene said, shifting his weight and crossing his arms. "You see us in here playin cards and whatnot and you think that's all we're about."

Ike shrugged. "Looks that way sometime."

"Tell you what, Ike, you come check out the downtown tutoring program, or the workshops at Uhuru or the dance performances or poetry readings we've sponsored." Gene gauged his tone carefully, giving it equal parts of reprimand and encouragement. "There's a whole lot more goin on than you think. You might be surprised."

Without waiting for a response—none was coming—Gene walked back past the playing tables and left the cafeteria with Juanita. Ike wondered if she had told Gene about seeing him with Cheryl that first time, not that he should care, or if she had seen them together just the week before at the Italian restaurant in the Village. But she had probably forgotten him by now. That, at least, would not surprise him.

The line outside the theater was a bitch, and so was the weather. Ike had caught a ride right away: beginner's luck. Hitching was something he had never even thought about doing before he got to college—Elizabeth would have kittens—but everybody seemed to do it all the time. Going to another town was pushing it, but he didn't have enough money for the concert and round-trip bus fare both, and getting back would be more difficult. After he was out there, it dawned on him that some black students from campus might come by on their way to the concert. Would they pick him up? If so, it would be an opportunity for him to build some bridges. If not—well, he had gotten used to doing things alone. Since Cheryl had been back the weekend before, he had thought about asking Rosen if he wanted to go—you could do that with Sly—but then he began to understand that it was being seen as a black event; in any case, Art had a date. And as it turned out, he was picked up by a white guy heading through to Pennsylvania who didn't want to talk about anything heavier than how bad 81 got when it was snowing.

All the warmth he had saved by not having to stand out on the road for a long time was quickly spent. The hawk was having a field day, ripping and biting at the vined-up folks who stood wrapped around the block like they were waiting to be taken away. It was a good thing Ike had gotten to the box office early and picked up a ticket. He was in the ticket-holders' line and he was backed up around the corner from the theater. There were just as many people on the other side waiting to get their tickets. It was the longest line he'd been in since Elizabeth had taken him to see *Bambi*. It hadn't been hot then, either, and he'd had to talk her out of giving up at least twice. He could see her point now.

Along the cursing and hopping line it was easy to tell the difference between the college crowd, from in town and away, and the local kids in snow-covered Converse. There was even a healthy smattering of whites, less heavily wrapped and mostly in front of the ticket-holders' line, braving the downtown venue for an event they would have dominated at a campus auditorium. As if to reinforce the distinction, someone returned to the line behind Ike with a pint from a nearby liquor store. The odor of reefer, a more common denominator, came in frigid puffs from up ahead.

"Wonna take you HI-YA!" someone howled.

"Haha, go 'head, Sly," a companion urged. "I know he *be* high, too, boy. That muhfucka *stay* fucked up."

"He just better bring his ass out on that stage and not pull no shit."

Two hours and one pitiful warm-up act after Ike had gotten seated, he and hundreds of other folks stared restlessly at a solid wall of amplifiers and instruments on the otherwise empty stage. Occasionally a long-haired stage hand would come out to test the equipment, but that only got people going. "Get the fuck off the stage," they yelled. "Where Sly at?" "Tell them Stone motherfuckers to get out here!"

The building was one of those old, real theater theaters, the kind with pillars and balconies that were only found in the inner city and only came to life for dirty movies, soul concerts or local symphonies. The kind of place where Ike, along with the rest of the city, had been baby-sat by the all-day Columbus Day and Memorial Day cartoon shows, and where he had seen Gordon Scott's Tarzan lead legions of brainless, expendable Africans.

Tarzan and all his elephants couldn't do anything with this crowd. The management tried piping in music, but the Johnny Mann Singers or whoever doing "Love Is Blue" was clearly a bad choice, and Sly tapes made things that much worse. A fat man who obviously had something at stake came out at regular intervals to update Sly's whereabouts; in two hours the group had progressed from being snowbound in Pennsylvania to warming up in a local hotel. The man was booed and cussed every time he appeared.

Finally, two hours and forty-five minutes after the listed show time, the fat man came out sweating. "Please, please let me talk," he shouted over the noise. "I'm very sorry to have to say . . . " Ike ducked to the side as people behind and in front of him leapt to their feet. "I've been informed that Sly is not feeling well and the group will not go on," the fat man was yelling. There were simultaneous surges toward the exits and toward the stage. The man took a few steps back and tried to give refund instructions. The vendors who had been hawking souvenir pictures and loose joints scurried for cover. A bottle from the balcony crashed near the stage. Ike vaulted over the back of his seat and made it to a side exit before he got jammed up.

"Jive motherfucka! I knew this shit was gonna happen!"

"What you come for then, fool?"

Right in front of Ike somebody wanted to start a fight because his woman's foot had been stepped on. Down front, a few people were trying to get past the security guards to attack the equipment, and women were screaming as though the roof were collapsing. Out on the street Ike could hear sirens approaching. He had finally gotten himself into the middle of a riot, and it wasn't about anything at all.

The cold felt good when he reached the sidewalk, sifted through the throbbing crowd and escaped to the other side of the street, narrowly avoiding a beat-up car that splashed him as he hopped to the curb. Looking around to figure out his next move, he didn't realize that the car had stopped and was honking at him.

"Richard!"

He heard his name and even saw the girl open the front door and stick her head out. But it took him a while to realize who it was, Barbara Hinman from Southwest. "Get in," she called, and he did, giant-stepping over the slush to tumble in beside her on the springless front seat. She hugged him immediately. "I can't believe it!" she said. "It's so good to see you."

"Same here. Thanks for the rescue. It's gettin crazy out there."

"Richard, this is Doug," she said, nodding to the driver with the blond pony tail.

"How's it goin, man?" Doug said, reaching across to clasp Ike's hand soulfully. "You guys went to high school together, huh? Far out. You came down for Sly?"

"Yeah, but he didn't show. That's what this is all about."

"We know," said Barbara. "We were there, too, isn't that wild? Doug started getting bad vibes, so we left a little while ago."

"Good timin, huh?" Doug said. "We heard the place go apeshit soon as we got outside. Sounded like somebody dropped a fuckin bomb or somethin."

"It's like the worst thing that could have happened," Barbara said. "There's been a lot of tension in town, and you could just feel that people were waiting for one more thing to go wrong and they'd explode."

"Say, we're headin back to campus. Is that cool, or you want us to drop you someplace?"

"Stay awhile, okay, Richard? Have you got time?"

"Sure, why not?" he said, catching a last glimpse of the mob outside the theater as the car turned and headed for the highway.

Ten minutes later downtown was a memory. The state campus was new and low, carved unnaturally out of a gentle hillside like a shopping plaza. Right away, Ike could tell that it was in a funny way whiter than his own campus, where ancient buildings and the natural environment dominated. This place was white like summer camp, where kids from other suburbs were imported to play. It didn't seem entirely like going to college, and he knew that was precisely why Barbara was there, though she probably could have been anywhere. It was an easy way not to be at home, and a fuck you to everybody who expected more.

She had changed by senior year into a self-styled intellectual and pseudo-radical who gave her valedictory speech in jeans and bare feet with a peace button on her robe. She had always been pretty in a peculiar, off-center kind of way, but few noticed because she was so strange. It wasn't worth the trouble. Nobody knew that better than Ike; it was a lesson he learned in tenth-grade spring when her father had stopped them walking home together. Did the fastest U-turn Ike had ever seen, got out of the car and planted himself right on the sidewalk. The words were kind, but the eyes and the body language weren't. And Barbara, another person then, got in the car without saying peep and left him out there hanging. Her confusion and insecurity were what had drawn him to her; he didn't find it so charming after that, and apparently neither did she. The killer came after the sidewalk humiliation, though, when the bus finally carried him back home out of enemy territory. Elizabeth was waiting with the news that some man had just called about his daughter and all hell broke loose. He'd never shouted at her like that before, and couldn't imagine being slapped any harder if he lived forever. *You may be startin to look like a man, but you ain't grown yet.* They hadn't been right since; Barbara stretched the cord before Cheryl cut it. *If that man calls here again tellin me what to do with my child there's gonna be trouble in both our houses.*

They parked the car—there were parking lots all over the campus—and, with the wind sweeping across the vast spaces, hurried into a pub that looked like a converted school cafeteria with the lights turned low. Doug and Barbara went straight for a large round corner table that was obviously their regular spot, where several people were already gathered. One of them looked like a Halloween Hendrix, a scrawny black guy with thick, uncombed hair trussed by a headband. The rest looked like everybody else, including Barbara. He imagined that the very day high school ended she had ripped off the pastel sweaters and pleated skirts emblematic of the life she had already given up and donned her new uniform: torn jeans, a huge flannel shirt covering a T-shirt and no bra. Her dark hair, grown long, was swept back. It was a sexier look, in a scrungy sort of way, but it didn't look like her.

Over pitchers of beer and through a haze of cigarette smoke, they—mostly Doug and Barbara—told tales of the aborted concert. That yielded talk of the Hell's Angels riot at the Stones concert on the coast, which led to a round of testimony about run-ins with cops and dogs and tear gas in pursuit of justice or good times or both. The tone was not bitter or remorseful; they could have been talking panty raids. Hendrix's specialty was urban conflagration. He claimed to have been in Newark and apparently had spent many a night regaling the campers with his exaggerated-dialect account of bad niggers challenging police and shitting their pants when the cops shot back. Even Barbara, who had clearly become less of a zealot, was entertained. Ike had thought her silly before, but was disappointed that she had been corrupted by cynicism. He wanted her, at least, to mean it; somebody should.

Ike noticed something going on between Barbara and Doug, a hassle of some kind that everybody pretty much ignored as if it happened about this time every Saturday night. He wanted to listen, but the beer called him away to the bathroom, where a guy who had just finished puking asked for the time, and Ike realized he had missed the last bus. When he returned to the table, Doug had gone, and somebody was bringing the conversation full circle by comparing the Sly riot to the reaction at Newport when Dylan went electric. Barbara reached over to him and indicated that they should leave.

"Where's Doug?" he asked.

"Tell you later," she said, wrapping her peacoat, clutching his arm and steering him out into the cold.

"Come on, Barb," he said, although the wind wasn't conducive to conversation. "What's going on?"

"I told him I wanted to talk to you alone and he got pissed. I mean, hanging out for a while was okay, but we didn't have a chance to say anything, you know? I thought we'd go back to my room. Is that okay?"

"Might as well be. It's not far, is it?"

The room, although darkened, looked huge. "Just fall down anywhere," she said and turned on a small lamp whose feeble light made it look darker. When she dropped her keys on a dresser on the other side, he realized why it seemed so spacious.

"This all yours?" he asked from the edge of the bed.

"Yeah, it's supposed to be a double, but my roommate moved off campus with her boyfriend."

"In my dorm they would have had somebody else in here the next day."

"Well, they should have, but the dorm director let me keep it. It was more convenient for him." She had pulled off her boots and settled in beside him with a baggie in her lap.

"I see."

"Then he stopped coming around but I told him I still wanted the single." She rolled a joint as she spoke. "It was the least he could do after the abortion. Wanna smoke?"

"Wait a minute. You wanna run that by me again?"

"Surprised?"

"No," he lied. "I just wanna know if you're okay." He took the joint. After passing the first night in Carl's room, he had given it a shot at Art Rosen's friend's party in the Village. Because it was less personal, maybe—more anonymous. This was the opposite, a shared communion.

"I don't know, Richard. I mean . . . it seemed like the right thing to do. I know it was the right thing. What else was I going to do? I had thought about leaving before that, 'cause school didn't seem serious and nobody was really serious about anything else, you know?" She took the joint back and, although she had rolled it expertly enough, held it with two hands like a little kid. "But after that I didn't want to go anywhere. Especially home. But then I met Doug, and he made me feel better, but I think he wants too much. I don't feel like I have anything to give." She put her head in his lap. "I'm sorry. It's just that nobody ever really wants to know how you feel."

"It's okay," he said. "I do."

"I know, thanks. How 'bout you?"

"I'm okay." He took a last puff and dropped the joint into the ashtray on the floor. "You know they had a lot of trouble up there last year, and I've been kinda worried about that, but everything's all right so far."

"Why?"

"Why is it all right?"

"No, why are you worried?"

"I don't know, I just don't want the hassle, I guess. I'm not sure what I'd do."

"I know," she said, turning to look up at him.

"Oh yeah, what?"

"The right thing."

"Whatever that is."

"That's what I mean," she said. "That's what I always liked

about you. I mean, a lot of people thought you were, like, a nice guy, but I think you can figure out what's the right thing to do, and some people might get pissed off, but that's okay."

"Glad you think so."

"No, really. When my father stopped us seeing each other I was mad at him and mad at you, and I wanted you to say or do something. But you were right, that would've been stupid. I didn't know what I was doing anyway."

"Neither did I," he said. "But thanks for the confidence." He squeezed her shoulder, then pulled back the flannel collar to rest his hand on her neck.

"Have you seen Cheryl?" she asked.

"Yeah," he said, surprised by the question. It was like he still thought of them as a secret, even though Barbara, as part of Jan's network of neurotics, knew all about it. The parietal rules at Cheryl's school added to the intrigue; their November motel weekend in Saratoga was fun partly because it extended the feeling of getting away with something. It was his own paranoia, on the other hand, that kept them in the shadows at his place. "She's fine."

"That's good," she said, and took hold of his hand. "I guess I never asked how you were going to get back. You want to stay here?"

"Well, it's either that or sleep in a snow bank."

She smiled and kissed his hand. "I'm glad I ran into you. I'm going to go get ready for bed, okay?"

She bounced off the bed and scampered out of the room. Ike stood up—his leg was asleep where her head had been—and roamed the room. There were several neat stacks of books that he hadn't seen before in the dim light. Gibran and Hesse and Kafka and Mao, the Bible—and Joyce. He remembered her discovering *Portrait of the Artist* in tenth grade and thinking anyone who couldn't get into it wasn't worth bothering with, although he managed to evade her scorn. Flipping through the books, he found notes scribbled throughout, emphatic, passionate comments that someone else might have written in her diary.

At the bottom of one of the piles he found their yearbook, which opened right to the page where they sat together at a table in the library, ogling a volume of the *Encyclopaedia Britannica* as if it were an ice cream cone, with dozens of books scattered around them, under the heading of Class Brains. What struck him, again, about the picture was that she actually looked like she was having fun, which did not at all fit his memory of her during senior year. Her tongue was poking out of a corner of her mouth, her eyes were bulging, and their hands were nearly joined in a mock attempt to grasp a page they might have been about to devour, literally. Cheryl, he knew, although she had never said so, resented his having chosen to be in that picture instead of joining her in the traditional floor-sweeping shot for Most Likely to Succeed; he had won both categories. But Barbara had asked, and he suspected that if he hadn't agreed, she would have declined the whole enterprise as bourgeois nonsense—and he wouldn't have that picture to remember her by.

He pulled off his turtleneck and his shoes, started to unfasten his corduroys and changed his mind, then got into the bed that looked like it hadn't been slept in in months. Barbara scooted back into the room in T-shirt and panties, her flannel shirt and jeans in a bundle in her arm. She dropped them and stood for a moment, puzzled. He thought she was about to look under the bed when she noticed him on the other side of the room. She kind of shrugged to herself and walked slowly over to him, holding down the bottom of her shirt and wearing an embarrassed smile that answered his question. The light stroked her surprisingly full thighs and the outline of her breasts as she passed the shaded lamp. She looked delicious.

"You okay over here?" she asked, standing over him.

He closed his eyes. The smoke, already melting his mind, released a warm rush through his body. "Yeah," he said quickly, and opened his eyes so she'd believe him.

She nodded faintly, reached for his hand and held it dangerously close to her crotch with both of hers. Then she took in a deep breath as if to say something but let it out wordlessly with a tight smile. Concentrating on his hand, which she was wringing like a rosary, he was startled by the whisk of her hair across his face as she bent down and suddenly kissed him hard. Her tongue licked his, gently, just before her lips pulled away. He surged up to hug her and they sagged back into the mattress, her slightly chapped cheek grinding into his neck and one leg struggling over his as if she were trying to secure herself atop a wall. When he found his hands kneading the muscles of her back beneath the T-shirt he let go, and she slid to her knees beside the bed.

"Good night, Barb," he said in what he hoped was a calm voice, holding her face out away from him.

"I told you," she said shakily. She kissed his hands again lightly, placed them on his chest and stood. "Sleep good, Richard. Thanks for being here." The light was off before he knew she was halfway across the room, and he fell asleep listening to her movements, half hoping she would call his name.

The sky hung heavy and low, and as Ike climbed the hill back to campus it seemed that when he got to the top he'd be able to reach up and grab a handful of cloud. Sundays were always like that—it could have been sundown at high noon—but this one was worse than the rest. Barb had let him sleep late. When he awoke she was fully dressed, sitting cross-legged on her bed sipping tea and reading a religion text. She offered to treat him to breakfast, but he declined. It would have seemed like bragging to go out in public in the morning with a woman people had seen him go off with the night before. So he had some tea and yogurt she had stashed away in her small refrigerator, and they talked a little about books and a little about high school, and they hugged and kissed and he left to hitch into town for the bus.

"Wow, that must've been some concert," Art Rosen said when Ike got back to the room.

"Oh yeah, the concert," Ike said. "It didn't even happen, but I ran into an old friend. What's goin on outside? I saw a mess of people standing around outside the union. Did I miss a round of fire drills, I hope?"

"No, it's probably a bomb scare. They've been havin false alarms on campus all day."

"Is that supposed to be part of the winter weekend fun?" Ike asked.

"No, it's more than that." Art was pacing now, his hands deep in his pockets, his eyes jumping from Ike to the floor. "I think somebody's tryin to get even. You didn't hear about what happened last night?"

"No, what happened?" Ike was beginning to get worried because Art wouldn't look at him.

"It's really—I don't know, it's fucked up, man." He gathered a breath and finally stopped moving. "The Uhuru House was bombed."

"Say what?"

"The Uhuru House—isn't that what it's called? Somebody fire-bombed it last night. It's almost completely destroyed."

There was a quick, suspended beat playing in Ike's chest as he walked toward the south end of campus. It was close to the way he used to feel at the starting line in a track meet, but then it was on him; he could determine the outcome. The panic he was now swallowing back with deep breaths came from being thrown into a situation he couldn't control. It not only speeded his pulse, it sharpened his eyesight. Two days ago he had walked past the white faces carelessly—it was the black ones he had been most conscious of—but now he was aware of everybody around him. It was like his first day in school after they moved out of Jewtown. All those colorless little people who didn't know who he was.

The only thing Art had been able to tell him was that there was a fight sometime Saturday night between black and white students in the Village. A bad one. Art had heard it secondhand and didn't know what the fight was about, but Lenny across the hall had been to a fraternity party later where people were talking retaliation. At five o'clock Sunday morning, Uhuru went up in smoke.

A forest of natural hair and knit caps surrounded the site of the building. Where the second story and roof should have risen above the crowd, there was a clear view of the upperclass dorms beyond.

Ike had gotten a call late the night before from an unidentified black voice, telling him there would be a noon rally at the ruins. Art, thankfully, was already asleep. After that, he hadn't slept, and he skipped his morning classes, not wanting to go out into the suddenly hostile world until it was time. He was only five minutes late, and the crowd had already formed. Today there was no Colored People's Time. He eased through the outer edges of the silent gathering to nestle into the womb of blackness. This was not about separate tables or parties or bullshit meetings. No credentials or passwords. Just be there, as he hadn't been before.

Ken Hollyfield was facing the crowd, standing on the steps that led to a useless pile of wood and introducing Garfield Bates. Bates stepped up, defying the cold in an open overcoat, and stared evenly at the congregation.

"While we're out here," he said in a dry, crackling voice, "I want you to look at what's left of this building behind me as a reminder. A reminder of what *time* it is in this country." Ike looked past him at the charred half building and tried to remember what it looked like inside. He had never been back after that first meeting. "Instead of thinking about the good times we shared in there," Bates said, "or even the serious work we did, think about last week in Chicago. Brothers Fred Hampton and Mark Clark were murdered by the police in a raid on the Black Panther Party headquarters there. There was no mistake. There was no accident. There was no even-sided shootout. The pigs went there to kill some niggers, and that's exactly what they did. Brother Fred Hampton was shot as he lay in bed. You see, they don't let you know when they're coming. We may be sad about this fire, but we have no business being surprised. We should know by the *time* to expect this kind of ruthless attack."

The crowd murmured but there was no response. It might have been a lecture, Ike thought, except for the narrowed eyes and tight jaws. "I know that when many of you came here for your education," Bates continued, his voice sharper, "you thought it would be safe. There are no Panthers here, you thought to yourselves, and no Ku Klux Klan. A few crazy niggers took over a building last year, but nothing much happened. Nobody was injured. So you thought you'd come here and get away—study and party in peace. But I know as you look at this building now," Bates said, "you're beginning to realize that you can run, but you *can't* hide. We're supposed to be here taking what we need to go back and help build our communities. You should understand that with the things happening in this country today, those communities may not be there by the time you get back. And even if you choose to ignore *that*, you can see very clearly that they are moving in on us here, too.

"Ken has some plans he wants to run down to you now, and I think you ought to listen very carefully so you can proceed in an organized manner. We don't need any more emotional bullshit. You have that big alarm clock standing behind me to remind you that the hour is very late, and we've wasted too much time already."

Ike shifted his weight from one foot to the other as the tempo in his chest picked up again. Something was going to happen. He looked around him from face to face and suddenly felt himself in the middle of one of those photographs from Selma.

"I really don't have anything to add," Hollyfield was saying, "except that this was our home on this campus. We may have taken it for granted, but you see now while we were jiving around we been kicked in the ass *again*." He was poised on his toes, flinging the words out before him. "I don't know what it is about us that we get through one crisis and we don't worry about it no more until we get slapped down again.

"What we're going to do right now is go over to Meade Hall and talk to Ellsworth. We're gonna tell him that we want a new building constructed to be ready for operation next fall. In the meantime we need temporary facilities with a twenty-four-hour guard, as well as a permanent guard around Brother Bates's home. We want full reimbursement for the materials lost in the fire, which includes our library and several people's personal papers. We're also demanding a full-scale investigation into who started the fire, but we're not waitin for them on that. We've got some idea of our own, and if we finish our investigation and get to those motherfuckas first, the shit's really gonna explode."

Ike flinched as the crowd was jolted by Hollyfield's last statement. He thought about leaving at that moment, but Hollyfield eased his voice.

"But right now, we're just goin to talk. Afterward, we'll do some planning in smaller groups so the whole world don't know what we're doin. Any disagreement with that?"

"Shit, let's go if we goin!"

"All right, come on." Hollyfield left the steps and strode toward the front of what was quickly becoming a line aimed at the heart of the campus. Nearly two hundred people, most of the blacks at the college, melded into a fluid force spreading like an oil slick through the snow. One brother jumped out into the middle of the road, walking right at an oncoming car. The car honked twice, then swerved to the side, sending up a spray of wet snow and bumping the curb. With that, people poured off the sidewalk.

Ike marched along silently, bodysurfing the wave of people that reminded him of the confusing crush at the start of a race before he could pull away and go for himself. When the caravan pulled around in front of Meade it was framed by a gallery of white onlookers. The blacks cut a path through the halls of the building leading to the office of the president. The building was surprisingly empty, and Ike got the distinct feeling they were expected.

All chairs, tables and windowsills in the outer office were quickly occupied and then people just came in and stood. People were hanging all over bronze busts and expensive lamps, while others were backed up in the hall outside. "They redecorated since last year," Ike heard somebody say.

Ken Hollyfield stood at the receptionist's desk, waiting for the crowd to settle. She was a small black woman who sat staring patiently back at them with arched eyebrows. "We wanna see Ellsworth," Hollyfield said.

"Just a moment," came the polite answer. "I'll tell him you're here."

"I think he knows, sister," Hollyfield pressed.

"Just a moment," she repeated and disappeared around a corner.

As she left, a man came out from the recesses of the inner office. "I'm Bob Perkins, assistant to the president," he said smiling. "Who's the spokesman here?"

"I know who you are and we didn't come to see you," Hollyfield said. "Where's Ellsworth?"

"He's inside. He said he'll see your representatives now. Who's coming in?"

"We all are." The group pushed forward before the man could react.

"Wait a minute! You can't all go in there—there's no room."

"You better *take* your hands off me!" A girl near Ike screamed as the man tried to hold people back.

Gene Mayford appeared in front of the man. "Did you touch this woman?" he demanded.

"What is this? I'm just trying to get a little order here."

"Apologize."

"Look, I don't want any trouble." His neck was flaming as his voice rose. "I might have touched her, I'm just asking you people not to stampede through here like a herd of—"

Bap! The back of Gene's hand sent the man's glasses flying under the parade of feet. Ike cringed as he passed by. He had not imagined that Gene could get like that. "I don't want no lip from you, cracker," he heard Gene say. "Just get on your knees and apologize."

"I *said* I was sorry," he blurted, a red splotch growing on the side of his face.

"On your knees." The hand was poised again.

"No wait—wait a minute." His face was trying to make a stand but his body was shrinking away.

"Shit, you ain't worth my time, boy," Gene said and walked through the man.

Ellsworth stood calmly in the middle of his expansive office. Hollyfield stood beside him, and they were ringed by a three deep and growing audience of black people.

"I trust you're going to let me stay this time," the thin, gray-haired president said lightly to Hollyfield.

"For the time being," Hollyfield answered. He wasn't smiling.

When the walls were completely lined with hunch-shouldered brothers, Hollyfield began to quote his list. Ellsworth listened carefully before he responded. He said that temporary quarters for the Black Studies program were already being prepared in a vacant fraternity house that was due for renovation. While new quarters, he said, were out of the question, plans for a permanent location in an existing building were being reviewed. Guards would be provided and funds necessary to continue the program would, of course, be appropriated. Any question of compensation would have to be negotiated with Dr. Bates and cleared by the trustees.

When Hollyfield raised the question of apprehending a suspect, Ellsworth cut him off. "You know, there's been no conclusive evidence so far that the fire was caused by arson."

The crowd groaned. "Man, don't give us that shit! You know it didn't burn by itself."

"The report from the investigators should be ready sometime this week," Ellsworth said. "We'll take no action until the report is in. And I suggest you don't, either."

"That's all you've got to say?" Hollyfield asked.

"At this time, yes."

Hollyfield walked toward the door. The group parted for him to pass and followed. One brother started back into the room to say something to Ellsworth, but Gene caught him and pulled him through the door. They trooped out, past the president's assistant, who stood in a corner with his broken glasses, and past the receptionist, who smiled and nodded at their departure. Down the hall the school's only high-ranking black administrator was pounding on the door of his own office.

"Wanna come with us, bro?" one of the crowd offered.

"Some other time, thanks," he said, smiling thinly. "Jeannie, goddammit, open the door," he hissed into the wood. "It's me."

Outside the building Hollyfield led them back in the direction of the Uhuru site. Ike didn't completely understand the gesture of coming to Meade and then going back, but he was glad nothing drastic had happened. There were others, however, frustrated with the marching back and forth, who wanted action. A handful of brothers bolted the line and charged into the chemistry building they were passing. Hollyfield called them back, but they kept on. So the group turned toward the building as well, picking up the pace to catch up to the mavericks and, at the same time, to make their foray seem part of the planned demonstration.

It was easy to follow their trail. Although the marchers had begun to clap and chant as they quick-stepped through the wide halls, angry shouts and shattering glass echoed around them. Several white students spilled out of a large room and, stunned by the number of blacks bearing down on them, stood pinned to the wall, their faces a mural of disbelief and hatred oddly distorted through plastic goggles. Behind them, Ike could see that experiments had been swept from the rows of benches. Grown-ups—professors and staff—ventured out into the hall, but they, too, were powerless before the wave. Doors opened and shut nearly in sequence ahead of them and behind. The chanting grew louder, the marching faster. They swept around corners and surged up stairs. More crashes and shouts ahead, sirens wailing plaintively in the distance. And a distinct but muffled *whoosh*.

Ike was nearing the top of a flight of stairs when the procession simply broke. The person ahead of him stiffened, and he was caught with one foot waiting to land on the next step. Amid a clamor of screams and curses, he realized as he was forced to step back that he had heard the word "fire." Since people were still coming up from below, there was no room to turn around. The mass knotted, squeezed from both ends, then bumped backward in awkward, helpless slow motion. The congestion didn't last; those nearest the top scrambled forward, either to find the source of trouble or, more likely, to find another exit, and the bottom fell out quickly with the awareness of disaster.

Blacks and whites filled the exits as bells clanged. The whites, for the most part, stopped outside and looked back; the blacks kept going. Pouring out of several different doors, the marchers began to re-form, sifting through the incredulous whites as in an elaborate halftime maneuver. But still, although brothers were urging people to fall into line and pick up the chant, the cohesion was lost. Many stumbled and ran from the site, like first-time criminals, not all heading in the same direction. Ike found himself off the curb in the path of cars honking and screeching in the slush, nudged on by police cars and fire trucks. He sprinted to the other side and, instead of turning toward Uhuru, ran on into the middle of the quad, weaving around people rushing to see what had happened. He ran for maybe two hundred yards, his best two hundred, through the deadly open whiteness of the meadow, before he slipped and fell.

Whoops, someone said lightly. He looked around and saw that people were still strolling. He had outrun the shock waves; nobody, right there, knew that something bad had happened yet, though they would as soon as they walked a little farther. They would know what he was running from. He rose slowly, felt the cold that had turned to fire in his lungs, and staggered toward the library, a vision now blurred by snow or tears.

He disappeared into the stacks and sank into a carrel. The sirens did not carry inside, but his head was ringing. He hadn't eaten. He put his head down on the cold metal desk, shut his eyes and tried not to think. It didn't work. Something had exploded in the lab. Somebody might have gotten hurt. *He* might have gotten hurt. Fighting fire with fire, the fire this time. Was that it, Even Steven? No, there would be more. It was a stupid, endless cycle. But you had to do something. The anger was real. And justified. They, somebody, had destroyed Uhuru. That couldn't be allowed to happen. Why couldn't they just leave them—him—alone? He got up and wandered about, looking for a book, any book, some solid truth he could hold in his hands.

He left the library hours later when the evening study force began to arrive. The tension of the afternoon had eased out of his body, leaving him tired and anxious to get back to his half-room home. He glanced at the mailbox and was relieved to find nothing. Lenny's grating voice carried down the corridor to him from the open door of his room.

"Just cause the place burned down doesn't give them the right to—"

"Get out," Ike said before he was completely through the door.

"I'm talkin to Rosen," Lenny protested.

The door crashed back as far as it would go. "Get *out!*" Ike stood by the gaping entrance.

Lenny's mouth twitched a few times as he looked at Ike, then over to Art, who had gone blank. He got up and eased past Ike. Art went over to close the door behind him and began to speak, but Ike cut him off. "Just don't say anything, all right?" He fell onto the bed. "I don't wanna hear it." He closed his eyes,

and when he opened them he was alone in the room. He didn't

know how long he had been lying there, but it seemed much later than it had just been. Art opened the door gently as Ike was getting up, trailing in a babble of voices from the hallway.

"You okay?" Art asked. "You were really out for a while."

Ike scratched his head and grunted. "What's all the commotion?"

"We just heard on the radio," Art said. "The police arrested two black guys for trashing the chem lab. Came and got them in their dorm. I guess there was a big scene."

"Great," Ike mumbled, trying to wake up. "Anybody get hurt this afternoon?"

"I don't think so. There was an explosion and a fire they put out pretty quick, but they said there was at least a couple hundred thousand dollars' damage. Were you there?"

Lenny came to the door of the room. "Hey, Isaac, what is all this?" he asked. "Everybody's goin crazy."

Too much. Art he could handle, but the jackals were going to keep coming. Ike moved toward the door. Lenny stood there as if someone owed him some answers.

"Get outta my way," Ike said.

Lenny looked at Art, puzzled, then back to Ike. "Christ, don't *you* start. What the hell's goin *on* here?"

"Just get the fuck out of my way, all right?" Ike's voice cracked but Lenny moved. Two steps out into the hall, he turned around, came back in, grabbed his coat and went out again.

"Where you goin?" Art called to his roommate.

Ike kept going without answering. He couldn't answer; he didn't know. He couldn't stay there, answering questions about things he didn't understand. Things everybody expected him to know. He wished he'd stayed with Barbara or had gone to visit Cheryl. He even thought briefly about catching a bus home, but that would be worse. He wondered, suddenly, where kids went when they ran away from home and didn't go anywhere. On TV they always had a playhouse in the backyard or a garage or they went to the park and sat in a tree or on a bench and never got stolen or molested.

He walked on into the cold, hearing noises and voices. The library was closing and the diehards were drifting back down into the Valley. He wandered in the direction of the Village, where he might be able to find a pay phone. He would call Cheryl. Hadn't he decided when she was down for Homecoming that he would share this stuff with her, not try to keep it all jammed up inside? That's what he would do. Go talk to his baby and let her make him feel better. She knew him; she could help him get through this.

Aw, shit! He slipped off his glove and reached into his pocket but found nothing but a pen and a stick of gum. No change. Where would he get change this time of night? Everything was closed.

A group of people were chattering toward him, probably from the library. He would stand there and listen to what they were saying. Maybe they'd be cursing out the niggers and he'd have to fight. Maybe they'd go off just seeing him. He leaned against a tree, looming past the edge of the light from a street lamp, tensed and waited. There were two guys and three girls in floppy sweatshirts carrying knapsacks—and they looked so *young*. They looked like . . . college students. Real college students. Their minds weren't on him or any riot, and they weren't even strung out about Vietnam. They were talking about biology. *Biology!* Didn't they know what was going on, that shit was falling apart? How could they be so naive, so out of it? Why couldn't he?

He followed them a little way, eavesdropping longingly, until he reached the bridge to the Village. And he stared into the gorge. The rocks were painted with snow, and the small stream of unfrozen water, in no particular hurry, eased its way down and out, toward the lake to rest undisturbed until spring brought the boats and the birds and the swimmers and fishermen. Must be nice. People went down there, too, at least one every couple of years, he'd heard, because of biology, and chemistry and physics. They went down there because nobody knew them and they knew nobody. Because their parents didn't understand. Because they knew they weren't going to grow up to be what somebody wanted them to be or what they wanted to be, and because nothing was the way it was supposed to be. But when you got down there, nothing ever changed. Ike believed that everything did change—that's why the shit was so fucked up now, somebody had rewritten the script—and he wanted to know how it turned out. He might not like it, but he wanted to know.

He turned back toward the campus. He was tired. So was everybody else, apparently. Nobody was out. Even on a day like that, everybody could just go inside a room somewhere, let the snow dust over the mess, and come back the next day to start all over again. Another class, another test. Nothing was real. Nothing stayed but the sets that framed the play. The quad looked just as it did a hundred years before, except for a few lights freezing the effect. And freezing him into a scene where he wasn't supposed to be. *He wasn't supposed to be there.* Somebody obviously thought so, or there wouldn't be all this commotion. Was it Ellsworth? Lenny? Maybe even Hollyfield. He bent over and scooped up a handful of snow—bad packing, but who cared—and fired a shot at the founder sitting there in his Abraham Lincoln chair watching for virgins, as the legend went, and probably trespassing niggers. He missed but tried again. And again and again and again until he had splattered the old fucker enough to bring out his mighty whiteness from head to toe.

When the ground around him was all green and brown, Ike stopped, suddenly sorry that he had torn a hole in the soft snow carpet; he had never liked the way Madison Park had looked on the first snow day after they'd scarred it with sled traces and snow forts. But having already spoiled the postcard, Ike went over to a fresh patch and drew a message with his numbed finger: IKE LOVES CHERYL. He stepped back, liked it, and drew another: ELIZABETH'S LITTLE BOY WAS HERE. Tickled, he sat down and wrote a postscript: FUCK YOU AND YO MAMAS TOO. He got up, knocked the snow off, and trudged on across the quad.

He headed for the building that housed the government department, because that was the way he was used to going. And he was cold. He tugged on the door and was surprised to find it open. Before he went in, he looked back and saw his tracks leading to and away from the brown patch in the middle and the love letters in the snow that were already filling in. He stood inside for a minute waiting to feel warm, but the heat wasn't on and there really wasn't much difference. After listening to make sure no one else was around—what custodian in his right mind would be around now?—he climbed the steps to the third floor where

Maier's office was. Maier wasn't there, of course, and the door was locked, so he kept moving, down the hall and back down the other stairwell and into a large, unlocked first-floor classroom. He turned on the light and noticed for the first time how truly ugly it was; who knew at nine o'clock in the morning? It looked like a room where the founder might have taught if the founder had known enough to teach anybody anything, which he hadn't. Ike had had more modern desks in grade school, and he had thought those hooked poles for opening classroom windows had gone out with Eisenhower.

Finals were coming up. If he could just block out everything and get through that, he'd be okay. It would be Christmas. Peace on Earth. He'd settle for a warmer coat. He had to think of something else to get for Elizabeth. He had been thinking that he'd present her with first-semester straight As, but that wasn't going to happen. It wouldn't impress her anyway, she'd expect that, and even if it did impress her it damn sure wouldn't be enough anymore. He didn't know what to get for Cheryl, either. Maybe a girlfriend for McFat. He looked around for some paper to make a list but couldn't find any; even the trash can was empty. So he went down to the men's room, no longer surprised to find anything unlocked, and grabbed several sheets of paper towels. Back in the classroom, he sat down at a desk, put the stick of gum in his mouth, took out the pen, and drew a blank on the Christmas list. So instead he started writing a letter to Cheryl that tried to describe the sound of breaking glass in the chem lab, and the incredible energy of being part of a mob, and the look on Ellsworth's face and the hatred in Gene's voice and the unbearable snottiness in Lenny's and Art's confusion and the willfully ignorant chatter of students talking biology and the music of the gorge and how he wished to God he had a dime because he'd never been so lonely in his life.

He sank out of the chair and kept writing on the floor, although the pen kept slipping out of his hand, too. The last time he picked it up he noticed that it wasn't so dark outside, and it pleased him to know that he would be the first one in class.

It was going to be a rotten Christmas. The dorm had emptied quickly during finals week, and he'd gotten through almost without talking to anybody—except Cheryl, whom he'd called to explain the strange letter. She would be in Michigan for the holiday, just for the first week but long enough to activate his sense of abandonment. Hodge wasn't well; he wouldn't be around much to ease the tension as he had at graduation. And Elizabeth was not going to act right. He tried to tell himself otherwise all during the bus ride, but reality hit when she got home from work and found him in his room unpacking.

"Hey, girl," he said easily. "How's it goin?"

She gave him a perfunctory peck on the lips and sat down on his bed. "You tell me. I'm payin all this tuition money and these niggers are down there tearin up the place."

"You're not paying much, remember? The scholarship covers most of it."

"That's not the point and you know it, Richard. I'm still supporting you, that's payment enough. And I want better answers than this 'you-know' I've been gettin on the phone."

"It's nothing, Ma. Just campus politics."

"Politics is when you vote. This ain't nothin but craziness." She slammed closed his suitcase. "Stand still and *talk* to me, boy. I don't know what's goin on down there, but I'm not stupid and I know it's more than what you say."

He stopped and threw up his arms, dropping a clump of dirty underwear on the floor. "Okay, what do you want? *I* don't know what's goin on either. Somebody burned down the black studies building, and people went off. I don't like it, nobody *likes* it, but what am I supposed to do?"

"You're supposed to stay away from everybody who had anything to do with that mess, that's what. I didn't send you down there to take care of nobody's business but your own."

"It *is* my business. It's everybody's business."

"Richard, you ain't got nothin to do with them hell-raisin niggers. If they got you so tied up in this thing maybe you oughtta just leave school for a while."

"And do what," he said, the contempt in his voice surprising him. "Go back to the stockroom? Pump gas? Get drafted? That makes a lot of sense."

"You can start all over again someplace else," she said. "Can't you see, honey? Those folks aren't interested in getting an education. They're just tryin to make trouble, and they're draggin you down with them. They said people are getting *arrested*, Richard. You could get ruined for life. I don't *want* that. I—I went to too much *trouble*—"

"I don't want that either, Ma," he said more calmly, suddenly sensing himself in control. "It's okay, I'm not getting ruined. But I'm not quitting, either."

"Boy, I'm not askin you, I'm tellin you—either leave that mess alone or get away from there."

"I can't do that."

"You mean you won't!"

"I mean I *can't!* It'd be the same anywhere else. I didn't know it was gonna be like this, but that's what's goin on. You know, ten years ago I probably couldn't even have gone to an Ivy League school. It's like the sit-ins and all that stuff, I guess, but now it's happening in the colleges up here." He was feeling his way through this and looked to her for a glint of understanding. "It's important."

"You listen to me, Richard. For the last eighteen years ain't nothin been important to me but gettin you to where you can make somethin of yourself. You don't have to fight nobody's battles but your own. This is what you've been workin for, and you wanna throw it all away for some stupid, bad-actin niggers."

"I'd like to be able to do like you want, Ma, believe me. But I can't."

She stood up and walked to the doorway. "Is that what you tell that frizzy-head white gal?" She slammed the door; he picked up a handful of clothes and tried to shatter it.

After stewing for half an hour he left his room to call Tommy Jackson. He had to get out of there. Luckily, Tommy was home and said he'd come by later. To pass the time, Ike went to the front closet, slid out the Howard Clothes box that had once contained his seventh-grade winter coat and carried it to the living room where Elizabeth had, in clear defiance of his long-standing wishes, planted a pitiful, five-foot artificial Christmas tree. But where did she keep Nat? Most of the records had long since gone into his room and those were now at the dorm. He sure as hell wasn't going to ask her. It wasn't in the closet with the old record player where he had found the stash of 45s and 78s last summer or behind the magazine rack, where *Ebony* was still discovering the Natural. The end table! And there it was, leaning in the corner behind the plastic flowers that wouldn't fool Ray Charles and the heavy, ostensibly gilt-edged ashtray that had never seen an ash even before Hodge quit smoking. The tree may be fake and the woman may be evil, but as long as those chestnuts kept roasting all was not lost.

The honeyed voice brought her from the kitchen. "Oh, I was gonna help you with that later," she said, sounding like a regular person.

"That's all right, I won't be here. I'm goin out with Tommy."

"Dinner's almost ready, you know."

"Just leave it. I'll get it when I'm done." He was dying to see her face but refused to turn around. He knew she wanted to say something, too, but he was gambling that she wouldn't want to push him anymore. And Nat always softened her up a little.

Even in the best of times, dinner would only be a distraction now. He took this job seriously and had since he was twelve and was able to reach the top by himself. First the bells with the chipped green paint. Then the red and blue balls that seemed to disappear every year, although he knew *he* hadn't broken one since he'd lunged through the branches to plug in his new black and white portable TV. The wax snowmen, Santas and soldiers were next, followed by the wooden sleds and reindeer. He saved a special branch for the sole surviving ugly faded purple teardrop, and he decided not to bother with the little fuzzy bear he'd bought on campus as this year's addition. He looped around the two long, crumpled tinfoil garlands just so, countered them artistically with the last string of heavy, solid lights, and filled in the gaps with last year's new strings of snowflake blinkers. He would need two packages of icicles; that would wait until tomorrow, and, just in case they signed a Christmas Eve truce, he decided to leave the star as well.

Punctuality had never been among Tommy's strong points, which was not surprising; Elizabeth always said Dessie would be late to her own funeral. Ike had time to finish the hard cubed steak and cold mashed potatoes she left for him, read every inch of the paper and watch more TV than he cared to before the doorbell rang.

"Hey there, Ike. How you been, boy?" Tommy came into the apartment looking harder and burlier than he had six months before. He was now a carbon copy of Big Tom, and that made Ike wonder if he had grown to look any more like his own father, a prospect that would hardly thrill Elizabeth.

"Not too bad," Ike said. "It's good to see you."

"Come on in, Tommy, and let me have a look at you," Elizabeth said from the couch.

"Hi, Miz Isaac."

"How's the army been treatin you?"

"Well, I could complain, but it wouldn't do any good."

"Yeah, I know how you feel," she said. "How come you're not wearin your uniform?"

"I don't like to wear it when I'm home, you know, I get kinda embarrassed."

"Why? You should be proud. Besides, your uniform must look better than some of the other things I've seen you wearin."

Tommy smiled and Ike eased him toward the door.

"Tell your mother I said hi. I have to call her later this week," Elizabeth said.

"Yes, ma'am."

"What time you be home, Richard?" she asked when they were almost out the door.

"I'll be here when I get here," Ike said.

"Whatever you say, Mister Man," she said without looking up.

"Somethin wrong?" Tommy asked as they got into his mother's car.

"She just been actin a little strange lately, that's all."

"Don't tell me her Boy Wonder done done somethin bad."

"Nah, she's pissed off cause I been into some of the demonstrations and things at school."

"You?" Tommy laughed. "What you demonstratin for, longer library hours?"

It was like neither of them had ever been away. Although he looked almost like somebody else, somebody grown, piloting his mother's Chrysler, Tommy talked and Ike listened, just as before.

"Say, you wanna hear about a real demonstration?" Tommy asked, leaning and wheeling. "Man, you ain't *seen* no demonstratin."

"You're gonna tell me anyway."

"Yeah, I am. But first I gotta tell you bout Chico. Real heavy dude on the base, you know, always got his head stuck in a book. Like you, but he ain't quite so dull. He's always tryin to politicalize the brothers. Hates the army, hates Georgia and hates white folks. He was drafted—said he woulda left the country but he didn't know no bloods in Canada. The brass is always down on him cause they say he's a troublemaker. Tell the truth, sometimes we wish he'd shut up, too.

"Anyway, one time this summer Chico had a weekend pass and he hitched into Columbus to see his old lady. Everything was cool, you know. But on the way back, he was hitchin and this car picked him up. Turned out it was some crackers from the base goin back, too. They were drunk and they all hated Chico so they decided to give my man a hard time. He tried to get out but they held him in the car and started fuckin with him. Took him out on a side road and whupped his butt. They musta stayed on his ass 'bout all night, man, cause when he got back he was hurtin. They told him if they ever caught him alone again they'd kill him, less he quit raisin hell on the base.

"Well, when the brothers heard about that, *ev*erybody got militant, you know, even the dudes that always told Chico to go fuck himself when he went around the rec hall quotin Malcolm X. We couldn't just let 'em get away with somethin like that. So a few days later somebody jumped one of the crackers who did it in the mess hall and all hell broke loose. I mean dudes were pickin up knives and all."

"You too?" Ike asked.

"Well, you know me, man. I didn't run into no knife or nothin but I was in there puggin a good little bit. The MPs broke it up before anybody got killed, but there musta been at least fifty guys into it. The brass picked out Chico and a couple of other brothers and got 'em transferred. The rest of us they just locked up for a while. I couldn't get home till now cause of that."

"You call that a demonstration?"

"Hey, we made the point. A few of them crackers ain't healed till yet."

"By the way, where are we going?"

"Oh, yeah, I wanna check out Lorenzo's. New place around here somewhere in the old ward. My Moms said it usedta be called the Oasis. Daddy worked there sometime."

"You mean we're going to that place where our *mothers* used to hang out?" Ike asked.

"Yeah, kinda sick, ain't it? But I heard it's supposed to be happenin."

It couldn't have looked too different all those years ago. The flooring was new and halfway shiny, but the little square Formica tables looked vintage. The crowd was younger than Ike would have thought, but then Elizabeth was right out of high school when she used to go there.

Ike wondered if this was one of the places Hodge had told him about, that he used to take Elizabeth to in the days after Lonnie. Get her back in circulation, put a little pep in her step. He'd said he didn't want to take her to the joints where old cats like him hung out. She wouldn't have any fun, and besides, he might have to fight somebody who thought she was a hot little number. That wasn't his style. So, as Hodge told it, they went to younger spots, probably like the Oasis, where he could celebrate her youth and at least make her laugh at the spectacle of him dancing his fool behind off.

"You know, I've never seen you drink before," Tommy said. He was pouring a Miller's down the center of a glass, and Ike was ordering a CC and soda, like the one Hodge had bought him at the Greek's.

"I've never seen you drink before, either," Ike said, "except for that Ripple Hez brought to the night meets."

"Gotta keep up my strength, burnin off all those calories keepin in shape," said Tommy. "And it's good to have somethin in your hand while you scope the room for babes."

"I see. Well, I have to unwind from all the academic pressure." They leaned at the bar in silence and watched people drift in. It was still pretty quiet because the band had not started playing yet; it was warm-up time.

"So how you like it down there?" Tommy asked.

"Honestly, man, I don't know. Everything's up in the air. I'm all the time either tryin to study or goin to some kind of meeting."

"Yeah, well don't work too hard there, Ike. You get too many more ideas in your head you liable to hurt yourself. Say, whatever happened to that girl you usedta be with?"

"Which one?"

"Far as I know it wasn't but one. That white chick from school."

"She's still around. Why, you wanna give me some advice about that, too?"

"I don't never give no advice, buddy. I just make suggestions. I gotta look out for you cause you smart in some things, but sometimes you need help. You know what I mean?"

"Yeah, man, go ahead."

"Naw, brother, I ain't got nothin to say. I was just curious. Hey, will you look at this?"

Ike supposed Tommy had just spotted a fox. When he turned around there was a tall shadow.

"Hezekiah!" Tommy yelled.

"Turkey Trot Tommy," Hez said, grinning. "And I be damned if he ain't got the professor here, too."

"How you doin, Hez?" Ike said.

"I'm doin, baby. You know that. Jackie, gimme a Colt. I sure didn't expect to see the Odd Couple in here. Come on. Let's sit down."

Hez engulfed a chair. The noise level in the place seemed to increase. "Ain't this a bitch," he said. "What you doin back here, Brother IQ?"

"It's Christmas," Ike said. "Came to see my mama."

"I don't blame you. She's fine."

"Hey, wait a minute."

"Just tellin the truth, man. You oughtta be proud. I woulda thought you'd get your jive ass blown up in Vietnam by now, Tommy."

"Not me, Hez. If I do go the Cong's gonna have to come get me. I ain't lookin for no trouble."

"I hear you. You know 'bout Wilbur, don't you?"

"No, what happened?" Tommy asked.

"Stepped on a land mine his first week over there, man. I didn't go to the funeral, but I heard the coffin was real light."

"Oh shit."

"Wilbur Harrison?"

"Yeah, the little monkey dude used to fuck with you all the time, Ike."

"How'd you get out, Hez?"

"Shit, baby, you heard of feet do your stuff? Good for jumpin, bad for marchin. They didn't want me and I didn't want them. 'Sides, I'm a family man now."

"You lyin."

"Y'all remember Tina?"

"The white Mustang?"

"It's parked outside, baby."

"You married her?" Ike asked.

"Signed, sealed and delivered. Got one in the oven, too. Hey, you didn't think I was gonna be a jitterbug all my life, did you? Close your mouth, Ike, you're gonna catch flies."

"Congratulations," Ike said.

"Yeah, man, that's all right," Tommy added.

"I know you all thought I was jivin all along," Hez said, still smiling. "But remember I'm older than you cats. Got all my serious jivin done while you was still playin stink finger. That's why I finally finished up, man. Time to settle down and TCB. But don't feel bad, we surprised everybody."

Tina was a legendary blonde with a weary face and Amazonian body, who was definitely not the cheerleader type but reputedly did her boosting in private. In fact, she and Hez were well matched; they both seemed like real-world visitors floating through the make-believe of high school. Ike rarely saw her in the halls, but she occasionally showed up at track meets—one of the much-advertised objects of Hez's attention, for whom he stocked a variety of ghostkiller lotions and powders in his gym bag so he'd be smooth and ready for action afterward. She had been there with the white Mustang waiting for Hez at the last meet, the city championships, a siren poised at the far end of the field. And Cheryl was waiting right alongside her.

For Ike, Tommy, Hez and the other seniors on the team, that meet had brought an end to a dubious career marked by half-assed practices and mostly mediocre results—Tommy getting left behind at the starting line when he couldn't pull his sweat pants off over his spikes, Ike knocked flat by the wind on the hilltop track they'd dubbed Choctaw Ridge. But on that day, Tommy ran four strong laps and finished a close third behind the fabled Kenny Dumpson, the black housing commissioner's son. Ike, meanwhile, pulled past Wilbur on the far turn of the quarter and, for the first time, got close enough to try the finish-line lean he'd been practicing for three years—although someone else's chest hit the tape just before he got there.

As always, the last event was the high jump, and they had all gathered to watch Hez do his thing. The only remaining competition was Walt Obrynski, a football player booked for Notre Dame, who, like Dumpson, represented the Catholic school that had already sewn up yet another title. On his first attempt at six-two, Obrynski hit the metal bar, and it fell to the foam rubber mat with a groan from the audience. Hez then stood, tall and loose, a scarecrow with a watermelon head, rocking back and forth until he felt ready. Five quick steps and he was in the air twisting above the bar in silence until his trailing foot clanged into it.

Obrynski took a little more time on his second try. He glared at the bar as if he were trying to intimidate it and shook his arms and legs like the wrestler he also was. A deep breath and he was moving slowly, gaining speed on the last two steps and lifting off the ground with a hard push. He soared over, barely brushing the bar, and hit the pit looking up anxiously. The bar rattled but did not fall, and Obrynski leaped to his feet with his arms raised in triumph. Almost before the bar could be steadied Hez was back in the jumping circle. Stare, rock, five steps and up. He did everything the way he should have, but his back knee scraped the bar. "Get out the *pit!*" Ike screamed, knowing the jump might then count, but Hez lay on his back until the bar danced off the stand and fell across his body.

He had one jump left. They called out for Hez to take his time, and Sonny, one of the brothers on the team, stepped out to settle him down. He rocked in place longer than he ever had, before setting himself in motion. At the end of the fifth stride Hez's body angled up and collided squarely with the bar. He landed on one foot in the pit, caught the bar and hurled it to the ground. There was light applause and Obrynski started forward to shake his hand but thought better of it. Hez stalked off, and the others didn't follow. He hadn't lost the jump in two years; nothing they could say would make it right.

The officials raised the bar to six-three to give Obrynski a chance to make it, although the meet was over. Most of the assembled team members from all the schools—who made up most of the audience at the meet—hung around to see him make three unsuccessful attempts at the height, only one coming close, and began to disperse. Then Hez reappeared in the circle.

"Mothafucka, I said put it back up!" he bellowed to the reluctant officials. "Six-four." The crowd turned back to see what was happening, and it wasn't only the Southwest brothers who rushed to the front. Angry but relaxed, Hez made his approach and propelled himself smoothly over the bar with two inches to spare. "That's the way you do it, chump," he said, pointing a long, crooked finger at Obrynski. He plucked the cigarette from behind his ear, fired it up with the lighter in his sock and pimped off to the locker room, not bothering to pick up his second-place ribbon.

"Hey, ain't that Delores just came in?" Tommy asked.

"Who?" Ike asked.

"You 'member Delores—usedta go with Sonny but that fool cut her loose. She lookin better than ever, too. 'Scuse me, I gotta go on a little detail here."

"See what I mean, Ike?" Hez said, shaking his head. "Too old for that mess, hang out all night beggin some bitch for a piece. Not that I ever hadda beg, mind you. Wonder if Tommy got a new rap since he been in the army."

"Don't see why he should," Ike said. "He's had the same one since eighth grade. Didn't work then, either, but he's got it all memorized."

Hez laughed. "So what's up with you, man? Didn't you say once you was goin to law school? You still thinkin 'bout that?"

"Yeah, thinkin about it. One step at a time, though. Got a long way to go yet."

"Well I hope you do. We need that, man. I just started workin over at the public safety building. I'm a guard."

"Oh yeah?" Ike said.

"Hey, they always said I'd end up in jail. But I fooled 'em, baby, I'm on the other side of the bars. I tell you, though, I see these young brothers down there and they be so fucked up, man. They got nobody to trust. These lawyers don't give a fuck about them. That's why I hope you do that law. Like Malcolm said, we got to get our own shit together, you know, take care of our own selves."

"Yeah, I know what you mean," Ike said. Even Hez was quoting scripture to him.

"Tell you what I'm doin. Real estate. Yeah, bought a place this summer, fixed it up, gettin ready to sell it. Got my eye on a couple more, too. Folks gonna always need a place to live, and they need better'n what they got. Tina's old man's givin me some pointers, but I think I got the touch, man. Now I got the steady income I'm ready to deal. You come back in a few years, Ol Hez gonna be a regular tycoon, baby."

"I don't doubt it," Ike said. "Maybe you're the one who oughtta go to law school, but I think you might do better anyway."

"Ain't no might in it, professor," Hez said, raising his huge hand for five. "You do your thing, I'll do mine, and we'll both kick us some ass. Uh-oh. Look at this. What happened, slick?"

Tommy came back to the table looking disturbed. "She don't look so hot close up," he said. "Too hard-lookin. I think she might be on somethin."

"The only thing she be on is that nigger's dick just came in, general," Hez said. "I coulda told you but you didn't gimme a chance."

"Hey, don't make me no never mind. They got a lot finer down in Georgia, man. Fuck her."

"Oh, no you won't," Hez said laughing.

"Come on, Ike," Tommy said. "I told Moms I'd take her shopping first thing in the morning."

"Yeah, I gotta do some of that myself," Ike said, rising from the table. "Good talkin to you, Hez. Congratulations on Tina, the baby, the job, everything."

"Only the beginning, baby," Hez said, stretching a paw out to each of them. "You all take care."

"Nice place," Ike said as they headed out to the car. "We oughtta come here again."

"Shit," Tommy said. "You can have it."

Alistair Sim had faced all his ghosts and along with Tiny Tim faded into the log that burned and was not consumed, and the carols had come down to "O Holy Night," the one he tried to stay awake for, the last they would play before "The Star-Spangled Banner" and the final, eternal beep that sometimes woke him with the thought that a bomb was about to fall. In the semidark, Mary,

Flo and the Mouth stared down at him from their supreme position on the wall—surrounded by yellow and green ribbons, a couple of heat-crinkled newspaper clips, three framed certificates and a Children's Day church bulletin with his name in it—as if asking whether this was the year he would break the spell. He usually turned off the set when the flag started flapping, darted into the bathroom with his eyes closed and tried to remember how he managed to get to sleep on the night before the first day of school.

It had never been that tricky with Santa. The pressure came when Elizabeth told him he could come on out and peek if he wanted to, but if he saw her putting his box under the tree before sunup he'd have to open it right then and she could stay in bed all day. That would defeat the whole purpose and get her off the hook. For a few years he listened for her as he never had for Santa, gradually got in the habit of staying awake and finally resolved to stay put so he could have the satisfaction of waking her early and making her do a full Christmas. This year, for the first time, he feared that she wouldn't play, even if he kept his part of the bargain. So what was the point? He pulled on his robe, waved to the girls, aborted the beep and left his room.

He went straight to the front window; his didn't have a view of the front, and he'd always wondered what the street looked like on Christmas Eve. It was, of course, quiet. It probably always was, except on Saturday night when he heard a lot of traffic and the voices of Jewtown creeping closer. The Coccaris did keep the lights on all night. When a single car chugged through the brown-sludge street, he couldn't imagine where it could be going.

The tree didn't look that bad after all—for a fake shorty. The lights, which he plugged in, made all the difference, if he did say so himself. He liked the way they blinked around the living room like a gang of Tinkerbells. Made the place look better than it deserved. What was amazing was that this stuff fooled anybody—like once a year everybody got to build his own movie set. Bad as this was, tomorrow would be worse. There would be a scraggly silver table-top model that Elizabeth had taken over with a few ornaments swiped from his careful arrangement. And the whole place would smell like old, a pissy medicine aroma as far from ham and potato pie as whiskey from candy canes. Hodge didn't belong there; Black Beauty looked like a panther in the zoo in the parking lot, and the women were at least twenty years past catching his eye. He must sure-nuff be singing the Lovesick Blues, that country tune he was always yodeling that got under Elizabeth's skin. Nobody's sugar daddy now. Even if his old building had been condemned, that senior-citizen highrise was no place for a man like him. Hodge ought to be there with them, if they had the room. Except there wasn't any them, which was why a hundred fairies and Rudolph himself couldn't keep the stupid tree from being a lie and why he was out of bed in the first place, spying on a Christmas that wasn't going to happen.

"What are you doin out here?"

He had forgotten about the red robe he'd given her; she made a mighty sorry Santa, shuffling and blinking and scratching her curlered head. "I couldn't sleep," he said.

"Aren't you a little old for that? You used to go right to sleep even when you were little."

"I know, but I've been lying in there awake for the last ten years. I just decided to get it over with tonight. So, where's it at?"

"Behind the preposition."

"Come on, where is it?"

"It's right over there where it's been since ten o'clock. I just came out 'cause I saw the lights and heard you rootin around."

"Oh, I didn't even see it."

"That's where I always put it. You been waitin for me to sneak out here in the middle of the night? Boy, you must be crazy."

"Can I open it now?"

"Can I sleep in the morning?"

"Okay, that was the deal. Oh, wait a minute." He turned on the record player and set Nat to spinning; it was the only way to open a present. Then he tore the wrapping off the heavy box and found a portable electric typewriter. "Ooh, yeah!" he shouted.

"You don't know how tired I got listening to you peck peck peck on that other one. Maybe you'll be a little faster now, since you got more work to do. Maybe you'll even write your mother once in a while. I never could read your scratching."

"Thanks, Mom. I'll save the others for tomorrow—I already figured out most of them."

"You did, huh? Okay, slide mine on over here before I go to sleep." She unwrapped the box too carefully, pausing to admire the paper—why did she *do* that?—and finally extracted the lavender gown. "Oh, Richard, that's *pretty*," she said. "You always were good with colors. I love this. Where are you going?"

"Hold on," he said, the spirit suddenly upon him. "Since you're not getting up, I've got something else I'll give you now." He rushed into his room and returned with a flat, unwrapped box.

Inside was a double 8 × 10 frame. One side contained a picture of him and Elizabeth at his graduation, the other Elizabeth and Uncle Sergeant Clarence at their last Christmas together, before Ike was born. "Oh, honey," she said. "This is wonderful."

"I like the way you look the same in both—give or take a few pounds."

"Yeah, a few." Her pose was remarkably similar, one hand grasping the arm of her main man, the other planted on her hip, her eyes daring the photographer—Hodge, in both cases—to take the shot *now*; she was ready. At both moments, in fact, her grip was coming loose, both men were going away (and both were looking more at her than at the camera, with a mixture of pride and mild embarrassment at her possessive pose), but when the shutter clicked she had exactly what she wanted, and so, she knew, could have it forever.

"You like it? I found the pictures at Thanksgiving and had them enlarged. I hoped you wouldn't miss them."

"Do I like it? Come here." He walked over on his knees for a kiss and a hug. "You couldn't have given me anything better."

"Sorry about yesterday," he said.

"I don't want to talk about that. I know you're doing what you think you have to, and I just have to trust you not to get yourself hurt."

"I won't. You remember that schoolboard meeting we went to when I was in junior high, when they changed the district to send us to the new high school?"

"I think so. Why?"

"I'll never forget this woman made a speech about us 'infesting' the new school, and you jumped up like you were shot out of a cannon and *demanded* to know what she meant by 'infesting.' I mean, you went off. I thought you were going to smack her."

"I almost did. You say that to say what?"

"I remember thinking I was real proud of you that night, 'cause you were fighting for what was best for me. It's the same thing that's going on now, except I have to do the fighting for myself."

"Oh, I get it." She patted his head, stroking the curly part near his neck. "You want a snack?"

"Maybe some eggnog and pie?"

They went into the kitchen and she fixed his, then got out a large glass and a pan from the refrigerator. "Oh, no, you're not gonna do what I think, are you?"

"You just eat off your own plate and don't worry about me." She poured a thick stream of buttermilk into the glass and crumbled in some pieces of cornbread, which she serenely spooned into her mouth.

"How can you eat that stuff, or drink it or whatever you do?"

"I used to ask Mama the same thing. But I tried it when I was pregnant and got to like it. It fed you pretty good for nine months, and you didn't even know you were getting it."

"Tell you what, if I ever get pregnant, I'll try it."

She snorted. "Where'd you and Tommy go last night?" she asked.

"We went over to Lorenzo's."

"That's the place that used to be the Oasis? Big Tom tended bar in there before you all were born. Dessie and I went in there all the time when I was at the business institute, when I first came to town."

"Yeah, I remembered you told me that."

"That's where they introduced me to your father—reintroduced, I should say. I met him once before. He hung out in there. I guess they called themselves doin me a favor."

He said nothing. He had learned long ago that this was the time to shut up and take notes.

"He was a good-lookin yella nigger, though. Before you got to know him. And he could dance, that was one thing he was good for. A lot of those niggers would just stand around tryin to look cute, but we would get out on that floor and just truck on down the line till closing time."

It was her turn to go silent for a while. When he thought she was finished, he said, "We ran into Hez Curry."

"He's not in jail yet?"

"Close. He's working as a guard. Doin pretty well. He told us about Wilbur Harrison."

"Didn't I mention that to you?"

"No, but you know there is something you did mention—a long time ago. It wasn't till after Hez told me he got killed that I remembered what it was."

"What?"

"That he was my brother."

"I never said that."

"You sure did—or at least made it pretty plain that he *might* be. You only said it once, when I was six or seven and we had been fighting in Sunday School. I never forgot that you said something that made me hate him, but I was too scared to mention it again cause I didn't want it to be true."

"Well, it's not."

"Then what the hell did you *say* so for?"

"Watch your tone, Richard. If I said anything like that I said that he might be your father's child. He could have been. Him and Wilbur's mother had a thing for a while, and I know some people thought it. She married Harrison in kind of a hurry. But I know it wasn't true cause Lonnie couldn't make no baby that ugly. Even with her."

"Aw, Ma."

"Aw, Ma what? You want some more pie?"

"Why do you *do* things like that? You said that on purpose to hurt me—or to make me hate my father, and I've been walking around thinking that might be true all these years."

"No you haven't. You didn't even remember till last night, and anyway, you should have asked."

"Damn!"

"Don't curse, Richard."

He put his plate and glass down hard in the sink. "I'm goin to bed," he said. "Merry Christmas."

"Richard—" He was already out of the kitchen. The needle was ripped from Nat Cole's throat, the tree lights went dead and his angry barefoot steps pounded away in time to the clinking of her spoon.

The woman sat at the kitchen table, slowly stirring the cornbread in her glass of buttermilk. The sound of heavy-soled shoes coming up the back stairs echoed the clink of her spoon against the glass. The door opened and the man stepped inside.

"You still up?" he asked. She looked at him, swallowing his stupid question with the buttermilk, and said nothing. He slid to the Frigidaire and took out a bottle of beer. "Didn't I ask you not to buy no more Utica Club?"

"It was on sale," she whispered between both of their slurps.

"Money ain't everything. It's not all the same, you know. Hate this pisswater."

"Where were you?"

"I was out. I hadda see some people."

"Over Ryan Court?"

"How come you always gotta think that? I told you I ain't seen that woman in over two months. I ain't had nothin to do with her."

"Where were you?" she repeated.

"Down to Rudy's. How's my man?"

"He's fine. How did it go today?"

"How what go?"

"Work, Lonnie." There was body in her voice for the first time. "Your job. How was it?"

He began to pace the room, looking at the floor. "That ain't no job. I don't need that nonsense. You know, I hear Snake Dumpson's got a gig with the city—housing administration or some shit. Word is there might be some work around some of these new projects."

"Oh, God, Lonnie." She turned to look at him. "You didn't get fired? Your first day?"

"Naw, I didn't get fired." He put the empty beer bottle down hard on the counter. "I left. I told you that wasn't no job. Baggin groceries and sweepin the floor. What's that?"

"It's a job, Lonnie. A paycheck. Who the hell are you to be picky? Ever since you left the railroad it's been one excuse after another."

"Hell, I can do bettern that. Get me a city job with real money and benefits. I don't need all these people's triflin shit, baby. This one bitch got her bags mixed up and came back screamin to the manager. It wasn't my damn fault—she run out fore I could tell her she made a mistake. But the man had to get on somebody so he jumped on me. I told him he could do it his own damn self."

"Goddamn you, Lonnie."

"*Look*, baby, that ain't *me*, all right?"

"You *promised*. And don't 'baby' me."

"I didn't promise to be nobody's fool. And please don't give me that shit about old Saint Clarence again."

She jumped out of her seat. "Don't *ever* mention his name!" She started to slap him, but he caught her hand.

"What the fuck's wrong with you?"

"He's dead."

"What?"

She pulled her hand loose and slumped back to the table. "He's . . . dead. DeeDee called me this afternoon."

He didn't move. "I'm sorry, baby," he said softly. "I'm . . . goddamn. That's a goddamn shame. Waste."

"What the hell do you know about it?" she cried. "*This* is a waste. This is nothin."

He stood in the middle of the floor shaking his head. "Played it straight by the book. Got himself killed. Goddamn shame."

"Shut up! You don't have no right to talk about it. You don't have a right to be alive."

"All right, girl. Let's not get carried away now."

"Clarence coulda been somebody. He *was* somebody, but look at you. Ain't got nothin and don't half try."

He took steps toward her. "I do try, dammit, and you know it," he hissed. "I keep tellin you ain't but so much a black man can do out there. Less the white folks fall in love with you, like . . . never mind."

"Well, why don't you just go crawl under a rock someplace if it's that bad?"

"Hey, we've been through this before, and I'm tired. The only place I'ma crawl is in there to my bed and go to sleep."

"Oh no. Not with me you ain't." She got up and blocked his path.

"Oh, you ain't tired?"

"I want you outta here, Lonnie. I don't wanna see you or hear you or smell you tonight."

"You always tellin me to come home early," he smiled, "and now you want me to leave. I think your trouble is you don't know what you want."

"More than you got, man. More than you can ever give me."

"Mommy?"

"Go back to bed, Richard," she said to their small son, who had stumbled into the kitchen rubbing his eyes.

"Hey now, buddy. Whaddaya say?"

"Hi, Daddy. I can't sleep." The man knelt and circled the boy's thin body with his long, pretty fingers, drawing it to his own.

"It's nothing, man," he whispered. "Go on back to bed."

They stood facing each other as the child toddled back toward his room. Then the man slowly started for the door.

"When he get up tomorrow, just tell him whatever you told him the last time, all right? Tell him his daddy's just a nigger and he can't do no better. Then tell him to look in the mirror and see if he don't see a nigger lookin back at him. You can lie to him all you want, but that's somethin you can't never change. Good night, baby. Sorry about your brother."

She watched the door close and listened to his steps on the old wooden stairs, echoing nothing but the hollow beating of her own heart. When the sound of the shoes was gone, she could hear the boy breathing an uneasy sleep in his room. She concentrated on the young snore until her own breath matched it. There was nothing else.

It was a waste of time and he knew it, but he always felt compelled to give it one more chance. This time might have done the trick. They had sat there, the twelve of them, around the conference table as if they were in some sort of seminar, debating a critical situation with the clock ticking away. The vice provost, an English professor who clearly didn't want to be there, tried gamely to keep the discussion on track, while the psychology professor berated Marvin for his calm conservatism. She couldn't understand, she kept saying between Camel puffs, how he, a black student himself, couldn't see that the court's decision had been purely a political one. Those students were doomed to conviction *because* they were black and had acted to defend themselves.

Marvin smiled patiently, waiting for her to draw a breath, and restated his belief that destroying thousands of dollars of lab equipment did not constitute a valid act of self-defense. They were guilty—nobody denied that they *did* it—and their conviction was in fact a foregone conclusion, and rightly so. Marvin was nothing but slick, an old-fashioned frat man given to blazers. The professor's salt-and-pepper Jewish-kink hair was more of an Afro than Marvin's neatly parted do. At the very least, she said, giving ground and appealing more to the others around the table, the university should have thrown its weight behind them rather than washing its hands and hanging them out to dry.

"It's not the university's place to shelter criminals," Marvin declared. "They should be responsible for their actions."

"They're *students*, for God's sake."

"Not anymore. They were suspended long before they were convicted, precisely because the university recognizes that such actions cannot be tolerated."

"Aren't we supposed to be talking about longer-term things?" That was Denise, the all-everything sorority representative who apparently was able to be involved in so many different activities because she believed fiercely in agendas. "I know the court case seems relevant but it's old business at this point and we have some things to get decided today."

One of the faculty reps, a physicist, leaned in ahead of the psych professor to reiterate the proposal for a series of human relations seminars. The vice provost, the lead played back to him now, declared that the seminars were indeed the main thing—they had decided on that at the last meeting—and the task now was to decide how to structure them.

They should, someone said, identify constituent groups of students—Denise rattled off a quick list as the vice provost jotted notes—and try to bring each of them in on it. But isn't the idea to bring people together? That's just reinforcing the barriers that already exist. All right, well how about the dorms? They've already got a good mix; we can hold a series of seminars there. Or the student unions. What about the frat houses?

"What about the faculty?" the psych professor asked pointedly. "I think some of this ought to happen in class. That's where education is supposed to take place."

"We can't force the faculty to take part," said the vice provost. "That's beyond our purview and would have to be a presidential directive, probably in the form of urging the deans to talk to faculty."

"Christ. What about staff, can we talk to them?"

"Then we've got the unions to deal with. That could be tricky."

"Who are we going to get to conduct these sessions?" asked the physicist. "If what we're saying is that we're all part of the problem maybe we should look for some sort of outside arbitrator."

"It doesn't matter," said Ike, almost to himself.

"Of course it matters. That's an excellent suggestion."

"It's too late. If the idea is to sensitize white students, you might reach a few who don't need it. But you're not going to bring anybody together. It's too late for that. You know what that conviction's going to mean, not to mention the cross burning last night. All hell's going to break loose anytime now. A week from now this whole proposal's going to look obsolete."

"Something's going to happen?" the vice provost asked, suddenly interested.

"Well, Richard's right, of course, there will be some response."

"No, I mean, Richard, are you suggesting that there's something planned—a massive demonstration of some sort?"

"What do you think? I don't know, but if you need me to figure that out, I think we don't have any business proposing anything."

It was downhill from there, but fortunately the meeting didn't have that much longer to run. They always ended on time, coming at that awkward, late-afternoon hour when people were running out of gas anyway, and things like family dinners and squash games and homework due tomorrow were on everybody's mind. At least he'd had his say.

That was just the beginning of what was likely to be a long night. The BLF had scheduled a meeting in the new quarters of Uhuru, a reclaimed, half-renovated fraternity house on the edge of campus. The downstairs lounge had become a lecture room and meeting hall, and rooms upstairs had been turned into makeshift classrooms. It wasn't, in fact, all that different from the old place and had the potential to be much better; the overall space was bigger and the fireplace and wood staircase were nice touches. But it was unsettled. Ike had only been in the old house once, but it felt more like home. It smelled blacker. In the new place, the large lower level was all dusty from the renovation, and crates were piled everywhere. And no one was sure if the arrangement would be permanent. It wasn't theirs yet, and it might never be.

Still, Ike spent a lot of time there. He'd attended the first meeting at the beginning of the semester, and Gene had made a pitch for folks to be around—to establish residency. Ike took him up on it, because he knew he wanted to make himself scarce in the dorm. He was also taking a Black Studies course that semester, one on white colonial imperialism taught by a light-skinned West Indian who seemed preoccupied with how white slave masters had had their way with black women throughout the diaspora. And so, two or three times a week, Ike would steal away to study in Uhuru, and he was surprised but not terribly unhappy to find that he was one of the few who did. There were plenty of meetings and card games and bullshit sessions in the lounge, and he enjoyed being close enough to hear them—and the music that accompanied them—while he worked in a classroom upstairs. What he heard was a different world but the same, black students expressing the very concerns that filled his dorm, the ass-kicking workload, stubborn professors, the weather, each other. They even took his presence for granted and drew him into conversations about this course or that, UCLA after Alcindor and Life Upstate. Art, who had returned for the second semester even more determined to be buddies, was clearly troubled by Ike's disappearances at first. But he asked only once where Ike was hiding himself. Ike told him, and they left it alone.

The plan that evening was to read for his Constitution course and eat a meatball and cheese sub from the hot truck. But it was difficult to concentrate, knowing that another riot could be imminent. He was surprised the university had dropped the two students so quickly and had pressed charges against them; he had supposed that some sort of amnesty was a given in these things. Whenever he'd read about some kind of demonstration, the first demand seemed to be that no action would be taken against the demonstrators. As far as he knew, no one had been charged with anything the year before. For all the confrontation, there was almost an understanding that black students could act up, which naturally upset many whites. It was this new hard line—more than the conviction, which carried only a fine and probation—that guaranteed an angry response. Ike wanted to think it would be something symbolic, but he knew it wouldn't be. It would be messy. So why was he there?

"I thought I'd find you here." It was Juanita, wearing tight, creased jeans and an oversized, gray sweatshirt—not her style—and the more traditional headwrap. Her attitude had seemed to change since Ike had begun to make himself, marginally, at home. Maybe it helped that Cheryl had not yet made an appearance on campus that semester. At least Juanita spoke to him, if only to tease him about being so studious.

"Want me to sharpen some spears?" he asked.

"No, as a matter of fact, I want you to walk me to the library," she said, strolling in with a sweet smile.

"The library?"

"The old building with the clock tower. Lots of books. I know you know the way."

"What about the big meeting?"

"Not gonna be one. Gene and Ken are going to talk things over with just a few people and decide what to do. Meanwhile, they figured the rest of us should just go on about our business and keep the white folks guessing."

"I get it. My mission is to lead the womenfolk to safety while the chieftains plan the attack."

"Well, I wouldn't put it quite that way. But would you please? I've got a lot of work to catch up on, and I'd rather not go across campus alone after last night."

"You promise to be nice?"

"I've always been nice to you, brother."

"Uh-huh. Okay, let's go. It's better than sitting around here waiting for the tom-toms."

She was, in fact, unusually nice; instead of trying to get into his business, she talked about herself for a change—how tough the year had been for her, trying to be a student and being involved in politics. But she knew it was important to do both, which was why she was glad she had met Gene. He'd been doing it for so long he made it seem possible, and necessary.

Why, he wondered, had she chosen to come there in the first

place? Why not stay in the city, where she could at least fight on home ground, or go someplace like Howard, where she wouldn't have to fight white folks at all?

The good black schools were too bourgie, she'd decided. All they seemed to care about was sororities, football and cotillions. Some of them had been real active in desegregation in the early sixties, she knew, but now the action was up here. And she'd had every intention of staying in the city, but she'd promised her mother she'd check out other schools—and when she visited this campus she fell in love with the place.

"You're kidding," he said.

"No, I really like it here. Truth is, I never liked the city—I mean, I love it, it's home, but I don't like being there. I've always liked the country. We were going to move to Jersey five years ago, but my father died and we were stuck in Harlem. Then so much started happening I didn't really think about it anymore till I got here, with the trees and the waterfalls and the hills and the lake. It's lovely"—he was charmed by her use of the word—"and when I realized there were righteous people trying to take care of business here, too, I figured I could have the best of both. I can't wait till summer. You weren't here last year, were you? It's gorgeous. It's even fun going to the library, cause it's not crowded and I can get my favorite seat looking over the lake."

"Really? I go by that room almost every night trying to catch that seat empty. It's fantastic."

"If one of us gets it tonight, we'll take turns."

In the room that housed the rare book collection, the overstuffed chair that commanded a view of the hillside across the lake was occupied, as always. Ike knew that everybody liked that seat but it was the first time he'd known anybody in particular who liked it—and Juanita was about the last person he'd expect to be it. She had to do some periodical research, so he went on up to his carrel in the stacks. Freshmen didn't usually have them, but he'd put in for one last semester when Lenny was getting on his nerves and it had come through a few weeks before. The little metal booth often made him think of visiting day at the state pen—an image drawn from Hodge's stories about going to see a busted union buddy—and he never could sit for more than about forty-five minutes without getting up to walk around. This time, he spent the first stretch with his Constitution text lying open before him but thinking about curling up in the big easy chair with Juanita. She was so little that he could easily picture her sitting in his lap—an image that never occurred to him where Cheryl was concerned, since she was nearly as tall as he was—and resting his head on the pillow of her unfurled Afro, looking out at trees and clouds in the distance.

On his first walkabout he cruised the area where he'd left her. She wasn't there. He flipped through a *Newsweek*, found a month-old *Sports Illustrated*, ambled over to the water fountain behind the microfilm machines and headed back. He got some serious work done then, read a couple of chapters, checked over his notes and pulled out his econ when he heard a mangled scream outside echoed by several more. Stressbreak. People streamed from the library, let out a traditional cry of anguish and eased over to the union for a cup of coffee before the final push. It was a good time for another tour. The mood in the library would lighten up for a while, conversation would rise from a whisper, there was an occasional contact high to be had in the men's room and a current copy of *Rolling Stone* might be lying around loose.

He found Juanita in the main reading room near the circulation desk. It was a huge, high-ceilinged room with rows and rows of partitioned reading tables and lots of easy chairs along the sides, most of which had been rearranged into facing pairs for feet-up study or sleep. Way up, a handful of balloons, left over from yesterday's promotion for a new beer at the union, pressed gently at the ceiling, like outsized sperm in a sex education filmstrip. Juanita was talking to two other black students Ike had seen around but did not know. He hovered behind her until they finished talking—she did not introduce them—and they went away.

"Report from the front?" he asked.

"They're still talking over there. Nothing's decided yet. I guess you're getting a lot of work done."

"Of course. How about you?"

"Some. I keep thinking about Gene, though."

"So where are you sitting?"

"I was in the bound volume stacks for a while, but I'm going over to the union for a minute now."

"I think I'll keep going here," he said. He had strained for a hint of an invitation in her voice and found none.

"Okay. I'll check you before I quit."

"I'm on the sixth level." He thought he'd tell her since she hadn't asked, and she couldn't check him if she couldn't find him.

"Okay. Later."

"Yeah." She was in a hurry, distracted, and suddenly he felt there was nothing particular to look forward to. It was turning out to be not much of a study date—not that that's what it ever was, exactly, but it had felt like one for a minute.

The small group of people strolling and chatting through Stress-break made him feel lonely, which, he thought, was a little weird seeing that he always came alone. The blips of conversation, about the hockey team, the Mobilization, the Knicks, next week's physics midterm—picked up like radio phrases on a late-night station sweep—did not hold the normal fascination for him. He went back to Econ.

It must have been another hour before he got up again. As he made his way back through the main room and past smaller reading rooms to the john, the mood in the building had once again become grim. It was oh-shit-I've-got-so-much-to-do time. Very little talking and even less hall roaming. Those who were less serious, or less desperate, had checked out.

When he reached out to push the men's room door, it opened before he could touch it, and one of the guys Juanita had been talking to breezed past him. Three others were inside. "Say, blood," one said, and Ike nodded his way to the urinal wondering what was going on. Maybe Hollyfield had assigned a revolutionary research project.

He took the long way back and stopped at the window overlooking the reserve reading room on the lower level. Several black students were congregated in one corner talking, ignoring the shushes and exasperated stares from the remaining hard-core white studiers around them. This was too strange. Ike hustled to the periodical stacks and did two laps around looking for Juanita. She wasn't there. The tingle at his neck intensified. Out of breath, and a bit unsteady, he walked back to his carrel. A folded piece of notebook paper—light blue, not his own—was sticking out of his Econ book. He took a breath and opened it.

Ike—meet me at back of reserve reading room 15 min. before closing time.—J

Shit. Something was going on, and as he'd feared—known, really—she was part of it. It was a little more than twenty minutes until closing. He sat down. He didn't have a clue what he would do next. Last time all hell broke loose he had come here. Now they were here, bringing the shit with them. There wasn't anyplace to go. But he couldn't just sit there all night. He heard chairs scraping back against the floor, books closing, people stretching and letting out discreet groans like during a workout. Fuck you, Juanita. He packed and rose.

Shuffling into the ragged parade of exhausted scholars, Ike felt an urge to call out. *Run*, you assholes! Don't you know? Can't you hear it? Shit, never mind that. You stay, *I'll* go. The main reading room was emptying out, but slowly. Passageways were clogged by people hanging out, meeting up. Looking past them, he could see that there was a bottleneck at the exit, where halfhearted student workers were required to check bags. Fuck. He sagged momentarily, then left the line, heading, without conviction, toward the reserve room.

"Ike!"

He turned and saw her approaching from the side. For an instant he was glad to see her. Bitch. "What the hell is going on?" he demanded.

"Come on downstairs," she said briskly. He stiffened and glanced toward the exit. The lights flickered. Last call. "It's too late. Don't try to leave, just come on."

"Too late for what?"

"Hold *on*, man, we're closing," someone said.

"Hey, take it easy."

"Don't *push*."

"Maybe they just remembered they've got a paper due."

Both Ike and Juanita paused to listen to the voices coming from the front. He looked to her for an explanation.

"I have to go," she said. "Wait downstairs." And she went off, bobbing and weaving through the stalled traffic. As he slowly stepped back, he saw an Asian kid who always patrolled the stacks to make sure everybody was out. He was moving reluctantly toward the door, in the grasp of a black student, one of those he had seen in the men's room, who was wearing the other kid's gray work jacket. Ike looked around. Over at the circulation desk, the middle-aged woman who usually closed up was walking away from the area with an agitated white student clerk. A black girl who also worked the desk stood impassively watching their departure. He sifted through the confusion of people moving forward and others stumbling back from the disruption at the front door.

Everyone had left the reserve room except the black students gathered in the back. "Yo, hit the light, brother," one of them said as Ike descended. He did. When his eyes adjusted, he saw more people coming in through the ground-level window. They were carrying boxes. He thought he heard chains. "Okay, you all know what to do. Let's get all these doors tight, right now." The guy who was giving orders—one of the ones who had just come in the window—brushed by Ike on his way upstairs. "That you, Ike?" It was Gene. "Hang loose, brother. See if anybody needs a hand. We'll meet at the main desk in half an hour."

Double fuck.

Having secured the window, the last of them trooped past Ike, who wandered back upstairs. The students and workers were nearly gone from the library; the last of them were being escorted toward the front door. Meanwhile, black students, a dozen, two dozen, he couldn't say, scurried about purposefully carrying pieces of rope, chains and boards. A few acknowledged him in passing, but basically no one paid him any mind. He was just there; it seemed they all were. In addition to the commandos, others were gathered around windows and desks, or settling comfortably in the main lounge, waiting. Ike went up into the stacks to look for a book.

Several minutes later he returned and took a seat, the same one in which he had sat breezing through magazines and looking for

Juanita a long, long time ago. There must have been close to a hundred of them. Was anybody *not* there? Did *everybody* know about this? He studied faces to see if anyone else was shocked, amazed. Afraid. Nervous was the best he could do; a few even seemed to be having a good time.

"You're probably wondering why I invited you all here," said Ken Hollyfield, strutting easy and talking loud as he entered the huge room. A smile fluttered quickly across his face, and a chuckle rippled back through the rows of chairs and tables. When he reached center stage, directly in front of the circulation desk, he turned to face the group squarely. The smile was gone. His muscles tensed under the Lawrenceville Prep football T-shirt, and he lifted himself slightly on his toes in his army boots. It worked. For a short man, he looked immense.

"Okay, no bullshit now. Listen up. This is serious business," he boomed, then added, menacingly low, "damn serious. This ain't no party. We're here to make a stand. We're here to get what's ours."

"We here to fuck with whitey," someone said.

Hollyfield flashed. "And anybody who can't listen can get his fuckin ass out right *now!* You all know what's goin down. They've convicted two brothers for destroying property but haven't charged anybody for destroying our home. Last night they burned a cross outside some sisters' house." He was walking now, stalking, still on his toes, his thick hand slashing, pointing, riding with his voice. Juanita sat with Gene behind the desk, along with some others. "They continue to treat us like dogs, like we ain't men and women, just like back home. Ain't no different. I figure we got two choices: we can leave, or we can fight to make it right." He stopped moving. "I don't know about you, but they're gonna have to *carry* my black ass out of here."

"All right now."

"Preach, baby."

"Okay, looka here. First thing, we demand to get the brothers reinstated, with full academic standing, and the university picks up their fines. We don't worry about the fire and the cross; we'll take care of that in our own way in our own time. We got other ways to make them pay. They can start by doubling the budget and staff of the Black Studies program, and making it fully autonomous. They can expand the academic support staff for black students. And we want a commitment to raise the enrollment of black students. They only let about seventy-five of y'all in here last year—oughtta be *at least* four times that many, with full financial aid.

"That's for starters. We get that on paper from the administration and the trustees and we'll give back their library—then we start dealing with these motherfuckers from a position of strength, and we'll have the power to make sure they *never* fuck with us like this no more. We give them twenty-four hours to deal. This here is our hostage. No library, no school. No deal, no library. They burned our home, we'll fuck with theirs. They start seein their rare book collection come flyin out the windows in pieces, they'll start to pay attention. We can build a bonfire right here that'll bring the trustees runnin' from New York and Washington. Anybody got a problem with any of that?"

"Fuck the books, man, burn the motherfucker *down!*"

"Shit, drag some whiteys in here and throw they ass on the fire."

"Dig it, roasted pig. Anybody got a apple?"

"You think this is some kind of movie?" said a woman in the front row, rising and turning on the laughing men. "Look, Ken, I didn't know what the plan was tonight. I don't think most of us knew. I just got the word to be here and be ready to deal, and that's all right with me. I agree with everything you said, and I'm willing to put it all on the line. But these fools are into talking trash and playing some kind of game and that's not where it's at."

"Sit down, girl. This ain't no peace march."

"Hey, I'm here to do everything I can to make things better for black students. That's what it's all about. If all you wanna do is play with matches and have revenge fantasies go on home and don't waste my time."

"Let's not get ahead of ourselves," Hollyfield said evenly. It seemed to Ike, who thanked God that she had said what he couldn't, that Hollyfield had enjoyed the exchange. "We're in control, we can take our time. We called the press and told them we'd have a statement in the morning. They're not gonna try anything tonight 'cause they don't know what we're gonna do, and we got their shit. Just to make sure, we're gonna secure all the critical positions. We got the doors locked up, and we want people at all the windows to see what's goin on. The campus police is out there now, but they can't do shit. For now we just wait. Relax, but stay alert. I'll see you all back here at seven." Hollyfield turned and huddled with the High Council behind the desk. That was it. The meeting was over. The possibility of violence had been expertly raised, and only partly doused.

As everyone looked for a spot to settle into, Ike stood and walked toward the rare book room. No one was there. He eased into the big chair and studied the large oil portrait of a woman in an elaborate green gown, the kind rich people had their pictures done in to make them look like the queen of something. She was the wife of the first president, who'd been a friend of the founder, and the gown didn't suit her. Supposedly she was the one who had talked the old boy into making something of this cow farm; her face showed more of the frontier madam than of the tea-and-crumpets type. She was probably tougher than the president and had more sense than the founder and neither of them could have made it work without her. Maybe if she were still around, or in charge, instead of hanging up here in fantasy rags, she could bring some peace to this town. Somebody needed to.

He noted a campus cop walking nervously by below the window, and finally opened his book. He had read part of *The Man Who Cried I Am* before, in high school, out of the library. Its notion of black and white conspiracies had seemed altogether too fantastic to him at the time, but he had been meaning to get back to it, and this was a good time for paranoia.

"I thought I'd find you here," Juanita said several pages later, perhaps trying to start the night over again.

He finished the paragraph. "Yeah, I'll do anything for a good seat." She had come closer, so he finally looked up. "So, was this part of the plan, too?"

"What do you mean?"

"I mean you tricking me into being here."

She snorted a sour kind of laugh and leaned, arms crossed, at the window. "Don't flatter yourself," she said, looking out. "I don't think anybody really cares if you're here or not."

"Then why'd you go through all those changes to get me here? And how come I didn't hear about this?"

"Maybe you didn't want to. If you'd stop hiding in those books and come downstairs once in a while you might learn something." She spoke over her shoulder. "Anyway, it was like I said. I needed to be here. And I wanted company. I thought you wouldn't mind."

"You knew I spend a lot of time in the library, and you thought I wouldn't mind spending the night. That's thoughtful." He didn't like his tone, but he couldn't help it.

She turned. "I didn't know you were going to stay, all right? When you were still here, I left that note because I wanted you to be safe. If you stayed with us I thought you wouldn't get hurt."

"I'm supposed to thank you?"

"Oh, fuck you, nigger. Stop feeling sorry for yourself. We're all in this now."

He hadn't expected such a violent rebuke, though he had asked for it. He sulked a few minutes—as he would have at home—then spoke. "All right, so what do we do now?"

"We wait." She was turned back to the window. "We stay until we get what we want."

"Shit," he said, almost laughing. He was too tired to cry.

"What's wrong with you?"

"I may be a fool but I'm not stupid. What happens when we *don't* get what 'we' want? By morning they'll be asking to make Eldridge Cleaver president of the university."

"Well, some of the brothers are a little out of hand."

"Out of *hand?* They're out of their damn minds."

"But Gene's gonna talk to them. It'll be all right."

"Yeah, okay. I knew I should've gone to the movies."

"Nothing's playing," she said—smiling—and suddenly beside the chair. "I looked."

He repressed a smile, looked down for a moment, then back at her. "How long we gonna be here?" His voice sounded strange to him. She sat on the arm of the chair. "I hope you all brought some deodorant and toothpaste."

"I know they talked about how much supplies we'd need," she answered absently. "Gene said—"

"Please. Look, I wish I had as much faith in Gene as you have, I really do. But this is some dumb shit. I don't want to be here."

"It's not safe out there now, Ike," she said, looking directly at him and placing her hand on the chair behind his head. "When word gets out . . ."

"I know, I'm not going anywhere. I don't think they'd let me right now." He hoped she'd disagree with him. She didn't. She looked away.

"Look, I'm going."

"I know. You're going to find Gene. I'm going to sit here and wait for the National Guard or some shit. And everything's going to be all right."

"You're learning," she said, and she smiled again. "Keep our seat warm. I might want to take a nap later." Her hand was on his shoulder now. He put his over it and she held on, tight.

"Power to the people," he said softly.

She got up slowly, turned off his light, and left.

Glass shattered like a breaking wave; Ike woke and dove. Two more windows exploded, then a lamp. Oh shit oh shit he moaned and hunkered behind a stuffed chair. The door crashed open, and Juanita crawled toward him quickly, like a lean jungle animal, wearing two bandoleros and carrying a rifle. Rising to her knees, she turned over a heavy mahogany table and tossed Ike a pair of pistols; he caught them and leaned in a crouch out over the chair. He couldn't see what he was shooting at, and knew only that his job was to make the glass fall out instead of in. After a fierce volley, she flung him a belt to reload, and they opened up again, until they realized theirs were the only shots. They sagged simultaneously, his back to the chair, hers to the table. He slid one pistol into his belt, wiped his brow with the back of the hand holding the other. They shook hands. Is that it? he asked. No, they'll be back. But not for a while. We have time. Time for what? She tumbled into him, arms fast around his neck, mouth clutching at his. She ripped off the remaining bandolero along with her sweatshirt, then removed his pistol. He peeled her jeans and jammed into her. They rolled, moistly, rocking between the hard metal of the guns and the soft carpet, his arms completely enveloping her tiny sweetness. It's all right, nobody's looking, she whispered urgently. What? She grew fuller, longer, as he did inside her, and the color seemed to drain from her and her mighty legs locked around him in a familiar brace, and her supple, pale body trembled violently, a dimple appearing in her chin.

BONG! BONG! BONG! BONG!

He awoke with his hand on his dick and a large bell ringing. The clock tower. That's right, he was in the Alamo Library, waiting to go down swinging against Whitey Anna's troops with a volume of Wordsworth. *BONG! BONG!* The sky was a dull, dark pink. He didn't know the chimes went off that early. They must've been on automatic. *BONG!* What the hell time was it anyway, he thought as the bells kept resounding in his head. He got up and limped out of the room with one still-sleeping leg to see what was happening.

In the main room, some people were still laid out in chairs and on the floor with jackets and coats thrown over them, as if a serious all-nighter had simply fizzled. A few were huddled in the reference room off to the side. As Ike walked aimlessly trying to wake all the way up, the numbing chime of the big bell fractured into a dissonant syncopation, landing at last on the first five unmistakable notes of "We Shall Overcome." More people stirred, and Ike spotted a small group heading for the door that led to the chimes tower. In the enclosed, Hitchcockian stairwell, the sound of the anthem was hypnotizing. It hung close, just around the next flight, but outside, distant, unattainable. He felt like Disney's Sleeping Beauty drawn to Maleficent's spinning wheel. The footsteps of the group ahead of him scraped above, marching in time with the beat of the song, and their voices, heard as a dim counterpoint, were disturbingly joyous. He might as well still be dreaming, but his thighs told him otherwise. None of this made any sense; nothing had for two days. He climbed on.

At last, the marching stopped, and the voices, multiplied, were as welcomingly close as a party on the other side of a door. The song—he had stopped counting after the eighth repetition—vibrated through him. One more flight, one more corner. There were maybe a dozen of them, slightly winded but relaxed, gathered around what looked like a small medieval chamber while a young-looking black student played Stevie Wonder on the mammoth chimes. Hunched over, head swinging dizzily, he worked the heavy wooden handles and pedals with his whole body. Somebody's church organist, no doubt, who had spent hours anonymously playing the alma mater by-the-numbers during lunch hour and dreaming of making those big bells *talk*. The brothers and sisters were digging it, and Ike felt crazily happy, and secure, in a way that had little to do with finally reaching the top.

"They're coming out," somebody called from above. Ike realized for the first time that there was another level, and, along with some of the piano-bar crowd, shuffled up the last steps. He didn't swim but knew immediately that this was what it was like breaking the surface after a deep dive. The top level was open, like the front porch of a big stone house, with a waist-high guard rail stretching between the corner pillars. The air hit him as powerfully as the final notes of the song ringing out one more time from the tier of giant bells suspended just overhead. As they faded out on the morning wind, Ike reached the railing and thought he was going to cry. It was the most beautiful thing he had ever seen. Without a word, he and several other students pressed against the east rail and watched a liquid orange sun lift like a living, alien creature from the horizon and ooze color into the world, gently animating the aerial photograph of the vast campus. Behind them, the lake and countryside lay peacefully, eagerly, awaiting the touch of life.

"It's going down."

They looked to the ground, where a small swarm of little people solidified around the front door of the library. Hollyfield was making his statement, although they couldn't hear him. Lots of campus police cars were around, maybe all of them, but no tanks yet. And there were several other cars with bright numbers painted on the tops. Ike recognized the blue 9 as the logo of one of the TV stations at home. Of course, this would be on all the local stations within a hundred miles, at least, which meant that by six o'clock that night, if she hadn't already, Elizabeth would hear about it. With any luck, they'd be out before she appeared out front with a police bullhorn. *RichardClarenceIsaac,ifyoudon'tcomeoutoftherethisminuteyoubetter. Don't make me come in there* after *you!*

Hollyfield was finished—the cops were moving the people away from the door—and a gray-haired figure in a raincoat appeared at the front. It was Ellsworth. Ike hadn't expected to see him there, not this early anyway. He probably hoped that a personal appeal might short-circuit some of the bullshit, and Ike hoped he was right. But after just a few minutes, he turned and left, signaling to the police to stay put outside. No sale. Ike's stomach growled.

The bells above spoke and they all jumped.

Lift-ev-ry-voice-and-sing—till-earth-and-hea-ven-ring. As soon as they picked out the tune, several of the students began singing loudly, trying to hear themselves over the peals and project their message over the campus. Ike didn't know the words; the Negro National Anthem was something reserved for church during Negro History Week, unless you were from the South, he thought. In fact, most voices began to fall out during the chorus, which made him feel better, and when the verse came around again people began to trail back down, covering their ears.

Again they gathered around the chimesmaster. It was obvious from the way the announcement had looked that nothing was happening right now, so there was nothing to do but hang out. After the anthem, he swung right into "Young, Gifted and Black," gave that a ride for a while, then took a break. One of the other students wanted to give it a try and sounded one tuneless bong before the young chimesmaster firmly waved him off. This may be a takeover, but nobody was going to fuck up his bells while he was around. He did, however, assent to demonstrate some basic technique and helped another student manage the first few notes of "Mary Had a Little Lamb." The group agreed that was sending out the wrong signals, so instead they set to arguing about what he would play next. He offered a few hymns and freedom songs, but the sense of the body was that those weren't revolutionary enough. A couple of people pushed for James Brown, not giving much thought to how "Mother Popcorn" would sound on the bells. Tired of the talk, the chimesmaster decided to try "Take the A Train," and nobody complained. After all, they'd been up there maybe an hour or so, and there could easily be plenty of time to play everything anybody could think of.

While they listened, they didn't hear anything on the steps until the sound of raised voices clashing between the bells prompted some of them to step over and look down. Almost immediately, several whites appeared at the top of the stairs. ". . . the fuck . . ." one of the black students managed to say before he was grabbed and pulled into the midst of the whites, who seemed to fill up the stairwell. Other black students rushed over—nobody, Ike noticed, was saying anything—and momentarily halted the crazy charge; the whites had to be leg-weary after their climb. But within seconds they fought their way into the chamber, and Ike, frozen but not alone on the far side, realized how big they were, though they were obviously students. The chimesmaster, who hadn't stopped playing, quickly switched to "We Shall Overcome" again, as if that might help, but the first white student snatched him away, spun him around, and slammed him into the big wooden handles. Ike felt himself moving forward, to do what he didn't know—and as it turned out, he didn't have to figure it out. A vicious backhand dropped him woozily to the floor, as the whites filled the room and began beating the remaining black students.

"Hey, Doug, how do you do this?"

"I got it."

Another one appeared in front of the chimes and began ringing out the alma mater, a signal, probably, that the tower had been taken. The chimesmaster, one arm hanging limply at his side, picked himself up and jumped on the intruder's back. Ike rolled over, reached up and got hold of the guy's leg, helping to pull him back. Suddenly, the most important thing in the world was to stop that song.

Some of the black students who had been dragged down into the stairwell reemerged to join the battle. They looked as if they had been knocked around pretty good, but they were able to keep the whites occupied; maybe there weren't as many of the invaders as there had seemed. Now the "fuckin niggers" could be heard, and the "honky motherfuckers" were flying. But it was all breath and grumble. The room had not been built to hold thirty or forty struggling bodies, and at this point everybody simply had hold of somebody else. There was no more free swinging and no derring-do—people vaulting from the chimes cables or pouncing from the stairs—just a grim, cursing slow grind, like in a football pileup. And it didn't last long before Ike, still with a handful of leg and a faceful of pain, heard more people on the steps.

"*Shit!*"

"*Bust these motherfuckers up!*"

It was the black cavalry; somebody downstairs must have seen the whites come up. Instantly they knew their plan—if they had one—for a quick strike was over. A few who were closer to the stairs, including the one Ike had hold of, broke and tried to get away. Some made it, scrambling back down the stairs behind the black charge, but more were clubbed in the head and stomped mercilessly. A couple of the whites, the larger ones who had led the rush, kept scrapping, dealing out more punishment until they were pinned by numbers.

"Get these fuckers outta here," commanded one of the black students, who seemed to be in charge of the rescue operation. "Dump their asses outside so everybody see what happens when they try some shit." With that, the white students were led, dragged and shoved down the tower steps.

Except one, a burly blond who continued to spit curses and struggle against the two blacks holding him. "You want it?" said an even larger black student standing before him, whom Ike recognized as the one called Zulu. "Come on, motherfucker, I got something for your sad white ass, you fuckin redneck punk."

"Shit-eating nigger bastard. We'll get you! We'll get all of you. You don't belong here."

"You'll get me all right. Turn him loose." Without hesitation, the two restrainers let go, and Zulu drove a mean right into the white kid's nose. "What you got to say now, blondie, huh? You want some more?"

"Suck my dick, asshole," he mumbled through the blood draining from his nose and charged into the black, knocking him back several steps and pumping in shots to the body.

Zulu danced back and looped an uppercut, followed by a solid pop to the side of the lunger's head. He crumpled. "Keep talkin, faggot," he said, smiling, and kicked the white dead in the balls.

The kid let out a scream that somehow turned into "Fuck you, nigger."

"You ain't fuckin nobody, chump." He kicked him again.

"Yo, Zulu, that's enough, man," said the leader. "You gonna kill the boy."

"Not yet I ain't," Zulu said. He picked the kid up by the collar and punched him again.

"Goddamn!" The word seemed to come from several people at once as the kid fell again bleeding to the floor. Everybody seemed to agree that that was enough, and a few others said so. But nobody was in a hurry to intervene.

"He's out, Zulu. It's over," the leader said again.

"Yeah? Well, I'ma wake his ass up." He got the kid in a bear hug around the waist and began dragging him up the stairs.

"Aw, shit."

"What's he gonna do?"

"This is gonna be good."

"Reggie, stop him."

No one moved. Once Zulu got his captive to the top, the others silently followed.

"Hey! Mother*fuckers!* Looka here!" He was at the railing, screaming at anyone, everyone, on the campus below. "You don't be fuckin with us no more, you hear? NO MORE! I'll fuck you all up! Send some more motherfuckers up here, goddammit!" He still had the kid by the waist. The other black students stood horrified, but Reggie went to get hold of Zulu's arm.

"*Enough*, man."

"Get the fuck off me, man," he screamed, elbowing Reggie back. And, with a single, sudden motion, he had the kid slung over the rail.

"Jesus, Zulu, *stop!*"

"*Shit!*" the white kid said, regaining consciousness with a view about two hundred feet straight down. "Get off! Lemme go, you fuckin crazy nigger bastard." He tried to heave himself back up over the rail but in the process kicked free and slid farther over. Zulu grabbed him around the knees, as the other blacks, gasping, rushed forward to the rail.

"That's right, honky, I'm crazy. Crazy enough to see how good you bounce. Hey, yo, everybody," he called out. "I got your hero up here. Any y'all want him?" Zulu started in to swinging him like a pendulum.

"Hey, don't! Lemme up!"

"Beg for it, baby. Talk to me now."

Reggie and the others closest to them tried to grab for the kid's legs.

"Oh, Christ, c'mon! *Please!*"

"That's what I wanted to hear," Zulu said, and raised his hands.

Somebody caught one of his feet, and they pulled him up. Zulu stood back and laughed. It was the scariest sound Ike could imagine. They set him down, but his legs could barely hold him. He was shaking, sweating, bleeding and crying. "Fuckin animal," he panted, wide-eyed. "I'll kill you, I swear to God, I'll fuckin kill you. Get your filthy black hands off me," he said to the others supporting him, though he still stared at Zulu. They let go and he slid to his knees. "I swear to God I'll kill you all, goddamn niggers."

Zulu, suddenly, stopped laughing and slapped him to the floor. The bells couldn't have made a louder sound. "Get him the fuck away from me," he said in a voice so thick with anger Ike thought Zulu was going to cry, too. He walked to the rail on the other side and stood, hunched over and spookily still.

Reggie nodded toward the stairs. One of the blacks half lifted and half pushed the white kid toward them. The kid stumbled, fell, rose and dragged himself toward the steps. Two of the blacks followed close behind; the others gave them a long head start and went down after.

Ike fell in behind the chimesmaster. "You all right?" he asked.

He stopped, turned and looked at Ike. "No," he said.

The stairwell was like a multileveled tomb. No one spoke. Everyone was sore, at least. And they all looked as if they had just gotten death's autograph.

Inside the library, several people came over to see about those returning from the tower. But it wasn't exactly a hero's welcome. In fact, there didn't seem to be that many people around. The siege was clearly still on—everybody's stuff was lying around—

but most folks had scattered around the place, keeping watch, making plans, maybe fucking in the stacks for all Ike knew, or cared. Feeling damp everywhere, his head throbbing and his knees threatening to give out, Ike kept walking through the big room, down even more stairs to the hall where a bank of pay phones stood. Time to call Elizabeth. Maybe she'd talk him into leaving. Maybe she'd come and take him home. Maybe she'd tell him he was a good boy, or a damn fool. Tell him anything. The phones were all busy. All of them. And there were at least two people waiting to use each one. What made them think their mothers were more important than his? Without stopping he went back to the main room and simply got down on the floor—he had done that so many times, sitting on the carpet holding her coat beneath a mannequin outside the fitting room while she tried on dresses—and he curled up and fell asleep crying softly.

Someone tripped over him and Ike sat up screaming. Something splashed onto his head. "Sorry, brother. Take it easy." The guy walked off shaking his head about the orange soda he had wasted. Ike looked around. He didn't know how long he'd been asleep. People were congregating around the circulation desk and coming away with sandwiches, chips and cans of soda.

"Hello, Richard. Or is it Ike?" It was Marvin, standing coolly in slacks and a cardigan sweater pushed up to the elbows. "You look like you've been in the thick of things."

Ike wiped the sticky soda from the side of his face with his sleeve. "What are you doing here? I didn't see you around last night."

"You didn't? Maybe that's because I wasn't here. As for what I'm doing here now, I could ask you the same thing. I mean, this isn't exactly how members of the student-faculty ad hoc committee on human relations normally go about their business, is it?"

"I don't get it," Ike said, easing to his feet.

"That's because you take yourself too seriously, man. This is the place to be, right? Last night I was tied up—had a dinner date with a lovely young coed, trustee's daughter. But today is another day, and it's time to show some solidarity with the brothers. That's why you're here, that's why we're all here."

"Who let you in? I thought the police had the place cordoned off."

"Oh, I see. You think I'm some sort of spy. No, brother, that's not how it works. In fact, the police have instructions to let black people pass through. I came with the food, and you're the first person who wasn't glad to see me. You can ask Hollyfield—we go way back. See, he knows it takes all kinds to make a revolution. You'll learn, little brother. Things aren't always what they seem. Now you better get some lunch before it's all gone." He sauntered off, greeting people as he passed them.

Confused, Ike wandered over to the food and asked no one in particular what was going on. "Administration's been meeting all morning. Shit in the tower got 'em all shook up. They know we're for real. Check out the crowds. Them crackers is pissed, boy."

Ike took his bologna sandwich and diet ginger ale—Marvin was right, the food was almost gone—to one of the side rooms with a window on the front. Several people were standing around, and they made room for Ike to have a look. The cops were still there, more of them, and some hippie-looking white students, radical sympathizers probably, had formed an outer ring. Beyond the two incongruous lines were dozens of other students, maybe even hundreds, some drifting by and pausing, some standing by to see what would happen, and many of them obviously upset. Ike wondered if Art was out there, wondering if he was in there. It was midday on a school day, and by now everybody knew the score. The blacks in the library were the center of attention. Something would have to give.

"I hear the administration's been meeting," Ike said hopefully. "Look like anything's gonna break?"

"They ain't gonna do nothin, not before the deadline."

"Any word on what'll happen then?"

"We're supposed to have another meeting tonight and decide."

"They say the rednecks been circling around campus with guns, man."

"Yeah, the frat boys might try again, too."

"Naw, man, not after this mornin."

So much for hopefulness. Ike finished his sandwich in silence and took another glance outside. He had tried to read the gathering as an agitated rally or a crowd of curious onlookers. The pessimism in the room, however, made it seem more like a lynch mob. He went back to the rare book room, back to his chair, his novel, his window and the madam. He thought about what Marvin had said. If they were letting people come in, maybe he could just walk out. But Juanita was probably right; it wasn't safe out there, not now, with who knows how many people beaten up, one almost killed, a campus full of irate students and people rumored to be cruising with guns. See what your children done done, woman? he thought. All I wanna do is read your books, and look what it's come to.

Sometime later, there was a quick knock. Juanita came in, shielding her eyes. He hadn't noticed, but the sun, falling lower in the sky, was beaming straight through the window.

"I see you're right where I left you," she said as she approached the chair. "Damn, you look like shit."

"I was up in the tower this morning."

"Oh, no. Are you all right?" Her concern sounded genuine.

"I'll live."

"I heard Zulu went off."

Ike said nothing for a moment. "He almost killed that guy. He *did*. He let go. Somebody else caught him. But it didn't matter. He knew we killed him. He was crazy. Scared, angry, humiliated. And Zulu knew what he'd done. Everybody knew. It was like there was a murder, but the body walked away. Even after this is over, nobody's going to forget that."

"I'm sorry you had to go through that," she said. She was sitting on the arm of the chair again. He was still looking down at his book.

"Well you were right anyway. It's not safe. I don't know if it ever will be."

"That's why we've got to stick together. Oh shit, what's that?"

Ike looked up. Squinting into the sun, they saw a group of people coming up the hill, fast. The police had maintained only a token presence on that side of the building, and it didn't look like any were out there now.

"They're going to try something," Juanita said. "I better go tell Gene."

"For once that sounds like a good idea," Ike said, not wanting to be alone in the window when the mob arrived. Somewhere glass broke. "I'll go with you." She ran for the door and began to call out. "Hey, wait a minute," he said suddenly. "Something's happening."

She came back to the window. The mob had paused at the crest of the hill, just across a small paved road from the library. Several people were pointing up. Faintly, Ike and Juanita could hear a sharp but muffled sound. The people in the front of the mob dropped back; some turned around. There was a lot of yelling, inside and out. Ike tried to get the window open.

"What is it?" he asked.

"I don't know," she said cautiously. That sound again, and the crowd turned and ran, several of them falling as they scrambled back down the hill. "Oh, God," Juanita whispered. Ike looked at her hard. Last night he had seen, he thought, a shade of doubt; now she looked scared. "They didn't."

"Didn't what?" he pressed. She shook her head and continued to squint into the sunset. "Juanita, what is it?"

"I've gotta go." She ran from the room. Ike started to follow her but paused. He heard sirens at the foot of the hill.

By the time he got out of the room Juanita had disappeared. A lot of people were drifting over to find windows on that side of the building. There was a hum of curious talk, punctuated by distant whoops of joy.

"Did you see that?"

"No, what happened?"

"They were trying to charge the building."

"Looked like somebody got hurt."

"Fired their asses up is what."

Standing in a hallway with people excitedly coming and going around him, Ike still couldn't quite put it together. One brother who'd obviously had a ringside seat burst into the hall with his fist in the air.

"Got *damn!*" he called out and, pointing his finger straight out, said, "*Bam! Bam!*"

"All right, cool out everybody." Gene came striding through the hall. Juanita was with him. She caught Ike's questioning eye for a moment, then looked ahead. "Y'all gather out by the desk. We're gonna fill you in in just a few minutes."

The group shuffled back into the big room. This time more remained standing. They'd been sitting around all day and were eager to hear the news. Ike wasn't.

Hollyfield again took the floor, a general addressing his troops. "Okay, you know we had us some excitement here," he began. "Bunch of crackers tried to charge up the hill. Figured they were just gonna come on in here and get us out. They been watchin too many John Wayne movies, but this time the Indians were ready.

"You all heard about what happened this morning in the tower. We knew then that just having people at the doors and windows wasn't gonna be enough, so we brought in some insurance. This afternoon brothers have been stationed up in the tower with rifles—to make sure if anybody got hurt it wasn't gonna be us." There was—astonishingly, Ike thought—little outward reaction to the announcement. Some grunts, a few smiles and *all rights* and a lot of clenched faces.

"When they saw the guns they held up. But some of 'em kept comin, so the brothers fired a shot to let 'em know we weren't playing. Another shot was fired and somebody got hit. We're not sure where it came from. It might've been ours, it might not. Anyway, the crackers split."

Ike shot a glance at Juanita. Who else could it have been? Did someone in the crowd have a gun? The police? One of those rumored rednecks with a hunting rifle? She didn't look up.

"Our deadline is still a few hours away," Hollyfield continued. "This here is the crunch time. We've gotta hold fast. Nobody leaves. You can bet somebody out there's waitin to get some payback on the first nigger that shows. We had talked about trashing the place tonight, just fuck it up and split before daybreak. Now it looks like we oughtta stay put. We can do all that later, but right now the most important thing is we got the building. We'll see what happens come midnight. Sooner or later they're gonna have to deal. But now is the time to be strong."

Now is the time. He's got his nerve, Ike thought as Hollyfield walked away. Time to study for midterms, maybe. Time for the NCAA tournament. Time for a ride in the country with Cheryl playing Name That Tune on the radio. How could it be time to hole up in a library and shoot people? It's too late for that, or even too early. A time whose time should not have come. His feet carried him forward to Juanita and Gene, who were about to follow Hollyfield to the reference room command post.

"Juanita?"

"How you holdin up, man?" Gene asked.

"Okay, I guess. No, not really. I don't know. Listen, what's this mystery shot stuff?"

"Not now, Ike," she said.

"Like Ken said, we just don't know yet. All the reports we've gotten say there were at least two, maybe three rounds. We're trying to find out more."

"But they can't just let us go, can they? I mean, if we shot somebody?" The pronoun sounded strange slipping out of his mouth. What do you mean "we," paleface?

"It's not entirely up to them, now is it?" Gene remained calm, but he was beginning to get a little annoyed. "I mean, we got the cards. Just hang on, man. We'll take care of it."

Take care of it, my ass, Ike said to himself, and they were gone.

Hungry, sweaty, headachey hours passed. Ike stayed in the big room after the announcement, at first drifting around in hopes of finding someone as upset as he was. He had known, though, that it wouldn't work. Hello, my name is Ike, you don't know me but I'm scared and pissed, how about you? But at least there were no windows, and if he wasn't exactly with anyone he wasn't alone either. He had passed part of the time watching women braiding men's hair; he had seen brothers walking around the campus with the braids sticking up all funny from their heads and he had wondered how it was done. Some even got into neat cornrows. Great planning: no food to speak of, but lots of combs and grease. It was a disarmingly domestic little ritual that reminded him of how Elizabeth used to toil over his hair for what had seemed like hours, especially on Sunday mornings. *This little light of mine, I'm gonna let him shine . . .*

Back by the periodical shelves, he dropped in with a group of students, mostly freshmen, it turned out, including Carl, in whose company he had first met Zulu. Gathered among scattered notebooks and texts, they didn't seem pleased with the way things were going. There was a lot of I don't know and Not what I had in mind and a fast-building anger toward Hollyfield for leading them into what had become a trap. Carl complained that he was missing a critical physics review session, that he had actually planned to slip out and return before the deadline but this business with the guns had made him reconsider. But that was bullshit, another said; maybe they were being selfish. Okay, Hollyfield maybe didn't figure all the angles right, but damn, they couldn't just eat shit for four years. You heard about what happened when King was killed? They were shootin at brothers downtown, man. That's when they started collecting the pieces. They knew the shit was gonna come down like this, I'm tellin you. This is so fucked up, I can't believe this. We got to be strong 'cause we're the ones have to live with these people. The seniors don't have to be doin this. Yeah, well, I don't like it but I'm here. This ain't no place to die, man. Believe this? Come way the fuck up here and get *killed* behind some school shit? All I know, I bust out of engineering, my father's gonna kick my ass.

There was a flurry near the circulation desk. Bates had come in, for the first time since the occupation began, and was conferring with the leaders. The group of freshmen, Ike included, stood and clasped hands all around: this was going to be it, whatever it was. As they gathered their things to move nearer the front, Ike said he was going to try to find out something. He strolled up to the glassed-in reference office and sat down on the floor. He could hear Bates's low voice, occasionally interrupted by an agitated Hollyfield. It was getting hotter. Bates was pushing something. Hollyfield didn't want to buy it. Other voices cut in; Hollyfield abruptly went silent. Ike wanted to stand and peek, but just then the door opened. Gene, Juanita and the others came out and called the meeting. As they spread out to round up everybody who wasn't in the room, Ike got up and saw Hollyfield sitting angrily on a desk, his arms crossed. Bates stood with his back to him, pocketed hands drawing his trench coat tight around his shoulders.

"All right, Brother Bates has something he wants to say," Hollyfield finally announced, straightfaced, when everyone had assembled. "He's got a proposition for us. We're gonna hear him out, then we got some deciding to do."

"Thank you, Ken," Bates said, stepping forward. Unlike Hollyfield, he stood absolutely still when he spoke, achieving the same illusion of size—he was slim and of average height—with less effort. "First I want to salute you all on your courage and determination. It's not easy to make a stand, and you have made one, at great risk to each of you. But now," his voice dipped, "it's time for an end. I have been in discussion with the administration much of the day. They have, in fact, agreed to several of your demands. The two brothers who were expelled and convicted will be offered readmission in the fall. The budget of the Black Studies program will be increased, as will the size of the academic support staff. And there is a commitment to increase nonwhite enrollment dramatically beginning with the acceptances being sent out this spring.

"For the record, I should say that the administration insists it was planning to do these things all along. That may, in fact, be true. And it may not be. I can say with some confidence, however, that had you not taken this action, those efforts would not have been made with the same urgency, and it is doubtful that the brothers would have been readmitted. They are in a position where in order to be consistent they would have to consider expelling all of you, should any harm come to the library. And at this point they simply cannot afford to do that. Because of what you have done, I am certain they will honor these commitments. If they do not, I assure you, I will resign and join you the next time."

"How come Ellsworth didn't come here himself? You his messenger boy or somethin?"

"The president did not come because the administration does not wish to publicize these terms. They will in fact deny that any deal has been made. I am no one's 'messenger boy,' as you put it. I volunteered to talk to you myself. The decision is yours to make. If you accept, you will surrender the arms to me and vacate the building by midnight. The Black Liberation Front as an entity will be banned from campus, and no charges will be brought in connection with the takeover.

"The shooting is another matter. Apparently the student who was wounded was only slightly hurt, and according to witnesses he himself was in the act of destroying university property. There is, as I'm sure Ken has told you, some question as to the origin of the shot. If you surrender the weapons to me, in the absence of other evidence, it will be impossible to identify any of you as the one who may have pulled the trigger."

"Well, if you're right, we got nothin to lose. We still got the libe, we got the pieces, we can stay and get more."

"That's right," Bates snapped. "You can get arrested. You can get shot. I'm not sure you understand what's happening here. I want you out before you are forced to defend yourselves again. I want you out before someone is hurt. I don't care how many guns you have pointed out of here; there are more pointing in. This is not make-believe. You are not, any of you, Huey Newton. He isn't even what you think he is. The Panthers may be willing to die, but I guarantee you none of them expected to. They're playing a game they can't win, and they play it far better than you can. But they're buying time. They and others dodging bullets in the street are creating a diversion, so you all can get in here and get out and take care of business. That's your job. I admire what you have done, but once the shooting started the game was over. That's the deal. You have a little more than an hour. I'll wait upstairs for your decision."

Bates turned to give Hollyfield a quick, hard look and walked out of the room. The murmuring began before he was out the door and didn't stop when Hollyfield, arms still folded, ambled to the front.

"Well, you all heard the man," he started. "Maybe it makes sense, I don't know. But I don't like it. We came in here to do something, and it don't feel finished to me. I've heard a lot of promises around here the last four years, and with all respect they don't sound any better comin outta Bates's mouth than they do outta Ellsworth's." He looked down, took a breath, and looked back up. "But he's right about one thing. We brought in the guns because we felt they were necessary for our protection. I still think so. But now that we've used them, it's going to be a lot harder to get out of this. This so-called deal gives us a chance to walk away clean. I'm not for it, but I can't ask you all to give up everything. So, what do you say?"

"Stick it out, man. What they gonna do, send in the Marines?"

"Maybe," Hollyfield said evenly.

"Meantime," Gene said, "we got no food or supplies or nothin. I've seen the way some of you been draggin around since this afternoon. Suppose they get smart and just decide to wait us out? This is one day. You wanna try for two, three? A week?"

Hollyfield looked at him but said nothing.

"Hey look," someone else said. "I'm down with the program and everything, but let's look at the facts. Seems like the only thing that's missing is some kind of public statement from Ellsworth. And I think you're right about the lies, Ken, but that means that even if he came here and gave his word it wouldn't mean anything. They could always change up later and say the faculty or the trustees overruled the deal. So this may be as good as it gets, you know? I mean, it sounds to me like we won."

"Yeah," Hollyfield said sourly. "It sounds that way. So how come it feels like we lost?"

The debate went on as he leaned back, almost disinterested, one elbow propped on the big wooden desk. Whenever someone spoke out in favor of leaving, there were nods and words of approval. Those who wanted to stay were met with fidgety, guilty silence—and Hollyfield himself offered no encouragement. The flame was flickering, but he refused to bring out the bellows. He seemed to have determined that it would live or die on its own; the room was growing cooler by the minute.

"All right," he said at last. "Who wants to stay? Let's see the hands." About a dozen went up, their owners searching the room defiantly for support. "That's it," Hollyfield said. He nodded quickly to Gene and walked out in the direction Bates had gone.

"Okay, pack up," Gene called, taking the lead. "We meet back here in fifteen minutes. Line up, be cool and get ready to walk when you get the signal. We march straight to Uhuru, and nobody makes a sound, understand? We don't know who's gonna be out there, but we don't give 'em anything. No matter what happens, we keep moving and say nothing till we get home. Got it?"

Ike noticed, among the freshmen, a few smiles and as many shrugs. A lot of people simply looked tired. He was unreservedly happy. They would have been crazy not to take the chance to get out, no questions asked. If only ten people had voted to leave, he would have been one of them. He'd take his chances with the rednecks; better than sitting on the plane when somebody else's number was up.

He went back to the room to get his coat and books, straighten up and say good-bye to the madam. On his way to return the novel to the stacks, he realized what a stupid idea that was. As he saw others pick up their personal belongings, it became clear there was a conscious effort *not* to put things away. Without being told, most people had left the place as messy as possible. In addition to the soda cans and orange peels left lying about, the furniture remained in disarray and scores of books and magazines were scattered everywhere. Trashing the library would have been redundant. It was a small fuck you, all things considered, but one, he supposed, that was richly deserved. He slipped the book into his coat pocket, found a potato chip bag he had stuck there earlier and dropped it to the floor.

They lined up like paratroopers, in the exact spot where Ike had been trying to get through the crowd twenty-four hours before. At first he figured they were waiting till the guns had been taken care of. But when he glanced at his watch, he knew they were waiting till midnight. He also realized, for the first time, how appropriate all this was: these were the waning minutes of April Fool's Day. He didn't bother looking for Juanita; she would be in front with Gene. He hadn't seen Zulu since the tower. Marvin had vanished as easily as he had appeared. He heard locks and chains at the front door and tried not to think of Butch Cassidy.

"It's time, brothers and sisters," Hollyfield said quietly from the front of the line. "Be proud."

Bong! And they were moving. *Bong!* He hadn't heard the chimes all day. The automatic mechanism must have been reset. It was twelve on the dot. *Bong!* He could feel the cold reaching in to him before he hit the door. It smelled good. The library was a big place, but it would probably be funky for a while. *Bong!* The campus police had formed a corridor for them to pass through.

As they walked the gauntlet a few camera flashes went off. *Bong!* Where was everybody? There weren't as many spectators as Ike had imagined. Uneasy as he had felt watching the mob during the day, he felt almost insulted that they hadn't stuck around. *Bong!* Beyond the police line the hippies had gathered to cheer them on, as if they were a band in a parade. *Bong!* They spread out along the sides of the black line and kind of followed along. A safety escort. Some, he knew, wouldn't like it. He didn't mind. *Bong!* They swung past the union. That's where everybody was. The place was letting out and dozens of students hung out to watch the procession. *Bong!* Most were as silent as the blacks, but Ike distinctly heard the word "nigger" at least twice. *Bong!* The lights of the campus thinned out past the union. *Bong!* A rock hit the pavement not far from Ike's feet. Another thudded into someone's back. A small group of white students stood by the side of the street beckoning the blacks. No one broke stride. *Bong!* The notes of "We Shall Overcome" propelled them toward the edge of campus. Ike smiled. The escort had fallen back, as if on cue, as they turned onto the path to Uhuru. Their steps grew stronger in the darkness. There would probably be another meeting once they arrived, instructions on how to proceed over the next few days. It wasn't a bad idea; there were certainly precautions to be taken. But as far as Ike was concerned, it was over. He was going straight to the phone to make two calls. He would tell Elizabeth he was all right. And he had to talk to Cheryl; she was supposed to come down that weekend.

The sun took too long to go down, so he didn't get to sleep until the third bus, and then it was almost too late. Most of the passengers were going on out to the new campus, which was about ten years old and would probably still be called new for a long time, around there anyway. But to the few people on the bus—the traffic went mostly the other way on Friday—that was the destination that mattered, and because the driver knew that, Ike had to stay awake to remind him to stop at what was left of the bus depot in town, a corner with a Greyhound sticker in the window of a drugstore. It was right across the street from the Springs Motel, which was nowhere near the springs, wherever they were, and not too close to the track. Ike had no idea who stayed there. As far as he could tell, the place existed for his convenience, although last-minute tourists during the summer season probably ended up there as well as parents who neglected to make reservations a year in advance for commencement. In fact, he thought as he trotted across the street with his bag, they should be thrilled to see him; he may be the only person who actually intended to stay there as a first choice.

They did a good job of masking their excitement. But it was enough that the desk girl ignored all the blank spaces he left where you were supposed to indicate what firm you represented and what your business was and the make and license of your car. The questions had thrown him the first time. Like the line in the college applications that demanded Where did you prep? they were questions that had never occurred to him, and he had never liked questions he couldn't answer. This time, however, he knew they didn't count, as long as he signed his name and paid in cash. He also knew, now, that he didn't have to worry about somebody wanting to take his bag and show him to his room—a problem because he didn't want a shuffling black man or a pretentious white one, obviously wondering who the hell he thought he was, showing him the way and opening doors and windows and turning on faucets and fiddling around with the TV and hanging around for a tip, when Ike didn't know how much he should give. Upstairs to the left, she said, and that was just fine.

He passed a young black woman by a laundry cart and wondered why she was there. It was the same reaction he'd had when he'd seen a handful of black people moving furtively around town before: what are you doing here? Working at the track, maybe, but that was seasonal and so were the tourists. The college would need people to change beds, and maybe her mother cooked in the dining hall. But those didn't seem like jobs to come all this way for. Unless the rich folks who lived there year-round had sent for them, and the ones who came to the springs brought their girls with them. And maybe some of them met up with the porters back when the trains brought the big-timers, and they all settled into a little runaway servant colony on the fringes, still cleaning and cooking and braving the winters and building their own little churches and bars and living free, if less comfortably, and waiting for the next migration to God knows where although they'd all be dead by then and most of their kids had already bused out to New York. Except for a few, like the woman who had just put clean towels in his room and didn't have to turn around to wonder who or what he was going to be rubbing with them. Maybe Lonnie had done some portering in his railroad days. The high rollers would have loved him, for a while, and he wouldn't have stayed with them but he wouldn't have stayed here, either. Still, he wouldn't have to stay to leave something behind, and she could be it. Is that it, Sister sister? We both a couple of random seeds? He could have 'em strung out all across the state, to hear Elizabeth tell it. Or if Wilbur wasn't, maybe he wasn't either.

The room was like a dorm room with a real lamp and a painting and a rug and a TV. But instead of trying to make it his, as he'd done in the dorm, he felt obliged not to disturb anything, so no one, not even the room itself, would know he'd been there. He dropped the bag, sat on the edge of the bed and studied the phone dial to see how to call out. She picked up at the end of the first ring and he closed his eyes to taste the hello; she was ready and didn't seem to be upset.

"Two-oh-seven," he said hoarsely. "Hurry." He loved the secret-agent efficiency of it.

" 'Kay. Bye."

Pure communication. It was at that moment he realized, guiltily, how much he missed her. The trip itself had been automatic, like going to class. There was somewhere he was supposed to be, so he went. He had been, without thinking about it, expecting a rebuke, the protests he'd sensed on the phone two nights before but hadn't given her a chance to express. He knew she was pissed, knew she thought she had a right to be, but he didn't want to hear it then and hoped he wouldn't have to hear it now. The three words she'd spoken sounded like everything was cool, so he turned on the TV, dialed past the news to *Star Trek*, and lay down without mussing the bed.

He preferred it this way, though he suspected she didn't. No, he knew she didn't. Bonnie and Clyde shit, she'd called it on his last visit two months before. She was tired of hiding out and insisted that he stay closer to the new campus, at a place known as the No Tell with the other boyfriends in for the Santana concert. He'd gotten to meet her roommate, Judy, daughter of an English-educated Saudi scholar. Having grown up in Cambridge, a kind of native exotic, she moved too easily among the preppie crowd and seemed to draw Cheryl along in her wake. Judy was okay, wickedly funny and gorgeous in a way you couldn't place if you didn't know. But Ike didn't like the way Cheryl, when she was with her, chummed up to the Williamstown boys at the party after the show.

It didn't help that, when he did get her alone, she wanted to reminisce about her Christmas vacation in Michigan, some party at a friend's house on a lake, which, she had said pointedly, was *her* Madison Park. She hadn't said any of that when they'd gone to see *Woodstock* right after she got back—he'd been going on and on about Elizabeth and Lonnie—and so it had the force of an eruption.

The knock came soon, two quick raps that opened his eyes and rolled him off the bed. When he opened the door she took one long step inside.

"Oh, wow," he said, holding the knob and blinking.

"What's wrong? Door says 207. You expecting someone else?"

"You look fantastic." He closed the door and leaned against it, one hand still on the knob and the other in his pocket. She seemed enormous, like someone he'd never seen up close before. Had it been that long? Her hair tumbled out behind a black beret, where it mingled with the collar of a red wool cape. All that was supported by an interminable pair of navy blue bell-bottoms that let go of her legs reluctantly at the knee to make way for the suede boots that boosted her to at least six feet.

"My bag," she said, producing it from under her cape.

"Neat trick. Did you leave a good number?"

"Yeah, Judy came up with a good one this time. An art gallery in New York."

"I like it."

Because of the prehistoric rules at the college, girls going away for the weekend had to leave an emergency phone number, and if, as was often the case, they were staying in town, they simply left a friend's number or chose from an impressive list of bogus alternatives. Judy, who was good at this, had once affixed a Connecticut area code to the number of a Rome boutique. Nobody ever checked unless your parents died, in which case the fact that you were at the Holiday Inn down the road or in an Amherst fraternity house wasn't terribly important as long as somebodv knew where you really were. Of course, nobody knew where Ike was.

"I wonder if they'll go through all this next year," he said, gently removing her cape.

"When the boys arrive? I doubt it. Too bad, it's kinda fun. They'll probably do bed checks."

"Not a bad idea," he said, and kissed her neck. "You keep looking this good I may check myself."

She turned and kissed him. He dropped the cape. Her pale glossy lipstick, as always, tasted faintly of banana and coconut, the dominant odors of the tropical fruit Lifesavers he used to help himself to from her bag in high school, the way he used to dig mints out of Elizabeth's. They'd each had a couple in their mouths the first time they kissed at a party in Jan's basement.

"You must think I usually look like shit."

He shook his head and pulled off the beret, then went back to licking off the gloss. She closed her arms around his waist.

"This is weird," he said after a while.

"What?"

"Kissing up."

"Oh, really, shorty? Now you know how it feels."

"Is she tall? Well, I gotta look up."

"All right," she said, and sat on the bed to unzip her boots.

"Where did you get those pants?"

"My father. U.S. Navy."

"Now *that's* weird. I bet they didn't fit him like that."

"I hope not."

He knelt beside her for a closer look. "You sure you got enough buttons there?"

"Thirteen. Need some help?"

"Hey, just because I've got a student deferment doesn't mean I'm not able-bodied," he said working the buttons.

"Oh no?"

"Hold on, I'm just admiring the cute little anchors. You know, if everything they say about sailors is true, they must have some pretty nimble fingers."

"Maybe that's why my father's getting arthritis already."

"You look like a Crackerjack box."

She smiled and lay back. "Yeah, and there's a surprise inside, too."

It was worth the unwrapping. But after he'd poured himself into her, he realized that they had made love like strangers—or like people who knew each other too well, which came to the same thing. That should bother him, he knew, as he drifted to sleep and noticed that the TV was still on. It didn't, though. Instead, he was glad she had made it so easy, without a lot of demanding questions, that he could take her for granted, wrap himself around her and relax. The most important thing was being able to come home safely. Tomorrow would be better. He stroked her leg in a vague promise. Tomorrow they would talk.

Before it got to be tomorrow, he turned and touched pillow instead of hair. Still asleep, more or less, he moved his arm around but felt only cold sheet. He peered down the length of the bed to see if her pants were there, where they had peeled her out of them. They weren't. Jolting himself awake, he lunged toward the foot of the bed. Her cape was gone from the floor. Only then did he see her by the window. She was bent over, her arms braced on the sill, as if she were studying a tiny drama just on the other side of the glass. Her skin shone like moonlight.

"Bad dream?" she asked over her shoulder.

"I just woke myself up. I thought you were gone."

"Guilty conscience?"

The question was beyond him. "What are you doing?"

"Watching. I think half the campus is out there."

"Come out of the window. Somebody might see you." The curtains were wide open.

"Ashamed of me?"

"No, I don't wanna get raided."

"Come here," she said without turning.

He walked up behind her and rested a hand on her long, narrow back. Since the motel was right on the main street, they were only about twenty feet above the parade that must take place every Friday. Girls in army jackets and ski parkas and men's overcoats, laughing loudly, wandered back and forth on the brightly lit street, into and out of more bars than any one block of Jewtown had ever seen, which couldn't possibly have had anyone inside for very long, so busy was the sidewalk. Roving bands of white female youths. Several had athletic-looking young men in tow, not so much as escorts as prizes being dragged along for show.

As he caught up on the view, she reached behind for him, straightened and pulled both his arms tightly around her. Without the boots she was perfect. His thighs pressed warmly against the backs of her legs, the inside of his elbows caressed her ribs and he rested his head easily on her shoulder. Looking down at their double-crossed arms just under her breasts, it occurred to him that she was awfully white. It must be her; he wasn't that black.

"You wanna go down?" he asked.

"No. Yeah. In the dorm it sounds stupid. I'd rather work or read. Or be with you. But when I'm with you sometimes I think I'd like to do some of those things. It wouldn't be like I was really doing them, you know? Like we could pretend and that would be okay." She turned his wrist. "They're closing soon anyway."

"I guess for me it's the other way around. It's okay not to do things I don't want to do. We can just . . . be. It's selfish, maybe. I want to keep you for myself."

"What for?"

He shrugged. "Look out windows and talk about everybody else, I guess."

She lifted one of his hands, kissed it and placed it on her breast. She slid the other between her legs.

"Any better ideas yet?" she whispered.

"I'm workin on it."

He felt her turn him around; his back was shocked by the cold glass. She held his face and guided it to her breast and pressed against him so firmly that he could imagine them tumbling through shards of glass to the sidewalk, where the drunken paraders might or might not notice them. She straddled one leg and he circled her hips strongly enough to grasp an elbow with each hand as she ground herself fiercely onto his thigh, rough and bristly at first, then with a wet smoothness. He thought he would gag on her tit, or hurt her as he sucked the nipple toward the back of his throat. But the tension broke suddenly and she melted down on him, kissing his neck, his shoulder, his chest, rubbing his sides, his waist, his legs as she slid from his thigh down to her knees. Then she took hold of him, and he barely had time to lock his legs behind her back while her mouth was covering him, pulling him into a frenzy that left them in a damp, clutching heap on the floor beneath the window as last call brought the happy wanderers below inside for one more round.

They nearly slept through Rocky and Bullwinkle; he discovered them on a routine check coming back from the bathroom. Still, they didn't leave the room until much later, when Cheryl steered them to a hangover diner where breakfast could be had at noon. The show they'd put on at the window had them both feeling loose. He felt so good that he didn't want to spoil it by bringing up the events of that week, and she seemed willing to let it ride. So instead they recited lines from "Fractured Fairytales" and hummed snatches of cartoon themes. And when he caught her studying him in the gaps, he got her to telling Judy stories. They danced through the afternoon that way, from the diner to the back aisles of her favorite used-book store, where she hunted a cheap *Sons and Lovers*, to an attic-like record store where she bought him a copy of her favorite Laura Nyro album, which, she said, she played when she was thinking about him and drove Judy crazy, and an old Jackie Wilson for herself. (Her uncle had played on a couple of sessions, she explained, and as a result even her grandfather, who thought blacks were mostly criminals and not very smart ones at that, had started to come around before he died. It wasn't the music that got him but the clothes; he liked their style.)

Then they went on a porch tour. They walked away from the main drag for maybe two miles, out past rows and rows of great old houses with porches that could sleep a family of eight, easily, with furniture. The one she liked best was right next door to a surprisingly seedy place where, she said, once lived a woman who had a dorm named for her because she was a trustee's mistress—but not really, because that would be too obviously scandalous, so they'd christened the place Dickinson in honor of her pet Angora, Emily. But the guy died shortly after and his wife inherited his seat and his money—she was the first woman trustee—and paid to have the building renamed after her. None of which mattered, because they tore it down when they built the new campus, and the house next door was the nice one. They decided to buy it one day as a summer place and put a carousel on the wraparound porch, but only if he could also buy and restore the Emily place as a guest cottage which he could legitimately advertise as the Cat House. She wanted to knock and ask how much they wanted for the house, but he restrained her and held on to her hand all the way back to the motel, where they made love in 5/4 time to *Mission: Impossible.*

He said he would treat her to anything for dinner, and she led him to a dingy pizza parlor several blocks away. It was the best in town, she insisted, but only a few people knew. It was empty except for two old people waiting for the bus and a thirtyish man who she said resembled a cousin she couldn't stand and who eyed her fishily from behind the counter where he was patting dough. Because there was no jukebox—it would be all Sinatra in this place anyway, she assured him—it wasn't the same as the night of the prom they didn't attend, after the city championships, when they wiggled to the Ronettes and Shirelles in the pizza parlor booth until she asked: what did your mother say?

He had squeezed her hands, started to look away and came back to her eyes. "I didn't tell her," he had confessed.

"Richard!" she had nearly shouted, snatching her hands back. "You said you were going to tell her."

"I said I'd think about it. Look, school will be over in a couple of weeks, we get through the summer and then we're on our own. It won't matter."

"I told *my* parents."

"You told one."

"That's all you'd have to do."

"Funny. That wasn't my idea, either. You told her because you wanted to."

"So I have to risk everything and you get to pretend nothing's going on."

"Risk what? Your good name? Your social standing? I don't have any of that."

"Oh, cut the crap."

"You told your mother because you thought she'd be okay, and she was."

"Yeah, as soon as she figures out whether to take me to a gyno or a shrink. It hasn't been a lot of fun, you know."

"Well, at least your daddy still loves you." After all the complaints about her mother, he had thought it strange that she told her instead of her father. "She's all I got, Cher. I don't want to hurt her."

"You don't mind hurting *me*. I hope you two will be very happy together because at this rate she's all you're *ever* going to have."

"That's not fair."

"*You're* not fair! You don't have any idea what I've been through, do you? You think everybody loves you, but I'm the one who's put myself on the line and they all look at me like I'm *dirt*. My own mother thinks I'm crazy and my father would strangle me. And you don't want to hurt anybody's feelings. Well *grow up*, big shot. *Everybody's* hurt except you. I *hate this*, Richard." She unpinned the corsage he'd given her and threw it across the table at him, along with his red second-place ribbon. "Oh, God, I hate this."

It was a conversation they had never discussed since. It wasn't necessary; he had made his choice by confessing to Elizabeth that night. He had no stomach for reliving that controversy, and recent history was even more troublesome. So when it seemed that he should say something to break their cozy but somehow edgy silence, he began to recall a place where he and Tommy Jackson used to go for 25-cent slices after school in junior high.

"Uh-oh. Set the Wayback, Sherman. I was wondering how long it could last," she said.

"What do you mean?"

"After a while, whenever you start feeling really good, you start talking about things that happened before you met me."

"I do?"

"I don't mind. It's been twenty-four hours, that's probably a record. But I'm glad you want to share it with me. I like the things we have in common, but I like what I find out about you when you talk about things that don't have me in them. Like, sometimes I feel like I grew up with Tommy Jackson."

"I guess maybe I do get carried away sometimes."

"Not enough."

He looked a question at her and immediately knew it was a mistake, like following Ali into a corner.

"What happened at school this week, Richard?"

He picked up another slice.

"I know there was some kind of riot or something. They occupied a building. I guess you were there, I don't know. Somebody got shot. It was all over the news. People kept asking me didn't you go there and what was going on, and I had to say I didn't know."

He made an annoyed face.

"I know that's not important, but I was worried. I was going out of my damn mind—do you *know* what that's like? I didn't know if you were in a hospital or in jail or what."

"That's why I called."

"No, you called to tell me not to come, because my being there would have embarrassed you. I guess you didn't hear me slam down the phone, and believe me, you don't want to know the things I was saying about you afterward. Once I knew you were okay I was pissed. I don't know if you thought you were doing me a favor, maybe it wouldn't have been safe or something, but Richard I *wanted* to come. If you wanted me."

"I know you would have been willing," he said. "I appreciate that, really, but I felt like I had to get away."

"Away from what? What *happened?*"

"I don't think I want to talk about it. It won't do any good."

"It'll do *me* some good. Doesn't that matter? How can I help if I don't know what the trouble is?"

"You're doin fine. Just drop it."

"But you're not going to drop it. Or it's not going to drop you. It's been all over your face since I came into the room last night."

"Okay, Cher, but not now, all right?"

On the way back to the motel he picked up a bottle of wine, hoping it would make up for his stubbornness. But in the room she sat coldly in a chair reading while he sprawled on the bed and sipped, feeling a force field hardening between them. A few times he started to say something, but he ended up offering to refill the glass she hadn't touched yet.

"I didn't know what was going to happen. I knew there'd be something, some kind of demonstration, 'cause these two guys had just been convicted over that riot in December." He talked with his eyes closed. She lowered the book to listen. "I was in the library and I could tell something funny was going on but I didn't want to be part of it. It was closing time and I started to leave. But then these guys came pushing through and everything got confused, so I went back inside to wait. And in a few minutes it was over. They took over the library. They put out all the white students and the staff and we stayed there waiting for some demands to be met."

He opened his eyes and looked at her. She was waiting for more. "Next morning some of us were up in the bell tower, watching the sunrise and just hanging out, and a bunch of white students crashed in. There was a big fight, and this one guy . . . " He tilted the bottle to his lips and swished the wine around in his mouth. "This black guy beat up one white kid and tried to throw him off the tower. He let go, but the others caught him. Later, around sundown, the white students tried to charge the library again, but there was a shot. They said they had guns in the tower. I never saw them. Somebody was wounded. There were more negotiations and at midnight we just walked out. And then I called you. That's it."

"Oh, God. Richard, that's terrible."

"Yeah."

"How do you feel about it? What are you going to do?"

"Cheryl, I *told* you what happened."

"Not to you. I mean, why did you stay?"

"I don't know." He looked into the bottle and had another sip. "I didn't *want* to be there; but it felt like I was supposed to be there. We were all there. Nobody knew what was going to happen, at least not most of us."

She came and sat beside him on the bed. "Are you in any trouble, you think?"

He shrugged. "I don't think so, but I don't know. Who the hell knows? I still can't believe it happened. I don't know what it means. I don't know why I was there. I don't know how I feel. I have to figure it all out. You can't help. Nobody can. I just want to be with you and not think about it right now."

"That doesn't make any sense, Richard. How can you not think about it?"

"None of this makes any sense, Cheryl."

"Is it just that you don't want to talk to me about it because I'm white?"

He jumped off the bed and stood before her.

"Don't *ever* say that again, you hear me? Don't."

"Well then why won't you *talk* to me?"

"*I did!*"

"You told me what happened, but now you just wanna sit here and drink wine and sulk. If you're not going to let me help you, I don't know what you came here for."

"I didn't come two hundred miles for some white pussy."

"Well that's what it looks like if you're going to come here and fuck me and not say a word about what's tearing you up. Look, I'm white, all right? Big fucking deal. I'm also supposed to be your goddamn girlfriend, and that means when you're in trouble we talk about it."

"Look, Cheryl," he said slowly, "I give you everything I can, but there're parts of me that—I don't know, that aren't ready yet. I can't explain it to you because I can't explain it to myself. If you can't understand that, I mean if you think that makes you some kind of whore or something, I'm sorry. Maybe I shouldn't have come."

"Oh, Jesus, Richard, cut the shit."

He went to the closet and snatched his coat from a hanger.

"What the hell are you doing?"

"Sorry, I forgot," he said and took $20 from his wallet and slapped it on the dresser.

"Richard!"

The door slammed.

"You *fool!*"

The place is not too crowded. There are only about half a dozen people at the bar. At one end, a light-skinned colored man shares drinks with a white woman who is growing loud and unruly. No one is staring, but everyone is paying attention. "Goddammit, Lonnie," she says suddenly, her voice rising above Louis Jordan's "Choo Choo Ch'Boogie." "What's the matter, baby? You don't like me, do ya? You sit here gettin me all hot and bothered, then you don't wanna do nothin about it." His words cannot be made out; he is trying to quiet her. "You know that black bitch of yours ain't givin you nothin!" The murmuring in the club ceases as he snatches her off the stool with one hand. He smiles but his hushed words cut into her as surely as the strong, lean fingers that hold her. His release sends her halfway to the door.

The laughter begins before she is outside.

"What happened, Ike? She foun out you ain't got no money?" one man says, easing down the bar.

"Shit, man, she looking for more than cash. More than dick too. That trashy bitch want a husband. I don't know no spook be fool enough to get himself into that. Cept maybe Hezekiah there. He sell his whole family for a shot at that pussy."

"You ain't lyin, brother. Thass some sweet shit you threw outta here. She sho must want yo ass."

"Can't blame her choice. She know quality when she see it."

"Sheeet."

"What you laughin at, youngblood?" the light-skinned man says to a younger man seated near him. "You think I made a mistake? You think I shoulda gone home with that bitch?"

"Naw, I ain't sayin that."

"See there. The boy knows I done right. You ol horny sumbitches ain't got no principles, that's all. I tell you what, though. I'm goin home tonight. She probly don't want me, but I'm goin anyway. I can hear her now: 'Don't be crawlin in here beside me, you ol drunk bastard. You ain't got no money and you ain't been home in two days, so don't come snugglin up to me now!' " He throws back his

head and laughs at his own falsetto imitation. "She so sweet. Never usedta cuss like that before we was married."

"Shit, bein married to you be enough to make somebody cuss."

"Yeah, I guess you right. I'm gon straighten up, though. That baby's comin soon and I'm gon get me a job if I hafta get on my knees and beg them ofay mothafuckas. That's right, youngblood," he says to the face studying him. "Crackers make you beg for your daily bread, but I'm gon give it one more try. Ain't nothin else I can do. You see that, don't you?" The young face nods. "Say, you sure you old enough to be in here? You look like you should be drinking wine up in Madison Park or diddlin some young gal under the stairs someplace."

"Yeah. I'm old enough. I just ain't never been in here before."

"What you drinkin, son?"

"Gin."

"Well allright now. Tom, give this young man another one. We gon drink to my homecoming."

"Thanks."

"That's all right, son. Just don't go gettin so drunk you start actin foolish. Like bustin your butt over some ofay tail. That shit get too expensive sometime, and you know what they say—pussy ain't nothin but meat on a bone. You can fuck it or suck it or leave it the hell alone."

"Mind if I sit down?"

The woman was back, no, another one, Long Tall Sally in a red cape, Superwoman, dragging coolly on a shore-leave cigarette.

"How long you been doin that?" he said, beginning to recognize her.

"Judy's," she said. "You okay?"

He wasn't. He didn't even like gin. Hodge told him about that shit. Worse than them Mexican cigarettes. You know what I mean. Don't tell your mama I said so. Seemed like a good idea at the time.

"What," he said carefully, concentrating down to just one of her, "are you doing here?"

She blew smoke out of her nose, like a dragon. But sexy as hell.

"I watched you out the window," she said. "When you didn't come back I followed you." No big deal.

"Oh," he said. Where'd everybody go? And who was this nasty-looking guy on the other side of him?

"You know, it doesn't have to be this hard, Richard," she said. Oh, right. He remembered that conversation. Weren't they finished? "You . . . we're doing this to ourselves. So some people think we shouldn't be together. Fuck 'em, you know? We don't have to care about that."

"I do," he said calmly. It was coming back to him. "I mean, it's everywhere. If I'm in the library, I'm the enemy. If I'm not, I'm somebody else's enemy."

"Since when did that bother you? You know why I fell in love with you, Richard? Because you got along with everybody and you were still yourself. Do you know how hard that is? I mean, being friends with Jan and Tommy Jackson at the same time is weird. And that guy, Hez, and even those bubblebrains I used to hang out with. They used to talk about you all the time till they figured out *I* was serious. But there was always a you inside of all that, like you had your own compass. That's the part I love, but now it's getting all spun around. I'm worried about you."

"Yeah. Me too."

She turned away and took another puff. "I'm worried about us, too," she said more quietly.

"What do you mean?" Knowing he had to be careful here, he made a conscious effort to steady himself.

She shook her head, eyes closed, and snorted a furious cloud of smoke. "Maybe it's not them. Maybe it's not any of that. Maybe we're just drifting apart."

"No," he said, with a clarity that surprised both of them.

"It happens, you know. You're there, I'm here, life goes on."

"Uh-uh. Bullshit."

"What bullshit? You don't think that could happen?"

"No. I don't want that."

"Oh, so, what? What you want, that's what happens?"

"Absolutely," he said and smiled. "My mother promised."

"Oh, God. Well, I guess that's that, huh?" She crushed her cigarette.

"Yeah," he said, and took her hand and pulled her from her stool. She towered above him, but he stood and looked evenly into the eyes that had grown darker—maybe it was the light—and more probing. "That's that."

"You know," she said, forcing a sad smile, "for once I hope she's right."

Ike hadn't spoken to Art Rosen since before the takeover. He'd come back to the room the night after to sleep and pack his bag and had left before Art woke up. Although he hadn't taken the time to notice it then, he felt bad about that. All things considered, his roommate had been pretty decent. Throughout the semester, while others on the corridor had seemed oblivious to the racial situation on campus or openly incredulous about the black students' activity, Art had been genuinely concerned. It wasn't out of deference to Ike, either; Art was the kind of guy who liked people to get along and was personally disappointed when they didn't. Ike knew that his withdrawal had hurt Art, not because he missed Ike's company—they hadn't gone around together since their first few weeks on campus—but because he thought Ike could help him come to terms with what was going wrong. But Ike had held himself aloof precisely because he knew he would be no help. That, too, was a shame. As he came to realize during that second semester, Art was just the kind of friend he'd hoped to find at college, someone who, for all his superficial hipness, was as naive and well-meaning as Ike was. Unlike the white guys he'd known in high school who had seen him primarily as the exception to a distorted rule, Art took him at face value and wanted nothing more than to pass the time pleasantly and make sense of the world.

Settling into his desk for a round of study, Ike was tempted to give it a try. But when Art walked in and froze, wondering for an instant if he should turn around and leave, Ike knew it was too late. Art asked where he'd been; Ike said out of town. It had been pretty bad around there, Art muttered, his eyes averted. He knew Ike had not left until after the takeover but did not ask the obvious question. So Ike continued reading while Art poked around his desk, first with an uncharacteristic listlessness, then, suddenly, with a roughness that exceeded his usual haste. A ring binder smacked the floor.

"Shit is *fucked up*, man!" Art shouted.

Ike started but turned calmly. "Lose something?"

"Come on, Rich. You know what I'm talkin about. Everything! All this, this *racial* shit. I'm just tryin to go to school, you know, tryin to be a regular guy, and every time I turn around people are burnin shit down and blowin shit up and takin over buildings—"

"You're startin to sound like Lenny."

"Yeah, well maybe he's got a point." He was standing in the middle of the room gesturing wildly. "I mean, *guns*, Rich! For chrissakes, enough is enough."

Ike sagged in his seat. "What do you want me to say? You think I wanted this?"

"Then why can't you *stop* it, man? Why can't somebody stop all this bullshit?" He stopped moving; Ike had never seen him stand still. "Friday I was playin basketball in gym. I went up for a rebound, you know, and this black guy, he's been ridin me pretty hard all semester, he gave me an elbow right in the ear. It wasn't an accident, right, 'cause he's grinnin and talkin shit. So I threw the ball at him and called him a black s.o.b. I'm sorry, but, hey, I didn't mean nothin by it. He's black and he's a son of a bitch, okay? He came at me like I figured he would and we got in a clinch till they pulled us apart. But the point is, I've been in fights before, but this was different, man. He really looked like he wanted to kill me. And he started it! And the other black guys there, they all looked at me like I was the bad guy, like what I said was supposed to be worse than gettin hit in the head. Like whitey-this honky-that all the time ain't supposed to count."

Ike couldn't look at him. "I'm sorry," he finally managed to say.

Then, in a moment of boldness born of pure exasperation, Art stepped across the line and stood before Ike's desk.

"I don't understand," he said. He looked and sounded frightened, seriously, like someone who'd just been told that the Russians had fired off the missiles and there were twenty-five minutes to figure out Why.

Now, Ike thought. They could go for coffee, order pizza, fetch full-suicide subs from the hot truck and earnestly debate The Situation all night, as others in the dorm had discussed sex, Descartes and whether Paul was dead. That was what roommates, friends, people did; that was how learning and understanding came about. He looked up, smarting from the pain in Art's face, and considered the possibilities of the moment.

"Neither do I," he said.

It was the first bit of completely honest communication they'd had in months, maybe ever. It wasn't enough; they both knew it would have to do. Art shrugged, grabbed the binder from the floor and walked wearily toward the door.

"Oh, Rich, your mother called last night. I told her I didn't know where you were but you wouldn't be back till late. That okay?"

"Oh, shit. Yeah. Thanks, Art."

He shrugged again and closed the door, mumbling, "Sure."

Ike reached for his econ book and found the birthday card, right where he'd left it so he wouldn't forget to mail it, but he'd been busy getting beat up at the time. And he had made a big deal about never forgetting because of what had happened two years before. He'd brought flowers to her office after school (three dozen, one for each year) and taken her out to dinner, and later they'd sat stunned before the television when *Ironside* was interrupted by news of King's assassination. He would definitely remember that. But he didn't. First time he was away from her he was in a motel room with Cheryl shaking off the gin and trying to pull his own life back together. No wonder she'd sounded funny when he called last week, like she was waiting for him to say something else. He thought then that she just wanted more of an explanation of the takeover—which, of course, she did—and so he cut the conversation short.

This was the last thing he wanted to be bothered with right now, but it would only get worse. He took a deep breath and dialed. The phone rang a long time. Even she couldn't be in bed yet; maybe she was giving him the benefit of the doubt and getting the curses out of the way first.

"So how was the first day of your thirty-ninth year?" he asked, trying to sound casual, when she finally picked up. He knew how much she disliked him putting it that way and thought that might derail her.

"Well," she said, as if emerging from a coma. "I guess your finger isn't broken after all."

"No, I'm sorry. See, there were special review sessions for midterms yesterday. And there was an emergency meeting of this committee I'm on, the one with the faculty, I told you about it, to improve race relations on campus." He was grasping at straws, but that was all he had; he knew she'd just as soon have him flunk a course—and didn't care at all about race relations—if it meant forgetting her. "Anyway, Happy Birthday. How was it?"

"Not bad, considering I didn't know where you were."

Mad would've been better. She sounded pathetic. But he didn't want to give her an opening to start rehashing last week. "So, what did you do?"

"Nothing, really. They had a dance at the Elks but I didn't feel like going. Dessie and I went out to dinner earlier."

And then you sat home waiting for me to call, he thought, filling in the silence she had trailed off into, and then got pissed when you called and I wasn't here and probably slurped buttermilk wondering how Lonnie's lowdown genes could have overcome your perfect mothering.

"Look, I'll make it up to you when I'm home. School will be over in another month or so."

"You don't have to make anything up to me," she responded in her best don't-do-me-any-favors voice. "Just let me know you're alive once in a while. I thought I was sending you to school. Tommy's in the army and he hasn't been shot at." He held the receiver away from his head for a moment. Perfect diction was her worst rebuke; it marked him as a stranger. "Your uncle was worried about you," she was saying when he brought it back.

Yeah, right. "Tell him I'm okay."

"He has a phone too, you know."

"Okay, I'll call him. And I'll call you next week. Listen, I'm sorry, really. Okay?"

"Yes, Richard. You know you're getting to be a mighty sorry child."

Tell me about it. "Yeah, I guess so. I'll do better. I gotta go, all right?"

"Go ahead." A washing of hands. "I suppose I should thank you for calling."

"Hey, anytime," he said. "Hope you have a good year."

"Well, it has to be better than the one I just had. Bye."

Hanging up, he thought for the first time in a long time about Jack, the boyfriend who'd given up nearly ten years ago and finally married somebody else. He had never really tried to picture him as a stepfather, but that was before. It wouldn't be a bad idea to have somebody else around now to keep her occupied. He had too many other things on his mind.

School the next day was a different place. Reading the Sunday *Times* with Cheryl, he had told her that the front-page portrait of a jittery campus convulsed by hostility was exaggerated. Now it seemed accurate. Either everyone was acting out the roles assigned for this drama, or the spotlight had illuminated deep strains of animosity that Ike had refused to see. Of course it had been bad. Certainly people had been on edge at least since the bombing, but it was the nervousness of people caught in a crossfire. What he saw on campus that morning were the faces of people who had taken up the battle themselves. Every significant nod or clenched fist from a passing black student carried more than the symbolism of brotherhood; they were the acknowledgments of co-conspirators, and with every one Ike quickly searched the suspicious faces of nearby whites, as if one would surely blow a whistle summoning the patrollers.

Entering the Monday-Wednesday-Friday classes from which he'd been conspicuously absent for a week, holed up first in the library and then on a Greyhound, he sensed eyes shifting toward him and bodies away. Like he was somebody dangerous. In economics, the guy he sat next to, his chatting partner who had schooled him in collegiate hockey, made no effort to remove his stuff from Ike's usual seat, so Ike kept walking till he found one in a half-empty row that stayed that way. He made sure to get to his Constitution class early to get his normal spot down front, only to have the professor, who always winked and checked the time with Ike before beginning his lecture, fix him with a withering stare, as if he had slept with the man's wife. Ike stared back but was distracted by something behind the professor on the blackboard. Someone had recently drawn—and no one had erased—a cartoon of King Kong, with an Afro, atop the libe tower, about to be shot down by a plane bearing fraternity markings.

Ike's last class was at Uhuru, usually a pain because, like most Black Studies classes, it was held late in the afternoon and so made for a long day. This time it was a relief to go where people wouldn't be looking at him like some alien invader. When he got there, he discovered that the house had been vandalized over the weekend. Several windows were shattered, and the message "Niggers go home" was sprayed on the front steps. The bombing last semester had seemed a more distant attack; this he took personally. He spat on the words and tried to rub them out with his shoe. When that didn't work, he dug out a highlighter and wrote in large letters next to the slur: WE ARE HOME.

Inside, a group of students was descending the stairs from a previous class. Juanita was among them.

"Well look what the cat dragged in," she said loudly.

Ike, who had been about to greet her, swallowed his hi and eyed her warily.

"You couldn't wait to get out of here, could you?" she continued. "Did you tell her the part about the tower? I bet that made her just holler."

She was right up under him now. Her remark drew nonverbal I-guess-she-told-him kinds of sounds from the others, all women. How did she know?

"Why don't you get off my case?" he said, although he muted his voice as if that would keep the others from hearing.

"Why don't you wake up?" she shot back. "There's a *war* goin on out here, man. I thought you finally figured that out last week, but no, nigger gotta go snuggle up to some white bitch to make him feel like a man then come strollin in here all simple like everything's cool. Well check it out, brother, everything is *not* cool and we don't need no damn visitors around here."

She held his eyes for a moment daring him to say something. He blinked. She turned for the door.

"What the fuck do you care what I do?" he called after her. "It's none of your goddamn business, all right?" She kept walking. "Kiss my ass," he added, and headed upstairs.

Ike stayed on at Uhuru long after his class and got more work done that night than he had all semester. All the shoes had dropped, and he no longer found himself staring off from the pages worrying about what was going to happen. Or what anybody would think. Or what he would do. And he didn't have to strain to hear what was brewing downstairs; all the postmortems on the takeover had apparently been conducted over the weekend. At one point, well ahead of his planned schedule, he went looking for someone to talk to. He found Carl wrestling with physics problems in the lounge.

"When's the test?" Ike asked.

"Tomorrow night," Carl said without looking up. "They're layin for me, too. I knew this shit cold last semester, but they lowered the boom with 102, boy."

"I heard. That's why I don't mess with that stuff. Usedta think I was pretty good in science, too."

"Yeah, you and everybody else. You know what they say about the gorge—they dug it as a mass grave for premeds."

They weren't the only casualties. Ike had heard that Carl's roommate, Freddie, had checked out after one semester, simply overwhelmed. There would, they all knew, be others.

"Hey, where you been since the libe?" Carl asked. "Don't you usually hang around here and book?"

"I was out of town."

"Must be nice to live close enough to get away from this craziness for a minute. I got jack shit done this weekend."

"When did all that happen out front?"

"Saturday night. We were gonna fix it up yesterday, but Hollyfield's waiting on the university to do something." He rolled his eyes.

"You takin a break anytime soon?" Ike asked.

Carl looked at his watch. "Ouch. I don't know, maybe in a few. Why?"

"Well, this may sound a little weird, but I was wondering if you could teach me how to play whist." Hodge had gone only as far as blackjack and tonk.

Carl raised his eyes, put down his pencil, sat back and smiled. "Oh, man," he said, giggling. "Sure. Why not? Let's see if we can get a foursome."

The radio woke him too soon the next morning. Something told him that the concept of school nights should still mean something and playing cards till two didn't fit the definition, even if it was his idea. It was a good time, though, like he'd picked up where he left off in Carl's room his first night on campus; like track practice, a rare reminder that he did know how to play. He had no regrets, except that now he had to get up. Normally the young voices on the college station did a slow job of arousing him—they sounded no more official than a bunch of Lennys outside the door—but the news opened his eyes: students, white students, had reported being mugged by unidentified blacks in two separate incidents the night before. There were descriptions, but they were meaningless; everybody at Uhuru fit them. Art was still asleep. Ike turned off the radio before the news was repeated.

Over coffee and danish at Paradise Lost in the basement of one of the humanities buildings—he'd long ago forsaken the union so he wouldn't have to walk past the black tables—he looked for more word of the muggings in the campus paper. No suspects, but the story didn't neglect to mention the heightened racial tension that was becoming almost a perverse source of identity for the university. Also on the front page, he read that Ellsworth had issued a proclamation banning all guns from campus, now that all the horses were way out of the barn. The bigger news, though, was on page three: word had leaked that an unnamed government professor planned to introduce a resolution at that afternoon's faculty meeting sharply restricting the Black Studies program, on the grounds that it was academically fraudulent and served as a Trojan Horse for subversive activity. By the time Ike came out of his first morning class the campus had blossomed with flyers for an SDS-sponsored rally to denounce the resolution.

Without giving it a lot of thought, Ike decided to go by Maier's office hours that afternoon, before the meeting. He knew his advisor would quiz him about the occupation, even though he had resolved to admit nothing, but it was worth the fencing if he could find out something about the faculty's plans for Black Studies. As he'd kept reminding himself in the library, the program was worth defending, and if the backlash was coming from government he could at least make a direct personal appeal.

But as he approached the main quad later, it was obvious that he wouldn't make it to Maier's office. Hundreds of people had gathered there facing the founder's statue, the traditional podium for rallies. Ike had expected a couple of guys with bullhorns haranguing a few dozen onlookers. He hadn't thought the radicals had that much pull anymore, and from what he had witnessed since his return to campus, he thought most white students had soured on the black cause. But here they were, not just idling by but listening, even cheering and occasionally waving clenched fists in the air. Only a few blacks were scattered in the crowd, but beside the headbanded speaker bellowing into a portable sound system at the base of the statue stood Ken Hollyfield, arms crossed and eyes shaded.

As Ike had heard others from the same spot try to persuade middle-class white students of their solidarity with downtown workers, migrant laborers and Vietnamese peasants, the speaker was playing a chord that stressed their harmony with the blacks. Incredible, under the circumstances, but it seemed to be working.

He kept the crowd's interest by playing on the fact that nobody in power had bothered to tell them what was going on since the occupation began; Ellsworth, except for his gun ruling, had remained silent. He argued that the blacks had brought guns into the building only after they had been attacked by a bunch of self-righteous thugs who probably needed directions to the library. Nobody had gotten hurt, he pointed out, except some asshole who was throwing rocks and yelling racist insults. And—this was news to Ike—tests had proved that he wasn't wounded by one of the rifles the blacks had used. They were keeping that quiet, the speaker charged, because the kid was probably shot by a campus cop pointing the wrong way and Ellsworth would rather have them believe the blacks had done it. Like the unsubstantiated reports of muggings, which nobody had proved were done by students if they had happened at all. Most effectively, the speaker comforted the students by reminding them that the blacks were really the victims all along. The old Uhuru House had been bombed and nobody was ever caught, and then two black students were thrown out of school without due process before they had been convicted of anything. A cross was burned and the new Black Studies building was vandalized and Ellsworth wanted them all to think that the blacks were responsible for everything that was going on.

The reason for all that, the speaker concluded, was so they could justify getting rid of the Black Studies program because it threatened the power of the faculty. That got a big cheer, and Ike realized why they had all turned out. They wanted an explanation they could relate to, and double-dealing bureaucracy in the service of status-quo authority fit the bill. They did have something in common with "the blacks" after all. Nobody was out to get *them*; it was the big shots, out to screw everybody so they could keep a lid on things. Confident that he had the audience where he wanted them, the speaker brought Hollyfield in for a solo, and he hit a heavy riff: he told them of Ellsworth's promise to beef up the program, which meant that if the faculty moved to cut it they had been betrayed. They had dealt in good faith, ended the occupation before the violence escalated, because they had been assured of the security of the program. If the resolution passed, all bets were off, and the faculty would be responsible for any further actions that might be taken—although, of course, since the BLF had been banned from campus he could only speak for himself.

The speaker took the beat and, in so many words, charged the crowd with the duty of proving they weren't racists and maintaining the peace on campus by letting the faculty know they wouldn't stand for it. And they didn't. With remarkably little persuading, as if not a one of them had a thing else to do, they followed the speaker's call to march on the building where the faculty was meeting. Ike, too late to make his plea to Maier and fascinated by this unexpected show of support, went along. Picking up chants of "Stop the Racist Cutbacks" and "Power to the People," the oddly energized mob surged toward the walls of Jericho. Though sturdy with stone and ivy and guarded by a hastily dispatched patrol of campus police, the hall seemed diminished and vulnerable as the students first massed before it, then coursed around, ringing it with youthful energy.

A few, apparently part of the organizing force, tried to push inside, directly challenging the cops so as to provoke a confrontation. But when the masses failed to storm the ramparts in support—most of them wanted to stop the faculty; they hadn't planned to *attack* the faculty—the leaders quickly changed tactics. They would stay there and shout the motherfuckers down. So they stomped and clapped and howled and chanted. It was a righteous party, a happening. For some of them it might have been a reenactment of the Vietnam days a year or two before, but less intense because it was, really, charity work. This wasn't the draft lottery, after all; there was no danger to them. They were doing this to show support for the blacks and to show up the faculty. For others, freshmen like Ike, it was a debutante ball, a chance to act out in the kind of big-time collegiate demonstrations they'd watched on television.

They were there for well over an hour, and Ike wasn't sure how long they could keep it up. Most of them didn't know how long these things went on, and no one knew what other arcane stuff they might have been discussing in there. When the collective spirit flagged, one leader or another would rise to repeat some of the same things the first speaker had said and to remind them of the importance of being heard. As the late afternoon air turned chilly—spring was a long time coming on the hill above that lake—the demonstration took on a meaning of its own. The students wanted to stay because leaving too soon would mean they hadn't been there at all. It became a test of endurance, a contest of wills. They were holding their breath and turning blue.

Finally, Bates and two white professors emerged from the hall. The crowd grew silent, less, it seemed, out of anticipation than out of surprise, as if they had almost forgotten the question and had to think about what they would do next if the answer was no. But Bates told them that the resolution, which would surely have had the effect of killing the Black Studies program and marking the university as a symbol of racial intolerance, had indeed been defeated. He thanked them for their support and urged them not to abandon the fight. They were not enemies, he said, but partners in the quest for truly progressive education freed from the liberal hypocrisies of the past. One of the white professors then saluted the students for both their enthusiasm and their restraint, which, he said, proved that they could be a positive factor in helping to shape university policy.

A few of the protest leaders jumped up to seize the moment with announcements about further meetings to force permanent change in the university governing structure. But that was beyond the patience or interest of those who had gathered for a specific purpose and were cheering lustily at their success. *Right on, brother,* a white student said, slapping five with Ike, who felt a little silly but good. Something had been accomplished after all. The white students had rallied to their defense and beaten back the faculty. And no one had gotten hurt.

The students began to disperse, joyously and irrevocably. Soon the faculty filed out, and Ike, wandering away with the rest, caught sight of a lone figure in a trench coat crossing a nearby parking lot.

"Professor Bates," he called. The man paused. "Congratulations." Bates looked at him blankly. "The faculty proposal," Ike continued, "you said it was defeated. That's good, right?"

"Yes, well. Actually it was more a nuisance than anything else."

"But all these people turned out. That's got to be a good sign."

Bates started walking slowly, with Ike beside him. "Yes, it is.

I'm sorry, I'm just tired of these foolish bureaucratic games. I'm glad that so many students were involved in this, but it doesn't really have anything to do with the program itself. And it doesn't negate the racism we've seen on campus."

"Couldn't hurt," Ike said, disappointed by Bates's negativism.

Bates smiled kindly. "It's been a long year for all of us," he said. "I don't blame you for trying to find some reason for optimism. There haven't been many. But understand, this is only the beginning. I'm afraid it will get worse before it gets better."

How could it be worse, Ike thought.

"Do you need a ride?" Bates asked.

"No," Ike said. "Thanks."

"Take care of yourself," Bates said before closing the car door.

"I will."

"I hear that was quite a show on Tuesday," Maier said creaking back in his chair, one foot propped on the open bottom drawer of the desk.

"I was mostly surprised by the turnout," Ike said, poised on the edge of the divan to signal the briefness of the visit. He'd learned. Making himself comfortable in previous trips had only invited more football recollections, which then led to attempts at the kind of probing discussions Maier used to have with Gene. In a way, Ike enjoyed the conversations after the fact, but at the time he always felt suckered. And the man could go on forever.

"I guess I thought there'd be more hostility at this point. You think it made a difference?"

"What do you think?" the professor immediately responded, eyebrows arched in perverse pleasure.

"I don't know, really. There were an awful lot of people out there."

"Oh yes. That didn't go down well. All this rabble hollering through the windows, you know, and that sort of thing. Didn't go down well at all. There was quite a lot of business about academic freedom and professorial prerogative. It changed quite a few minds, all right. I think several gentlemen who didn't give a hang about it one way or the other were afraid not to support the resolution because it would have been seen as yielding to student pressure. Can't have that, you know."

Ike leaned back, confused.

"You mean it almost backfired?" he asked.

Maier snapped upright and wheeled around the corner of his desk so he could bore in.

"Let me tell you something," he said. "That resolution was going nowhere. It was a bad piece of business, and most everyone knew it. Oh, sure, there are questions about the program. No one knows where some of these instructors are coming from, because Ellsworth made an arrangement with this Bates fellow and bypassed some of the normal procedures, you see. So some clever colleague of mine thought this would be a good time to get the faculty back in on it. Wasn't necessary. Clumsy, really. You have to be concerned about the public perceptions of these things. As you see, these are very paranoid times."

"Was the vote close then?"

Maier waved his hand in petty dismissal and wheeled back behind his desk.

"Didn't come to a vote," he said. "Threw the whole review back in committee where it belongs. We'll work it out. These things need time, but it'll be all right. Good thing the paper caught wind of the resolution, though, eh? A little insurance doesn't hurt."

"I see," said Ike, and in fact he thought he did. "Well, thanks for your time. I just wanted to get some idea of how it went."

"Certainly, uh, Richard. Say, why don't you stop back when classes are over? We'll talk about how the semester was for you. Pretty hectic time, I imagine, eh?"

"Yes sir," Ike said, standing.

"Oh, listen, you know I heard the darndest thing the other day I thought you might get a kick out of. There's this story going around that it was a black student who burned that cross."

Ike looked blankly.

"You know, that business right before the occupation, the burning cross in front of the house. Can you imagine?"

chapter 12

Soon, none of it seemed to matter. Even weeks later, getting the final notes for his Black Studies paper and closing out his carrel, Ike couldn't get over how everything had stopped, as if somebody simply turned a faucet. There was no organized public black-student activity. Hollyfield had dropped from view after the faculty protest, evidently taking the BLF with him, and the other black students Ike came in contact with, like himself, spent their time trying to salvage the semester. The radicals, who for a few days had seemed intent on using the momentum of the takeover to relight the home fires, had turned instead to fry other fish; there was the Panther trial up in New Haven, and the antiwar circuit beckoned. The note of common struggle struck up by the faculty protest somehow legitimized the plan for race relations seminars that the ad hoc committee had submitted, virtually unnoticed, during the takeover. As a member, Ike went to one of the first—he was the only black person there—at which participants cheerfully concluded that they probably were racists, but it was their parents' fault and they didn't mean it. Ellsworth did his part for normalcy by telling the trustees at their April meeting that they could get themselves another boy. There was a lot of speculation about whose idea that really was, but even if he had walked the plank he had a lifeboat ready: he was going to join some commission planning new directions for higher education in the year 2000.

But more than anything else it was the weather that wiped the slate clean. Temperatures in the fifties had already brought out some shorts and bare feet, but when the canvas top that covered the middle of the state was dropped to reveal an endless, honest-to-goodness blue sky, the world changed as if new leaves emitted radiation that caused amnesia. White flesh was everywhere, jiggling beside dogs on the quad, lying on the hillsides and fraternity roofs, falling out of cars, bouncing down hallways. Had a building been torched, a lab trashed, the library taken? Had names been called, fists thrown, shots fired? Last night, maybe, last week, last year—*in the winter*; summer's here, or close enough, and there were parties to drink and finals to ace and the hockey team went all the way and the Knicks were a cinch.

Ike told Cheryl all of it. He wrote regularly and called often, expressed his frustration and confessed his relief. He was glad things were back to normal but didn't think they deserved to be. It looked like there wouldn't be any fallout from the takeover, although there was rumor of a civil suit against Zulu, who, it turned out, had dangled a lawyer's son from the tower. He told her how upset he was about the cross-burning rumor—how even the possibility that it might have been true was enough to make him swear not to let himself get manipulated by anybody even if he did agree, sort of, with what they were after (and even, he realized, laughing, as he wrote the letter out in longhand at his carrel, if it made him sound too much like Elizabeth). And just to prove something—he didn't know what—he even told her about Juanita, whom she would remember from the bus station, about how he had thought things were easing up between them and why he thought that was important to him and how she guessed that Ike had been with her after the library and had gone off about that, but it was okay because he really didn't give a shit anymore. *They're not going to make worm's meat of me*, he wrote. *Me and you, baby. Nightingales and carousels.*

That was how the politics had ended, or so everybody thought. But then Nixon bombed Cambodia and they shot four kids at Kent State and spring died quickly. It wasn't angry and bitter like before. It was empty and sad, like when Kennedy was shot, except that they all knew none of them would have been riding in a motorcade but they, or people who could have been them, had danced around in front of cops and thrown rocks and insults, or had walked peacefully to class while somebody else was raising hell and might have been in the line of fire, too. It didn't even have anything to do with blacks in military gear or African costumes; they had done it to each other.

And so, within days, Ike again stood outside the stone fort while the faculty conferred, but this time there were even more of them, and some screamed over and over "Shut it down!" while most stood quietly and waited, as if for the mailman. They didn't have to wait long before word floated back through the masses: they could go home. In the face of a threatened massive student strike, the faculty, which had pretty much had it with that particular semester anyway, had approved a set of options. Students could stay and take finals or they could leave with the grades they had or they could take incompletes.

"You just won yourself a single, man," Art Rosen said, waving a fist in the air. "I'm *gone!*" They had gone to the rally, if that's what it was, together. It made as much sense as anything, since all the rules had gone out the window. Most classes were canceled that day; there was nowhere to go and nothing to do but hang around and find out what the deal would be, which was why everybody was out there, and without even discussing it they had figured they might as well do it together. They even talked on the way back to the dorm about how the year might have turned out differently if not for The Problem. But it was a discussion that would not be continued; Art would be moving into the ZBT house—"Zionist Bankers Trust," as someone from a rival frat had called it during rush, evidently thinking Art Italian—and Ike was in line for a single in a smaller dorm.

People on the corridor started figuring out how to polish their averages—which papers to write, which finals to take, which books to sell back that afternoon because they weren't ever going to open them again. The scheming itself was fun, but most of it turned out to be talk. When the first few left, Art Rosen among them, others started telling themselves that even if they got an A on the exam they couldn't do any better than the B- they already had, and anyway it was tough to study with people packing all over the place. So they went home too.

A bang, then a whimper, and Ike was left in peace. At least, now, there weren't a lot of people frolicking in forgetfulness; there weren't a lot of people at all, so that was all right. Those who were around, even if they had no memory of the mess on campus, couldn't help but remember how the semester finally ended. So something would stick, anyway. Somebody's pain would mean something, if Ike's didn't. Meanwhile, during the last few days, he had discovered the kind of freedom Juanita told him she had found during the summer. A few small classes—the only kind left—a little work, and a lot of time to be a real person at last.

"Hey, Ike," someone called as he dropped his last book on the circulation desk.

He paused near where he had lined up for the midnight retreat. It was Gene Mayford, looking like an ordinary person, in fact like an older version of himself.

"Where is everybody?" Ike said without smiling. "We can do it again for auld lang syne."

"No thanks," Gene said. "Once a year is plenty. Say, you got a minute?"

Ike looked at his watch.

"A couple," he said.

"Let's get a cup of coffee."

They walked over to the union. On the way, Gene talked excitedly about Willis Reed coming through in the clutch and how he must have fucked with Chamberlain's mind. Ike didn't say much because he didn't trust the conversation; he had never thought of Gene as being so interested in something as trivial as basketball. He also didn't want to think about what he had missed.

James Brown was jamming "It's a New Day" on the jukebox in the cafeteria, another takeover. They cruised through the line, where unhurried workers seemed more pleasant than they had all year, and settled into a table near another bid whist game.

"This okay?" Gene asked, obviously referring to the fact that they were in the black seats.

"Sure," Ike said.

"What I want to talk about is the BLF," Gene began.

"I thought there wasn't supposed to be one anymore."

"Well, there isn't, but that's no big deal. We'll change the name. But there's gonna be more changes than that. First of all, Ken's out."

"He's graduating, right?"

Gene suppressed a laugh and shook his head.

"What? A coup?"

"Not quite. He's been about a half step away from bustin outta here for the longest. There was no way he was gonna hang on behind all the shit that happened this semester. I think he knew it, too, especially after he realized Bates wouldn't go to bat for him. That's one of the reasons he wanted a big finish. But anyway, he's gone."

"So what does that mean?"

"It means, for one, that there'll be new leadership."

"You?"

"That's right. And some new directions, too. Confrontation's going to ease up for now. We don't need to keep woofin, we made our point. You know, we came close to being Jackson State, but they know it would've been a two-way thing here, not just black folks dying."

It made sense. They had been to the brink, though no one was killed as at Jackson, right after Kent. Ike could certainly go for something new. "Okay," he said, "well what about these new directions?"

"Everything's not set yet, but I know we have to spend more time takin care of our own business. The tutoring program's a priority. On campus and downtown. And I think that without compromising the integrity of the BLF, or whatever it's called, we've gotta start dealing more with the university on its own level. You know, getting people into committees and boards and shit like that—infiltrating the process and having a say, while the group maintains its separate identity."

"And why are you telling me this?"

"That's obvious, Ike. I want your support. I want your help. I've talked to Maier about you; he thinks you're pretty sharp. And I know you volunteered for that ad hoc committee. You do your work, you spend time at Uhuru and you stood by us during the takeover."

"I didn't know I was scoring points."

"Well, that is the point. A lot of the freshman brothers and sisters are like that. They take things for granted. That used to drive Ken crazy, but I think it's probably the way it should be, up to a point. You all haven't been fighting over the same ground for two, three, four years, or more, like some of us. And you shouldn't. It's time to move on, and that's what I want to do."

"But I still don't know what you want me to help with. I mean, you want me to be some kind of spy or something?"

"No, man, I don't want you to be some kind of spy or something." There was a touch of exasperation in his voice. "This ain't the Panthers and the FBI. I'm not interested in all that undercover shit. I basically just want to know if I can count on you to help out next year."

"Let me ask you a couple of questions," Ike said, emboldened by the flattery.

"Shoot."

"What about the cross?"

"Goddammit," Gene said. "You mean that shit floating around about did we burn it?"

"Yeah."

"What the hell do you think, man? I mean, that is the dumbest piece of white propaganda bullshit I've heard since I've been here, and I've heard a bunch. It's crazy. It's ridiculous. Next question."

Ike noted that there was more outrage than denial in the response, but he plunged ahead anyway. "Who shot that kid outside the library?" he asked.

This time Gene simply looked perplexed and shot Ike a sideways glance. "Whose side are you on, anyway?" he asked. "Look, Ike," he went on, "I don't know. I'll be honest with you. I wouldn't tell you if I did know, because it wouldn't serve any purpose, and I'll bet that you wouldn't really want to know if I could tell you. It didn't come from the library, we know that. I will say that all the pieces weren't inside, all right? But there were a lot of guns around, and we weren't the only ones who had them. It could've been anybody. Any further questions, counselor?" Gene let the question hang for a moment, and then smiled lightly.

Ike sipped air from his cup and let all the implications sink in. "No, I guess not."

"So, you in?"

"Somebody's slumming, but I don't know who."

They both looked up and saw Juanita at the end of the table. Hands on hips.

"Hey, babe," Gene said. "Sorry I missed you, but I wanted to talk to Ike. I figured you'd find me."

"That's okay. He's probably gotta run anyway," she said. "Business, right brother?"

"Come on, Neet, ease up," Gene said.

"No, she's right," Ike said, meeting her gaze. "I have some very important business to take care of."

"Well, don't let us keep you," she said.

"I won't," Ike said.

"Wait a minute," Gene said. "Talk to me."

"It sounds good," Ike answered, turning his back to Juanita. "We'll talk next year. I'd like to help." He reached out his hand.

Gene took it, like normal people, without a lot of carrying on. "That's all I ask, brother. It's gonna be good, man, I promise you that. Take care, hear?"

"Yeah, you too. Excuse me," he said to Juanita, and left.

He could tolerate her foolishness and deal with Gene on an even level because he had Cheryl, and she was waiting in his room. Once Art had cleared out, he called and asked if she wanted to keep him company while they both finished up—her classes were over, too—and she had agreed. It was weird, having her at Art's desk, under the blank wall where Raquel Welch had been, and he stared at her chewing her fingers, tugging her hair into a

Medusa wig, and felt good imagining what it would be like to *be* together, all the time. He felt bad leaving her to go to the library, but she had her Lawrence paper to work on, and that was part of the deal: being comfortable enough to go about their business and knowing that they would fall asleep wrapped up in each other without even having to make love, although they hadn't reached that point yet.

And the days had been good. That little park by the lake—she gave him shit for not knowing they had a carousel—and hiking down the gorge below the waterfall and walking out by the apple orchards. Back to the garden; they *were* stardust. They'd even sat out on the slope last night, facing away from the damn tower and reading the stars until they ended up splendoring in the grass. And for once, he didn't care if Juanita, Malcolm and Eldridge Cleaver found them, so convinced was he that this was the way it should be, and could be. He looked at his watch, saw that it was almost twelve, and opened the door to find her in darkness, sitting on the bed, smoking, looking out the window and listening to Otis.

"I've been—loving youuuuwoowoowoowoo—a lil too lo-ong," he crooned with the record.

"You know, you really should stick to mouthing the words," she said.

"What do you mean?" He tried to look hurt. "All my peoples can sing."

"I'm afraid somebody lied to you, sweetie, or else all your peoples is deaf."

"You'll get used to it." He closed the door and made his way to the bed before her. "Ooh, baby, please—down on my knees," he sang.

"You're gonna do the whole thing, right?"

"Shut up, this is the good part. *Ah love ya, ah love ya, ah love ya, gootgodamighterahloveya!*"

She applauded dutifully, helped him up beside her and turned back to the window, where she was studying the sky.

"Find any signs yet?" he asked.

"You know that funny set of lights I told you about last night? It's still there," she said. "And it's definitely getting closer. It's obviously some sort of probe, and if we stay right here for, I don't know, maybe a few weeks and then go up on the roof and light a flare I bet they'll come get us. We'd be perfect specimens, young, healthy, smart, reasonably attractive, and we can start a whole new branch of humanity. What do you think?" She looked at him seriously.

"It's an interesting proposition."

"We have to stay right here, and we can't tell anybody."

"They're closing the dorm day after tomorrow."

"Does that mean no?"

"You know, you look great in the dark," he said.

"What, is that supposed to be some kind of compliment?"

"Yeah, it is," he said, working his fingers through her thick hair and turning her head to the moonlight. "You look more like yourself. It's like this fierce beauty comes out, you know, with the eyebrows and cheekbones and all."

"Great. He thinks I'm a goddamn werewolf." She grabbed his hand and bit it.

"Ouch! Listen, what time you leavin tomorrow?"

"That's nice. First you turn down an offer to colonize the stars, then you tell me I look like Lon Chaney and now you want to throw me out altogether."

"I just wanted to know if we'll have time to do anything."

"I don't know. Maybe I'll just slip away at dawn," she mumbled, curling up in his lap.

He didn't say anything for a long time. If he hadn't been holding on to her, he would have thought she'd left the room. Part of her, it seemed, had. "Have a good time?" he nearly whispered at last. He knew she was back because he could hear her sort of purring as he wrapped her hair around his fingers. She nodded.

"I wish it could have been like this all year, you know?" he said.

"Oh, I don't know if I would have been able to stand it. I've decided too much happiness isn't good for you."

"Just so much happening all the time. Not even the work so much, just—so much to do, figure out."

She closed her eyes and sighed. "I understand, Richard," she said turning up to him. "It's not your fault."

He bent down to kiss her, sensed a brief hesitation, and pressed on with the almost polite gentleness he had practiced since that gin-soaked night in Saratoga. She had expressed doubts then, and his every touch, every stroke, carried the sure, soft message of reassurance. He wasn't going anywhere, he tried to tell her with his body. Didn't she know that? He finally let his head drop to its resting place beside her neck and stopped moving. She kept her legs clamped around him like a tightly tucked blanket and then, slowly, she hooked the sheet with her foot and pulled it over them, wiped the sweat from his back and turned a damp face away from him, toward the window. He licked salt from her cheek and searched the night sky for the strange lights, thinking, as he drifted to sleep, that maybe the time was right for them to be lifted away from all this.

Back in the room after his shower the next morning, Ike pulled on his pants, dropped onto the messed-up bed and surveyed the room. He was going to miss it, he decided. He had made it his, finally, by outlasting Art Rosen and by having Cheryl here, celebrating while the last few jerks on the corridor sweated out chemistry.

He pulled out one of her cigarettes and lit it as she strolled in wearing his robe.

"These things are nasty," he said after one puff. "I don't know how you can stand it."

"I'm a nasty person, darling," she said. "Didn't you know?"

"It's goin on ten. So what's the agenda?"

"I decided I'll take the eleven-fifteen. I can get a cab downtown." She was working on her face in the mirror.

"Isn't there a later bus? We could go find some French toast or something."

"Has some French toast been reported missing?"

"Come on, you know what I mean. We can look for a place and have brunch. I like brunch."

"Uh-uh. I have to get back. Besides, nobody eats brunch during the week."

"Aw, man."

"No, Richard."

"All right," he whined. "Well, are you still going to the country with Judy next month?"

"Yep."

"Did you figure out where I'm supposed to meet you?"

"Nope."

"Why not? I have to figure out my cover story."

" 'Cause I don't want you to come."

"Okay . . . " Ike said and forgot about looking for a shirt. "Then when will you be back home?"

"I'm not telling." She was brushing her hair in front of Art's mirror.

"All right, I give up. No brunch. No country. And you're not going to tell me when I can get in touch with you. I don't get it. Is something wrong?"

"Nope. I'm just not going to see you anymore." She still hadn't looked at him.

"Excuse me?"

She turned then. It was a Bette Davis turn. "Am I smiling? Do you see a smile on my face?"

"Don't play that, Cher."

"I'm not playing, Richard."

"Wait a minute. You *serious?*"

"That's what I said. Read my lips, since your people are deaf. I'm not going to see you anymore." She picked up her suitcase and walked past him to put it on the bed.

"You mean—just like *that?*"

She carried her clothes to the suitcase without answering him.

"Wait, this is crazy." He jumped over and grabbed her arm. "I said *wait* a minute, now! Will you please tell me what's going on?"

She pulled her arm free and sat down carefully beside the suitcase. "Don't you have business to take care of?"

"What are you talking about?"

She sighed. "I can't do this anymore, Richard. You have no idea what this year has been like for me."

"You think I've been havin a picnic here? Look, I'm sorry. I know it's been rough, but we got *through* it, that's what counts.

You can't tell me these last few days haven't been good. And next year—"

"Next year, Richard," she said rising to face him, "it'll be the same damn thing. This summer you'll lie to your mother about being with me so she won't get pissed off even though she knows you're with me. And next year there'll be more meetings and demonstrations and we'll get together on a few weekends when nobody's looking and fuck our brains out and everything will be great and it won't *mean* anything."

"The hell it won't!"

"Oh, Richard, will you please wake up? I told you I don't mind when you talk about the past, but you never get around to talking about the future, *our* future. I'm not sure we have one anymore."

"Of course we do. But we have to live through the present first. We have to settle all this now so the future will be worth something."

"Spare me the speeches, Richard. It's too late. That's the point, you're always looking for something to settle, trying to fix things when nothing's broken. I don't *give* a shit about all that other stuff. We won! We were happy! Why couldn't that be enough?"

He turned abruptly, then began wandering in little circles. "I don't get it, Cheryl. I thought you were on my side."

"I *was*. I am. But you keep moving."

He started to say something but couldn't.

"I'm glad things are working out better for you," she said quietly. "Really."

"But that means they're going to get better for us, too," he said hopefully.

"I wish. What I think it means, though, is that you don't need me anymore. I can't live with that. I won't do that to myself, Richard. Not even for you."

He put his hands on her shoulders, fingering the flannel lapels of the robe that fit her almost as well as it did him. She stood with her arms folded and did not bend to his touch. It was daylight, but she had never looked more fierce. Or more sincere.

"I love you, you know," he said.

"So what?" she replied softly, holding his gaze. "If I didn't love you so much I could keep on playing the game and go on with my life and we could have great times together. It won't work. You *know* it won't. You won't let it."

He dropped his arms to his sides and took a step back.

"Nobody likes a smartass, Costanza."

She almost smiled. Just for a second.

"Come here," she said, and grabbed both his hands. "Tell me I'm wrong, and I'll take it all back. We'll go find some French toast and forget I ever said any of this."

He looked at her for a long time and with a shiver of fear pulled her to him.

"I didn't want it to be this way, Cheryl," he said, clutching desperately through the fabric for a firm grip of her.

"I know."

He let her go and sank to the bed. She continued packing.

"I can't believe this," he said. "This can't be happening. Just like that, and it's over?"

"I don't know any other way to do it. You're just mad because I thought of it first." This time she did smile.

"Fuck you. Hey, you know we haven't seen *Bambi* yet." He had told her through repeated viewings of A *Man and a Woman* that it was *his* favorite movie.

"Call me if it ever comes around and I'll go with you."

"Never mind."

"Give up?" She was smiling freely now, and he tightened his face so he wouldn't smile, too. "Would you call me a cab, please?"

"You're a cab, goddammit. And take off my robe."

Fifteen minutes later they walked out of the dorm.

"You know, if you apologized right now, I might still forgive you," he said.

"I'm going to grab that suitcase and hit you with it if you don't stop."

"You want it? Okay, take it." He put the suitcase down on the sidewalk. "I don't know why I'm carrying it anyway. I ain't no damn redcap. I mean, it would be different if we were going together or something."

"You're sick, you know that?" She picked up the suitcase. "I want you to remember that. You have no sense."

She eyed him as if expecting a response, but he was spent. Maybe that's what it had been like when she had something on her mind and he insisted on playing.

The cab was waiting in the parking lot behind the dorm. He had hoped that it would be late, get a flat, explode on the way up the hill. He took the suitcase from her and hoisted it into the back seat.

"Thank you, sir."

"Yeah, sure. Don't mention it."

"You want a tip?"

"Like what," he said, trying gamely for old time's sake, "don't fall in love with a girl who can see the fuckin future?" He was twirling his fingers through the back of her hair with one hand and brushing a piece of lash from under her eye with the other.

"I'm glad you did," she said. "Good-bye, Richard."

As she was about to slide into the cab, he pulled her to him and kissed her. She tried to keep it short, but he held her tighter until he felt her arm around his neck. Then he let go, leaving her to break it off. He hoped she wouldn't, but she did.

"Bye, Cher," he said, or thought he said, an instant before the door closed with her inside. *Don't go,* he thought as the cab pulled out, leaving him standing there alone. He took one quick step, measuring the angle to sprint down the embankment and lunge at the car, but stopped. Cheryl didn't look back.

If the room he'd shared with Art Rosen was a jail cell, the one his body inhabited the next year was solitary confinement. And that was fine. The closest he had come to this was the evenings he'd spent in his room during his first year at Southwest, freshly arrived from the multicolored, polysyllabic chaos of junior high. But that was, in hindsight, a pose: the misunderstood loner; he knew better things were coming and he was biding his time until they did. Janet showed up, smart and fresh like a TV sidekick, to ease his way into the bright upper tracks. Tommy rooted him back in the dark bottomland of the track team. And even at his mopiest, Elizabeth was a room away, always ready with the Sergeant Clarence pep talk: you can do anything, be anybody, go anywhere. Finally, there was Cheryl, who had lifted him away from all the rest, and then left him wrecked on the face of the moon. The summer home didn't count. He wasn't there, really. He returned to the department store where he'd worked two years before (and where Elizabeth had worked, briefly, years before that), thinking she might wander in. She never did, and in the evening he simply went back to his room. Elizabeth may have suspected something was up because he didn't have anyplace to go. He wouldn't give her the satisfaction. Hodge knew, and he kept his distance so he wouldn't have to acknowledge that he had squandered both potential and squaw. All he wanted was to get back and serve his sentence in the little corner room with the angled ceiling, the one that had seemed to offer such intimate possibilities when he saw it the semester before, but which now mocked and reinforced his isolation.

He still had the newly named Afro-American Society. That was a good one. When he had spoken to Gene at the end of freshman year, participating seemed more attractive because it was optional. Now it was more like coercion; meetings were the only place he could go, besides class and the library, to escape the whorish screams of Laura Nyro he perversely subjected himself to, over and over, in his room. Because he never bothered with the parties that came after or between meetings—too much work—they did not become a way of life for him as they apparently did for others. He came and went, the phantom of Uhuru. Who was that masked oreo? Juanita didn't even hassle him anymore. The issues were less emotional, which gave him more room to operate without engaging: recruitment, financial aid, tutoring, curriculum, programs and speakers. Things did get warm when a black football player was declared academically ineligible, and again later when a black administrator was accused of making improper advances to black women students. He skipped those sessions, and the situations resolved without public demonstration. Perhaps he wasn't the only one who was tired.

Often he would leave the meetings and go alone to a movie on campus. It didn't matter what was playing. Once he ran into Art Rosen afterward, heading back to the frat house with a flock of ZBTs. They spoke of a party that weekend, and for a moment he actually considered it. But when the time came he walked aimlessly past the waterfall and the Greek House and ended up spending the night again with Laura.

By the end of the semester, Cheryl had neither written nor called, and he knew she wouldn't. So did Elizabeth, apparently. Confident that her son was miserable, she went out of her way to stage what she considered a pleasant holiday. Hodge had come to stay at the apartment, bunking on the sofa as he had in the past between living quarters. Less resistant than in the summer, he allowed himself to become their boy again for two weeks, joining in the illusion that the last two years had not happened. They ate, watched TV, went to the tree-lighting ceremony downtown—the event that once preceded the visit to Santa in Hall's transformed annex, with what must have been the world's longest electric train forever circling the vast room. He went along to show off for church folks in their sweet-smelling, heavily carpeted homes. He even submitted to the ritual of the photo album: here's little Richard in the park with Tommy, on his bike with Hodge, Easter parading with Elizabeth, displaying birthday toys with Elizabeth, at the fair with Elizabeth, at the Enchanted Forest with Elizabeth. And perched on a car fender with Lonnie Isaac. Hodge said it was taken in Madison Park on his first birthday. Elizabeth said he looked like he wanted to cry. He didn't think so; he thought the little boy, for once, looked a lot like the handsome man who was plagued by other people's expectations and checking the horizon for a way out. Later that night, he looked behind the yellowed library card in his wallet for the long unseen scrap of paper with an address scribbled in Hodge's shaky hand. Satisfied that it was still there, he moved Cheryl's graduation picture behind it and began to pack.

Into the second semester, turning to study the sky outside the window in history class, he found Rachel. She sat next to him, and at first she reminded him of Jan: a bit short, kind of dumpy and unkempt. But Jan had simply been ahead of her time; an awful lot of white girls at college looked that way. The real similarity was in the conspiratorial chatter, which he at first tried to ignore. She didn't stop, though, and she had this unnerving habit of looking at him when she spoke, her small, dark eyes gleaming. Although she seemed fidgety, always pushing a tumbling lock of curly black hair from her brow and working her shoulders as she whispered through a lecture in a rapid Boston accent, the eyes centered her, promising a calming depth, and they drew him out.

He wondered why she focused them on him. There had to be something wrong with her, she'd have to be a misfit or crusader, and Rachel, it turned out, was both, her labor union father and retarded sister combining to endow her with unusual sensitivities. But he did not question her motives, or his warming response, as classroom chatter turned over the course of weeks to coffee at Paradise Lost, joint study sessions, gently deflected social invitations and finally a hand extended the countless miles across a notebook in his dorm room. A few tentative probes—are you sure you want to do this?—followed by a thrilling near silence in lecture the next day, when railroad strikes gave way to the sensation of accidentally touching knees and the concentration required to maintain contact. He did not stop to question on that weekend when they wrestled wordlessly in the cushioned wooden armchair of his room, and he lifted her sweatshirt to feast on her large breasts and massaged the thick hair inside her jeans. He did not, in fact, question the improbable flow of events at all, until the night he lay breathlessly beside her, his room without music for the first time he could remember, and she pushed back her hair, fixed her eyes on him and said: "Thank you."

That was not what he wanted to hear. Was he supposed to be doing her a favor, easing some guilt, salving some pain? He had wanted her, had wanted not just to know what another body felt like, but had come to want *her*. Her sincerity had touched him and her manner amused him. Her eyes had offered a clear path to a safe place, her body a secure harbor. But he had not wanted her in his debt. She didn't even smile when she said it, lying still on her back looking up at him like an invalid. So serious, even now. So . . . needy. The thought contorted his face. What he had taken for serenity was instead an empty space. Could she be expecting him to fill it? With what?

There was only one thing, and if that's all she wanted, he decided, she would have it. He climbed between her legs and braced his weight on his outstretched arms. Meeting her gaze, and feeling himself harder as he did, he pushed. And pumped. She lifted her head to kiss him, but he remained out of reach. Raised up on his toes, a push-up posture. Her head bobbed, curls tumbling. She clutched her hair with both hands, clearing the way for her eyes, which now began to reveal her helplessness. The lines of her body, which had once seemed so solid, softened and blurred, jiggled and melted. He heard his own back-turn breathing and the sound of his chest, stomach and thighs rhythmically slapping hers. Sweat dripped from his head, one drop acidly closing her eye and oozing down her cheek like a tear. More followed. She wiped them away frantically, almost drying her face with her hair, still trying to see. Until, at last, she held her eyes shut, covered them with her hands, and turned her head with a choking sob of release. Or sadness. Or pain. It didn't matter.

He ached. He wanted now to collapse on her, gather in all the pieces and hold them back together. But he fell to the side, apart, and said nothing. Eventually she rose, said she had to go, and dressed. At the door, head bowed, blushing lightly through the hair she no longer bothered to push aside, she said she would see him next week.

What for?

The next evening, a Sunday, he had promised to meet Gene at the apartment he shared with Juanita, across the street from the community center downtown. He had been to the center once, when he had agreed to do some tutoring. But nobody was expecting him, and the kid was late and didn't seem interested. When Gene had asked how it went, he said he'd go back only when they got their shit together. So now he was supposed to help get the shit together. Working directly with Gene, even with Juanita lurking about, he thought they might be able to get somewhere.

When he arrived, after a long walk down the hill, he found two police cars, lights flashing, parked in front of the house. A problem at the center, he thought at first, but why were the cars here? Then, remembering that nothing was that simple, he angrily recalculated: some subversive shit. And he had almost walked right into it. Damn. He had half a mind to turn back, but he couldn't do that. Gene had always been straight with him. He thought. But what was this? Two cops were dragging Gene from the porch, a third leading the way. He was struggling, grunting, spitting blood and curses. He went forward to intercede, but Gene's face froze him, and the suddenly unfamiliar voice bludgeoned him. *Fuck you! Get the fuck away from me! Fucking niggers ain't shit!* And then, more loudly: *Bitch!*

He looked to the house. More cops remained inside. One put a hand to his chest, stopping him at the doorway. Another was speaking to Juanita as if to a child. She was shaking her head no, and holding her arm awkwardly. All right, the cop said. It's up to you. What about this one, the other asked. It's all right, she said. The cop dropped his hand, smirked, and they left.

Juanita turned her back to him and wobbled to the sofa. He looked around. The room was a mess. Chairs had been overturned. Books thrown. Pictures knocked cockeyed.

"Did they do this?" he asked.

"Oh no." She snorted. " 'They' didn't." She looked up at him as he passed her, surveying the damage. There was a cut beneath her eye, and her lip swelled.

"Oh, God," he said, and tumbled to her side. The questions appeared on his face but did not emerge from his mouth. He reached out, carefully, because her arm seemed to be injured and because she seemed so very tiny. His arms settled clumsily on her, one on her back, the other where her small knee bent the fabric of her African print robe. He sat that way for a long time, not holding her but surrounding her, and, not knowing where to begin the discussion, didn't. After a time, he felt something that startled him, like a rock bending, and he realized as her muscles relaxed how tightly she had been holding herself. In slow motion, she swayed back onto him and slid insensate across his lap and drew a ragged breath like a newborn baby's and cried without sound.

He placed his hand on her hair, as he had wanted to the first time he saw her. So soft. He tried to reshape it into the Roberta Flack crown he knew, and felt her voice vibrate through his leg:

"Never really hit me before. Thought he would once or twice. Last year. He'd get so angry. Tired. Tense. Maybe throw something and go out. When he came back, he'd be fine.

"Yesterday there was a letter. From Ken Hollyfield. Something about last year. He got real quiet. Wouldn't say anything for hours. When I tried to talk about it he exploded. Said he couldn't trust anybody. More hurt than angry. Confused. Nothing I could do. He left, took the letter with him. Came back this afternoon, but this time he was worse. Said I was like all the others. He hit me.

Knocked me around. Tried to choke me. I went in the other room, locked the door. Called the police. Didn't know what else to do. He tore up the place. Went after them when they got here. Tried to get the gun. That's why they took him. Don't know who he was going to shoot."

She stopped. After another long while she rose, so quickly and easily it surprised him. She looked at him briefly, her expression blank, walked briskly into the bedroom and closed the door. He stayed for an hour straightening up.

In the morning, he took a seat on the far side of the auditorium for history class. He would not be able to keep it up and no longer wanted to. It could not work as a friendship; there would be little to talk about now. The fleeting notion of romance had been a mutual delusion. Still, he had thought about continuing, but climbing the hill from Juanita's he had identified, with a surge of shame and power, the emotion he felt as Rachel stared desperately up at him through damp fingers: the urge to leave dark red handprints all over her soft white flesh. *Smack!* You're welcome. *Smack!* You're welcome. Now, even at a distance, the dark eyes seemed swollen with hurt neither unexpected nor unwelcome as they followed his all over the room and burned into his back when he pushed through the crowd at the end of the hour.

The roles were reversed when Juanita appeared a week later in the urban policy class they shared. He did the looking, she the avoiding. When he got the chance to ask if she was all right, her reply was indignant: "Why wouldn't I be?" Watching her turn to move past him, disappointed but not entirely surprised by her response, he grasped another fact. She was pregnant, a few months, and beginning to show. A quick check of others leaving the room, watching him bemusedly stare at her, told him that this was not news. Everybody probably knew. Like people walk around pregnant in college all the time. Where was he from? But this magnified the repulsiveness of what Gene had done. How could he hurt her like that when she was carrying his child—and there could be no doubt that it was Gene's, even if his rage might have made him imagine otherwise.

He trotted after her and spoke softly because others were nearby. "Listen, if there's anything I can do," he said.

"Do I look like a damn charity case to you?" she replied, still moving. "I don't need your pity, all right? I told you. I'm all right."

"The hell you are," he said and stopped.

She paused. "Look, I'll let you know, okay? Thanks. You must be havin a slow year."

What was left of it began to move more quickly. Without Gene, who disappeared as Hollyfield had the year before, the meetings became less frequent. He had brief but pleasant conversations with Juanita, who never mentioned Gene or the baby. Rachel stopped looking and Laura Nyro stayed on the shelf. He signed up for a summer internship offered through the urban policy class. He made dean's list. He forgot. Until he got home, checked the paper in his wallet again, and found the picture. And knew he had to be sure.

And so, thirteen months after the cab had pulled away from his dorm, he showed up at Jan's door.

Her father opened it and contained his puzzlement pretty well.

"I'm Richard Isaac," he said. "Is Jan home?"

He told the stranger to step in, called for his daughter and wandered away.

"Richard!" Jan screamed, appearing from around a corner in worn bell-bottoms, an outsized denim shirt and bare feet. She ran up to him and threw her arms around his middle, which was about as high as she went. "A blast from the past. How are you? Daddy, this is Richard. We went to high school together. Remember you had that list of people who were smarter than me? He was one of 'em."

"Good to know you, Richard," he said from a chair in the living room.

"See, I do have parents. At least one. I haven't seen my mother in days. Come on downstairs."

He hadn't thought he would ever enter that room again, the scene not only of the Trojan debacle but of the first tropical-fruit Lifesaver kiss. That had come the night after Bobby Kennedy was killed, and Jan's zoo of sensitive rejects had gathered in the dying days of a troubled school year. It was the first time he had been with Cheryl away from school, a sympathetic communal where they were free to touch and not talk, with "Scarborough Fair" playing on the turntable and "Stay in My Corner" in his mind.

The room now looked smaller because there was so much more in it. The posters on the wall were the same, Don Quixote and LBJ on the toilet and Hendrix, but a futon commanded the middle of the floor, books were stacked on the bar and clothes were thrown all over the place.

"Not quite the same, is it?" Jan said. "I've been living down here since I dropped out last semester. Did you know about that? Too much bad shit, all kinds. My parents—my alleged parents, that is—have been taking it pretty well. I've been working at the drug counseling center down on State Street, and I'll probably go back in the fall. Social work. I guess you're still hangin in, huh?"

He had plopped down on the sofa and didn't respond because he wasn't listening.

"Richard?"

"Have you seen her?"

"You know, it's really weird. I almost never see anybody from high school anymore. You'd think I'd bump into a few people around town, but considering where I work that's probably good."

"She's never home. I even drove by and waited but she never came out."

"Richard—"

"I thought you might know where she is."

She stopped in front of him, pushed up her sleeves and crossed her arms.

"She's in Europe."

He sat blankly. Jan took a deep breath.

"She's doing her junior year abroad. She and a friend are going to tour the continent first. She left a few days ago."

"You saw her?"

Jan sat down heavily.

"She was here a week ago. I haven't really been keeping in touch. I did run into her once last summer, and she told me about you guys."

His face began to show pain.

"Then she just dropped in out of the blue like you did. Actually, she called first, but it doesn't matter. I'm just here, you know."

No response.

"I think she just wanted to let me know she was going. I thought it was because I'm sorta the one who's supposed to keep track of all you guys, and it sounded like it was supposed to be a secret. But now—she didn't say so—but I think she wanted me to know in case you asked. I told her I hadn't seen you either. Funny how she knew."

"I called her house last week. She wasn't there."

She reached over and pulled his head onto her shoulder. "Still hurts, doesn't it? God, it must be awful."

"I don't know what happened," he said finally. "I thought I understood for a while, and then I guess I thought it was like a test, you know, and if I waited long enough it would be all right, and then I waited and nothing happened, and I don't know what to do."

"This must sound really dumb, but in a way I think you're so lucky," she said, pulling her long, straight hair to the other side so he could nestle closer. "I mean that. I can't imagine what it would be like to love somebody like that. That's something, you know?"

He lifted his head to protest but nothing came out. She put a hand to his face, tracing the top edge of the week's growth.

"It'll be all right, Richard," she said softly. "Really."

He kissed her. Her face was so close and he needed it so bad. She pulled back and studied him—his eyes were still closed—and then led him back to her mouth, their tongues wrapping around each other. She turned her body toward him and he collapsed onto it. When she turned her head to whisper something soothing, he nibbled down her neck into the collar of her shirt. She shifted completely underneath him on the sofa, the better to hold him like a child having a fit; he kept biting and licking and began to press against her with his hips. She took his face in both hands and kissed him fully once more. His breathing began to ease, but then he pulled at the buttons on her shirt. *Easy,* she whispered. He bit her breast—she wasn't wearing a bra—and she yelped. *You're hurting me,* she said, but he nuzzled deeper under the denim and began pulling at the snap of her jeans. When he tore open his own she grabbed both his hands. *Richard, it's me. Jan. I'm your friend. Not like this.*

He stopped, looked at her hands on his, and then at both of them. She was flushed, her hair scattered, a reddened breast exposed, her jeans down on her hips and he was about to come out of his.

"Where was all this passion a few years ago?" she said. "And I thought you didn't care."

"I'm sorry," he said.

"Listen." She tried to pull him to her, but it was as if rigor mortis had set in. He wouldn't budge. She wrapped herself around him where he was, kissed his shoulder and ran her hands over his body; his remained in his lap. "I understand. Let's go for a ride, or a walk, and talk awhile."

He shook his head vaguely.

"We can go out tomorrow, then. Start over and see what happens."

He stood up, without looking at her, and fixed himself in his pants. "It's too late," he said.

"No it's not. We're still friends, Richard, and maybe we can help each other. You haven't heard about my problems."

"I'm leaving tomorrow."

"Well when are you coming back?"

"I'm not," he said, and walked out the door leading to the driveway.

The next day he was on a Greyhound to New York. Sort of a reverse migration. He thought of all the colored folks who had gone there from the South and wondered again about the families like his that had overshot the mark and settled, instead, upstate or in New England; it was as though he were returning to first base to tag up. It was even stranger that he had never been at all—no Statue of Liberty, no Empire State, no U.N., although they had managed excursions to the Thousand Islands and Corning and the Adirondacks. But he knew why, and that was precisely why he had signed up. The Black Studies program was offering a summer project working for a group called the Tenants Rights Action League. Twelve students would be doing fieldwork, learning urban government from the ground up by helping people in Harlem deal with landlords. Afterward they would each write a report and get four credits. All had been carefully screened for serious intentions, but the fact remained that it was ten free weeks, with modest pay, in the Big Town.

He arrived at Port Authority, disappointed that the bus had come through a tunnel that deprived him of an inspirational skyline view, and, without recalling his carefully memorized directions, found the Eighth Avenue subway. The caverns smelled of food: hot dogs and donuts and the sticky residue of coffee, soda and wine. Everything, in fact, seemed to operate on a sensual level, on scent and sound and fleeting visual cues, like the presumably colorful but worn signs that no one apparently noticed (just as it was years before he had noticed the Route 11 signs on State Street). And on sheer motion. You got where you were going, wherever that was, simply by *going*. Reflection, contemplation, reconsideration, hesitation—all the things he was good at—were good for getting trampled. Better simply to move on, which he did, right through the open doors of a train that a quick visual sweep told him had a bright blue A on it somewhere. He remembered reading something, in Langston Hughes probably, about the A train being a trap for unsuspecting colored folks who could find themselves whisked out to the far reaches of Brooklyn. But he was sure he had seen an "Uptown" sign on the platform, and even if it was the wrong direction he could always turn around. It was like reaching the Mississippi; one way or another, once he got there, he'd get there.

So he settled into a seat, clearly a precious commodity, and tried not to look like what he was, a perfect victim. The vulnerability was kind of thrilling. For all he knew, people could be buying drugs, stealing, killing, making sexual contact with each other all around him while he fixed his eyes on the words PLEASE KEEP HANDS/OFF OF DOORS printed across the sliding doors. That was only good for one stop, since a dangerous-looking young man parked himself in front of the doors, and he thought it best to avert his gaze. On doing so, he discovered that everybody else was doing the same, as if each had a designated spot to look at, most of them involving the floor, the advertisements above the windows of the car or a face-shielding newspaper. Encouraged by that realization, he gazed the length of the car and decided that, unless there was some conscious predator he couldn't detect, no one was paying him any mind at all. It was absolute freedom: if no one would look at you, you could do *anything you wanted*. He could jack off right there in his seat if he had a mind to, and as long as it stayed in his lap, no one would care.

Even before he stepped off the train, there was an even more profound discovery: surging along beneath the city, he had entered a world more broadly, more deeply, more completely black than any he had ever been in. It was more than the people left on the train, a cast expressly assembled for the destination of 125th Street. Everyone, on the platform, in the token booth, in the ads on the walls, was black, as was everyone in sight when he emerged aboveground. The music blasting from storefronts and carried in tremors along the pavement was black; the odors were black, the *air* was black. He had been in black houses, on black blocks, in black neighborhoods before, since the day he was born; no amount of cultural exchange, no extended diplomatic missions could change that. But this was different. In all those other contexts, the whiteness was just around the corner, right outside the door, like a parent in the next room or a cop cruising down the street. Here it was distant, left behind underground somewhere (and even down there less white than the sho-nuff, red-cheeked whiteness of home). The blackness was safe, as if it could go days, years, maybe forever without being called to account for itself, without being reminded that it was Something Else. He wondered for an unreasoning moment whether, if he turned on a television set, any white people would appear at all, or whether everyone from Huntley and Brinkley to Matt Dillon would be transformed into a darker version, or at least have their voices dubbed as in a foreign movie.

He found the address, an old stone apartment building, mounted the stoop and, since the door was locked, searched for the name of Mike Thurgood beside the buzzers. Thurgood was the coordinator of the program, a former student of Bates's who had agreed to oversee the internship in return for some cheap legs; Bates had arranged for a foundation to pay their salaries and housing costs. A tall, thirtyish man in undershirt, jeans and socks came to the door so quickly that he at first seemed to be just another resident. It was Thurgood, who had seen him coming, "ten miles away," he said without a big enough smile, from his first-floor apartment window.

"You guys stand out like narcs," Thurgood said, shaking his head and ushering the newcomer into his place.

"Thanks," he said, without sarcasm. At least it wasn't just him. "Now which one are you?"

"Richard Isaac," he said. "Ike."

"Okay, Ike. Here's your homework."

Thurgood handed him a folder including a manual on the league, some newspaper clippings and copies of various forms they would be dealing with. He also gave Ike a set of keys, quickly demonstrated three of them on the outer and inner front doors, and led him upstairs to his room.

"Carl, your roommate, isn't here yet," Thurgood said. "But everybody's due in by this afternoon. We'll have a meeting at seven in my place, and you start work tomorrow. Later, man."

The room they shared was a one-room apartment with kitchenette and bath; his first big-city place, and it was the Harlem equivalent of a dorm. There were three such rooms on the third floor, where the men would stay, and three on the second floor for the women, another reminder of collegiate segregation. Carl came in a while later carrying a deck of cards in his pocket, which Ike took to be a promising sign. He had played only a few halfhearted hands during the year, but he thought, now, that he could get over that. The two of them had already begun to reconnect when they joined the others at the meeting, where all the students introduced themselves, primarily for Thurgood's sake. Reggie, who had led the rescue operation in the library tower, was there. Going into his senior year, he was the oldest; most would be juniors like Ike, several from his urban policy class, and there were a few sophomores, including the one whose body language defied anyone to make something of the fact she was from Westchester, and whose slightly Asian-tilted eyes forced Ike's to his shoes when she caught him staring.

They left Thurgood's apartment as a group, to walk the streets for a while—better a team of tourists than individual gawkers. A guy from Queens took the lead as the unofficial guide, but the outing was less about landmarks like the Apollo, the Theresa and Small's than about checking out the folks and riding the rhythms. Afterward, they returned to one of the rooms to talk and listen to music—no one had serious equipment, but you could trust the radio in New York—into the night.

The next day, as Thurgood had promised, they went right to work. The league office was around the corner, on Eighth near 125th, a storefront cluttered with paper and soon crowded by the eager recruits. There weren't enough desks and chairs for all of them, so after more introductions to the permanent staff and a little this-is-here-that's-over-there talk, some went back to their rooms to work, studying case records, familiarizing themselves with names of landlords, agents and lawyers and city bureaucracy. When Thurgood thought they knew enough not to embarrass themselves, he sent them out into the field, following up on old complaints to see if anything had been done, interviewing tenants who had called with new complaints, canvassing people in buildings owned by problem landlords to turn up new complaints. Working in rotating teams of two, they spent half a day in a building, took a break, logged reports at the office and stayed to work the phones or returned to apartments where no one had answered. About half seemed familiar with the landscape, though only two or three had actually lived in neighborhoods like that. The rest were getting a crash course in the reality they always talked about in Uhuru classes.

Yet they all managed to get used to it fairly quickly. In the evenings and free hours they took to the Muslim bakery and fish store on 125th, hit the black-owned Mickey D's for lunch and sometimes La Famille for smothered chops on fat days. They roamed the tiny aisles of Michaux's bookstore, stockpiled hair-care supplies for the remote winter and sampled authentic fashions like the latest in men's high-heeled shoes. They went across the river when Oakland came to the Stadium, and they drifted to the legendary courts to watch the Rucker tournament, some of them even matching their own educated moves with local talent; Carl, for one, wasn't half bad, although his game, in that context, was more like that of an old-timey, earthbound City College guard. They made dependable reefer contacts, but only for outside consumption—Thurgood was a bloodhound. They did the Studio Museum and the National Black Theater and the Schomburg library. Occasionally they ventured farther, most often to a jazz club on the Upper West Side, but time and pride kept them mostly in Harlem.

Actually performing their duties, however, was a bit more difficult than settling into the routine. The tenants, invariably, were suspicious, indifferent or too gabby, like the woman who kept Ike and Carl sitting for three hours going on about her husband, her children, her daughter's boyfriend, her relatives in South Carolina, the women in her church and everything else but the landlord. Gradually they learned to become more official the friendlier the client. Yvonne, the sultry (or was it surly?) suburbanite, was notorious for charming her way through a door and then, notebook in hand, cutting the crap. And if a tenant copped an attitude, she would pull a reversal: instead of acting the efficient social worker, *she* would become the outraged sister, putting the client on the defensive for not cooperating (as if she were the one with bad plumbing and a broken fire escape) and stalk out of the apartment. After that, the tenant was often more receptive to a visit from another team.

Late on a Friday morning at the end of the third week, Ike got a chance to witness her performance. She hadn't walked out—Ike was waiting for that—but she had stopped a fussing old woman in the middle of a harangue about outsiders stirring up trouble. When Yvonne finished telling her that she would be *ashamed* to spend her good money and have to live like that, the woman slipped her eyes quickly to the water spots on the wall and the tattered drape that didn't conceal the broken window and said well, maybe you do have a point and invited them to sit down. After she had told what she had to tell and they had stood to go, she reminded them that it was her trouble and she had always taken care of herself just fine. Yes, Yvonne said, putting a hand on her bony shoulder, but you don't *have* to. Just remember that.

"So what do you think?" she asked Ike as they started down the stairs.

"I think she'll be in the office first thing Monday morning."

"I hope so. You didn't see the bathroom."

"How'd you do that?"

"That one was easy. She was just like my grandmother. Always told me never to talk back and stayed in my face until I did. Then she was happy."

As they hit the bottom step, Ike noticed two teenagers burst through the front door. He shifted his weight to give them a clear path to the stairs and took Yvonne's arm to ease her to the side. By the time he realized their first step was *not* to the stairs, it was too late. Before they had even completed the side step, they were thrown into the darkness beneath the stairway.

Give it up!

The corner of his eye saw the blade, about as shiny as an old butter knife, licking Yvonne's throat; he envied it, even as he figured out that was what he was feeling in his ribs. There was a clatter as the bag was torn from her shoulder and spilled on the tile floor. He felt a slap on his behind and knew his wallet was gone.

C'mon, man, get it.

Yvonne's body sagged slightly. His shadow lingered for a second and parted. He saw her things scattered on the floor, the money obviously plucked from the remains, and two forms scurrying for the door. And then he remembered.

"Hey, *wait!* I need that," a voice hollered, and Ike lunged toward the door. The figure recovered its balance and whirled.

"The wallet. I need the wallet. Take the money—"

The blade came up and hesitated.

Shit, muhfucka.

"Ike—"

"Take everything—"

A strong left hand seized his collar. The blade was at eye level.

"I *need* the wallet."

The blade wavered. Ike flinched. A door opened. He fell back.

They were gone. He felt Yvonne's hand on his back but scrambled to his feet and ran out the door. The wallet was on the sidewalk. The rapid sound of rubber slapping pavement dissolved into the traffic. The paper was still in his wallet. Yvonne appeared at the door.

"You all right?" he asked her.

"Yeah, but what's wrong with you? You nearly got cut."

"I know, but I'm okay."

He put his hands on her shoulders, although he wasn't sure which of them needed steadying more.

"Your girlfriend's picture?" she asked, noticing the wallet in his hand.

"No, it's an address. I remembered I don't have it copied down anyplace else."

"Hm. Sure hope it's important."

He helped her throw the stuff back in her bag and they left the building.

"Let's take a cab," she said when they got to the avenue. "I want to get away from here."

"With what?"

One foot already off the curb, she looked down at her bag.

"Shit. All right, we'll have to take the bus."

"You got tokens? I was going to buy some."

She sighed. "It's twenty blocks."

"Nice day, though." Her frustration was beginning to make him feel better.

"Damn, Isaac," she said as they started down the street. "Your luck always this bad?"

"Not at all. I thought it was you."

Reading the near miss as an omen, Ike decided to begin his search the next day, while Thurgood had some of the group making follow-up visits and others went to check out *Shaft* at the movies. He told himself he had stalled because he wanted to get to know the neighborhoods better; he knew that he probably needed to know himself better. There was no time, though, and he didn't even have Clyde to cling to, just the piece of paper he had stolen from Elizabeth's dresser ten years ago, with an address Hodge had scribbled down. It was old then. He had planned to write a letter and put it back, but he couldn't think of anything to say, so he kept it, waiting for *her* to mention it, to acknowledge the connection and begin a conversation that went beyond snide comments. In all those years, even when he had changed wallets, it had never occurred to him to copy the address. The paper itself came to be a sacred relic, although he had actually forgotten it for years, and if it did not force her to give him back, it would, one day, lead him to the answers himself. And this was the day.

The address was not far. Somebody had already canvassed a

building a couple of blocks down on the same street, and Ike himself had casually glanced around when they went for walks, hopelessly searching for a tall, light-skinned, gray-haired man—before it hit him, chillingly, that he would only be in his early forties. That alone had put him back several days. It was one thing to confront an old man about an irreclaimable past; it was another to meet a relatively young man and deal with possibilities of a future. On this stretch of Eighth Avenue, though, it wasn't easy to tell young from old. There were men barely past his age who looked tired and used up. He did not bother to search those faces. No matter what had happened, and it could have been literally anything in all that time, the idea that Lonnie could have landed itching and empty among the junkies on the curb was inconceivable.

The building itself nearly sickened him, though he had been in sadder ones just that week and there was no reason to believe that, seventeen years ago, it was any worse than the one in which he had spent that other Saturday morning waiting to say goodbye. He went to the door and was relieved *not* to find the name—but then, there weren't any names, and the inner door was locked.

"He'p ya?"

An old man loomed on the sidewalk behind him, wearing a greasy brown sports jacket, dirty plaid slacks and a Yankees cap.

"You live here?" Ike asked.

" 'Chu want?"

"I'm looking for somebody. Man named Lonnie Isaac." The old man tilted his head and squinted his eyes. The odor, more wine than bodyfunk, finally reached Ike. "I'm with the Tenants Rights League."

"Isaac, huh?" For a moment it looked as though he were going to fall asleep. "Don't think I know him."

"You live here?"

"Tenants League? Whas that?"

"He needs our help. The door is locked, do you know how I can get in?"

"Isaac. No, that was Isaac sumpn, not sumpn Isaac . . . "

Ike turned his back and started knocking on the door.

"Aks Wilson."

"What?"

"Wilson. 1B. Aks him, he might know."

"Thanks," Ike said, and found the buzzer.

"Say, bro, you, uh . . ."

Ike scooped some change out of his pocket, looked around to make sure there wasn't a line forming, and slapped it into the old man's hand.

"Isaac . . ."

A short, fat man opened the door and replaced it with himself. "Yes?"

"I'm looking for somebody," Ike said.

"Yes?"

"Lonnie—Alonzo Isaac."

"Who are you?"

"I'm with the Tenants Rights Action League."

"I'm sorry, there's nobody here by that name."

"Do you know if somebody in the building might know him? He used to live here."

"I don't recall anybody by that name living here."

"Well, it was a while ago."

"I've been here a while."

"It was, uh, seventeen years ago."

"You say you're with the Tenants Rights Action League?"

"Yeah, I am, but . . . my name is Richard Isaac." The man-door didn't budge. He was going to make it hard. "He's my father. I'm looking for my father."

"I see. Well, I'll tell you. If he did live here, Miss Hill might know him. She's been here a lot longer than that."

"Is she in?"

Something moved in his face that Ike thought might be the idea of a smile. "Let's see," he said.

Wilson moved, like a tank reversing direction on a narrow road, and Ike followed him upstairs to a dark corridor where he momentarily lost sight of the man and heard only fat breathing. Wilson knocked.

"Hello?"

"Miss Hill?"

"That you, Wilson?"

"Yeah, it's me, baby." The door cracked open. "Sorry to disturb you. Have you got a minute? There's a young man here wants to talk to you."

The door opened to a woman leaning on a walker. The place smelled of Wizard. She wore a wig slapped carelessly on a hair net.

"Hello. Richard Isaac."

"What can I do for you?"

"He says he's looking for his father. You remember a man named—"

"Lonnie Isaac. He came here about seventeen years ago. From upstate. Tall, light-skinned. Curly hair."

"No, I don't . . . wait a minute, now. Isaac. Say he your daddy?"

"That's right."

"Come on over here." She peered up spookily into him. He felt a surprisingly large hand on his face. "Talk."

"Well, like I said, my name is Richard Isaac, and I just came to town a few weeks ago and I'm looking for my father." He tried to recall the voice, an inflection, a rhythm, but he had nothing to work with. "I haven't seen him since I was about three." Self-conscious, he glanced at Wilson, who nodded. "My uncle wrote down this address. It was a long time ago, but this is where he stayed when he came to New York . . ."

"Good-lookin yella nigger," she said.

Oh shit. "You know him?"

"I think—yes, yes. Railroad man."

"That's right," he said, reaching out for her hand.

"Wasn't here long. Not him. That was a movin Negro." She looked at Ike and away. "Moved out after a year or so."

"Do you know where he went?"

"No, can't say that I do. Up on thirty-somethin, I believe. Saw him back around here sometime. He always spoke. Yes, he was a charmer. I do remember him."

"But do you remember where he went?" He was squeezing her hands.

She pulled loose, shook her head and moved away. "I'm sorry, son. Oh, you know . . . wait a minute. Mattie Taylor. You know her, Wilson?" He shook his head. "She used to go down, oh, one of them big buildings downtown, you'd know it but I just can't call it, she used to clean down there, you know. I believe she mentioned him one time, that he was somewhere by her, you know. Maybe in her building. I'm just not sure. But it was over thirty-second, thirty-third, over from Lenox there. Yes. She might be able to help you. If you can find her. She might still be there. I haven't seen her in years. Mattie Taylor, that's her. Little fast-talkin woman. She should be retired by now."

"Thank you, Miss Hill. Thanks so much."

"That's all right, son. Hope you find him, that's what you want. You know, you do favor him. I can see that. Do him proud."

"Don't get your hopes up too high," Wilson said as he sank, step by step, down the stairs.

"What do you mean? She said she knows him."

"Yeah, but at her age the mind plays tricks. She didn't look too sure. I took you to her because you wanted something to go on. She might have seen the same thing."

"We'll see about that. Either way, thanks."

"All right, brother."

Ike ran out into the street looking for a phone booth. When he found one, three blocks away, it had no directory. The next one didn't even have a phone, so he kept running all the way back to the league office.

"Thought I gave you the day off," Thurgood said when Ike entered panting.

"Hey, I just love my work."

"Well look here, man, we got some follow-ups."

Ike held up a hand. "Just passin through. I gotta check somethin." He grabbed a Manhattan phone book and a pad of paper. There were a couple of Matties and several M. Taylors. But with Thurgood hovering he couldn't do much. He wrote down some numbers and addresses and dashed out. Slow down, Ike, he told himself. Enough for one day. He lives. Sonofabitch, it wasn't all a dream. Knowing it would be much too weird to call home and ask to talk to Clyde, his old teddy bear, he went to his room, pulled out a subway and a bus map, and fell asleep planning his approach.

That night they all went to see the Stylistics at the Apollo. Ike thought the place a bit tacky for its reputation. The building, despite all the old-theater touches, was worn and musty. The crowd, perhaps inevitably, was young and not nearly as fly as they thought. And the show itself was well on the hokey side: the MC with the jive DJ rap, all rhyme and rhythm and resplendent adjectives without a shred of sincerity; the warm-up acts with maybe one modest black-radio hit who all looked, sounded and moved like somebody else; even the stars of the show, who drew a magical response as much from the steady increase in quality as from the act itself. But with lyrics like "stop, look, listen to your heart," the youngest kid in the audience could have predicted the choreography—or in fact have staged it. After Woodstock and the monster tours playing sites like Madison Square Garden, this was like a time warp—fifties doo-wop theater. It might have been fun, in a nostalgic sort of way, if he'd been in the mood.

Although the show started late (of course), everything moved along briskly; the choreography between acts was tight. This wasn't no be-in, love-in, drop-in. This here was a *show*, and there were more folks waiting outside for another at ten o'clock. There had been some talk among the group of where they would go after, but Ike hadn't participated. He'd only agreed to do the Apollo because it *was*, and he was hoping it would take his mind off Mattie Taylor. It didn't. But he was dressed, and there was no TV in the room, so when they voted to grab two gypsy cabs down to a midtown club, he was in.

It was amazing that New York City was as democratic as a college campus, where word circulated that there was a black party and everybody simply showed up. He would have thought that in a place that big, there would be dozens of different spots for different folks. And maybe there were. But in this barn of a place two blocks into the darkness off Broadway, it seemed that every black person in Manhattan between eighteen and twenty-five with the price of a ticket (or maybe just everyone who had heard the promos on WWRL, which was about the same thing) turned up.

College students and secretaries, stockboys and bank tellers, sales clerks and transit workers, nurses, drug dealers, social workers—there was no telling who they were unless you got into a deep rap, and then everybody would be lying. It was a party, a professional party, with none of the chummy intimacy of a dorm lounge and all the grim abandon of people who worked all week and had this time to purge the demons and regenerate their souls. Run this line, work this step, get high, get happy, get laid *to*night.

Ike, dancing from dim memory, finished a three-song set working out with a big-leg woman who clutched her shoulder bag and never once looked him in the eye, and then caught his breath at the endless line at the bar. His rayon shirt was pasted to his back, and his chest was sore, having been beaten to death by the Cancer medallion he decided would have to go.

"How you doin?" Yvonne showed no trace of sweat, although she had been hopping, too; he'd followed her body bouncing on the floor.

"I may have lost a few pounds."

"You seemed out of it earlier," she said. "I thought you might be upset about yesterday."

"Oh, no. Thanks. I haven't thought about it much, really." He had already decided, walking back to the office and getting her to share uptown insights she'd withheld from the group tours, that the Evilonne tag she'd been given wasn't entirely fair. He appreciated her asking. "What about you?"

"It wasn't the first time," she sighed. "Niggers're probably in here, if they're old enough. Buy me a drink?"

They sipped and surveyed the floor silently for a while. It was one of the more comfortable awkward moments Ike could remember. A slow song came on—the Stylistics again—and she took his hand and nodded toward the crowd. Several men, he noticed, must have timed the DJ the way Lou Brock timed pitchers; they were already in position to move in. And maybe he had done the same thing without thinking about it. Maybe he was better than he thought.

The song seemed less silly without the gestures. The genius of those musical candy bars was in the possibilities they offered for your own movements, from the shoulders to the knees at close range, and the way they absolutely dared you to break into a loud, shit-talking falsetto. She didn't look at him either, at first, but he liked floating over her face, and the feel of it lightly on his chest.

"What is it?" she said, opening her eyes and catching him looking.

"You're very pretty."

"You think so?"

"I've thought so for a while."

"Why didn't you say so?"

"Never got this close."

"Maybe you should have."

"Maybe."

"Well, thank you."

"You're welcome. Can I ask you a question?"

"You always talk this much when you dance?"

He shut up, and when the song ended, they moved toward the stairs to the balcony, away from the group table. He kept a hand on her back until the crush of people forced it off.

"How come everybody thinks you're so evil?" he asked as they settled into the last free table.

"Do you?"

"Yeah, sometimes."

She looked out over the floor, and there was a sudden silence as the music cut off and the featured act was about to be introduced. He was startled when she turned back and spoke, not loudly but not softly.

"I don't like to play," she said. "That bothers a lot of people. I know who I am and I feel good about myself. If people don't like what they see, that's their problem. And I don't have time for people who feel they have to apologize for who they are."

"I see," he said, but the offensive continued.

"I know I've been lucky. Most of the people I grew up with were in pretty good shape, financially. Because their parents worked hard to get there, and to teach them they were just as good as anybody else. Then in high school all of a sudden people started feeling guilty about not being poor. Like anybody *wants* to be poor. Same thing in college. There's this collective guilt trip about being Ivy League, like it's not a legitimate thing for black people to be. Nobody says it, but it's like you're supposed to pretend you're sorry you're smart or that your parents aren't poor. Well, I'm not sorry. I like it. And so do they."

"I just figured that you thought you were cute," he said.

"I do. I think you are, too. Now can I ask you a question? What was in that wallet that you were willing to get sliced up for?"

"Got some time?" he asked. She nodded yes, and he told her the story of Lonnie Isaac, what he knew, down to Mattie Taylor. The group had begun to sing, so he had to edge closer, his arm around her chair, explaining his history to an occasionally nodding 'fro and a gold hoop with a half-horse archer. When he finished, the head remained still for a moment, then turned, bringing her face an inch from his, before she put her hand on his shoulder and leaned to his ear.

"We can all help," she said. "It shouldn't be too hard."

"No, thanks. I don't want to turn this whole thing into some kind of search party."

She left her hand on him and kind of peeked around the corner to his face.

"Is it all right if I help you find her?" she asked.

"I'd like that."

After that, they often asked Thurgood to team them if his Mattie Taylor charts indicated a suspect near a building to be canvassed. If that didn't work, and it never did, they separated themselves from the group once or twice a week—*everyone* noticed and read more into it than there was—to go on a Mattie hunt. When Manhattan ran dry, he combed the league records and she checked outer-borough phone books.

In the middle of July, on a muggy Saturday morning, they rode the train out to the backside of Queens. It was a miserable ride. The novelty of the search had begun to wear off for her—she had begged off a trip to the Bronx earlier that week—and he was lousy company. This would be the one, he was sure, and that certainty, along with the heat and the unswept Friday night debris in the rattling car, made him tense and irritable. As if that weren't enough, he had turned twenty two days before, and nobody knew. Except Elizabeth, of course, who called him at the office. The rooms didn't have phones, either. And maybe Lonnie, if he was still keeping track, but since there hadn't been a card since he was four there wasn't much hope of that.

When the hour-long train leg ended, they stood before a dry cleaners on a wide, busy avenue that would have put downtown back home to shame—could this still possibly be the same *city?*—and argued over where to wait for the bus. She'd hardly ever been in Queens before, and he was the one who had pinpointed all the addresses and planned all the routes and they'd always gotten where they were going. But when the bus came she turned out to be right, and they had to sprint a block across traffic to make it, which under normal circumstances might have made at least one of them laugh but this time only left them both sweating and glaring out of opposite windows. It was turning out to be such a hassle that he was beginning to think he should have called first. He usually didn't, because it was such a weird thing to try to explain over the phone—and because he kept hoping that seeing him might make a difference, as it had with Miss Hill. No, this was the right way to do it, but as they trudged the last six blocks from the bus stop, he tried desperately to think what he would do if she was not at home.

A dog barked as they opened the gate to the small yard and mounted the steps of the kind of house Ike didn't know they had in New York: the same aluminum-sided, crammed-together places they had in the rest of the world, the houses where nice, normal colored people lived. A man whose Afro was slightly too big for his age—the hairline gave him away—answered the door. Through the screen, Ike introduced himself and explained that he was looking for Mattie Taylor; he was trying to locate Lonnie Isaac, somebody he thought she might know. The man told them to hold on a minute, a look of confusion defeating the one of suspicion on his face, and retreated into the house.

"Mama," they heard him say. "Some kids out here looking for somebody name Isaac. They think you know 'im."

"*Bingo!*" Yvonne whispered.

Ike raised an eyebrow and shrugged slightly, trying to see into the house. His fingernails were strip-mining his palms.

"Well what you leave 'em standin out here for?" said a squeaky voice over the quick flapping of sandals.

"I ain't never seen them people before."

"Don't mind him," she said pushing open the screen. "Come on in the shade. Too hot out there, must be eighty-five already." She was a small woman with a red wig and bifocals and a flowered housecoat. "Now, how may I help you? You ain't no Witnesses, I know, 'cause I done shooed them away already. They get here early."

"Thank you," Ike said. "I wonder if you could give me any information on a man named Lonnie Isaac."

"Lonnie Isaac?"

"A tall, light-skinned—"

"Yeah, I know who you mean, I just ain't heard the name in a while."

"A Miss Hill, on 117th Street, said you might be able to help me. He's my father."

"Oh, I see. You children sit on down. Tyrone? Ty*rone!* Help me with that pitcher of iced tea out here. How is Mabel Hill anyway? Wasn't doin any too good last I heard."

"Well, she seems to be getting by."

"Yeah, I guess that's about all you can ask. Sit down, sit down. What's wrong with this boy?"

They sat lightly on the plastic covering on the sofa on the enclosed porch that was more of a room, with its furniture, flowers and carpet. Yvonne stroked the back of his hand.

"Relax," she said. "It's over."

She was right. They had found Mattie Taylor, and she knew his father. But she didn't know where he was. Tyrone came out with a pitcher of iced tea on a tray, and Ike decided he resented Tyrone, who was old enough to be his father, for being there.

"I sure didn't know Lonnie had a boy," she said, flapping back out to take a seat on the porch.

"He never said anything about a family?"

"No, as a matter of fact he didn't. Reckon he didn't seem old enough to me. He was 'bout the same age as my Tyrone, but he was overseas at the time, and Lonnie was just like a son to me. Stayed down the hall and ran errands for me and things, you know. And I helped him out a little when he was out of work. He was down at Penn Station for a while, then gave that up, always looking for somethin new."

"Do you know if he's still in town?" Ike asked. He took a sip of the tea, which was good, laced with mint, but put the glass down when he felt his hand shaking.

"I don't believe so. He wandered off 'bout the time Tyrone came home. Said he was goin down South. For what, I don't know. I like to think if he come back he woulda been in touch, but you never know. That was some time ago."

Bile eased up the back of Ike's throat. He grasped the tall, frosted glass and squeezed it hard, drawing the coldness into him. He heard ice rattle and felt Yvonne take the glass from him. She said something to Mattie Taylor and Mattie Taylor blathered on. She had her son; one was as good as another. Yes, it was over. Yvonne would close the interview. She knew what to do, and even kept a hand gently on his knee as he slumped back into the plastic. Outside, just a few feet from the porch, two boys stepped by, talking loudly. They were thirteen or fourteen, their faces bearing an anger they couldn't explain. Most likely they were orphans, too, their fathers, maybe knowingly, maybe not, watching them without expectation from cars, storefronts, the bedroom windows of women who were not their mothers. Somebody's sons. And now Ike was one of them. Lonnie would not be coming back. The amnesia wasn't temporary. It was willful and permanent. Another mother fucking rooster, that's all. But if what he felt was hatred, it wasn't for the man, if you could call him that; it was for the woman who had failed to hold him, who had been right about him all along.

chapter 15

It really was beautiful, spectacular in fact. Driving over the crest of the hill to see the lake, parting the earth to the horizon, Ike felt as though he were entering a hidden paradise. But he had entered the town a hundred times before, and, except maybe for the first time—he couldn't remember—it had never had that effect on him, even before he became accustomed to the flatness of Princeton. How could he, and so many others, spend so much time here and not realize how magnificent it was? All he had to go on was the boarded-up memory of that free week at the end of freshman year. Everybody else remembered mostly the Halloween-to-Easter snow, which along with the relentless pressure and bleak interiors conspired to rob them of their sight, to keep their very surroundings a secret. If he tried to tell Yvonne and the others who were so eager to leave, they'd think he was tripping. Better they all figured it out for themselves someday.

Right now, they were probably too busy getting fucked up; that was the routine. All-week jams and round-the-clock whist and bottles of Brass Monkey and seedless smoke and furtive, furious coupling with people you'd had your eyes on for four years. Ike had been rather looking forward to it. But when it had been his time, a year before, he had spent the final days hanging around with Juanita and Malik, which he could do because Yvonne had left for home right after exams to start working. It had been a good time, brief but long enough to remember the closeness they'd almost shared after Gene went away. They were getting ready to go away themselves, back to the city; she had given up on waiting for Gene to get better and come back for them. She didn't put it that way, of course. She talked about not wanting Malik to grow up around all those rednecks and intellectual hypocrites, bourgie college Negroes and downtown folks who acted as if they had simply fallen off the underground railroad and forgotten where they were going. They tried, her people, but they were just stuck there, and although she had worked with them full-time since she came off the hill, she had her baby to think about. That was what she said, while refusing to discuss the things they'd both heard: that Gene had returned from Cuba and was into some weird shit down South with a worker's party fringe group—when he was able to function.

He had almost forgotten about her until, in his senior year, he had finally gotten around to working with kids downtown, as he'd promised Gene he would. His schoolwork was no longer an excuse—he had that beat by then—Uhuru politics were wearing thinner than ever, and the social whirl with Yvonne left him feeling he ought to do something more substantial. (How many hours of community service would it take to balance one Howard Homecoming and two Penn relays?) So he bopped down to the center to volunteer, and there she was, extending Gene's work after she'd dropped out to have his baby. He ran into her fairly often after that when he came down for his twice weekly tutoring sessions, and even more often he ran, literally, into Malik, who knew a dozen ways to escape the confines of the day-care room and zoom heedlessly around the halls, through the gym, up and down the stairs. You couldn't walk into the place without meeting the kid, usually with your legs, and if you didn't have your balance together, he was liable to take you down. Everybody, at some point, bitched about it—the weather, white folks and that hardhead boy were equally handy topics of passing conversation—but without him, they all knew, there would be no Juanita, and nobody else was going to spend twelve hours a day there, filling in for day-care teachers, teaching African dance and double-dutch, opening up for Cub Scout meetings, organizing basketball tournaments and after-school parties. So they tolerated him, braced themselves for his kamikaze assaults or occasionally dodged and let him bang himself into a wall for spite. Ike took special pleasure in gathering him up and returning him to Juanita, if he could find her, and if not, trying to hold him in his lap for a few minutes while he explained the New Deal or Julius Caesar to an earnest ninth-grader.

But they never had much chance to talk, he and Juanita, until the last week, when they were both settling up affairs and he offered to take Malik to the park to give her a break and then help pack. She still lived in the first-floor apartment of the house directly across the street from the center. The living room was much as he remembered it, dark and sparse. (There was no TV; no wonder the kid went berserk.) Most of the pictures on the walls, of Garvey, Nyerere, Guevara, were the same ones that had been knocked cockeyed, that he stared at with her slumped across his lap. There was a new one of Malik, a giant Woolworth's portrait special that made the rest seem out of place. But he would have thought that, if she wasn't going to move, she would have changed more.

Boxing a shelf of books, several with Gene's name still in them, he gave in and asked, as casually as he could manage, if she'd ever found out what was in the letter. She ignored him to answer the tea kettle and returned momentarily with a pot of chamomile. Not exactly, she said sipping, but she had a pretty good idea. She thought that Hollyfield knew something about the burning cross freshman year. And how that white boy got shot. Knew something was funny all the time but lied to Gene because he'd been crossed, too. When he finished with the books, she asked, could Ike reach the wood carvings on the top shelf, too?

The last couple of years at the center would be good training, she said, redirecting the conversation, but she needed to go back to school, and life would be more stable for Malik at home, with her relatives around, than on that block, which had all the negatives of the city and none of the redeeming virtues. She talked about the things that had made a difference for her growing up, not so much the cultural institutions as the people themselves. The shopkeeper who watched her in his store after school, baby-sitting, without letting on, until her mother got home from work, and who would leave his nephew behind the register to take her down the street to hear Lenox Avenue orators, including Malcolm. The Sunday School teacher, a young widow, who took her to movies and bought her books from E.B. White to W.E.B. Du Bois. The junior-high boyfriend who became a junkie, kicked, and finally won an electrician's card. All were part of that self-contained shadow society that Elizabeth had degraded enough to propel him away from without a thought. And for the first time, all those endless harangues about going back to the community, cheered on by an elite-in-the-making who had no intention of ever setting foot again in Harlem, if indeed they ever had, began to make some sense.

It must have been four o'clock in the morning by the time he left her apartment, and he went back the next night although there was no packing for him to do. He went back to talk, for the first time in a long time, about his father and Elizabeth and Tommy and Hez and, indirectly, about Cheryl; he went back to try to explain who he was, because otherwise he feared he would leave without anyone ever knowing.

Ike briefly considered and rejected the notion of driving past the center and went straight to Yvonne's. Even her place, an old house perched near the top of the steep street that led downtown, looked brighter as Ike pulled up to park. But that, he knew, was because it was a typically leaden, snowy day the last time he'd been there, and he was pissed about having to leave early to go show himself to Elizabeth, who was pissed because he had cut out early on her at Christmas. The best thing about grad school, he decided, as he toted his bags up the wooden steps, was that he could honestly plead that he had so much work to do he couldn't worry about offending either of these women.

The first thing he noticed was that her 'fro was shorter; she'd had it trimmed for the occasion, and that, along with the sleeveless leotard, made her seem slimmer and more muscular.

"It's about time," she said at the door, with the pulled eyebrows and pursed lips that once earned her the name Evilonne. "I rushed out and did everything I had to this morning because I thought you'd be here by noon."

He ignored the pout and picked her up, the bangles that ran halfway to her elbow clattering musically behind his head. "I never said that," he told the gold hoop dangling from her ear.

"Well, I just thought you'd want to spend as much time with me as possible, since we're leaving tomorrow."

"I do, so stop bitching and kiss me already. You're getting heavy."

"I like your nerve," she said, returning to the floor after a quick, deep kiss. Despite the tone, her face had relaxed into the surprisingly broad grin with the small gap in front and dimples on the side. "I can remember you carrying me all the way into the bedroom, and I weighed more than I do now. How do I look, by the way?"

"Fantastic," he said, and she did. Not that she'd ever been fat, not even close, but she worried about it. Her constant workouts, including kung fu, hadn't so much taken off inches as solidified them.

"I take it the VIPs aren't here?" he asked, looking around belatedly at the apartment, which even in a similar state of disassembly looked more luxurious than Juanita's had.

"Not hardly. They took one look, a quick look, and headed for the hotel. I left it a mess so I'd have a good excuse to stay here tonight. Assuming I'd have some company, of course."

"You got it. Just let me stretch out for a few minutes and I'm all yours. What's doing tonight?"

"Dinner with the Josephs and Mr. Howard."

"Really? The living legend himself? I don't know if I'm up for all that."

He was lying on the sofa. She sat beside him and produced two joints.

"Don't worry," she said. "I'm going to get you up and keep you up."

Although he had seen the transformation many times, and again just minutes before, Ike marveled at what a little makeup and a dress could do. What looked like a bad mood in jeans and braids became regal haughtiness in clothes, an illusion she could maintain for hours before dropping her shoe and pressing his crotch under the table with her foot. Not this time, though, because the Josephs were waiting on the porch of the French restaurant, a small country house painted a dull yellow and set back from the road on a long gravel drive. And Bo Howard stood with them.

"Good to see you again, Ike," said her father, a vaguely nervous man whose smile would become much easier after a martini or two. The gap was his, Ike noted again. Her mother, who was not as big as Yvonne but whose gracious stillness made her seem more formidable, offered a smiling cheek and gave Ike a little hug. That was as good as it would get with her. Even Hodge had not been able to thaw her out that one Parents' Weekend when (despite Ike's and Yvonne's discouragement) they had all converged on campus. Always quick to sense a tough audience, Hodge had left her to match airs with Elizabeth and gone off to toss back a few and tell lies with Mr. Joseph.

"Ike," said Mrs. Joseph in her surprisingly light voice, "allow me to introduce our good friend, Bo Howard."

"It's an honor, sir," Ike said. "I've been hearing about you all my life."

That was true enough, although the things he'd heard in recent years he wouldn't care to repeat. Maier had told him how Howard's strong influence had helped bring more black students to the university, but Ike had also learned that Howard bitterly opposed the Black Studies program and the increasing separatist trend on campus. He had even tried to dissuade a white trustee from making a personal gift of one million dollars to support black student programs unless there were more guarantees of complete integration. And that was *before* the library takeover. Among black students, Howard came to be known, derisively, as "Uncle Bo," and even Yvonne, who had known him much of her life, rarely complained in public. Ike wasn't entirely comfortable with the label, knowing what he did about Howard's past and having heard his own share of Tomtalk. But he did wish the guy could be a little more cool.

The big man surrounded Ike's hand with his. "I know a few things about you, too, son," he said. For some reason, no reason, really, Ike had expected him to have a trace of a Southern accent, or a deep, rich voice; he sounded like a colored schoolteacher from home. "I made it my business to find out after Lilly told me about you, 'cause I can't believe anything she says where Von is concerned. Come on, let's go in so we can get served by midnight."

"I didn't know they had places like this around here," Ike said as they waited for a table.

"There's a lot of things you're not supposed to know when you're a student," Howard said, not softly. "The trustees make a big thing of meeting on campus, but when we get here, everything's always planned so we come into contact with as few students as possible."

"I guess that's why I never saw you around—or any of the others for that matter. I didn't even know you were on the board for a long time, until Yvonne told me."

"Well that's no accident. If they had their way I'd show up for every two-bit function that had anything to do with black or football and then go away. So I like to pick my own spots, and that means keeping what they call a low profile."

"Your table's all ready, Mr. Howard," the hostess said—so much for a low profile—and led them to a spot by a window where they would be able to watch the sunset. Heads turned, not because they were the only black people in the restaurant but because the customers, nearly all of them parents with graduating children, recognized the wide-shouldered man with the large head: the Ebony Flash, who, without a football, moved with all the speed of someone bound for the principal's office.

The waitress took drink orders and removed their pewter plates; Mrs. Joseph told Yvonne to sit up straight, and Ike fished for advice on his upcoming law internship in Washington. Howard confirmed that the firm was a good one, dropped a couple of names, doubted that Ike would get to do much interesting and suggested simply that he do whatever he was told an hour before he was told to do it. As he spoke, his eyes wandered toward the window a few times, but nothing else, even his mouth, seemed to move.

"Ike, didn't you tell me that Bo was the reason you came here?" said Mr. Joseph, sweeping the inside of his glass with an olive and beginning to thaw.

"That's right, I did."

"Well, I'll tell you, you made a good choice for the wrong reason," said Howard, a little looser himself. "I'm not sure mine was much better, but I didn't have as many options. I came because I knew they didn't want me. The football coach did, but he was the only one. He figured after the war others would be taking in more blacks, and you know we'd already had Levi Scruggs back in the thirties. Turned out the coach was further ahead than he bargained for. But once they took me I had to come, and he had to play me, though I suspect he was under some pressure not to, because it was his fault I was here."

"And the team was bad," Joseph added, signaling the waitress.

"Pitiful. They sure didn't have anything to lose."

"Why don't you tell these children what it was like, Bo," said Mrs. Joseph. "Yvonne knows all about Morgan, but you know they think they're the first to do everything." Having put the ball neatly into play, she turned her full attention to the just-arrived menu. Yvonne rolled her eyes.

Ike had hoped to hear more about Howard's Washington law career, his stint in Nixon's administration (at least he'd had sense enough to bail out after the first term) and the urban development stuff he was doing. But so far shoptalk had proved futile, and it was obvious he was going to have to sit through a few verses of The Way We Were.

"There were about a dozen of us at the time," he began, rolling his shoulders and leaning into the monologue as if approaching a huddle. "You don't hear about the others; three or four of them never graduated. One was a woman. We hardly ever saw her; she lived with a family downtown, and I think she went out with a fella down there. Anyway, you know how they say we never hear about the best ballplayers because they never make it off the block? Let me tell you something: these cats were good. I mean, they *scared* me. I was just a hard-workin small-town boy from up the road who knew how to carry a ball. These guys, some of them had been in the Pacific, they'd been working in the cities, they'd been around. And *sharp* . . .

"Most of us lived in this rooming house off campus. By that time we could live in the dorms, but nobody cared to. We went to class, worked, studied, stuck pretty much to ourselves and partied downtown at the Elks, late, after the Nu-Tones finished their fraternity gigs on the hill. Of course, we had 'em all to ourselves for a couple of years after word went around that the trombone player was caught in a room upstairs with somebody's date."

"Whaaat?" Yvonne interrupted.

"Well, the official version was that he was looking for the bathroom and she followed him. I was never convinced myself, 'cause I was in the kitchen at some of those jobs and saw what went on."

"Bo, please," said Mrs. Joseph; Mr. Joseph got a kick out of it.

"Anyway, about once a week we'd have these big poker games at the rooming house. This one fella was an engineer, and he had a big prelim coming up, the kind the white boys had nervous breakdowns just thinking about. Well, it was poker night, so he dropped out of the game for a couple of hands to go over the material. Blew that test away."

"What happened to him?" Ike asked.

"He just up and left one day. He was too smart for them and he wouldn't sweat for them, and they couldn't handle it and he couldn't be bothered. Went out to California. Has a small firm, gets some DOD money."

"Why didn't somebody do something when he left? We wouldn't stand for that now."

"Yvonne," Mrs. Joseph said.

"There wasn't anything to do," Howard replied. "What's the point of keeping somebody in school if he doesn't want to be there? I thought he was a fool for leaving, but that was his choice. Turned out he was right. He did okay. I think they make it too easy now, for everybody but especially for us. They've got these programs to bring you all in here and keep you here, and they don't care whether you learn anything. Don't care if you care, either. So they let you run around and tear up the place and give you Black Studies to keep you happy 'cause they know it ain't gonna do you no good. Meanwhile, the rules are still the same, but they've got you playing a different game."

Ike and Yvonne traded glances, choosing up to see which of them should try for the tackle.

"I understand what you're saying," Ike said—maybe he could

just kinda strip the ball—"but don't you think it's important to try to effect change? I mean, sometimes the rules are wrong. That's what the civil rights movement was about."

"But you didn't see anybody in Birmingham bargaining for amnesty. They broke the law and went to jail. Nobody went to Woolworth's trying to get a meal for free. And they were trying to get *into* the game—they weren't talking about black buses and black schools and black elections."

"That's just because it wasn't time yet," said Yvonne, arriving with the pursuit.

"Maybe it's not time now," said Mrs. Joseph calmly, seeking to even up the odds.

Yvonne ignored her. "I don't see where white rules have done us a lot of good," she said. "We have to affirm our own values, our own culture. Black Studies should be part of the curriculum; Europe isn't the whole world, you know. And besides, we should be able to learn things we can take back to the community."

Howard leaned back and smiled. "You're going to take Black Studies back to Westchester and do what, Von? What kind of marches you going to lead on Capitol Hill this summer?"

"But if black students don't take advantage of the opportunity to change the institution while they're here," Ike said, "how is it ever going to be made more equitable?"

"Don't worry about this place, man," Howard said, back in the huddle, and this time calling the play. "This doesn't count for anything. You wear yourself out fooling with these eggheads, you won't have anything left. You all didn't get here because of anything I or anybody else did on campus; it was what was happening out there. Get your paper. You want to make a differencc, go on out there and do it where it *makes* a difference. Then you come back with something in your pocket, and make all the rules you want to when you know what you're talking about."

"On that note," Mr. Joseph said, as Howard cruised into the end zone.

"I'll have the fish," said Mrs. Joseph.

After they dropped Yvonne off, Ike showed the Josephs a secret place behind the chapel to park the light blue Caddy, where they wouldn't have to walk for half an hour or struggle up the hill from the Valley to get to the quad. It was also appropriate, since they looked like they were going to church. It never failed: people who wore suits and ties all week looked ordinary on special occasions, while others, like the relative handful of black parents, *looked* like they were going someplace. It was the janitor-as-deacon syndrome, and in this context, it even applied to the Josephs, who were no strangers to finery. Their little girl was graduating from *college*, no matter that the feat was preordained, and every step announced that they were some*body*, you hear?

At least, nestled inside their aura, Ike could be fairly certain he wouldn't receive any surprises, like last year, when he'd arrived at the quad and found himself face to face with Rachel and those gleaming dark eyes, the ones that always asked and never expected. On the edge of the quad, two years after the fact, she had smiled the sad, triumphant smile of the accomplished victim and said simply: "You could have said good-bye."

There weren't any other wild cards in the deck, which was at once comforting and mildly disturbing. Yvonne had filled up his last two years—three, counting grad school. For Ike, that was almost a lifetime. But he'd gone over all that when he and Yvonne started to get serious, the wondering about whether he was missing something with his penchant for monogamy. Not that he'd had that many opportunities to do otherwise. He simply didn't *know* how to play the field—it obviously took some talent and determination. So he took solace in the rationalization that the sexual revolution was a fraud and he would rather have the security of a Somebody. As a result, to anyone who recognized him out there on the quad, he was unquestionably Yvonne's Ike. And that was okay.

He and her parents took a position by the founder's statue, one of the more popular venues, where he could stand on the base to see better and Mrs. Joseph could sit to rest. Elizabeth and a visibly aging Hodge had stood deep in the corner of the quad the year before. And although he had, of course, felt proud for her to be there, partly because those were the occasions when he could appreciate how young and attractive she still was, he was also pissed that he had to spend so much of the procession looking for her. The point was for her to see him, but God forbid he should miss returning a wave and have to hear about it the rest of his life. In fact, he probably would have missed her, but out of the corner of his eye on that last turn before they headed toward the stadium, he had noticed Juanita over on the library steps, draped in kinte cloth and holding up a grinning, waving Malik. Nothing could have surprised, or pleased, him more. Saluting them in the knowledge that he might well never see them again, he spotted Elizabeth in the foreground, discreetly returning what she had thought was a wave to her.

Now it was his turn to watch as the graduates, having shaped up like a mobilizing army, paraded around the quad by colleges, some engineers holding slide rules to distinguish themselves, architects brandishing T-squares and a batch of hotel students donning the traditional chef's caps in place of their mortarboards. Although most played it straight, there were plenty of dirty sneakers, worn jeans and even shorts beneath the academic costuming, the kinds of things that not long ago signified a kind of protest and now represented a status quo of unexceptional individuality. The ritualized combination of solemnity and mischief in the parade crystallized the irony of the moment for them: as students they were now undeniably adult, but as adults they were willfully, almost embarrassingly, childish.

But that was the white folks. Where in years past there had been considerable debate among black students over how much to buy into the symbolism—there had been lots of dashikis, shades and berets worn in recent processions and not a few black students who didn't bother at all—the vast majority of this year's class did as Ike had done, put on the stuff and make like A&M marching Purdue into the turf. Yvonne, toting her hat so as not to mess her do, strode by in the midst of a small tribe of black students who looked singularly out of place yet compellingly noble in that procession. Niggers could *wear* some robes.

"You see her, Lil?" her father called out after she had blown an all-purpose kiss in their direction.

"Mm-hm."

"Look good, don't she?"

"Yeah, but these others don't look like anything."

As their children marched past, parents split off from the perimeter to walk to the stadium. It saved a lot of time, although the procession was designed to allow all the parents to be seated before the students entered, even if they had to stand in line outside in those hot robes for half an hour. Ike was glad the weather was warm, though, because his graduation had been inside the gym, the alternative site for bad weather, which was not unusual. That had cost him a chance to be in the stadium, which he'd only visited twice, once during the bleak fall of sophomore year, when he'd been to every movie on campus and even found himself at a hockey game, and once in his senior year when all the folks had turned out for the debut of the first black drum major. They all left after halftime, just to make the point.

It wasn't a big stadium by major-college standards; everyone would probably have fit in the end zone section at Ohio State. But that was its charm. Like a minor-league baseball park, it was not a self-contained environment. The field was simply there, surrounded by some seats, and life went on just beyond. The seats on either side of the field were not divided for the home crowd and visitors. The wooden bleachers on the west were reserved for students; the steep concrete crescent on the east, looming over the hill and facing the lake, was for grown-ups. Sitting there for the first time now, Ike could see neat civilian neighborhoods across the tree-lined gorge a long kick from the end zone, school buildings where on game days nonfans went about their business barely a hundred yards from the field, and, stretching out behind the dais set up before the bleachers, the rest of the world.

The ceremony moved fairly quickly, helped by the tradition of eschewing outside speakers to avoid the hassle of deciding who would get honorary degrees, a practice that had seemed increasingly wise in years when the obvious choices, a Kissinger, for example, would have been entirely too controversial. Instead the no-longer-new president, a man less elegant but more solid than Ellsworth and pinched by fiscal, not political, pressures, gave his routine pitch. This time he added a dash of caution about corruption in high places and the responsibility of the educated man or woman to uphold order and justice in society. But except for the faculty and generous alums, to whom the speech, like a state of the union address, was really aimed, it was little more than the Last Lecture. Parents spent the hour digging the pageantry they had paid for, and students, like a baseball crowd tolerating "The Star-Spangled Banner," waited only to erupt in timed spontaneity. Which of course they did, the black students led by the drum major, who produced a baton and whistle and high-stepped them through the chaos.

Afterward, Ike and the Josephs met Yvonne at the chapel, and they drove back to her apartment. Ike had already loaded his stuff back into his car that morning before her parents picked them up, so the fact that he had spent the night at least seemed less obvious. Now he briskly helped load the Caddy, said his good-byes and split. He would do a long day of depressing face time with Elizabeth, leave instructions for shipping some stuff to DC and fly on out of there. It was Yvonne's idea; he hadn't planned to bother going home at all. But she wanted time to tend the home garden even if he didn't. So they agreed she would share the ride back to Westchester in the Caddy and tell them everything they wanted to hear, and nibble a few of her mother's meals (protesting all the time, no doubt, that they would spoil her beach shape) before meeting Ike at JFK to begin what he insisted on calling their honeymoon.

"De islands, mon. Jus like I pictured it!" Ike declared, looking up through his shades and wagging his head. "Coconuts . . . and *evryting*."

"If you're going to act like a tourist, you can just keep on walking. I know people here."

"Sorry, dear. I'll try to behave. I'm just a li'l ol country boy ain't never been noplace is all."

"I know, but you don't have to show it."

The air he drew in deeply as they crossed the tarmac was hot and sweet. The sunlight glaring on the hard, smooth ground and ricocheting off the terminal windows before them and the silver plane behind seemed to reflect color. If Europe was anything like Onondaga, he knew before he had taken a dozen steps why the white boys first came to the islands and kept coming now as tourists, as if this paradise were something handed down from generation to generation for family pleasure. But those proprietary notions were immediately refuted, at least to Ike's mind, by the reality of what he saw. This was a black place, a feeling he had more strongly even than that first day in Harlem, possibly because of the security guards and customs officials. The people in uniforms, the power suits, were black, too, not just all the workers, and he knew it wasn't his imagination or Yvonne's aura of familiarity that got them more gracious treatment than the elaborately ironic politeness shown the whites in line with them. She, naturally, was used to it; she was the first person he'd known who exceeded his own capacity for expecting to be treated well. He, however, feasted on the less-automatic smiles and the near-winks that surrounded them until they closed the doors of their rented Ford, turned on the air conditioning and cruised out onto the wrong side of the street.

"I forgot how much I hate running that gauntlet," she said, apparently unbothered by the left-handed driving.

"Really? I thought it was hip," he said. "Looked like they were happy to see us."

"I suppose so. They would have been even happier if I'd been alone, not that that fazes them much. It's true they don't get nearly as many black tourists, so it's kind of a kick. But they know the only way they're going to get big-time tips from us is to make us feel more important than the white folks."

"Damn, baby, you sure know how to bring a guy down. Here I was getting all into a homecoming thing."

"Sorry. For what it's worth, Daddy says it's even worse in Africa."

"Thanks. I guess."

But there was little time for disappointment, as Yvonne dutifully began describing the sights they passed as they swept around the edge of the island, past the waterfront and downtown shopping district, the cruise ships hovering like predators out in the bay and the luxury hotels guarding the far tip.

"So who did you hang out with—the guys on the boats or the homeboys?" he asked.

"Which would make you more jealous?" she asked, perversely fingering the stick shift. "Actually, when I've been here I spent the whole time shopping and eating with my mother."

"Uh-huh."

"See there. It doesn't pay to tell a man the truth."

They drove on around the far end of the island and there, overlooking the spot where the ferry left for St. John, stood the apartment building. It was a great deal her father had lucked into, she explained, leasing the apartment for business. It didn't get used as much as he had planned—a couple of regular clients used it for a week in the winter—but it had proved a good write-off and off-season retreat for the family. And he was certain there would be more developments in that area and hoped to buy in.

Inside, they dumped their bags, and Yvonne lit up while Ike perused the record collection her father kept there, a self-conscious sampling of jazz and show tunes, and a Harry Belafonte album for the colonially minded. Ike gave Miles some play and decided to jump in the shower; Yvonne, bless her heart, read his mind and joined him. The shower cap spoiled the fantasy a bit, as he realized she actually intended to get clean. He pressed on anyway, and when she slithered away he managed to drag her down on the bath mat, with the water splashing out over them and her protesting that the floor was *hard*. But the wet felt good, all of it, and they toweled off lightly and crawled into the living room, where they sat, still nude and damp, sharing a joint in the lazy, hot breeze from the open balcony door. Ike felt himself beginning to melt away, like a man who had sat down for the first time in a week, and staggered into the bedroom, this time hoping she wouldn't follow.

She didn't. When he awoke about an hour later, he did not see or hear her, so he pulled on a pair of shorts and walked to the balcony that hung out over the pool. She was there, as he expected, gliding slowly and powerfully from one end to the other. She had abandoned the cap and goggles she sometimes wore for serious workouts. This was showtime. She was premiering a shiny, pink two-piece just substantial enough to hold everything in place and skimpy enough to hint that the next stroke might set her free. And instead of endless laps, she frequently raised up languorously out of the water, arched her back and strode to the end of the diving board, flexing her buttocks and rolling her shoulders. She knew that Ike would, sooner or later, be looking, and in the meantime she knew that it was about time for whatever dishraggy white women there might be around to show up for their afternoon dip. She also, certainly, had noticed, as Ike just did, two young men who worked at the complex standing in their hot polyester uniforms at the pool entrance admiring her form. They were obviously used to sneaking out to size up the women who came there in search of color and texture, some of them certainly quite attractive, although Yvonne no doubt would say that was a matter of coincidence; buzzards weren't choosy. But they knew, as she did, that this here was the good stuff. In fact, Ike found that he was even more drawn to the sight of them watching her than he was to her. It was, after all, a reflection on his good taste—and his incredible luck—that he was there with this golden lady.

He had a better chance to show her off that night, when they ate dinner in a hotel restaurant overlooking the harbor and later danced in the lounge, the kind of place where rum-punched white tourists got crazy over old Motown hits. That was just the warm-up. Afterward, Yvonne led him to another place, not quite the real thing but closer to it, an upstairs club a couple of blocks away from the waterfront shops. Islanders mingled with black visitors under the spell of a patois-rapping DJ who easily mingled reggae and calypso, Stevie and Barry White and the Ohio Players. Diaspora boogie: bumping and jumping-up through the funk, Ike laughed down the memory of practicing lame steps from *Hullabaloo* and *American Bandstand* for his hapless, tentative forays to Douglass Center, at least two lifetimes ago.

In the morning, with remarkably little sleep because of the night's activities, public and private, they returned to the waterfront, where he impressed her with his apparently unmasculine tolerance for shopping; he was not only patient but an active participant as well. And while he was not immune to predictable lures like stupid straw hats and T-shirts, he also showed an eye for tops and dresses, watches, earrings and more bangles. He even understood her resistance to buying swimwear, on the principle that you don't buy things on vacation to wear while you're there. He had been raised well, for some things, although when Yvonne offered that observation he insisted that the skills were innate.

Afternoon found them at heart-shaped Sweetheart Beach, strolling past the restricted public section, where the locals could get an eyeful of the yellow-suited Yvonne, and on to the nearly deserted tourist section, where they photographed each other in seductive poses and played backgammon till sundown. In the process, she changed his notion of sun and sand from the smug, provincial playground of the Beach Boys he had bitterly resented growing up. It still wasn't exactly his thing, but it was definitely Yvonne's, which meant it wasn't simply a white thing either. On the following day, after a comical round of tennis, they ferried to an even more luxurious beach on neighboring St. John and played *From Here to Eternity* in the surf, but a downpour caught them before the climax and they pulled everything back in place and ran soaked and breathless to wait for the boat and raced laughing with anticipation into the apartment to finish what they'd started on the living room floor with the balcony door open and their pent-up screams bouncing off the surface of the pool below.

It didn't take long, however, to reach the far side of paradise. The sense of impending loss, like that moment you begin to feel the carousel slow down, closed in on Ike toward the end of dinner at an Italian restaurant nestled in the hills above the harbor, on the last night. As if to prolong the ending, his mind retreated to the beginning: her defiant pose in Thurgood's Harlem apartment; the fleeting thrill he felt when he saw her pinned but not subdued beneath the staircase; the surprisingly soft feel of her against his chest, dancing to the Stylistics; and most of all, the saving touch of her hand on his leg on Mattie Taylor's porch.

"What is it?" She was licking her Courvoisier glass, scanning the sky, when she caught his gaze. She always caught him; that hadn't changed. But he liked it when she looked up, her smooth throat suggesting unsuspected vulnerability in a body that grew more powerful in the sun. And absorbed color like Polaroid glasses.

After three days, she was nearly two shades darker, and the red-shaded bronze gleamed in the light of the burned-down candle on their table. Even more than the constant swimming and the futile tennis instruction, the sun shaped her arms and legs by highlighting curves more subtly than the Vaseline on Valerie's ebony legs in junior high.

"I was thinking about New York."

"Him or me?" Most people would have thought the question vaguely threatening. It was the way she seemed to will her eyes to slant by dropping the lids just so.

"You." The trick was to know that the threatening look, was halfway to a smile. It was always there, lurking around the corner if you dared to take the step. And sometimes, like after an evening of rum and cognac, you only had to wait.

"Good," she said, giving him the gap and taking his hand. "Let's go back and make some more memories."

She didn't like him to dwell on his father—would just as soon he never mentioned it. That had taken some getting used to, because she'd been so good about it then. She nursed him through the crisis, first sympathizing with his sense of loss and then taking him past it. Lonnie had left them, after all, and had never tried to get in touch. He probably didn't want to be found—what would he do with a grown son that he knew he had and had ignored? And most important, Ike didn't need him. Hadn't he gotten that far on his own, he and his mother? Everything was open to him now, and everything he'd always wanted was there, in the future, not the past. Since he wasn't interested in gloating—the impression given was that that would have been *her* only motive—why not let it go?

She never said much then about her own parents. Ike had wondered, and finally asked, if she was going to see them at all during that summer—they were so close. She laughed, bitterly, and he chalked it up to her wanting to preserve her first summer entirely on her own. When he did meet them, at school that fall, she was unmistakably rude. But he knew that she was something of a spoiled brat, and they had slept together for the first time, at last, the night before, and he wasn't always exactly civil to Elizabeth, either. It was a long time before she told him about returning from one of their regular just-us-girls trips to the island with her mother, at the beginning of the summer in New York, and finding a necklace that wasn't hers or her mother's in their bedroom. She never told her mother, or her father, but she knew he knew. And he paid. If she had gotten nearly everything she wanted before, she got things she didn't even want after that, and spent some time thinking of them. That was how she got this graduation trip, the first time she had been back to the island.

"Fuck!" The strap on her sandal broke as they climbed the steps to the apartment. Ike grabbed her waist. The long, belted white cotton dress felt better than a nightgown, smoother and cooler than just skin. Half drunk anyway, she sagged into him as he opened the door. He pushed it ahead of them, slipped his free hand under her legs and lifted her inside.

"What are you doing?"

"I gotcha. Told you I was going to carry you over the threshold."

"Oh, no. Isaac, put me down." He faked dropping her onto the floor; her arms seized his neck. "Wait! Okay, you win. But it doesn't count."

Kicking the door closed behind him—a nice move—he surged toward the sofa, fell atop her and attacked her with kisses.

"Does this count?"

"Mm-hm."

He pulled back and left her eyes closed, her lips puckering against air.

"So how come you didn't gimme no nooky in New York?"

The eyes snapped open and began to narrow. "Damn, are you back there again? You didn't ask me, that's why."

"What about that night after Small's you had me pokin through my pants on the stairs? I call that asking."

She chuckled. "We were still getting to know each other, sweetie. Listen, if you're gonna do another history lesson I'm gonna smoke." She kneed him off and walked through the broken sandal to the ceramic bowl on the kitchenette counter.

He hadn't meant to ask that. He knew why. It had taken the imminent arrival of her parents—of her father—to get her to open up. Only after he knew about the necklace did he understand why she had insisted he take off his watch and why he couldn't find it for two days afterward. Casual evidence, a little twist of the knife. He'd been a setup, but by the time he figured it out it hardly mattered. He was where he wanted to be.

"I don't want to go to New Haven, Von," he said with a weary conviction that pulled her attention from the joint she was rolling.

"H.G. Wells here. From the past to the future. Why don't you take a break and stay home sometime, baby?"

"I'm serious."

"I know." She inhaled deeply and sat close beside him. He picked up the sound of the ocean outside and took a mental stroll on the beach before she exhaled and turned to face him. Great lungs. "We went through all this before you graduated. When I finish my master's in DC I'll join you and we'll conquer the world together. Meantime we've got the whole summer."

He accepted the jay after she took another hit. She watched him carefully as he put it to his lips, as if it were a thermometer that would tell whether he simply had a fever or was really crazy.

"These last few days have meant a lot to me," he said. "More than I thought, really, even with all that honeymoon shit I've been talking." She looked away quickly, then came back for the joint idling between his fingers. "It's just us, alone in the world, and it's *good*."

"Of course it is. It's always been good. That's why I didn't 'give you no nooky' the first time you squeezed my thigh. I knew we could build something special, because we both knew what we wanted."

"I thought I knew. But this is different. This is real. *This* is what I want, being with you, and now that I know that, it's hard to wait."

"See, that's the problem with time travel," she said, grinding out the roach. "You *don't* have to wait."

The heavy, floral air—not to mention the rum and reefer—had been floating him into a quick and swirly sleep every night. Not tonight. He lay for a long while, propped up on one elbow, watching her curled on the white, wrinkled sheets, her left hand between her drawn-up legs—interesting how they snapped shut the moment he rolled away—and her right thumb in her mouth. He had no idea how many men she'd slept with and didn't honestly care. But he wanted to believe that no man—except her father—had seen her like that; it was more than a year before he'd caught the thumb, and six months after that he let on.

He got up and softly left the room. Nudity was a new thing with him. Yvonne spent so much time alternately admiring and castigating her body that it seemed unfair to be priggish about his. Still, it was being there on the island that made it finally all right. Watching men move along the beach, and in town, as if their clothes were no more significant than a hat worn against the sun—the same way he had, long ago, watched others dance until he could internalize the rhythms—had done it. He liked himself. His body was beginning to grow out past his belly button, and his chest and shoulders looked like somebody had hung a suit on a wire hanger. What was once an outline had shape, definition. The promise of solidity. Yet his legs were still in track shape, even developing muscles that could have helped him in those last hundred yards. It was not too late, he thought, moving through the living room to open the sliding glass door to the terrace. The distances were longer and the comp was tougher, but he was ready to run this one, not as Elizabeth's boy but as Yvonne's man. Maybe even make some little men, show *them* how to run. Funny he had never thought about that before. Yeah, Jim, ready. He began doing stretching exercises at the rail, pushing forward, crouching down, feeling a power that could lift him out over the pool, barely touching the sand of the beach with his toes and striding easily across the waves all the way to DC. She's not ready, but that's all right. His mission, which he chose to accept, was clear: give her back what she'd lost, what he'd never had. What good was training without a race to run, a prize to win? And what better prize?

Isaac, Isaac, he's our man, if he can't do it . . . aw, *dig*, baby. Kick!

All of DC, or at least the part that called itself Washington, was caught up in the case—not surprisingly, since it was the biggest political scandal of the century. One of the partners at Ike's firm was defending a "Good Guy," one of the few Bright Young Americans just trying to do the right thing who had been perfectly cast in the televised hearings the summer before, replacing the soaps in the witness chair a few feet from his pretty-but-not-showy heartland wife who had persuaded him to come clean. He could have been the handsome young lawyer, a Brad or a Cliff, blinded by greed and ambition who had been caught in the machinations of his evil and powerful client, a tycoon running for governor, but was redeemed by the love of a Jennifer, the good woman he had married only to join her father's practice. That was the way it seemed to play on afternoon television, anyway. In fact, it was only a coincidence that he was sort of a nice one, something that made the secretaries and receptionists feel better about their vicarious relationship to the affair. It could just as easily have been one of the Hitler youth snots, or even—which would have been better for the firm—one of the Big Fish; they all needed counsel, and everyone wanted a piece of the action.

Everyone, for that matter, claimed some piece, however small. The connections were well worn by the time Ike arrived: somebody's neighbor had been to a party with one of the defendants, or used the same dry cleaner, or saw him regularly buying bagels and the Sunday *Post* or knew his wife from the produce counter or had a boyfriend who went to undergraduate school with him. But the new batch of young blood in town for the summer allowed for another wave of name dropping, and, of course, the impeachment hearings revived the whole epic saga like a rerelease of *Gone With the Wind*.

Yvonne was in the thick of it. While he slogged through busywork reserved for the greenest kids, distinguishable from the permanent clerical staff only by his age and gender, she was a key grip in history. Her man was on the Judiciary Committee, a moderate Republican who had virtually inherited his seat. Some staffers called him the Phantom—the Ghost Who Walks—not for his airy presence but because he was the third in his line, all with the same name, to haunt the halls of Congress. He was the only representative whose initials were carved on his desk, it was said. The nameplate was actually the family tombstone. Every twenty years or so Congress would reconvene in January and there would be a different man sitting there and no one would notice, although the Gentleman from New York did seem remarkably well preserved for a man of 110. Recently, however, the spell had been broken. Even the constituents who hadn't read the name on a voting machine their entire lives might have noticed when Number Two, retired but too stubborn to die, took out newspaper ads defending the President, whom Number Three was in the process of deciding whether or not to impeach.

For that reason, the office was a madhouse all summer. Other congressional interns proofread newsletters on dairy price supports and welcomed touring church groups. Yvonne got to field passionate phone calls, edit polls, tally letters, write press releases and meet with delegations of citizens who weren't interested only in autographs and flags, including one officially named "The Coalition to Throw the Bum Out." One day she was drafted to greet a busload of senior citizens bearing "Get Off His Back" buttons and reprints of Number Two's ad. Her job was to smile and listen, thank people for their time and input and reassure them that the congressman was considering all views and carefully weighing all the evidence. But, as she told Ike, she had nearly lost patience with the old black man who was the President's loudest defender, who wanted to know what she was doing on the staff anyway and accused her of poisoning the congressman with her militant drivel. He'd reminded her of other pea-brained oreo shufflers back home who never got the trick of playing it both ways, and it was all she could do to get them back on the bus and over to the White House before she started getting personal with his old monkey ass. Even Mr. Joseph, whose ruthlessly nonpartisan business connections had helped land her the job, was perfectly willing to let the Old Prick, as he called the President, get squeezed now that he'd been caught in the zipper. And since that was one battle she didn't have to fight with him, she certainly wasn't going to take it from some colored fool in a red, white and blue straw boater.

Such incidents were an annoyance for Yvonne, a distraction. But they were among the high points of Ike's days, even in hearsay. Law was boring enough in its daily routine; he'd made his peace with that because he was good at the small stuff and knew in the long run it was the only way he'd get to play with the big boys. But since he hadn't even started law school, he was simply there to soak up atmosphere, pick up the cadences and, as Howard had predicted, do the shit while he kept his face in view for the EEO establishment. Yvonne, meanwhile, had the benefit of a shortcut she didn't even appreciate. He was sure she would have been just as happy in a bank, where the relationship between power and money was more out in the open. And it was enough for her to be there, in Chocolate City. The fact that she had one of the choicest assignments in town hardly mattered.

The place was still a mystery to him, although he and Yvonne had passed through a couple of times on weekends. He had missed the high-school senior trip with laryngitis, and had often blamed Elizabeth for somehow spoiling what he'd planned as a retreat with Cheryl, even though she didn't, he thought, know about her then. Now he wished he had done all the things he wasn't going to do if he had made the trip—the archives, the Library of Congress, the Smithsonian, the monuments—because the up-close-and-personal sleaziness of the case worked better as melodrama in contrast to the grandeur of the backdrop. Yvonne politely but firmly refused to do the tour bit; she gave him a drive-around on their first Saturday and told him he could take it from there. What intrigued him on that first view was how much a city it was, and a fairly unexceptional one at that. Sort of like Buffalo with marble. Everyone knew, for instance, that real life mingled with edifice in New York, that your pocket could be picked on the sidewalk beneath the Empire State Building, that you could be mugged in the shadow of the U.N. But the Washington of the mind was a masterful creation of camera angles. Who would have guessed that a Fred Williamson movie would be playing across the street from the White House, that the twin brothers of the once-men who lined Eighth Avenue shuffled now and then past the spot where network correspondents did their Capitol stand-ups? The closeness of it all surprised and appalled him. Real Life wasn't even around the corner; it was right there in the way. It was good, he thought, that the government was even less insulated than some college campuses, like the ones he'd been on. But what powers of will could allow an entire nation and its representatives to ignore the truth when it blew up daily on the curb like fast-food garbage? Fucking with the Constitution seemed a small crime in comparison.

But within days, Ike found how easy it was to lose sight of the city. Some of Yvonne's Howard and Georgetown homeboys were still around, between excursions to the Vineyard, and she and Ike spent the early weeks of the summer making the rounds of clubs and restaurants that existed for the pleasure of aging Jacks and Jills and their darker, well-schooled cousins who had already infiltrated the federal bureaucracy or were in training to invade city halls and executive suites from Newark to Atlanta and points west. The guilt and self-recrimination that had so bothered Yvonne when she first went to college were little in evidence; here, affirmative action was another phrase for manifest destiny, the inevitable rise of the children of doctors and teachers and social workers and accountants.

To Ike, at first, they seemed to be playing grown-up with their suits and business cards and Tanqueray, but he quickly changed his mind. They had been playing at rebellion; this was their natural environment, a cynical world where street protest was an old joke and parliamentary accommodation with a Southern congressman or a slight concession wrung from a utility company were acknowledged as historic triumphs. It was a great way to pick up tennis tips and Black Caucus gossip, and the people were pretty, in a brittle sort of way. But Ike was not disappointed when Yvonne's work quickened and they began to fall from the scene. She encouraged him to continue to circulate, and he did. But after one long night clinging to a barstool surrounded by some of the BT Express, an eager bunch assembled by the black transportation secretary, listening to Amtrak stories and thinking, in spite of himself, about his father while waiting for Yvonne to show up, he started spending more evenings in the one-bedroom apartment they shared, reading, listening to the radio, and eyeing the Orioles with the sound off on the color set she'd had at school, another of Mr. Joseph's payoffs.

He avoided the clubs because they represented her life, but he did not feel compelled to establish one of his own. Instead, he stubbornly waited for her to join him in crafting one that would be theirs. Their schedules were such that they ate dinner together only a few times a week. Because Ike's work duties were fewer, and because he didn't mind cooking as much as Yvonne did, though she was better when she got into it, he occasionally surprised her with recipes from a cookbook he bought. Simple ones, because they didn't have a lot of stuff, and he wasn't above his old standby of Shake-and-Bake and Rice-a-Roni. But he did some interesting things with chicken and bread crumbs and played around with fish. When she insisted on going out, he tried to steer her to small neighborhood restaurants they could claim for their own. For special moments together, he said. Or he'd get her to go to movies or listen to music or stay home and watch late-show musicals. He wanted to grow something that sprouted in a private place—the middle of the small table where they shared breakfast, the depression left in the bed when she turned to suck her thumb, the hole burned by a hot seed in the middle cushion of the sofa, where they too rarely shared a debriefing joint at the end of the day—and spread out to form a whole, unique world with them entangled at the center.

As far as he was concerned, that was the entire point of their living together. Officially, it was an act of practical defiance; it saved a lot of time and money. They didn't tell their parents, and they kept separate phone lines, but neither would have been terribly upset if they were found out. She, he suspected, hoped they would be, and so made a point of dialing them up without telling him so that he might wander into the room making noise. He, on the other hand, was not interested in rubbing Elizabeth's nose in anything; he simply wanted her to leave him alone and didn't much care what she thought about what he did. He saw the summer, very clearly, as an experiment, an audition for life. The only roommate he'd ever had was Art Rosen, who now, according to the alumni magazine's class notes, was in med school in New Orleans. He wasn't at all confident that he knew how to act around people—freshman year certainly didn't count, and neither did Elizabeth. But he wanted to, more than anything, particularly with Yvonne. He wanted to practice all those little adjustments you were supposed to have to make, not so much where you squeezed the toothpaste and whether you kept the bread in the refrigerator, but when to shut up when you wanted to say something, when to stay up when you wanted to go to bed, when to do nothing when you wanted to do something.

This was hard work, and he approached it seriously. After all, he had hardly ever been around married people. There had been Dessie and Big Tom, but he saw them while running through the house with Tommy, and they seemed *too* married in a way; whatever alterations they'd made had been made so long ago, and so completely, that you couldn't tell what had begun as his and what as hers. The Josephs didn't offer many clues, either. When Ike saw them, Mr. Joseph seemed almost as much a guest in the house as he did. He didn't believe it was always like that, and even if it was, that model did not appeal to him: the husband relinquishing his voice in the home in exchange for authority and independence in his own life outside. That would not do. Ike knew that he wanted a blend, not a split, a sharing of control and submissiveness at home with each having responsibilities elsewhere. Since he was a boy, he had delighted in declaring to Elizabeth that he had no intention, ever, of supporting any woman. She had always worked, hadn't she? But she *had* to, she would reply, her own frustration more pronounced than the implied indictment of his father. Sure, he answered, and she did just fine. And since she had made him learn to clean and cook, even though he had schoolwork to do, there was no reason to have somebody sitting around all day doing things that he could do, too. So there!

Still, even though he definitely did not want Yvonne to be a homebody, he was jealous. They had been apart for a year, while he got his master's, and would be for at least another, while she got hers. This was the time they should be laying a foundation, but he was left playing a solo while she was busy, busier than he was, with more interesting things and more interesting people. She wasn't able to attend his firm's summer outing, inexplicably held during the week, which left him one of a few black people and not too many more young people sprawled out at a suburban country club for golf, tennis, swimming, drinks and shoptalk. There were two black associates, one of whom headed straight for the golf course with the managing partner. This guy had shown no interest whatever in buddying up with Ike, although he had taken him to an early-summer lunch, probably on orders, and spoken tellingly of the flaws of the other associates without laying a glove on any of the partners. The other, a woman who wore a perpetually hapless expression, always made a point of smiling at Ike and asking how he was doing. But he had to make his answers brief, because she was always in a hurry and usually seemed nervous, possibly because someone was always praising her black colleague in her presence and possibly because she was aware of the smirks that appeared when she consulted, often, with one partner. At first Ike guessed that something was going on, but he later decided it wasn't that juicy; others in the office were simply pleased that she wasn't cutting it. Estranged from her peers and afraid to consort too openly with her mentor—she obviously still believed the first smirk theory—she sat by the pool trying awfully hard not to frown. Ike sat by her, and she asked again how he was doing, and he managed a full-length response before she jumped up and announced she was going for a walk.

So Ike got himself a vodka and tonic from the poolside bar and eased his way into a circle of men standing around talking—even at a *picnic* they stand. Luckily, the conversation was political, and Ike was able to trade on his hand-me-down knowledge of the Judiciary Committee. It seemed to work well. He dropped the names of a couple of key committee staffers and offered the latest wisdom on how the swing vote would go and detailed the Republican strategy to stall for time in hope that the President would comply with the subpoena. None of it was big news, but a few first names and suggestions of personal bickering went a long way. When the talk went legal, he lobbed in the name of a hot young lawyer he'd met at a black-mafia Princeton Club function. It was a gamble. The worst thing a young black man could do was praise another who was considered a loser by white men. (That was true for a young white man, too, judging by the expression on one partner's face when an intern spoke admiringly of the black associate hustling out on the links.) But Ike guessed right with his man, who was considered golden within the circle. Having made points on what might have been his best day's work of the summer, he retired from the group while he was ahead.

The following week, he was able to join Yvonne for her staff social, held more sensibly on a Saturday afternoon at a senior aide's townhouse. These seemed, in contrast, like real people, barbecuing on the patio with little sense of hierarchy or gamesmanship. The atmosphere was further eased by the absence of "Mr. Walker"—the Phantom—who would not be dropping by because he was back home taking the pulse of the people. The staff interpreted that as a sign that he had made up his mind and wanted to show the flag before the storm, and that, too, added to the high spirits. It wasn't so much that they wanted him to vote yes, though some clearly did, but that they were tired of the straddling and uncertainty that kept them from performing effectively.

Shortly after Yvonne and Ike arrived, a tall, bearded young man was greeted by all with the question: "Where's Hubbard?" That, Yvonne explained, was a reference to the *Post* reporter for whom the staffer had become a Prime Source. Nobody seemed to mind. The committee itself had become an absolute sieve—there had been a lot of pieces lately about loose lips and how they might sink the investigation—and this guy had enhanced his stature by propping up the Phantom, usually portrayed by the committee folks as a problem at best, an idiot at worst.

"When I read about this on Monday," Frank, the host, said, his arm locked around the leaker's neck and a long fork waving in his face, "I want it clear that the steaks were magnificent."

"And that the house was spotless," added his wife, who worked somewhere in Treasury. "Bernice was off this week and I killed myself for you guys. Be sure to get that in."

The Redskins, who had just opened training camp, got equal time with the hearings in the conversations that followed. Frank was excited because he had moved into likely range on the RFK Stadium waiting list and concerned that the Phantom would blow it for him before he hit paydirt. Fat chance, they all agreed. They'd *never* dump him, even if he turned up on the tapes telling dirty jokes. Maybe the gaps were him waiting to get the punch line. Well, maybe if someone told Hubbard about seeing Frank in a phone booth with Tony Ulasewicz. Or if they found Ellsberg's psychiatric file in his drawer, along with the tape recorder and Liddy's gun. Or if they caught the Phantom in a parking garage with Woodward. Or fishing in Key West with Barker. Or at a stag party with Segretti on Bebe's yacht—with Rose Mary popping out of a cake. And with all that, counseled Frank's wife, who'd heard the game before, he'd come back with 51 percent and maybe have to give back the Old Man's cuff links.

And so it went. Yvonne, who was normally fussy with strangers, especially white ones, cheerily accepted compliments on her yellow halter and shorts, appropriate for the weather and occasion, though daring for the company, which leaned heavily toward alligator shirts and khaki. Obviously, she had carved out an identity for herself as something of an exotic, an advantage as long as she didn't *act* like one. The women marveled at her elaborate earrings and armload of silver bangles, the men at her native behind, and none seemed to realize that her deep Caribbean tan was as temporary as their tennis blushes. She even, to Ike's surprise, joined in singing along with the *Woodstock* soundtrack and danced a little when the party got silly. They had often discussed how white people danced only when they thought of themselves as acting silly; she had bet him a dollar that that would be the case as soon as the sun went down, although she had never seen her colleagues in a purely social setting before. Smiling conspiratorially at him over the shoulder of a dance partner doing the jerk—the eternal standby—she confirmed for Ike what until that moment he had refused to believe: she was even better at this than he was.

The thought, after a rush of resentment, actually comforted him. In the space of a few weeks, without trying—at least, he didn't think she was trying—she had shown him how easily they could move back and forth across the line without compromising integrity, identity or ambition. It also made him more desperate than ever to solidify their interior life, because he feared he needed her to make the round-trip, but she managed fine on her own. Just how fine he realized one evening when she came home raving about Barbara Jordan's performance on the committee.

"My girl was *bad*, you hear me?" she exclaimed. " 'My faith in the Constitution,' " she intoned deeply, " 'is whole. It is complete.' I said *whooo*, get it, girl! She may look like Ugly's mama but she can rap her ass off. Took all those white boys right *off* the hook, too. Got half of 'em believing they're not just out to get the Old Prick. It's 'the Con-sti-*tu*-shun!' I told Frank and he tried to say that was our position all along. Well, why didn't we *say* so, I said. Why didn't *he* write that speech? I told him, the Republicans owe her more than the Democrats. We're the ones who *need* an excuse for this shit. If they had elections for the Supreme Court she'd be on it tomorrow."

She was high. It was just the kind of thing that Ike wanted her to rush home and share with him. But her recounting the exchange with Frank put a damper on it, which, he well knew, was completely unreasonable. Frank was there; he wasn't. She worked for the man. No big deal. That wasn't quite it. Maybe it was that he could picture her telling the same story, with the same excitement, to a bunch of anonymous black policy analysts at a nightclub—or to white congressional interns at lunch. Where's *mine,* he wondered—the quote, the anecdote, the detail, the comparison that would have made sense only and especially to him?

He was beginning to work himself into a pout when she landed on his lap, straddling and facing him, and gave him a kiss.

"You should come Saturday," she said. "A lot of it is boring, but you'll appreciate the good parts. I think they might vote, finally. I want you to be there. We can have a 'moment.' "

Saturday was hot as hell, the kind of day, apparently, when outwardly mobile residents, as in New York, usually left the city to the poor and the visiting. But not when two years of prime-time drama were about to reach a climax. The gallery filled early for the noon session, and the press section, she said, was busier than ever; you knew the deal was about to go down when the columnists and anchor types turned out to upstage the beat reporters. For a while the sense of anticipation, combined with the heavy, muggy atmosphere, seemed as if it would spark an electric storm. *This is it,* everyone's body language suggested. Clearly, even in a ponderous bureaucracy, there was a recognizable moment when something happened, the legislative equivalent of a fourth-period touchdown against the Cowboys, and the team was now coming onto the field for the fateful drive.

The drama, however, was excruciatingly subtle. For one thing, the chairman didn't gavel the session to order until nearly an hour past schedule; the Democrats had been caucusing, Yvonne explained, in yet another effort to get it together. The first signs were promising. The Republicans immediately withdrew a stack of amendments and dropped their torturous tactic of clarifying the wording in the articles of impeachment. All they had accomplished was an embarrassing rehash of the entire case for a national audience—and even the Phantom had conceded that they were only prolonging the agony. But the energy soon began to drain out of the room when a Democrat, a Southerner who needed a little song-and-dance for his constituents, began an equally withering approach of detailing the evidence. This time the Republicans objected, and the audience, a knowledgeable crowd, chuckled as the members sniped at one another.

The laughs proved rare. As the recitation stretched on into the afternoon, the committee itself was visibly restless. Some members seemed to be sharing jokes. Others shuffled papers, tapped pens, yawned and even strolled about the dais, though rarely in camera range. Yvonne, bless her heart, obviously would rather have been back in the office, at least until the vote got closer, even though there was nothing to do there but watch on television. All the action was in and around the hearing room. It was the committee staff, and the congressmen themselves during breaks, who fed the reporters. Instead, she kept up a steady whisper, explaining who was who and what one had said to the other last week and what that one's problem was, keeping her own head in the game and keeping Ike awake. By late afternoon, though, she picked up a change in tone. A couple of motions went through almost automatically; once, even a member who had proposed an amendment declined to support it.

"They're laying down," she said. "They're gonna do it. Look at him." She nodded to the Phantom, who seemed to be hyperventilating. Ike recognized the starting-line jitters. "Poor baby. You'd think they were coming to get him for the electric chair. Get tough, now, Junior. You can do it. They'll still love ya, baby."

The girl knew her stuff. As if someone had given a signal, the huge room hushed, and the chairman called for a vote on Article 1. Ike had watched enough conventions on TV to be able to dig it, and this, by comparison, was pretty routine. No balloons and signs and strategic spontaneous demonstrations. They played it straight, and only by watching eyelids and neck muscles could you tell that they knew they were writing a chapter for every eighth- grader's social-studies book. One by one, their names were called, and though there wasn't much to be done with an "aye" or a "no," each gave it his best reading. The deed was done before the Phantom's turn—there was a marked rustling, but no outburst—yet he aimed his "aye" carefully, as if the body were still kicking and his the decisive bullet.

"O*kay*," Yvonne said, aloud, squeezing Ike's hand.

The chairman kept talking after the vote, but nobody seemed to be paying much attention. Ike's mind flipped suddenly to *Birth of a Nation*, the scene with the shiftless nigras eating chicken in Congress. Yeah, he thought, but they'd know when to party. Be turnin this motherfucker *out* right now. This here was like Wimbledon or opera, so cool it was frozen. Someone came up and whispered to the chairman, who till then looked slightly more tired and not a bit happier than he'd appeared since the coverage of the hearings began. But now he seemed shook as he called for attention and asked everyone to clear the room. The show was over, so nobody seemed to mind much, even though the vibes were wrong. It was, Yvonne said, backing his own perception, like when the teacher calls a fire drill and something tells you it's not a drill. But it was a good excuse to make a clean break. If she'd hung around to touch base with cronies, there was no telling when they'd leave—like Elizabeth making him miss all those kickoffs while she chatted on the church steps.

It wasn't until Monday that she was able to fill him in on what hadn't made the late-night news: someone had reported a kamikaze pilot en route from National Airport to crash into the Capitol after the vote. Maybe, he told her, he had taken the togetherness business too far; that would have been a bitch of a moment.

The sound was halfway to a party. The voices, exuberant but modulated, overpowered the music that sounded like someone in the background trying to make a point. The event had been planned for a day or two, in anticipation of the announcement, but it had come together with impressive speed. When Yvonne moved to ring the bell, Ike noticed that it wasn't necessary: the catch was taped back. Too cute by half. Inside, a blow-up poster of Watergate security guard Frank Wills, in whose name the party was being held, dominated the living room, accented by colorful WILLS/KENNEDY and JORDAN/WILLS bumper stickers. Yet for all that bravado, there was a definite undercover feeling to the gathering. It didn't start late because of nostalgia or C.P. Time; it was because everyone had felt compelled to watch the resignation speech with his white colleagues or in private. Only after a respectful interval and some serious discussion did it seem cool for a few dozen young black political operatives to come together and rejoice at the passing of the Prick.

Congressional staffers were there, and lawyers and apprentice consultants and journalists and representatives of the Democratic establishment-in-exile who were counting on the scandal to carry over for two more years. Even a few Republican retainers, relieved that the nightmare was over, turned out. One of them was testifying in a corner of the room about the heroic job Haig had done, holding the White House together in the final days and finally getting the President to Say Good Night, Dick.

"Well that's what he gets paid for, isn't it?" sneered a dissenter.

"Sure, but he could have stonewalled like the other guy."

"And the elections would have turned into a referendum on the trial, and by next year you guys would be bloody as hell. I could've lived with that. He did what he had to do, okay? But let's not pin any medals on his ass. He's got too many already."

Yvonne seemed unsettlingly familiar with people Ike had never seen before; she touched men's arms when she spoke to them and reacted to everything that was said around her, flashing her gap all over the place and never once narrowing her eyelids. She laughed off cracks about Bo Howard—apparently it was known that she was an acquaintance—who had shown a sharp sense of timing by shuffling to the President's defense the day before the smoking gun tape turned up. Name dropping wasn't going to get it in this crowd. Ike felt himself fading into the background—was he stepping back or was Yvonne moving away?—until, standing near the stereo, he eased the volume up a notch. He nearly got something going. A shoulder dipped over there, an ass twitched over here, a foot patted and a finger popped. Then a guy slid in beside Ike and turned the music down lower than it had been in the first place so he could continue rapping to a woman about the night the special prosecutor was fired.

Ike retreated to the kitchen. He had seen people coming out of there with bottles of beer, but someone had his head stuck in the refrigerator. Ike scoped around for a cooler or something; when he turned back the guy was holding a bottle out to him.

"This what you need?"

"Yeah, thanks. Pretty heavy out there."

"Well that's DC. Company town, everybody's in the game. People still be playin when they playin, if you know what I mean."

"I'm catchin on." Ike twisted off the cap and saluted with his bottle.

"Isaac, right? I'm Paul Spencer. We met last month at Mario's. You said you're on your way to law school."

"You've got a good memory," Ike said.

"Part of the game." Spencer swigged and winked. "Yvonne says you guys met at school."

"You gonna tell me my sign?"

Spencer chuckled. "Hey, give me a break. I remember cause we were comparing college notes, and when you all came over we were sayin these must be some bad niggers here. We thought we were into some shit in Cambridge, but damn, guns and what-not. That was serious."

"And a long time ago."

"I hear you. Seems a lot longer than it was. Did you know a brother named Gene Mayford?"

"Why?"

"You wouldn't have any idea where he is now, would you?"

"I haven't seen him in three or four years. What's up?"

Spencer took a long drink, peered into the bottle, then peeked up at Ike. "You heard about that business in Atlanta?" His voice had changed. "With the judge?"

Several days before, the White House death watch had been briefly interrupted by a quick burst of news from Out There: the attempted assassination of a federal judge, who was black, in front of the courthouse. It was like something out of *The Godfather*. The judge had dived back into his car and survived with serious wounds. A cop on the sidewalk was killed.

"A group called the People's Liberation Army claimed credit," Spencer said. "Marxist outfit. One of the gunmen was black, the other white."

"Yeah, and?"

"We think Mayford might have been involved."

"Bullshit."

"Relax, brother. Let me run it down. He wasn't at the scene, but we know he's got ties to these folks. Strong ties. You know he spent time in Cuba?"

"Yeah, I know. Who's we?" Spencer, he finally remembered, was a Black Caucus brat.

"Everybody, man. My guy's got a tough run down there this year. The district's still more than fifty percent white, and the opposition's gonna run this into the ground. Even the niggers get restless when an integrated bunch of outlaws starts shooting down black cops and judges on the street—although, just between us, the man is a major pain in the ass. I don't know how he ever got to be a judge. The bureau's all over this, and we can't afford to come up soft."

"So you think turning up Mayford will do the trick," Ike said, not nearly as acidly as he'd hoped.

"Damn straight," Spencer shot back. "Look, buddy, you may not want to believe it, but your boy's in this to his eyebrows. You all had some fun shaking up the university back in the old days, but this shit is real. It's dangerous. These are crazy motherfuckers out here, man, and they're trying to tear down everything we've all been working for."

Ike sipped silently.

"You know I'm right. We're gonna nail these bastards one way or the other. But I'm thinking that maybe your boy can still be reasoned with if somebody can reach him. We don't want to see a Panther thing go down here."

"But you wouldn't mind."

"Hell, I wouldn't cry myself to sleep. Would you? You think the black community's gonna rally behind a band of Marxist murderers? Look here, brother, you think about it. Take the weekend. Talk to whoever, make some calls, see if you can come up with something to make this happen easy. Meet me Monday morning for breakfast at the Adams."

Spencer walked out. Ike sucked his beer dry. When he reentered the living room, a room filled with black people presumably joined in common cause, he thought of the library. They were cocky then—and full of shit, some of them—and also scared, as scared as he was, though he hadn't wanted to admit it at the time. They all had something to lose and were putting themselves on the line. And when they won, or at least didn't lose, even their joy was tempered by the remaining risks and unknown consequences.

These jokers here, though, were just grinning and patting themselves up and down each other's backs. And they hadn't done diddly. Half the people in the room must have taken over something sometime or other, or sat in or marched or boycotted. The results, obviously, were small by comparison, but it was something they had done, together. The Prick had done *himself* in, other white folks had finished him off, and niggers were partying like it was their show. And at the same time, scheming how to do each *other* in to look good for the other people. Some sorry shit, if you thought about it. But the sad part was that, for all the trifling arrogance, this was where he wanted to be. This was his life, the way he could make a difference. There had to be something to hold it all together.

"What's wrong with you?" Yvonne asked. At first he thought that she had sought him out, but then he realized he had been standing right in the middle of the room.

"Nothing. Let's get out of here."

A quick oh-lord-it's-one-of-those-moods looks passed across her face. She touched his arm, the same way she had been touching everybody else's.

"Okay," she said. "Just a little while longer, all right?"

He moved away to give her space, but positioned himself near enough to the door to remind her of his intentions.

"Say, blood." Someone attacked him with a thumbs-up slap-shake. "Fuckers on the *run*, baby. Who you with, man?"

Ike mentioned the name of the firm, waited for the not *bad* expression, and added that he was just an intern, though.

"Hey. Foot in the door. That's the name of the game."

"Wonder what he's thinkin right now," Ike said.

"Who?"

He nodded to the poster of Wills, who had discovered the original Watergate burglars.

"Probably thinkin 'bout a job. You know they fired his ass."

"I heard."

"Pathetic, man. Criminals get on TV, you know they'll all have contracts to write their books even if they do some time. My man can't catch a cold."

"Too bad he's not here. Free hors d'oeuvres."

"Dig it. Well, it's symbolic, you know. But that's where it all started, right there. He's like the Rosa Parks of the seventies."

"That's hip. I'll tell him next time I see him. Should make him feel better."

They got home a little after two. There had been a moment, just before they left, when it looked like a sure-enough party was going to break out; at that point—in time—somebody lowered the music *again* and left the spirit twisting slowly, slowly in the wind. There *was* work tomorrow, although it would be the closest thing to an official holiday. With the swearing in, and probably a mawkish farewell, all covered live, no one who wasn't actually involved in the transition would be getting much done.

Yvonne immediately stepped out of her shoes and peeled her pantyhose. Ike threw his jacket on the back of the sofa and slipped his tie.

"Von," he said, as she began to step toward the bathroom. He had meant to sound casual but knew he had put more into the word when she stopped. He held out his hand. She came back and took it.

"What is it, sweetie?"

"I've . . . I've been—"

"Thinking," she finished for him. "Let me guess."

She fell onto the sofa, not a casual flop but a deadweight drop, one that sounded like someone letting fall a heavy basket of wet things she had been carrying for a while.

"You don't like my friends. You don't like my job. You don't like your job. You don't want to go to law school."

"You're getting warm."

"Oh, God."

She moved to get up. He blocked her and grabbed hold of her shoulders.

"Let's get married."

"Baby, you need to go to sleep."

She tried to rise. He slid his hands around her back and squeezed. *Tighter*. Please. *Tighter*.

"I mean it," he said.

"That's what I'm afraid of."

"What?" he said, stepping back. "What are you afraid of?"

"I didn't mean that."

"Then why not?"

"*I*saac!"

She pushed forward again. He held and kneeled, so he could look her in the eyes.

"I love you, Von."

She sighed and sank back, freeing herself. "I know."

"Don't you love me?"

"Please."

"*Don't* you?"

"Yes, but—"

"But what? I need you. I need to know that, I don't know, that I can count on you. That we have a commitment."

Her face had turned slightly, as if he were a drunk begging for quarters, and as he spoke she slid, maybe six inches to the side, where the air was clear.

"What do you think we've been doing for the last three years? I'm not going anywhere, Richard. It's *okay*. We don't need some damn piece of paper."

"*I* do."

"It doesn't *mean* anything."

She stood and circled behind where he knelt, arms stretched out on the sofa.

"We sleep in the same bed," she went on. "That means something. We do things together. When we're apart we miss each other. That's all that matters."

"No," he said, turning to look up at her. "It's not enough. It's too easy. There's no glue. Either one of us can walk out of here anytime and that's that."

"Are you serious? You think paper's going to change that? You think a *promise* is going to make any difference? Look at my parents. Look at *yours!*"

He climbed to his feet. She took a step back but did not back away.

"So they screwed up," he said evenly. "We can do better."

"*Everybody* screws up, and we *are* doing better," she nearly yelled. Her arms were crossed and her eyes beginning to slant. "This is as good as it gets, sweetie. This is all anybody ever has. Words lie and paper tears."

She turned to walk away. He grabbed her arm and spun her around.

"Not if you don't let it."

"What's the goddamn difference?"

"The difference is that you *say* it. You give your word and it means something."

"Yeah, right." She laughed without smiling and watched him carefully. "*Today* it means something. You don't just lock it up and put it in a safe and not worry about it. It's an everyday thing. It's only as good as yesterday or last night."

"It's not the same." His voice slipped under the echo of hers. They had not turned on any lights, and her features were beginning to blur. "You can break a promise," he said, "but you can break it a hell of a lot easier if you haven't made it."

"That doesn't make any sense," she declared flatly and strode toward the hall to the bedroom. Before he could speak she turned and continued. "Look, you stupid motherfucker. I love you, all right?" Six feet away she had become simply a voice. Her legs, her hips, her lips, her eyes, were a memory. But he knew the voice well enough to know that she was crying. That was one thing they had never done together before. "I can say it every day, but if I wake up one day and don't mean it—or *you* don't—so what if we promised ten years ago we'd *always* mean it? You can't guarantee the future. You know that."

"We can *try!* That's the difference. We can put ourselves on the line. Hold ourselves accountable for what we feel now."

He knew he was right about one thing. At that moment, words were all they had. By stepping away, she had canceled his right to persuade with his hands, his arms. They couldn't even see each other's faces. And there was no sound but a faint tinkling: her earrings, as she slowly shook her head.

"What's the use?" she said. "I mean, if it works, it works. If it doesn't, it doesn't. That's all there is to it, Isaac. I'm going to bed."

He decided not to. If he did, they would cuddle, maybe even make love, in which case she would win, or they would lie restlessly, back to back, in which case no one would. Instead, he sat on the sofa, and at daybreak cleared his mind to write to Juanita. If the heat was on Gene, and if people knew that *he* knew him, they would be looking for her. Maybe she would want to join him, although he hoped not. In any case, the least—and most—he could do was let her know. After he had found her address in his book and made out the envelope, he had a second thought. He slipped the letter into another envelope addressed to Elizabeth, and scribbled a quick note asking her to mail it from there. Then he put on some coffee and made French toast for Yvonne.

They spent the weekend pretending that the conversation had never happened. There were moments, over dinner watching the news, at the market, walking hand in hand by the reflecting pool on Sunday, when she seemed about to say: See? This is now. This is real. But she didn't, so he didn't argue for freezing those moments to be thawed later for seconds, thirds and fourths, preserving the tangible remains for future sustenance as opposed to distant, wispy memories that offered no nourishment in the cold of winter. Yet he knew a frost was coming.

In fact, despite the withering temperatures, he felt downright chilly when he walked into the hotel restaurant Monday morning. It was a semi–power place, and it was packed with people confirming new arrangements in the new regime. Spencer stood and waved, like somebody's damn cousin, and Ike noticed someone sitting beside him. Someone he knew. It took until he was standing there at the table before it came to him. Marvin. From school. The committee—and the library.

"What are you doing here?" Ike said as he sat.

"You ask me that all the time, man." Marvin smiled. "The answer's the same. What are you doing here? This town's full of niggers who were a whole lot more radical than I ever was, all working for Uncle. It's the way of the world."

I didn't ask all that shit, Ike said to himself.

"You learn anything?" Spencer asked.

Ike saw the scraps left on their plates. A menu lay on his side of the booth. He reached for a croissant from the basket on the table and began to butter it.

"What's to learn? I told you I haven't seen the man in years." Spencer looked annoyed. Ike bit into the croissant and caught Marvin's eyes. "No," he said.

"Don't jerk me around, man. I know you all were close."

"I *said* I haven't seen him."

"That's okay, Paul," Marvin said. "Listen. I spoke to Juanita. She says she doesn't know anything either."

He's lying, Ike thought. Who *is* this sonofabitch?

"Just be aware that when the heat gets turned up, guys start trying to reach out. They get in touch all of a sudden. They show up at friends' apartments." He smiled. "They take an interest in their kids." *Cocksucker*. "If that happens, if you hear anything, we'd like to know about it."

"Don't count on it," Ike said. "Who the fuck are you guys anyway?"

"We're just looking for a little cooperation," Spencer said. "We're all on the same side here. Look, I don't know what your ambitions are, but everybody could use some friends—especially when you've got an armed building takeover on your record."

"That's weak," Ike said. "Shit, *he* was there."

"Says who?" Marvin said, with one of those piss-in-his-mouth grins Ike remembered from committee meetings. "Besides, we're talking about a murder investigation here, brother."

"Tell you what, brother," Ike said, standing with the tail of his croissant, "you keep talking, hear?"

He walked to work, pushing through the humidity and cutting across the grain of Banneker's concentric layout. It was supposed to be marvelously symmetrical and logical and civilized, but after two months it still didn't make any sense to him. Negro logic, maybe. Yeah, it was pretty with lots of wide streets and trees and shit, but you couldn't *get* anyplace, not from here to there, not unless you *knew* you knew where you were going. Goddamn Marvin. Juanita wouldn't talk to him about Gene, or Malik. She wouldn't talk to him about water in the desert. But maybe it was him; maybe that's what the letter had been about that drove Gene over the edge. It was too obvious—and, at the same time, too improbable: Marvin skulking through the night to light a cross on the lawn, or hiding in the bushes to shoot white kids like John Wayne gunning down Liberty Valance. An agent provocateur posing as Hollyfield's inside man. Even if that was it, these questions about Gene sounded like a fraternity joke, some kind of loyalty test, or one of those *Mission: Impossible* things where they build a whole fake world outside the guy's window and tell him everybody he ever knew is dead or has turned against him and it's not safe for him out there so he might as well give them the combination to the safe. But he didn't *have* no combination, you dumb mothers. He was surprised to find himself smiling as he strode through the lobby to the elevators. Until the old brother in the tan uniform and cap—its shiny bill tilted just a touch in memory of sportier times—smiled back, as he did every morning, Ike thought he was still angry. Everybody could use some friends. Nigger must think he Sydney Greenstreet.

As soon as he got past the receptionist, he took off his jacket and loosened his tie to let the air conditioning dry him out. And to hold him in the meantime, when he got to his desk he bent down as if to tie his shoe and slipped on some of the Speed Stick he kept in his bottom drawer—one practical lesson about working summers in the big city. He was still early, officially, but somebody was always around to make you feel like you got there too late or were leaving too soon. Another lesson: fuck it. He leaned back to consider his options. He could finish typing these or filling in those; he could pull the rest of the files that Boyce wanted—but Boyce was out of town. Or he could call Yvonne and get the number of that guy she knew in Justice, which was where he thought he might begin to get a line on Marvin.

Or he could answer the phone; these things always worked themselves out.

"Isaac." The receptionist got to recite the name of the firm. That saved everybody about half an hour a day.

"Hi, honey."

Elizabeth. "Hi. What's up?"

"I tried to get you at home this morning but you'd gone."

That's right. I work, remember? "Where are you?" he thought to ask, remembering that she did, too—and her boss wasn't big on personal long-distance.

"I'm at home. I just came from the hospital. It's Hodge."

"What happened?"

"He had a stroke. Early this morning. One of the neighbors found him. He had fallen out of bed and couldn't use the phone so he tapped on the wall for help. They called me, I went over and cleaned him up and called an ambulance."

She had slipped into official precision. He could see her giving the same explanation to a doctor, who probably wondered, as he did, what she was being so damn efficient for.

"How *is* he?"

"They're not sure. It looks bad. I'm on my way back." There was a break in her breathing. "Richard . . . "

Good. She was losing it. "Yeah. You need me?"

"I know you've only got another week, and then you have to get ready for school."

"Do you *need* me? Never mind. Look. Tell him I'll be there tomorrow."

"I'm not sure how much he understands right now. When I left I wasn't sure he even knew I was there."

"Tell him. He'll know. I'll make the arrangements and get back to you."

"Thanks, honey. I don't want to put you out or anything."

Oh, Jesus. "Get back to the hospital. I'll talk to you later."

What the fuck did you call for if you didn't want me to come? What was I going to say, no? Hodge, man, please don't leave me alone with this broad. An associate walked by eyeing him strangely; he had been talking out loud. Lesson number two. He eased on his jacket, tightened his tie and went to find the managing partner.

More powerful than a locomotive. Planes couldn't give you that. Once you were up, you didn't seem to be going anyplace. Awareness of movement meant bad news: weather, turbulence. It wasn't really faster; it was suspended animation. Go to sleep here, wake up there, and if you couldn't get to sleep you just floated, uneasy, like riding through a humid night waiting for sunup.

A train rocked. Blasted you out of there, the miles flying by right out the window, where you could count them, one after another, as he had invisibly swung from telephone pole to telephone pole on country roads in the back seat of Black Beauty until he lost track and fell asleep. But that was light stuff next to a train. Something about the metal on metal and the whole contraption shaking, hurtling relentlessly as if it might fall apart within seconds after arrival.

Gotta-get-there-gotta-get-there-gotta-get-there-gotta-get-there, Moooving! Gotta-get-there-gotta-get-there.

The urgency left you no time, almost, to worry about what *was* up there. Or back there. She couldn't meet him for lunch, which might have helped, and there was little time for dinner. He had to pack. This would make the connection at New York, which could get him to the hospital by breakfast. The final scene was a disappointment. Not her fault. There weren't any stairs. Back home, long ago, they used to have stairs, black, tar-papery stairs with tiny glistening specks that looked like way-out-there stars, and it was like you were climbing into a cold, dark, jeweled space deeper than anything John Glenn or Stanley Kubrick had revealed. That wasn't her fault, and it wasn't his fault that the station had all the romance of an office building lobby and that stuff like rent and phones and forwarding luggage had to get done before he could even begin to blame her for not getting back to the Conversation, so he didn't have any reason to feel let down and nothing in the script said to play it as a farewell, which meant a quick seeyalater as if, as if, as if what? As if he'd see her later, and she'd get to forget he'd asked but he'd have to remember, now, that she'd never answered.

A train took you away from that fast, no waiting, taxiing, banking, hovering—half an hour, maybe, and you were still looking down at the same spot and whoever you'd left was halfway home. And the routine violence of its movements, a roller-coaster that didn't climb, didn't dip and never stopped, was an unkind incentive to sleep. Like that poor baby out there on the treetop, even if you weren't tired before, you wanted to pass out because the shit was scary and *rough*.

Gottagettheregottagetthere . . .

• • •

Was he on his way to the bathroom, the dining car? He was out of his seat, struggling for balance in that little alleyway at the back of the car, where you have to set yourself and tug mightily—and maybe yell Geronimo (What was that Indian's name again?)—before you plunged out into the loud, raw space between cars. The door flew open, a sure, practiced pull, before he reached it, and the man stood in front of him, like a surfer, not even holding on. Did he really twirl that watch chain? Did he even have one, or was it the stance? Maybe, too, the hat, tipped way to the side in memory of sportier days. He'd had them, that was for sure. Tall, light-skin, curly-head, prettysmilin nigger. A dancer, maybe, a runner, yes.

Look like you been through it, son.

It's a rough ride.

Yeah, it is that. But it ain't the train. Train's like a reefer. You up, it keep you up. You down, baby, it grease the skids.

I hear that. Guess I am down. Goin home. Emergency.

Somebody die?

No. Close, maybe.

That ain't it, then.

Hell it ain't. He's like my father. (Why should that make him smile?)

If he ain't gone yet, that should be a up. You wanna get there, right? The go-to shouldn't get you down. Could be the come-from.

He grunted, eyes down.

I thought so.

It's not all that. It's just—

Talk to me, baby.

I don't know if she wants what I want. It's all there, but we can't pull it together. Can't get it in synch.

I knew it, man. They make you loop the loop, don't they?

No. I mean, it's not like she's tryin to fuck with me.

Let me tell you, son. I'm the come-frominest man you ever met. For me, that's a high. Shit get thick, I rock on, you know? You ain't there, zip, I'm ridin the rail, Jim. Course that's me. I can see it's workin on you different.

That's what I'm tryin to say. I don't wanna get away. I wanna make it happen.

Looka here. I can dig where you comin from, cause that was me, believe it or not. First time. I knew it was right, man, but I couldn't get it right. Drove me crazy. So I ran. Got good to me, and I kept on. But you know what? I figured out, long time ago, that all that rockin and all that ridin went back to that one time. Wasn't bout all the others. I was tryin to get back and when I knew I couldn't, I kept gettin away.

See I couldn't do like that.

Well check yourself, son. You could be headin that way. What I figured out for me, I was right the first time. That's right. The first time. Ain't that a bitch. Here, there and everywhere, and I had it right right off the bat. Couldn't get back, though, so here I am diggin the ride. You wanna get off, that's another story. It ain't the train, though. It ain't the train got you down. That's just transportation. Could be it's just movin in the wrong direction for you.

Yeah. Maybe not.

Mommy, is Daddy on the train?

No, honey.

I thought you said Daddy worked on the train.

Not this one. That was a long time ago.

Oh. We goin to New York?

No, Richard. You know better than that. We're going to Boston.

Uncle Clarence gonna be there?

No, honey. You know Uncle Clarence is dead. We're going to visit his family.

What time we gonna be there?

Long time, sweetie.

She went back to her book with the handsome man holding the pretty lady whose dress was falling off, and he looked at his Superman book again, the one where he goes back to Krypton and meets his parents but they don't know who he is because it's not real. Then he went up to the water fountain and this time made it both ways without bumping into any of the people sleeping in the seats on the aisle or spilling water on them from the paper snowcone cup. The train took a long time, but it was fun.

So was Boston, at least at first. His big cousin had lots of comic books, Mommy only let him have a few, and they read and played superheroes and tag and marbles. The little one was meaner. He looked mad and followed him around the whole time and wouldn't let him touch his stuff, especially the Zorro sword. His big brother told him to quit being a brat and beat him up once but that only made him worse.

Their new baby was nice, too, it was a girl and he never held one before. She had big dimples and little bitty fingers and toes and held on real tight to his finger and smiled at him a lot. Their new daddy didn't say much. He wasn't as funny as Uncle Hodge but didn't mind getting dirty like Mommy's friend Jack did and let them climb on him inside and in the yard and pushed them on the swing and tried to make his mean cousin share his toys.

He spent a lot of time with the boys and the baby and their daddy while Mommy sat around talking to Aunt DeeDee like they were girls whispering secrets and went for walks and shopping when Aunt DeeDee said, Girl, come on, I need to get out of the house for a while, I'm so glad you all came. And Mommy went along, almost like he wasn't there, because she wasn't at home and didn't have to clean nothing and could pretend she wasn't a mommy at all.

They all did some things together. He found Mother Goose's grave when they went around looking at history stuff and Mr. Davis, their new daddy, bought him a toy boat like his cousin's when they went to see the big old boat in the harbor.

One day when Mr. Davis was with the baby and Mommy and Aunt DeeDee were out his cousin showed him a picture of him and his real daddy.

I thought my Uncle Clarence was your daddy.

That's him.

How come he don't got on his hat? Uncle Clarence was a soldier.

Not all the time, dummy.

Don't call me that.

Aw, don't be a baby.

Yeah, you a baby, the little one said.

He pushed him and said, Shut up, and the big one knocked him down.

Don't push my brother. He's just a little kid.

He's callin me names.

So what? You are a baby. Leave him alone or I won't let you read my comics anymore.

They're stupid anyway. Just like you.

His cousin knocked him down again and said, Dumb brat.

The little one hit him and said, Baby brat, baby brat.

He kicked the little one and the big one grabbed him around the neck and the little one bit his leg.

He started crying and Mr. Davis came and pulled them apart and he ran outside until Mommy came back.

Later everybody apologized but the little one didn't mean it.

Next day Mommy took him shopping with her and Aunt DeeDee and that night they all went out to dinner and ate fish and it was okay but the little one kept blowing water on him.

Then it was time to go home. Aunt DeeDee gave him a wet kiss on the cheek and Mr. Davis shook his hand real mannish and the baby giggled for him and the big cousin gave him a comic book to read on the train but the other one kept his hands in his pockets and looked mad some more.

The train rocked his head in Mommy's lap and he said, I don't think they like me, and she said, Of course they do, honey. Some boys just like to play too rough and they don't know when they hurt somebody's feelings.

Later he said, It's not fair.

What's not fair?

They got two daddys, Mr. Davis and Uncle Clarence. And they got two brothers and a baby.

Yeah, but you've got me and I've got you, and we're better than all of 'em put together.

She played with his hair and he fell asleep with the moon smiling at him out the train window. And when he woke up it was time to get off and the moon was still there and so was she.

November 4, 1974

Yeah, the old machine still works.

I'm going to just jump right in here because I want to talk about how it felt, that week at the end of summer. The first four days were pretty rough. I sat with him for hours, as long as they let me (especially when you weren't there) and talked to him about everything. I didn't realize it had been so long. A lot of it was things I hadn't discussed with you—still haven't—or with anybody else. They were the kind of things I always felt I owed him. You know, man talk, the stuff I supposed I'd talk to my father about if you . . . never mind. It's not like I'd been doing that all along—having heart-to-heart talks with him. A lot of it had been in my head. But I knew he was the person to go to if I was going to talk. Maybe it was seeing him lying there, unable to respond (to tell me how full of crap I was) that made me open up. Or else the fear that he would be gone and I'd never have the chance again.

I talked about making it the way we'd all planned I would. He knew it better than either of us. You were the one pushing and worrying, and I had to jump through the hoops. He always sat back all cool watching it happen just the way he knew it would. Like he'd read the book before and didn't want to tell us all the twists and turns of the plot because it didn't matter, he knew the ending. Like he knew I'd have to do a lot of things you didn't want in order to do what you wanted and that I'd get to resenting you for making it possible.

I talked about Yvonne too. How I sort of kept her from you after you met her because you liked her so much. I didn't want to tell you how serious we were getting; I knew you'd approve and think you'd been right all along. I told him about how being with her made me feel responsible, and what a drag that could be. I know you don't want to hear that because responsibility has always been a big thing with you. But it doesn't work if you have to work at it, you know what I mean? If it's an obligation, a duty. Half the time growing up I thought you were responsible for me because you got stuck with me, not because you loved me. And in return, you wanted to be certain I got myself stuck with somebody I felt responsible for, somebody who was dependent on me, and my carrying that burden would vindicate all your own years of involuntary servitude.

I can just see you loving your grandchildren more joyfully than you ever did their father. Would you greet their accomplishments with a question about the next, or buy them ice cream for every fingerpaint picture and clay lump passing for a bunny? Would you enjoy watching me do the yelling, the spanking, the correcting of pronunciation, or would you perversely intervene (as only Hodge could do for me) and protest that I was taking my responsibilities too seriously? Yes, you might do that, especially if you saw, as you would, that I was good at it, that for all my righteous dominance, I gave them, as well, more freedom than I got. That would scare you. You might begin to understand that your way wasn't the only way or even the best way.

Anyway, here's the funny part—and this is the joke I shared with Hodge during those days last August. In fact, I waited until he was awake, with one eye fluttering with a hint of comprehension and the other half open but not seeing. I waited because I knew he appreciated a good punchline. I tried it, you see. Went out and got myself some responsibility and wore it around for three years like a block letter. And I begged for more, for all of it, to prove I could carry the weight my father couldn't and still jump all the hurdles (I'd found plenty you didn't even know were there) and win the race. And you know what?

She said no.

Hodge didn't laugh.

I thought it was a scream, don't you? I mean, this was the perfect setup, so perfect I didn't want to tell you. And she wouldn't go for it. Ain't that, as Hodge used to say, a high kick for a low calf?

But at the time I was more worried about Hodge. Here I had made myself a sitting duck for him. I was sure the Signifying Monkey would be in order here, or one of those dumb-house-nigger parables. He didn't move. I thought, for a minute, he looked sorry for me. It was something about the way his eyes kind of saddened up and drifted away. He could always pick me up or put me down before, but pity had never been part of the ride. He had his nerve. Here he was, old, poor and flat on his back and I'm off for my third Ivy degree and he feels sorry for me. I couldn't take it. I left.

The next day was the day I waited for you. I couldn't face him alone. Remember, the doctor—that young white guy you looked at like his name was Kennedy—said there had been marked improvement in his condition. And you strutted into the half room all sunny and positive, got partway to the bed and he kind of rolled his eye at you and squinted what he could of his face like you were from Mars. You froze in mid-step.

It's me, Elizabeth, you said. Baby.

And he said something that sounded like, "Who?"

You weren't ready for that. You stiffened up and took a step back, then turned into my arms. Right then, over your shoulder, I swear he winked at me and let out this little toothless wheeze that looked and sounded like a newborn baby laughing like Hodge. When you heard that, you knew you'd been had. It was a good one, and we went up to him, still absentmindedly holding on to each other and rejoicing in the knowledge that he was still there. I don't think either of us gave any thought to the way we held hands as we leaned over him.

I felt better the rest of the week. Since we knew he wasn't going to die just then, we started telling Hodge stories, all those dumb things with him and his cars and the Fourth of July picnic that would have had Noah worried and that grand two-and-a-half-hour camping trip.

What was it I meant to tell you? I got angry in the middle again and forgot why I started this. This was supposed to be the important part, how I've been thinking about those last few days. What Hodge did then. What I meant to tell you then. And didn't, again. I guess I was supposed to be telling you now, so when I get home again

Fuck it. This isn't going to work.

chapter 18

It was the last line that caught his friend Jeff's attention: "leader of the armed occupation of a university library in 1970 by militant black students, which left one white student shot and wounded." There had been no follow-up to the Atlanta killing and Gene's name had been little publicized—he was no Angela Davis—so his capture was not front-page news. If Jeff hadn't noticed that reference deep in the A section, put two and two together, and showed the paper to him, Ike might have missed it altogether. Yvonne hadn't known Gene, and Ike had never gotten around to telling her about the Atlanta business. She might have picked up something on the DC vine, but the vibrations rarely traveled that far north anymore. He wouldn't have heard it from her.

Spencer's congressman had already won reelection, narrowly. Others in the People's Liberation Army had been rounded up, including the triggermen, and the candidate, formerly a lieutenant in the movement, ran hard on the investigation. Gene had been arrested, the article said, in a Harlem apartment. There had been a brief exchange of gunfire, which was undoubtedly what had drawn the paper's attention. He was wounded—hence the ironic parallel. No mention of a woman or child. A relief, but not surprising. His letter had come back to Elizabeth's. Juanita had obviously been ahead of the game. By the time Gene had shown up in New York, she was long gone.

That, at least, was good news.

The bad news was Christmas—again—and he was already regretting his promise to come back. Not that there was anyplace else to go. That letter, retrieved from the waste basket, partially recopied, then angrily shredded, still lingered in his mind, but he'd learned his lesson way back from the paper towels. That hadn't worked. None of those sensitive, heartfelt outpourings had changed a damn thing. Why should this one be any different? It was all a cop-out, inadmissible evidence.

He'd have to do better than that. But he wasn't in any hurry to try.

He could still make it back on a tank. Good timing; he'd picked up the Maverick used in Jersey because it reminded him of the old Comet, not knowing that within a few months its most valuable feature would be its gas mileage. Elizabeth had moved up to a Buick, but she never went too far so it didn't matter that it cost four times as much to fill up twice as often. He still looked for the Comet, though, because they'd had it before they moved, so it always seemed more of a landmark than the two drab, three-story sandstone rows of apartments. They'd been there all through high school—he'd been gone longer than he'd been there, in fact—but it had never been home. He didn't have one. Canal Street, maybe, where he'd waited for Black Beauty on Saturdays and for his father one more time. It was now a stoney lot in the shadow of the interstate. There'd be Christmas trees there now. One year he'd convinced her to get one from there. I could understand if they *grew* there, she'd said, but the man just sells 'em there, you know. The selection really wasn't too great and they *were* overpriced. It made him happy, but he didn't complain when she went back to the large, brightly lit Tree City out on the boulevard, as advertised on TV. That was before the K Mart nevergreen.

The Coccaris still had their lights, thank God. At this time of year, daylight was a waste, especially around here, where the snow merely reflected the dullness of the sky. The day dawned instead at nightfall, when displays like the Coccaris' shone brighter than the Fourth of July and never failed to excite him. They had once made annual pilgrimages around town to see them, nativities and Frosties, Santa silhouettes perched atop light-form chimneys, forty-foot front-yard trees dressed to rival Rockefeller Center and whole houses lit up in toyland splendor. Tacky by day, no doubt, but at night, for at least a couple of weeks, the lights made him believe in things shiny and new. That was why he cheered aloud over the noise of the Maverick's heater when he saw that the neighbors had not only maintained the tradition but added a gaudy Rudolph to the front lawn, blinking his nose defiantly at the quiet, careless fraying of the block and flashing a beacon to a son with no Comet to look for.

Upstairs, Nat sang, a potato pie baked and a fresh tree twinkled; some hip Cratchetts had taken over the apartment. And this pleasant-looking woman, just hippy enough to convey maternal solidity, stepped forward to hug him.

"What you know good, girl?" he asked her.

"What's that on your face?"

That was more like it.

"Got too busy to shave. Liked the way it looked. Why, you don't like it?"

She grunted. "Well. Keep it trimmed. It's not so bad."

She'd been podded. He'd have to look under her bed for the empty, alien shell.

"Supposed to be Christmas in here or something?"

She crossed her arms.

"No, dummy, it's Yom Kippur. If you don't like it after all this work you can just take your behind back to New Haven and I'll find me somebody else to share the spirit."

He put his hands on her shoulders and kissed her on the nose.

"It's beautiful," he said. "Really. I didn't know you had it in you."

The ornaments were screwed up. Too much of one color in a couple of places. And there was a bare spot that could have been better covered or turned to the wall. He wished she'd let him do it, though he was glad she'd made the effort. But how'd she get the tree up there?

"Go put away your stuff and wash your hands," she said. "Your dinner's waiting."

"You mean it's waiting like on the stove keeping warm or sitting out on a plate getting cold?"

"You know, I hope you don't pretend to your college friends that your mother is as bad as you try to make me out when you're home," she said and went into the kitchen.

When he followed, after washing and flipping Nat over, she was standing at the stove like somebody who didn't mind cooking.

"There you go, Your Honor," she said, presenting a hot plate of fried chicken, macaroni and cheese and greens. "So how's school?" She sat down to watch and listen.

"About as bad as everybody said it would be, but okay. Hey, this is good. It helps that I'm a little older than a lot of the others. I get more respect that way."

"Are they giving you a hard time?"

That was code. She meant: do they call you boy, make you drink out of the colored fountain and have you picking cotton? "No harder than anybody else," he said. "They give everybody shit. Sorry. Friend of mine named Kaplan probably gets in more trouble than anybody else."

"Jewish?"

"Mm-hm. He catches it a lot more than I do. Nice guy, but he tries to show off a lot. Thinks he knows all the answers."

"Sounds like somebody else I know."

"I don't know what you're talking about."

He had introduced himself to Jeff, whom he'd seen in class, when he heard him singing "Corrine, Corrina" under his breath in the library. Turned out his uncle had owned a record store in a black neighborhood in St. Louis, and held on to the old stuff that he figured might be worth something someday. Meanwhile, Jeff had absorbed much of it, so he and Ike took to comparing notes. He started to share that with her, but he had realized a while back that she took no special pleasure in his interest.

"And, you'll be happy to know," he said, "I haven't taken over anything. No time, and nobody's doing that stuff anymore anyway."

"So you really like it?"

"Well, yeah. I mean, it's not a barrel of laughs, but it's what I want to do. Just a couple of years and I'll be ready to take on your boy Perry Mason."

"I don't know about that. You want some more? Did I tell you they took it off?"

"Really? How do you get through the evening?"

"I ask myself the same thing all the time," she said at the stove serving seconds. "I'm usually so tired I don't even pay attention to what they got on there."

"Guess it shouldn't matter. You went to sleep on Perry, too."

"All right now."

"How is he?"

He figured he'd timed it just about right; he hadn't reached for the crutch too soon.

Walking back to the table, she sighed, as she would have to, but also nodded, signaling that the cue was on time. "He's about as well as you'd expect, you know. He has some good days and a lot of bad ones. He's wearing me out, but he's still here."

"How's Maria working out?"

She snorted. "Well you know I had my doubts. But I'll tell you the truth, sometimes I think she's keeping him alive. She's good with him, she really is. She don't take no crap, and you know that's how you have to handle him, cause honey he couldn't hardly take care of himself when he was your age. It was always Momma or me or Aunt Milly or somebody, you know, lookin out for him. And I'll tell you something, just between you and me and the fencepost. I don't think she's all that attractive and she's certainly no spring chicken, but I think she kinda charms him just enough to keep his hopes up, you know what I mean."

"That's my Hodge. Seventy whatever and can't hardly move and he thinks he's shackin."

Next morning they quietly exchanged presents, reciprocal sweaters, and went off to Christmas service at church. They hadn't always done that before, especially when it fell during the week, but she was church secretary now, and he understood it seemed to be a bigger part of her life. Dessie was there, holding their seat on the aisle. Ike had once seen them force a whole pewful of folks—visitors, obviously—to slide down because they were trespassing. She had just returned from visiting Tommy and his family in Atlanta. Big Tom had been sick for a while, cancer probably, though nobody said it. The difference in Dessie's and Elizabeth's ages had always seemed greater than it was, probably because she had gotten married first and his mother seemed not to have been married yet. Watching them together now, like sisters, he realized that the gap was real. The changes of the last few years had acted on them differently; one of them seemed at the end of something, the other at the beginning.

When she sashayed back to her seat after reading the welcome and notices with special holiday sincerity, Ike noticed one of the ushers, a handsome, younger man, following her with his eyes. Dessie elbowed her discreetly and raised an eyebrow in the usher's direction; Elizabeth ignored it and looked straight ahead. After service, Ike braced himself for a round of who's-this-fine-young-man on the front steps, where Elizabeth usually held court. There was some of that, and he responded with modest aplomb. But she, meanwhile, spent time chatting familiarly with Jim, the straight-backed gentleman who bore a head usher's blue ribbon and whose white gloves had seemed grafted to his hands for twenty years. Once, long ago, Elizabeth had told him that Jim worked as a redcap at the old station along with his father when she first came to town. And in an unguarded moment he had heard her tell Dessie that she wished she'd let *him* take her bags instead. Because Ike had always thought of him as older, he looked younger now, his dark Indian features set but not sagged, in a way that any of the churchwomen would kill for. His wife had died fairly recently; Ike remembered Elizabeth being involved with the ritual mourning and doing-for. He also remembered, though it was not the kind of thing that one gave too much thought to at the time, that Jim had always been particularly solicitous of Elizabeth.

"Finally giving the old boy some play, huh?" he said as they slid into the car.

"Who, Jim? Honey, I've known him since before you were born." A nondenial denial.

After a quick dinner of stuffed capon and sweet potatoes, they went to see Hodge, confined in the old folks' highrise built on the Jewtown dust. They brought him a plate, although he didn't eat much, which was why they didn't have dinner there, and they brought one for Maria, too, despite Elizabeth's grumblings that she didn't know what to do with real food. Ike had never met her, and his image of her had shifted back and forth from Latin seductress to Mean Old Nurse. She was, not surprisingly, neither. It was a short, slender woman who opened the door, with black hair pulled back from a smooth, firm face.

"Merry Christmas," Elizabeth said.

"Yes. Thank you. You too," Maria answered, smiling slightly. "Come in. He watch television." She accepted the plates of food graciously but as if they were an unwelcome offering—the way Elizabeth might take a cake baked by a woman who kept cats—and spirited them into the kitchen.

"Hi, Unc, what's shakin?" Elizabeth called to Hodge, who seemed only then to notice them. "Look who dropped by."

"What it is, sport?" Ike asked.

He was sitting in pajamas on the sofa, wrapped in an afghan, looking like a small child allowed to stay up late for a favorite program. He smiled weakly but cheerfully, the left side of his face showing more flexibility, and managed to say, "Merry Christmas" in a Don Corleone whisper. First Elizabeth, then Ike, kissed him lightly on the forehead, and Ike pulled from a plastic bag several wrapped packages. The first, which Elizabeth opened when Hodge's hands proved too slow, was a blue bathrobe that she draped over his shrunken shoulders. Ike opened another, a blue Yale cap, which he placed on his uncle's head, and then another, a wide, garish paisley tie. Elizabeth had said he shouldn't waste his money on expensive things, a request he found offensive, even though she cleaned it up by saying she knew he didn't have much money. But he took it as a challenge to find small things with special meaning. The final item was his favorite, secured with the help of Jeff, who had another uncle in the car business: a

Lincoln hood ornament. Hodge grinned and whispered, "Black Beauty."

Maria had reentered the room without a sound and sat watching the scene obliquely, conscious of not intruding. Elizabeth opened her purse and handed her the small package Ike had asked her not to. It was an ornate gold-plated bracelet with purple glass beads that one of her Italian co-workers had given her. Elizabeth, who considered it hideous, had figured Maria would have similar taste and had rewrapped it; she had also told the woman she would save it for church, so she wouldn't be expected to wear it to work. Maria opened it, looked suspiciously at Elizabeth, pressed a thin smile and set it down on a table beside her chair.

Her main business completed, Elizabeth sat poised on the edge of the sofa and began to make loud, pleasant conversation like in a club meeting. Hodge's gaze had fallen back onto the college football game on TV—"Boy like Snake," he whispered to Ike, referring to one of the old high-school heroes from the neighborhood. So she was left to make a few comments to Maria about the weather, in the same voice she used with Hodge, as if speaking mostly Spanish was the same as having suffered a stroke. "That's typical though, around here," she chattered. "We never have to worry about a white Christmas." Maria knew, as Ike did, what game she was playing, but she nodded and said yes. Although her English was not good, she'd been living there for years, a fact Elizabeth tended to ignore. She fluffed the pillows on the sofa. She smoothed the thin, still-wavy hair on the back of Hodge's head, and mumbled something about a brush. She straightened up the magazines she had brought, most of which obviously had not been touched. Maria said something, though, pointing to a *Jet*. "Pictures. I show him. He like." The bathing-suit centerfold, probably, which Ike had found less appealing since the magazine went to color; the shading on the model's legs had been much more appealing in black and white.

Either embarrassment over this woman showing half-nudies to her uncle or sheer impatience prompted Elizabeth to get up and announce she would look in the kitchen. Ike could hear her banging cupboards. The refrigerator opened. "Has he been eating the oatmeal?" she called. "The cornbread? You want me to heat up these plates?" Maria followed. The refrigerator opened again, and Ike heard Elizabeth say, "Oh, really? Well, as long as he eats something." She went on oblivious to Maria's shadow, rummaging through the bedroom and bathroom, making occasional remarks, ostensibly to herself, about pajamas and razors. Ike caught Hodge's eye. He smiled weakly and shook his head.

"What's the score?" she said when she returned.

Hodge whispered and nodded toward the set.

"What you say?"

"More game after this, he say," Maria explained.

Elizabeth looked to her and back to Hodge, momentarily flustered by the need for translation. "Well," she said, recovering. "I guess I know when I'm not needed." She laughed quickly and alone. "I'll just come back sometime when you're not busy," she added in an exaggerated tone of nonchalance.

Hodge gestured her closer and whispered again.

"What do you know 'bout any Merry Christmas, you sittin up here lookin at some old game," Elizabeth said, fetching her purse.

He wheezed his baby woodpecker laugh, pointing at her as he looked at Ike.

"Good see you," he said.

Ike gave him a heavy hug. "You too, Hodge," he said. "Take it easy."

"He doesn't look too good, does he?" Elizabeth said a few minutes later in the elevator.

Ike shrugged. "About as well as I expected, I suppose."

"He's really gone down in the last few weeks, though," she said gravely.

Ike didn't try to resist the grin. "Must be the Puerto Rican cooking," he said. It was killing her, anyway. "He seems pretty happy to me."

Elizabeth began to respond in earnest but caught his expression.

"Oh, shoot, boy, what do you know?" she said petulantly. "Somebody's gotta look after him."

"And you've gotta look after somebody, right?" He took her arm to keep her from slipping as they tenderfooted through the parking lot. It was already getting dark, but on Christmas that meant the beginning of brightness.

The next day she went off to work complaining but proud in the new sweater he'd given her, very middle-aged preppie in a soft blue with a gold chain and pin. She half apologized for not taking more time off, but she never knew how long he was going to stay and had long since stopped worrying over it. He always just sat around anyway. Besides, she had taken the beginning of the week to get the apartment ready and had used up all her personal days on Hodge. Ike found odd pleasure in watching her get ready, triggered by her asking whether he thought a gray tweed or black wool skirt would go better with the sweater. He chose the black and stifled the urge to ask how she'd been getting herself dressed all these years. Obviously, she had been getting it done without him; it was enough that she had asked, calling up those frantic high-school mornings when, trying to coordinate himself and protesting that Rifkin, the accountant she used to work for, wouldn't notice if she showed up in a paper bag, he always relented and passed judgment on a blouse, a scarf, a pair of earrings. Only after they'd raced each other out of the apartment did he realize how much her unfailingly sincere "Thanks, honey" contributed to his day.

Her preparations took even more time now, possibly because he wasn't rushing her—and simplifying her decisions—but also because the extra pounds, the hair in a state of late-summer turning and the insult of forty, two years past, commanded increased diligence. Makeup, once a powdery, slapdash affair, had become a system of bases and creams, and she lingered for minutes adding color around her eyes from a battery of gear that replaced the single stubby red eyebrow pencil. It also occurred to him that one reason his fashion services were no longer needed was that she was not desperate to mix-and-match the same dozen pieces. His own closet was now pinched with the overflow from hers, warm-weather dresses and tops, light-colored skirts sheathed in plastic that made his adolescent sports jackets look archaic. Spring hats—God forbid a colored woman should go bareheaded on Sunday—covered old

Sports Illustrateds, school papers and certificates on his closet shelf like ivy, and the mess of letters he'd received from colleges, most of which he'd never heard of, was neatly stacked into a tall pile on the floor to make way for an assortment of shoes, all of them with at least the toe out and stratospheric heels that rivaled his track spikes. There was, after all, a limit to her sacrifices, which he had taken for granted as he was supposed to. She liked to look good; that was never a secret, and everyone always said she did a good job of it. But the woman he watched tip out of the apartment that morning was one who knew that she had not looked as good as she wanted to, as good as she might have had she not spent her cute years on him. Well, go ahead, girl, he said aloud out the window. Still, he was not really sorry that was the way it had worked out and was sad that she had apparently resigned her commission.

He had decided to walk downtown for the first time since he had gotten his driver's license. The stretch from here to there had grown blacker and poorer; that was obvious. When the interstate had sent them all scurrying like roaches to the west side, their impact had seemed minimal. One junior high school, not the one Ike had attended, became "black"—maybe a third—as the tar oozed with particular thickness down that one stretch contiguous with the old neighborhood. A good many of them, however, had elbowed in beside Poles and Ukrainians, wrongway Italians stuck on the other side of town from their own reservation and an awful lot of what Elizabeth called Poor White Trash, though they were far from the Appalachian depravity the term conjured up. Altogether it made for a surprisingly easy rehash of the prewar stew that had become, first, Jewtown in fact, and then, later, a blackface version that kept the name. As it turned out, that was a temporary alignment. The Bamas had tipped the balance, with a vengeance, and as a result the black population was now poorer and trashier than the PWTs had ever been.

There were lots more of them, and fewer places to put them. By the first year of college, Ike had begun to notice empty spaces flashing by as he drove down the streets, and because that process was predictably continuous, he hardly noticed anymore. On foot, however, he could see that the spaces were far more numerous than he had imagined. More perversely, grass had overgrown the once-fresh rubble and the openness had seemed to shrink, so that no one who hadn't bought a Payday or bag of barbecue chips in that spot would ever stop to think there had once been a building there at all. Many of the buildings that did remain had lapsed into parody, like the Chinese cleaners that had become the headquarters of a community service outfit and was now occupied by a fish-fry-and-numbers joint. The emptiness accelerated in the last long blocks between the residential area and downtown. Where huge industrial buildings had stood, some still operating, others given over to warehousing or discount outlets, there was now an unobstructed view ahead to the pathetic remains of the four main-drag blocks that had been the mecca of his childhood.

First stop was Louie's Record Shop. They used to keep some old stuff in the back bins with Sinatra and the original cast albums. Maybe he could find a Louis Jordan to share with Jeff. He got nearly to the end of the block before it hit him, and he retraced his steps with a quick fury. Right there, next to the Thom McAn's. That *was* it. He stepped inside to make sure. Louie's had become a cut-rate kids' clothing store. The bins lining either side of the long, narrow shop were filled with cheap snowsuits, tights, underwear and one-piece pajamas. Up on the walls, large, ugly pink and blue stuffed dogs and cats posed mockingly among red and gold tinsel garlands. A young girl, cute, about four, in a day-old lavender cloth coat, steered a baby carriage absently into one of the bins as she looked up at the animals. A soft gurgle from the carriage rose swiftly to a scream that turned heads throughout the shop.

"Taniqua!" hissed a small, sinewy woman nearby. "What you wake that baby up for?"

"Sorry, Mommy. It was a accident."

"How many times I gotta tell you to watch where you goin? You see it ain't no room in here for sightseein."

The rebuke, almost as loud as the crying, inspired the baby to higher levels.

"Hush, Malcolm," the girl said, jiggling the carriage. "You go back to sleep."

The mother sucked her teeth and swatted at the child with a handful of irregular Doctor Dentons. "He wake now," she said. "Come on, I can't shop with that noise. You just gonna have to wait for them shoes, too." She grabbed the carriage, swiveled it roughly and pushed toward the door.

The girl was neither repentant nor defiant. She followed with a slightly embarrassed impassiveness, as if *her* child had just acted up—these things happen—and she would have to continue her business another time. She looked, Ike noticed, exactly like her mother, which was not good news for her. The woman bore a look of permanent agitation carved in her face more sharply than age, although she was probably a year or two younger than he was. As they passed him at the door, Ike glimpsed a swatch of color, bright blue, that was out of place in the pastels of the carriage. It was the Doctor Dentons, buried in a far corner under the squirming and squealing Malcolm. Taniqua looked back and gave Ike a little shrug of a smile.

Outside he headed for the library. He liked to think that he spent much of his youth there, and in fact there had been many Saturdays when he begged out of shopping to rummage around alone in the children's room. But he couldn't remember much about the rest of the place at all. He knew, though, that they were supposed to have documents on the nineteenth-century rescue by local abolitionists of a runaway slave named, of all things, Jerry. It was the kind of thing that everybody knew something about vaguely and mentioned from time to time during Negro History Week. He'd been meaning to get the details for years and this was as good a time as any. What he would do with them was another story, but at least he would know.

Ahead of him on the street was a familiar figure, and without thinking about it he fell into a pace, a home-stretch rhythm, that would overtake her. Between the bottom of her short coat and the tops of her mid-calf boots, he saw enough to jog his most enduring memory of Valerie, his seventh-grade dream girl: riding his bike in measured laps around her house for just one more look at what God meant legs to be, full and sleek. It was lucky that she lived within his prescribed range. If there was a hope of following her farther then, he would have. It was odd, though, how, in those days, he almost never saw anyone he knew from the neighborhood downtown. Didn't they go in department stores? Did they all just stay home? There were lots more folks around now. Maybe they had more money, although that had never stopped Elizabeth, or maybe there were more tacky stores. Either way, if the abolitionists showed up today they'd have a bitch of a time figuring out who to rescue.

As she turned the corner, he considered calling out her name. But in that moment he realized it wasn't her. Of course not. Anyone who looked that good at ten would have passed prime a long time ago. Look worse than Taniqua's mother and, in Valerie's case, three times as big. It could be a sister. It was one of those families they never stopped coming from. They marched out of the apartment and through school, one after the other, mass-produced, and so apparently similar that Ike couldn't help being surprised when he heard that one had embarked on a successful career someplace.

The Valerie chase brought him within sight of the library. And it reassured him that somebody, if not her own parents, was still making them like they used to. But it also, somehow, opened his mind to a thought that must have been floating on the edge for some time. He shouldn't be alone. When you go home you hang out with friends. The excuse of Tommy being away had worn thinner than the knees of last summer's play pants. And what else was there? Drinks with Hez had been an accident, a happy one but one that couldn't be pushed. And it was a long time ago. Janet might be happy to see him, but her happiness would be too important a part of the equation. At this point, he knew, he would resent it if she wanted to remain just friends, and if they tried to be more they would end up with less.

There was that time he ran into Sonny, one of the track bloods, looking surprisingly suburban in his Izod and Adidas, at the car wash. He had studied accounting at the community college and held a nice desk job at the pharmaceutical plant while he finished his bachelor's at night. He mentioned that another teammate worked there, too, but he was out on the floor. The way he said it suggested to Ike some distance in the relationship. Sonny obviously sensed that he had more in common with Ike now than with his boyhood running buddy. His soft drawl, which had hinted at cautious understatement in the rambunctious world of high school, was more clipped. Ike imagined that he went through life now like the male Sunday School teachers who consciously abandoned their Saturday backyard diction for a more precise presentation. That would be difficult, and he may have been looking for someone who understood. So when Sonny said they should get together, he meant it, and it struck Ike as a perfectly rational and pleasant idea. But he was just passing through, as always, in a hurry to meet Yvonne somewhere, and they parted knowing that it wouldn't happen.

Ironically, later that day at a supermarket—Elizabeth had a policy of going out of the neighborhood for food—he had run into Lucinda, one of The Group whose attention he had craved. She recognized him first. He had to scramble for her name and slip it in near the end of their brief conversation. She looked okay but not as stylish as once advertised; the frosted hair and turquoise eye shadow carried a lot of the weight. She had finished school, was living temporarily at home and was engaged, which came as a mild surprise because Ike seemed to remember her always being engaged. Their encounter was sincere and devoid of any meaning. That, he thought, was fitting. He had spent so much time concentrating on Elizabeth that he had neglected his own long-term interests. As a result, the place was a ghost town, filled with things he hadn't done and people he hadn't done them with. Actually, that wasn't quite right. Slogging up the half-shoveled library steps, a magically animated figure being returned to his proper state, he knew the reverse was true. They weren't the ghosts. It was his own presence that was as smoky as the runaway slave's. He couldn't stay there.

The world turned, snow fell and Elizabeth wanted to go shopping. It was the natural order of things. Ike wanted to go with her. That, he had concluded, was natural, too. Downtown, however, was not where it was at; he should have guessed that from the way the natives had taken over. Elizabeth moved with the times, the styles, the stores and the white people. That meant the mall. They were no strangers to the outskirts of town. The Comet's first trip had been to Shop City, a now hopelessly old-timey strip of adjoining stores along a single sidewalk. The effect had been to recreate downtown excluding the bus and foot folks, with, of course, acres of free parking. The big change in that original setup had been the addition of a split-level department store that soon abandoned its original State Street site, triggering a mass exodus. A few years later, an enclosed, climate-controlled center had opened in an opposite suburb, so she reprogrammed the Comet to change directions.

But here at last was the environment she had been waiting for: indoors, with wide concourses branching out in three directions. Escalators. Gardens. Fountains. Hall's, the stately dowager, was there, though they maintained the downtown operation with the third and fourth floors sealed off. Sears held down another corner with its auto center and bare-floored efficiency, highlighted by a new cheery, pink-cheeked attitude. It seemed positively giddy at having left the city behind. The third corner was dominated by Corcoran's, a recent invader from out of state, far classier than Sears and less stuffy than Hall's. It was clearly The Big Draw. Ordinarily, Ike would have given them points for keeping downtown alive, almost single-handedly, with their massive store and parking garage. But that was also their sin. The city store devoured two-thirds of a huge block that had once included his two favorite movie theaters, also the last two centrally located in the city. Ike had been furious when he realized that never again could a ten-year-old, or even a fifteen-year-old, walk or catch the bus downtown to "the show" on a Sunday afternoon or summer weekday. The *only way* to get to the movies was by car. This mall had two theaters, perversely right next to Corcoran's. He could not have been more upset if he'd been denied a house or admission to college, and he vowed never to set foot in the place. Elizabeth thought he was crazy.

They roamed the streets of paradise for hours. It was as if Christmas had not happened. The rush before could not possibly have been greater than the sale-induced, weekend-after swarming. But after he had nudged her in every other direction and explored as many diversions as he could, the time came to make a stand.

"I thought that only went for downtown," she said outside the second-level entrance to Corcoran's.

"Same store, same principle."

"Oh really now. You don't have to *buy* anything. Just look. They've got a real nice men's department. I saw some jackets last month that would look real good on you."

"Getteth behind me, Satan."

"Honestly. You're just gonna stand out here and wait?"

"That's right. I might look around a little, but I won't go too far. I'll get lost."

"You know this could take a while. I'm not gonna rush myself on your account."

"No kidding. My hair could turn gray before you come out of there. But I won't step through that door."

"If I see Mr. O'Hern, you want me to give him any message?" She knew all the managers by name.

"Yes, please. You know what to tell him."

"You know," she said, laughing and leaning into him, "you're goin about this all wrong. If you could keep *me* out of there you might get someplace. Then their business would really start to fall off."

"I know. But I wouldn't want to impose my values on anyone else. Besides, I'd need a ball and chain to keep you out."

"You got that right, kid," she said, turning to enter. "And even that might not do it."

He leaned on the rail and watched the scene below. It was like looking down at an anthill of white people. There were few men. Most of those who had ventured forth, it seemed, were back in the TV department of Sears watching the playoffs. Lots of women and children, none quite as loud as Taniqua's mother, but not as different as either would think. These, too, had a worn edge to their voices that bounced off the hard, shiny surfaces collectively like shattering light bulbs.

In one of the center display spaces, the radio station that once kept him up till midnight waiting to hear Procol Harum again was raffling off a fire-engine red vintage Corvette. Farther up, brightly dressed elves were hawking half-price toys under the banner "North Pole Workshop Clearance." They weren't dwarves—that would be too scary—and they weren't children—that would be illegal—but all were properly short. He noticed that when one handed a balloon to a woman who straightened up after receiving it and towered above him. It was dark blue. She picked the last one from the bouquet of reds, whites and greens, and as she loped away it bobbed in rhythm with her head above the crowd. Strands of gray streaked her deep auburn hair, surprising because she didn't move like someone that old.

A starter's gun fired in his stomach. He scurried sideways along the rail, eyes still focused ahead, and pushed onto the escalator. The traffic was against him. Stumbling, he risked a glance downward between the shopping bags that pummeled his knees. Wrong way. The down escalator was too far. The stiffest resistance was along the sides, so he forced his way down the middle, pumping his legs to make room and keep balance. Step one. Skip two. Easy. Grab. Hop. Lunge. He had to keep looking ahead. *Sorry. Sorry. 'Scuse me. Watch it. Comin through.* He jumped near the bottom and hit the floor limping. The blue balloon had disappeared around the corner. He veered to the left side. Easier to dodge if they see you coming. Jammed up by the raffle crowd, he ran atop the brick curbing that surrounded the center displays—dance that sideline, Franco—and managed to pick up speed. Room to maneuver at the corner. His rubber-soled shoes squeaked a faint echo of squealing movie tires. The balloon paused. He closed. Wheelchair dead ahead. Fat woman on one side, kid on the other. Don't get stupid. He stopped for the traffic to clear. The balloon floated down a side aisle. He started again at a trot, building momentum again at the turn. Wait. There. No. Wrong balloon. *Was* there a right one? Fuck! He breathed heavily and jogged back to the last intersection. His head swiveled. Winded *and* dizzy. Shit. Yes. Down that way. Out the door. Push. Not crowded here. Flat out. Dusk surprised him. Half a dozen balloons, all suddenly gray. Icy wind licked all up under his open coat at the places where he sweated. Which way? *Call!* A car door slammed. No. His eyes swept back across the lot. A balloon swooped for freedom on the breeze. A long arm reached out once and drew back into the car. He was already moving in that direction when he heard the engine turn over. On the first try, no less. Can't get there. Check the color. Burgundy Chrysler. Okay. Popeye Doyle time. He scanned the parking lot markers for their section and went for his keys. No! *SHIT!* He had driven her car because she wanted to be chauffeured, and he was pissed so he handed over the keys as soon as they parked. The hard way, then. Swinging around for that exit. Get in the wind. He was on his toes in three strides; shouldered the coat back far enough to work his arms; finally the head, snapping in time. *Huh! Huh!* The cold worked down through his lungs and up through his nose to a spot right between his eyes. Fuck that. Push. Ice patch. Hop, step, jump. He lost his balance, caught it. The car surged ahead. Blew the angle. Stop sign. Maybe. The brake lights glowed. He waved his arm. *Wait!* The slush gave way beneath him, then plowed into his face as his body slammed the pavement and slid. A car honked and skidded. The lights of the Chrysler floated out of the lot.

He couldn't decide if the house was nicer than he'd imagined. Probably. She had never talked them down, but you didn't exactly get the impression of tastefulness. Not that it mattered. As far as he had been concerned, she didn't live there, any more than he lived at Elizabeth's. Neutral corners they had to go back to between rounds. *A friend from high school.* That neutral enough? Apparently not. When he gave his name, she knew. That didn't matter either. *Oh. Didn't I hear about you?* She didn't miss a beat. It wasn't as ditsy as it sounded. She knew, all right. And she didn't back down. *I wouldn't be surprised.* They nodded to each other ever so slightly. Understood. *She should be back any minute. Won't you have a seat?* She wanted to see this. He liked her. *Can I get you anything?* Don't ask, he thought. *No, thanks.* She lingered, arms folded. A few school questions. He noticed her checking his left hand. She gave up nothing. She was fucking with him. But not meanly. That would have been okay, too. She'd waited long enough, and what could she do? She was trying to decide whether to ask or let it go. Her eyes kept sliding to the window. If she knew she had more time, they would have gotten into something, he was sure. But she didn't want to start something she wouldn't have time to finish. Finally, and reluctantly, she retired to another room.

On the mantel above the fireplace he saw her high-school graduation picture. And started to get up. Even though he should have been ready; he'd cried in his yearbook the night before. Too obvious. She'd be waiting for a move like that. And then he'd have to tell her what she didn't know about the picture. The little gold cross on her neck was a fake; he'd given her one like her parents had on her sixteenth birthday, though not as expensive. She swore her mother wouldn't be able to tell the difference. It was his she wore that day, and on a dozen other special occasions. Right up in your face, honey.

The door opened. And Mom was on it.

"There's a young man waiting to see you, dear," she said.

She had no time, Ike thought, to say more. He was too close. But maybe she didn't want to. He looked to her first, watching her watch her daughter. He wasn't sure, anyway, that he wanted to see the first reaction. He stood, in fact, before his eyes settled on her, in case he wasn't able to afterward. The eyes got him again. With her hair shorter and stylishly tousled, the heavy eyebrows stood out even more, but so did the eyes—her mother's, he saw now. Too light and wide open, they took in everything, while the rest of her face gave it back.

"Hello," she said simply. He probably had that coming.

"Hello," he said. Mom was still watching and had shadowed the one step forward she took. But he was beyond that now. He was beyond help. This was as far as his imagination had taken him. He could have stood there forever.

"What brings you?"

An odd phrase, he thought. She knew it. God, it runs in the family. They were both fucking with him.

"I wanted to talk to you," he said. Look at you. Make a fool of myself. I don't know. I'm dying.

"Well, let's take a walk," she said.

Her mother started to say something, but insisting was obviously not her style. She knew she was trumped and held out his coat.

He took it, put it on, followed her out the door, down the steps, up the block.

"That was you, wasn't it? At the mall?" she asked.

"You saw me?"

"Sort of. I saw something. It crossed my mind that it might've been you. I guess I figured if it was really you, you would have caught me."

"I tried."

They walked silently for a while.

"I take it the war is over?" He didn't get it. Then he did. He hadn't counted on bitterness and subtlety both. "Who won?"

"Nobody," he said, resigned to absorbing some punishment. "Not me."

"Too bad," she said too quickly. "I would have thought you couldn't lose."

She still hadn't looked at him, not really. But she was walking faster than she did when she was lost in thought. She was stalling. Stalling and spanking. He knew it when she started asking the same bullshit questions her mother had. And giving the same information, as she might at a mandatory reception. Ph.D. program in economics at Columbia. No big deal. She slowed when they reached the playground at the crest of the hill. It was the spot where he had dropped her off. He had never considered how much time she had in that half block to reflect, consider, judge. He slowed even more, trying to think of something significant to say about the setting. She clomped on and dropped into a rusty swing. He watched her for a moment, waiting. When she felt him approach, she pushed off the ground hard, and her long legs gave her swing an exaggerated motion.

"So what can I do for you?" she asked.

Rescue me. Redeem me. "I don't know. Like I said, I wanted to talk to you. I wanted to see you. I still like to think that we're friends."

"You don't even *know* me," she said. She planted her feet in the snow and stopped her motion abruptly. And looked at him as she never had before. "We were only together two years, and that was four years ago. Four *years*, Richard."

"So what?" he said, moving closer. "I know you better than I know myself. Better than I knew myself then, anyway."

"Oh yeah? For all you know I could be married."

"I don't believe it."

She almost smiled, lifted her feet and rocked gently in the swing. "No, you're right. Close, though. I met him in France. When I went back this summer he wanted me to stay and marry him."

"Why didn't you?"

"I don't know." She swung harder.

"You belong here," he said with conviction.

"With you?"

"Maybe."

"For a minute, when I walked in the house, I thought you might be him," she said.

"Disappointed?"

"No."

"You love him?"

She stopped swinging. And shrugged. "What difference does that make? I probably loved you when I met him."

"He doesn't have a hairy chest, does he?"

She closed her eyes and chuckled, threw back her head and stared at him. "Very." She swung some more. "But he never heard of the Righteous Brothers. What about you?"

"I tried," he said again. He sat on the swing beside her. "Thought I had something. It's been more than three years, but . . . it's not the same. It could be ten and it wouldn't seem as long."

"You still see her?"

"Good question. We were supposed to get together now. We both made excuses. I haven't seen her since August. I think she's afraid I want to rush her into a commitment. So am I."

"That's a change. Do you love her?"

"Yes. I think so."

"Is she black?"

He was surprised and knew he shouldn't have been. That had never been her problem.

"Yes."

"Is she prettier than I am?" She was smiling freely now. It had become her interview.

"Yeah."

"But?"

"But nothing. She's definitely prettier."

"Thank you."

"Well." He started to swing. "She can't stand Otis Redding."

She caught herself and restarted so they were not in synch.

"How's Tommy?" she asked.

"Okay. Married in Atlanta with a kid. Judy?"

"Okay. Chicago. Single."

He stopped and stood. "New York's not that far from New Haven," he said.

She stopped. "You know, this isn't an easy thing you're suggesting."

"Yes it is."

"Stop that!" She strode to the monkey bars and turned. "You're talking about going backward. Digging up the past. That's dangerous, Richard. I mean, you just pop up like Marley's ghost and want to pretend it all happened last week. I don't believe this."

"That's the problem. You thought I was François."

"Henri."

"Henri?"

"Yes. Go on."

"You thought I was—Hen*ri*—because you didn't want to believe it could be me."

"Oh, brother."

"You knew I'd show up. Sooner or later. Maybe even after it was too late to do anything but remember. I knew. Soon as I saw you in the mall I realized I'd never stopped looking."

He moved closer. She looked up and said nothing.

"Cher, I trusted you once. You believed you were right about us then. I didn't get it, not for a long time. It turned out you were right. I wasn't ready, but I knew I would be. I thought it would be too late, by then. For us. But it's not. I'm right this time. You have to trust me. You owe me."

"Come here," she said.

A helpless moan slipped from him as she looked him straight in the eyes, touched his face and kissed him. Her lips were gone long before his eyes opened.

"Walk me home," she said softly. "I'll give you my address. When you get back, write me. Okay? No paper towels. And no promises."

"Okay," he said. "By the way, when I said you owe me I had something specific in mind. You know what next year is?"

"I give up. International do-it-in-the-name-of-brotherhood year?"

"No," he said scornfully. "*Bambi.*"

"Oh, God. How do you know these things?"

"It's easy to keep track of the important stuff," he said. "It all goes in cycles, you know."

Another Saturday. He couldn't say he ain't got nobody. That had never been true, after all, much as he had pretended it was. But he had one less somebody. The cars, four of them, mounted the hill as if in secret with their lights on but no horns blasting as they had every Saturday afternoon when wedding caravans swung by the park for pictures. They crept past the highway ramp covering Tommy's old house and his. Past the stubborn bronze Indian heads still planted in the sidewalk, which Hodge had taught him to spit on for luck. Past the spot where Hodge had let go of the bike without his knowing, freeing him to fly. Past the rose garden waiting to bloom once more below the Hump in Madison Park, and on to the final place.

He had wanted nothing to do with the arrangements. He was scared to death of dying. Whenever she tried to discuss it with him, he would first change the subject, then sing a little scat, and, if she persisted, leave the room. Don't you at least wanna know where you're gonna be? she would ask. Ain't goin nowhere, Baby, he would answer. She had once considered Springfield, with her mother, the little sister he adored, and even Tuskegee, the home he'd fled for France. But he'd always made it a point to be thankful to the Germans for liberating *him*, and she really had no intention of going down there herself unless he just wanted it. So, long before his stroke she had decided to do it easy. Even then she could get no cooperation. Surprise me, was the most he'd said. But his biggest surprise came when he laughed feebly one time for Maria and breathed no more. It was a surprise, too, for Elizabeth, who for all her planning halfway believed he'd put *her* in that hole, and for Ike, who had no way of knowing that people could in fact die.

The night before at Slater's, still standing proudly among the empty lots and new apartment buildings of the old neighborhood as if it were a tribal burial ground, he had seen her fall apart. J.T. Slater, the prince of darkness, left them alone in the dim, paneled room with the folding chairs, the flowers expertly deployed to seem more numerous, and the silver-colored casket. Ike remembered the *Jet* photo of a player propped up in a Cadillac facsimile complete with steering wheel and was glad he had asked J.T. to slip in the hood ornament.

As soon as he left them, she strode briskly to the casket, but her knees buckled when she got there. Grasping the side, she sank nearly to the floor and loosed a chilling, inhuman sound that called to mind childbirth. For years they had exchanged disdainful Sunday glances when sisters got happy, each with her trademark hop, wail or swoon. Not me, her look had reassured him. I'll never embarrass you like that. This, of course, was different, but it frightened him, and he moved toward her before she could call out again, before Slater reappeared or guests arrived. There was no need. As he reached her she pulled to her feet, forced out a convulsive sob as if she were coughing up gristle, sniffed deeply and said: He looks good, doesn't he?

Ike had picked out the clothes: a yellow shirt, wide tie—Hodge said they'd come back—with a pink and purple design and tan windowpane jacket. He doesn't have a suit, Ike had told Slater, who was remarkably sanguine about the whole thing. The Lincoln hexagon was nestled in the breast pocket with a white cotton H-embroidered hanky Ike had given him. Elizabeth, fearless, patted and smoothed while she fretted over his weight loss and admired

J.T.'s grooming. He was always, she said, good with hair. Then she put an arm around Ike and almost whispered, Just you and me, kiddo.

She was wrong.

He had been to New York a few weeks before. He'd wanted to do DC first; he hadn't spoken to her since they'd canceled New Year's in an awkward I-gotta-run call, and he thought it was important to see her again, first. Jeff told him to quit acting stupid. If he'd really wanted to go—and if she'd wanted him—they'd had plenty of time. Besides, New York was a lot easier for the weekend. So he went. On Friday they ate Chinese on upper Broadway, drank at the West End, talked late and he slept on her sofa. On Saturday they walked a hundred blocks to the Strand bookstore. A movie, more eating, more talking. On Sunday they roamed Central Park to the site of the carousel, though it was too early for that, and when they parted, as friends, he knew which way his train was running.

The wreath she'd sent, a tribute to his devotion to a man she felt she knew, was carried out of the hearse along with the other flowers. Hers was actually more appropriate than most; it read simply "Hodge" because she couldn't remember the name, Oliver Henry Hodges, that the preacher and the mourners felt dignity demanded. Jim stood close on the other side of Elizabeth at the edge of the grave. Beside him was Maria, to whom Elizabeth had already decided to give the veteran's flag. Dessie was there, and so was Tommy, with his wife, Sheila, and their three-year-old daughter, Titi. Shurley, the bartender, stood beside an old man named Chappie; he and Hodge had retired to adjacent stools at the Greek's. No one expected Aunt Milly, but she had sent the second-largest floral display, after Elizabeth's, the only evidence Ike had that this person indeed existed. She was represented in the flesh by some ladies of the church, all titled Mrs. but alone for the length of Ike's memory. A reciprocal agreement: Aunt Milly had no doubt seen the unknown menfolk of women like them laid in the ground sometime, somewhere.

The ceremony was brief and surprisingly lacking in gravity. Everyone was serious, but as if they knew they were supposed to be. I hate to just leave him, you know? Ike said as they shuffled back toward the cars. Well you don't wanna bring him home, now do you? she said through tears. A Hodgian answer; he couldn't complain. And the trembling of her hand as it clutched his arm gave her away. No, and I guess I'd just as soon not stay, he said. He sure wouldn't, she said. You know he wouldn't even go in the cemetery to bury Mama. He tried, got drunk as a skunk, but he couldn't do it. Always said the only way anybody'd get him in here was in a box. Maybe, Ike said, we could put a neon sign on the marker and he'd never know.

Not everyone returned to the apartment, which was fine. There was nothing to do, not even cook. Death, as always, brought food from everywhere, including places Elizabeth would rather not consider. Dessie busied herself ritually, acting out a blood-borne imperative to fill in for the grieving. Jim was all over, greeting and getting and rubbing her neck: the man of the house. Cool, Ike thought. It wasn't his house. He took the phone into his room and placed a call to New York. Long distance? she asked when he returned smiling. He nodded. New Haven? He shook no. Washington? No. Her eyes narrowed. She sighed. He knelt beside the chair where she sat. Don't worry about it, he said. Honey, she said, if I hadn't stopped worrying about you by now I'd be out there with Hodge.

Tommy approached with a request: Titi wanted to watch *Soul Train;* could he put on the set in back? Come here, sugar, Elizabeth said. You know I wanted a girl but this hair woulda been the end of me. Tell me about it, Sheila said, flexing her fingers. Elizabeth, her hands playing about the thick braids, looked into the little Dessieface. You wanna get away from all these people you don't know, don't you, sweetheart? No, ma'am, I wanna look at Sotrain. It was an honest Southern accent—Tommy's voice was bending, too—not like the ignorant bleats of the little Northern-born Bamas that scratched fingernails across her mind's blackboard. You know, my uncle, the man we buried today, he liked that show, too. Why don't you just go turn it on right over there. Titi! Dessie said, catching her at the dial, don't be turnin on no TV now, go on in back and play with your dollie. Desdemona,

Elizabeth said in a tone that hinted at more than punch in her cup, I told that girl she could put on *Soul Train*. If Hodge don't hear no music he's liable to come back and haunt me tonight, so let her go.

Lord, look at those children, Jim said. What is that mess? It's the hustle, Titi explained to the old folks. Shoot, said Elizabeth, that ain't nothin new. We used to do that at the Oasis. Sure did, added Dessie. Little more style, too. You remember I showed you how to jitterbug, Elizabeth told Ike. Oh, that's where you got your lessons, huh? Tommy said loudly. That explains a lot. Excuse me, young man? Elizabeth said, standing. I'll have you know I was a very good dancer. And a good teacher, Ike said. Oh yeah, that's why you couldn't get your back off them walls, Tommy laughed. Daddy, shh! Oh hush, girl, I said you could watch, nobody said we were gonna be quiet. Hey, I was just ahead of my time, Ike said. I had to wait for you Negroes to evolve. Come on, honey, Elizabeth said. Uh-oh, said Dessie. Uh-oh is right, Tommy said. See what you done done, Titi? All right, said Ike, I got your hustle right here, my man.

He took her hand. They pulled back, rocked side to side, drew close and she spun away. Titi scrunched up her face. Get it, girl, Dessie said. Up, back, grasp, turn, step. The song on the TV stopped. Titi, Tommy, Dessie, Jim, everyone faded. Hodge cackled. Elizabeth closed her eyes and smiled, as Ike took the lead—bless it now I've got my own—and danced them to the other side.

ABOUT THE AUTHOR

DENNIS A. WILLIAMS teaches at Cornell University in Ithaca, New York, where he lives with his wife, Millicent, his daughter, Margo, and his son, David.